Praise for
KRISTINE KATHRYN RUSCH

Kristine Kathryn Rusch is one of the best writers in the field.

—SFRevu

Whether [Rusch] writes high fantasy, horror, sf, or contemporary fantasy, I've always been fascinated by her ability to tell a story with that enviable gift of invisible prose. She's one of those very few writers whose style takes me right into the story—the words and pages disappear as the characters and their story swallows me whole….Rusch has style.

—Charles de Lint
The Magazine of Fantasy & Science Fiction

The SF thriller is alive and well, and today's leading practitioner is Kristine Kathryn Rusch.

—Analog

Praise for
THE RUNABOUT

[The Runabout] is so good, it will make you want to read the other stories.

—SFRevu

Amazing character construction, building a plot that riveted me almost from the moment it began. I will now absolutely have to read the preceding titles and I cannot wait to see what will come as a result of The Runabout.

—Tangent Online

Praise for
DIVING INTO THE WRECK

Rusch delivers a page-turning space adventure while contemplating the ethics of scientists and governments working together on future tech.

—*Publisher's Weekly*

This is classic sci-fi, a well-told tale of dangerous exploration. The first-person narration makes the reader an eyewitness to the vast, silent realms of deep space, where even the smallest error will bring disaster. Compellingly human and technically absorbing, the suspense builds to fevered intensity, culminating in an explosive yet plausible conclusion.

—*RT Book Reviews* Top Pick

Rusch's handling of the mystery and adventure is stellar, and the whole tale proves quite entertaining.

—*Booklist Online*

The technicalities in Boss' story are beautifully played…. She's real, flawed, and interesting…. Read the book. It is very good.

—*SFFWorld.com*

Praise for
CITY OF RUINS

Rusch keeps the science accessible, the cultures intriguing, and the characters engaging. For anyone needing to add to their science fiction library, keep an eye out for this.

—Josh Vogt
SpeculativeFictionExaminer.com

Praise for
BONEYARDS

Rusch's latest addition to her "Diving" series features a strong, capable female heroine and a vividly imagined far-future universe. Blending fast-paced action with an exploration of the nature of friendship and the ethics of scientific discoveries, this tale should appeal to Rusch's readers and fans of space opera.

—*Library Journal*

Filled with well-defined characters who confront a variety of ethical and moral dilemmas, Rusch's third Diving Universe novel is classic space opera, with richly detailed worldbuilding and lots of drama.

—*RT Book Reviews*

Praise for
SKIRMISHES

. . . a fabulous outer space thriller that rotates perspective between the divers, the Alliance and to a lesser degree the Empire. Action-packed and filled with twists yet allowing the reader to understand the motives of the key players, *Skirmishes* is another intelligent exciting voyage into the Rusch Diving universe.

—*The Midwest Book Review*

Kristine Kathryn Rusch is best known for her Retrieval Artist series, so maybe you've missed her Diving Universe series. If so, it's high time to remedy that oversight.

—Don Sakers, *Analog*

Also by
Kristine Kathryn Rusch

The Diving Series (Reading Order):

Novels

Diving into the Wreck (A Diving Novel)
The Application of Hope (A Diving Novella)
Becalmed (A Diving Universe Novella)
City of Ruins (A Diving Novel)
Boneyards (A Diving Novel)
Skirmishes (A Diving Novel)
The Falls (A Diving Universe Novel)
The Runabout (A Diving Novel)
Searching for the Fleet (A Diving Novel)

The Spires of Denon (A Diving Universe Novella)

SEARCHING FOR THE FLEET

A DIVING NOVEL

KRISTINE KATHRYN RUSCH

*wmg*PUBLISHING

Searching for the Fleet

Published 2018 by WMG Publishing
www.wmgpublishing.com
Parts of this novel appeared in different form as the
novellas *Dix (Asimov's SF Magazine,* March/April 2018)
and *Lieutenant Tightass (Asimov's SF Magazine,* July/August 2018)
Cover and layout copyright © 2018 by WMG Publishing
Cover design by Allyson Longueira/WMG Publishing
Cover art copyright © Philcold/Dreamstime
ISBN-13: 978-1-56146-035-9
ISBN-10: 1-56146-035-4

For Dean, who keeps asking questions....

SEARCHING FOR THE FLEET

A DIVING NOVEL

DIX
FIVE YEARS AGO

1

FOR THE REST OF HER LIFE, Yash Zarlengo would replay that last night in her mind, going over each and every detail, looking for something different—a clue, perhaps, a missed signal.

She never found one that satisfied her.

Yash and Jonathan "Coop" Cooper had been sitting in their favorite bar in the *Ivoire*. The bar was really just an extension of the main commissary, but the ship's designers had gone all out. The bar had twenty-five tables organized in small groups, some with counter running behind them, and plants shielding the patrons. The tables were made of brass and some teak-colored wood. The chairs matched the tables, except for the comfortable brass-colored cushions.

Alcohol bottles lined the two interior walls. The wall that was easiest to reach had once held the alcohol which had been easiest to find in what had been the sector the *Ivoire* traveled through. The wall behind the recycler cleaning unit had upper cabinets filled with bottles that were mostly one-of-a-kind.

Technically, everything in this bar was now one-of-a-kind.

Yash tried not to think about that. Instead, she stared out the floor-to-ceiling windows that revealed the vastness of space—or whatever planet the *Ivoire* orbited. The windows could be shuttered, then shielded, and often were when the ship was traveling from place to place.

But at that moment, the *Ivoire* was docked at the space station that housed the Lost Souls Corporation. A woman who called herself Boss in that bastardization of Standard everyone spoke in this time period had started the corporation to discover more about something she called "stealth tech," but which really had more to do with the Fleet's *anacapa* drives.

Boss had found the *Ivoire*. In fact, Boss had accidentally rescued the *Ivoire*. She and her people had inadvertently activated the equipment in a decaying sector base. That equipment had pulled the *Ivoire* out of a trap in foldspace, bringing the *Ivoire* and her crew five thousand years into their future.

As a cadet—hell, throughout her career—Yash thought she could deal with anything. But the loss of everything she knew—from the Fleet itself to the language her people spoke to the history that was just yesterday to her and so far in the past as to be unknown to these people—was overwhelming. Some days, she thought she wouldn't make it.

But going through this with the crew of the *Ivoire*, all five hundred of them, made it easier. She wasn't going through this alone.

She took comfort in that.

Hence the drinking sessions with Coop. They would meet in the bar not quite nightly, put their feet on the tables precisely because that wasn't regulation, and drink some of the old whiskey, the kind that they had brought from planets they would never see again, in a time period they couldn't return to.

After the first few sessions, Coop and Yash usually didn't get drunk. They sipped and stared at the edges of the space station and the edges of the sector beyond. Planets Yash still didn't recognize, nebulae that gleamed against the blackish-blueness, the red star so far in the distance that it looked like a pinprick of blood.

She wasn't coming to love those things, but they were becoming familiar. Anything could become familiar, given enough time.

That night, about a year after they had arrived in this strange future, Coop was staring at his whiskey, not drinking it at all. He was looking through the glass at the view, in an unusually contemplative mood.

He had been everyone's rock. A solid, broad-shouldered man who seemed even taller and more broad-shouldered since they had arrived, he now had a few more lines on his face, a hint of silver in his black hair. He had stopped wearing any kind of uniform a few months ago, and had said nothing about it.

He now dressed like Boss's people, wearing black pants and a black or gray T-shirt, quietly moving his association from a Fleet that probably no longer existed to Lost Souls Corporation and its vague connection to something called the Nine Planets Alliance.

He was shedding as much of the past as he could, and making it okay for the rest of the crew to do so. Some were already thinking of leaving the *Ivoire* permanently, taking jobs inside Lost Souls or becoming planet-bound somewhere in the Nine Planets.

Yash couldn't contemplate any of that. She still wore her Fleet clothes as well, although some of them were getting worn. She would have to replace her regulation boots soon, and she didn't want to. They were comfortable.

They were also coming apart.

"Hey, can anyone join this little party?" Dix Pompiono, the *Ivoire's* nominal first officer, spoke from behind them.

Yash tensed. Coop stopped swirling the liquid in his glass. His expression hadn't changed, a sign that Coop didn't want anyone to know what he was feeling.

But Yash knew exactly how Coop felt. Neither she nor Coop wanted to deal with Dix right now. This was their relaxation place, not a place for histrionics. And Dix had been all over the emotional map ever since the *Ivoire* arrived here.

Dix had actually suffered some kind of breakdown a few months ago after a mission Coop ran to Starbase Kappa to shut down a long-malfunctioning *anacapa* drive. The mission had nearly failed because of Dix. Coop resented that deeply.

Yash hadn't told Coop that she had found the mission joyous, in its own way. Yash had felt useful again, like she was back in the old Fleet, with a proper goal and a future.

Of course, after that mission, the *Ivoire's* crew had nothing to do. And, in some ways, that mission had been the *Ivoire* crew's last gasp. The mission had brought up too many conflicting feelings for everyone, not even counting what had happened with Dix.

"Gotta pour your own." Coop sounded welcoming, but the pause before he spoke probably told Dix more than enough.

Behind her, glasses clinked. Then she saw movement reflected in the windows before her. Dix had taken a tumbler out of the cabinet near the recycler. He had grabbed the whiskey bottle and was now pouring himself a drink.

Coop let out a sigh so small Yash wouldn't have heard it if she hadn't been sitting next to him. Yash patted his arm, not to comfort, but in agreement.

Coop glanced at her, blue eyes hooded. Then he shrugged ever so slightly with the shoulder closest to her, as if to say, *What can you do?*

She mimicked his shrug so that he understood that she identified with him. The nice quiet evening they'd been enjoying would be quiet no longer.

Dix rounded the table nearest them, carrying a tumbler of whiskey two fingers full. He stopped, looked at the view, then took a sip.

He was gaunt now. He had always been too thin, and abnormally tall for someone who ended up as bridge crew. His hair had gone completely white in the past year, and his cheeks were sunken inward.

The last time Yash had seen him, his hands shook as if he couldn't control them.

But they weren't shaking now.

"There's the future," he said, looking at the sector they still hadn't explored. "It's been there all along, hasn't it?"

He sounded like the old Dix, a little wry, intelligent, and maybe even a bit hopeful.

Yash couldn't believe that Dix was hopeful. He'd been the most distraught of all of the senior crew members, the one who had been least able to contain his heartbreak when he learned they could never, ever go back.

Indeed, his completely insane meltdown on Starbase Kappa had come from some cockamamie scheme he had developed to send the *Ivoire* back to its own time period—and Coop had thwarted him.

Dix had barely spoken to Coop since.

Dix sipped from his tumbler, tilted his head back—clearly savoring the whiskey—and then swallowed. He turned away from the windows, and set his glass on a nearby table. But he didn't sit.

Instead, he continued to stand, the light from the space station illuminating half his face, leaving the side closest to Yash in shadow.

"I owe you guys an apology," Dix said.

His voice had strength, which she hadn't expected. The last time he had used the word "apology" in her presence he had said, *I suppose you expect an apology*, and his tone had been as mean as the words.

Now, Yash didn't answer him, but she met his gaze. He still seemed sad, as if sadness had leached into his very soul. She wondered if someone who knew her well would think the same thing of her.

Coop didn't even move. It was as if Coop hadn't heard anything.

"I've been thinking about it," Dix said, glancing at Coop, then looking back at Yash. "I've been acting as if this happened just to me. It didn't. It happened to all of us."

Yash didn't wanted to react to anything Dix said, but she couldn't help herself. She nodded.

He gave her a faint smile, took that nod as an invitation, and sat down to the left of Coop. Coop rested his glass of whiskey on his flat stomach, and continued to stare at the universe beyond.

"I can make excuses," Dix said, "and I did. I know I did. The loss of Lenore made me crazy."

Everything made you crazy, Yash thought but didn't say. She didn't dare speak out at all, because everyone had lost family and loved ones, even her. She would never see her parents again, or her twin sisters. She hadn't had a lover at the time the *Ivoire* left on its last mission for the Fleet, but she had had an entire cadre of friends, all of whom had not served on the *Ivoire*.

She would never see them again. She would never see anyone she loved who hadn't been on the *Ivoire* again.

"Sometimes I think if we could access records of the Fleet, learn about what happened to everyone, I'd feel better," Dix said.

Yash stiffened. She'd had that thought. So had Coop. They'd actually looked through the information they'd pulled from Starbase Kappa, but it was minimal. Maintenance records mostly. No history of Fleet personnel, not even personnel who had come later.

As was proper. No information about the Fleet should have been available in any closed Fleet outpost. None.

"But I keep turning it over and over in my mind," Dix said, "and I realize that discovering that Lenore married someone else and had kids with him—or didn't marry anyone and died alone—that wouldn't help me. It's not just the loss of the *people*, selfish as that is to say. It's the loss of the future. The expected, imagined future."

Coop let out a small sigh. His fingers wrapped around the glass, but he didn't take another drink.

"How do you do it?" Dix asked. "How do you get through each day? How do you accept that you should put your uniform away and say goodbye to the Fleet, when the Fleet has been our entire life?"

Coop stiffened. Yash did too. Yash hadn't ever had that conversation with Coop, although she'd had others. About the Fleet. About where it might be now, five thousand years later. About whether or not it still existed.

About whether approaching it if it did exist was a good idea.

"You don't want to talk about it, do you?" Dix asked. "That's how you're coping. You're denying what's in front of you."

A surge of anger ran through Yash. Coop wasn't denying anything. Neither was she. They were moving forward each and every day, just like they'd been trained to do.

She swung her feet off the table, sitting up, about to speak, when Coop lifted one hand from his glass, forefinger out, stopping her.

"I'm using my training," he said to Dix. "You should too."

"Training?" Dix made a sound halfway between a laugh and a sob. "None of us were trained for this."

Coop's lips thinned. He sat up, then put his glass on the table in front of him.

Yash tensed. She would step between them if need be. The crew was still on edge; they didn't need to hear that their captain had physically fought with Dix.

Then she swallowed, thinking about her own reaction.

Coop wasn't a violent man. He had never hit anyone on his crew, rarely hit someone who had attacked him. He was the calmest person she knew.

That hint of violence in the air? Was she imagining it? Or had it come from her?

She shifted slightly, saw Coop's posture. No. She knew him well. He was furious. He was past furious. He was barely holding himself together.

"We are all trained for this, First Officer Pompiono," Coop said, enunciating each word precisely. He was using the captain speak he used only with the most recalcitrant crew members, the ones he would dump at the next port after dozens of write-ups. The hopeless ones.

Dix raised his eyebrows. "I never heard any of my instructors mention that foldspace could catapult us five thousand years in the future, making us lose *everything*, cheating us of our own march through time. Making us abandon our families—"

"Then you weren't paying attention." Coop handed his glass to Yash, as if she were his second in command, not Dix. And in truth, she had become Coop's second in command. She had been at his side for the entire year they'd been stuck here, working on the *Ivoire*, figuring out the way forward. Dix had been wallowing in his own losses and breakdown, and Yash had been working. Hard. Like most of the crew.

Yash set Coop's glass next to hers, out of the way.

Dix leaned back just a little, but there was something in his eyes. A kind of triumph, maybe? Relief that he had finally gotten an obvious emotional reaction out of Coop?

Coop laid his hands flat on the table's faux wood surface as if he were stretching them, as if he were pushing the table down so that he wouldn't do anything harmful to anyone.

"Our training," Coop said, "was about this, and *only* this."

Dix frowned, opening his mouth to speak, probably to disagree, when Coop continued.

"We were told that DV-Class ships ventured out *alone*. We could get lost. We might never come back. We often had no one to rely on but ourselves. I don't know about you, but my training included years of role-playing those very things, plus going over historical incidents of lost ships, coping with hundreds and hundreds of scenarios in which this very thing occurred."

"It's not the same," Dix said.

"It's *exactly* the same." Coop spoke softly, but used as much energy as if he had shouted them.

Yash was holding her breath. She made herself release it.

"It's not the same," Dix repeated. "In those scenarios, we would have had hope."

"Hope?" Coop spoke the word as if Dix had been using Boss's bastardized Standard. "What kind of hope are you talking about?"

"Hope that we could return." Dix was calm, like the Dix of old. The man that Coop had made First Officer.

Yash could remember when Dix inspired confidence in everyone, when he knew the exact right words to say. When he really was an extension of Coop, understanding exactly how Coop would approach something, and then anticipating it, so Coop never even had to give the order.

"You lack that hope now?" Yash asked. Because she didn't. She was still searching for a way back, even though she knew it was a long shot. They had gotten here, hadn't they? That meant returning was possible as well.

Coop turned his head slightly, as if he had just remembered that Yash was in the conversation.

Then he shifted his body, almost blocking her view of Dix.

8

"You think all of those scenarios," Coop said, "the hundreds and hundreds of them that we learned, would *always* have hope?"

"Yes," Dix said.

"Ship destroyed, crew scattered, the Fleet never notified before it happened, you think those kinds of scenarios had *hope*?"

"Steal a ship, buy one, get back to the Fleet," Dix said.

"Without an *anacapa* drive," Coop said. "Not possible."

"But the hope—"

"Is a myth, Dix. You were in the same classes I was. You had the same training, the same instructors. Did you *miss* the parts about ships getting lost forever in foldspace? Do you think those crews had *hope?*"

"Until they died, yes, I do," Dix said.

"Did *you* have this kind of hope when *we* were stranded in fold-space?" Coop asked.

"Yes," Dix said calmly. "I was convinced we'd get home."

Coop harrumphed. Yash thought back to those horrid weeks just over a year ago. She hadn't allowed herself to think about getting back to the Fleet. Nor had she let herself think about foldspace as much more than a theoretical problem. The Fleet used foldspace as a tool to travel long distances. The Fleet believed that the *anacapa* drive created a fold in space, so that ships could cross it quickly.

But Yash hadn't been sure that they entered a fold in space. She thought maybe they had traveled somewhere else, a different sector of the universe, somewhere far away. Or maybe they had entered some kind of interdimensional portal. She had kept those thoughts to herself when the *Ivoire* was trapped in foldspace, because she needed to fix the ship, figure out what had gone wrong, to create some kind of chance—

"I wasn't convinced we'd get back to the Fleet," Coop said.

"But you said you were." Dix sounded surprised. Apparently, he had trusted in Coop's words.

Yash had too. She had thought Coop amazingly calm throughout that entire ordeal—as much as she had paid attention to him. She had spent so much time in engineering that most nights she had even slept there.

"I said I believed we could escape foldspace," Coop said. "One problem at a time. Remember, Dix? It's part of the training."

Dix flinched.

Yash nodded. She was rather astounded that Dix had to be reminded. *One problem at a time* was a core principle of the Fleet. She had been operating on that very principle when the *Ivoire* had been trapped in foldspace.

"And I was right," Coop said. "We escaped foldspace."

"We didn't do anything to escape," Dix said. "These people we're stuck with, this Lost Souls thing, *they* got us out."

Yash clenched a fist. How dare he? He knew how hard everyone worked to get out of foldspace.

She finally spoke up. "You're mistaken, Dix."

His head swiveled toward her as if he had forgotten she was there. Coop, too. He frowned at her in surprise.

"We fixed the *anacapa* drive just enough," she said, "so that when a signal came from another *anacapa* drive, we had the energy to assist in the pull from foldspace. If that signal had come one week earlier, we would still be stranded there."

Dix's eyes narrowed. "You believe that."

"I *know* that," she said.

Coop nodded. "One problem at a time," he said. "That's what we did in foldspace. We worked the problem."

Dix's lower lip trembled, making him look like a little boy who got caught in a lie.

He squared his shoulders, then said, "So what's the current problem? Getting back to our time period? Getting back to the Fleet?"

If he had actually been doing his job the last year, he would know what everyone was working on and how they were coping.

Although not everyone was coping. And Coop was managing those people as well.

To his credit, he didn't say that. He leaned forward, putting more of his weight on his flattened hands, then peered at Dix as if unable to believe that Dix had no idea what was going on.

"We're five thousand years in the *future*," Coop said. "Five thousand years of technological advances. Five thousand years of changes. Five thousand years of Fleet history."

"Technology is backwards here," Dix said, interrupting Coop's flow.

"Here at Lost Souls, yes," Coop said. "It is. But we haven't found the Fleet yet. And once we find them, *if* we find them, we have no idea if they'll believe us, help us, or work with us. But I don't care. One problem at a time, Dix."

"We're searching for the Fleet?" Dix asked.

"We never stopped searching for the Fleet," Yash said.

Dix shifted slightly on his chair. "And you think that when we find them—"

"*If* we find them," Coop corrected.

"You think they'll help us get back." For the first time in a year, Dix sounded almost joyful.

"No," Coop said. "I make no such assumption. One problem at a time."

"But the new technology, as you said." Dix was smiling, but his smile was that intense weird smile he had had on Starbase Kappa. "Their technology will be better than Boss's. They'll know how to get us back."

"A lot of assumptions in that," Yash said. "We don't know if the Fleet still exists. We don't know if the Fleet of the present—if there is one—has better tech than Lost Souls. We don't know if they're going to *want* to send us back, because it might cause all kinds of problems. There are time lines—"

"And alternate realities, and yeah, yeah." Dix waved a hand. "I believe in that less than I believe in foldspace."

Whatever that meant. He had gone off the deep end after all. After the apology, Yash had hoped the old Dix had come back. She missed him. Before the *Ivoire* got lost in foldspace, he used to sit in this bar with the two of them, and work shipboard problems as if they were nothing.

The man in front of her only resembled that man. The man in front of her had Dix's shell, but not his courage. And she was beginning to think he didn't have Dix's brain either.

11

"Are we going to even try to get back?" Dix asked Coop.

"When?" Coop asked.

"What do you mean, when? If we get a chance. Are we going to try?"

Coop looked away, focusing on the windows. Yash looked too, saw the lights of a small ship as it left the space station on a mission she probably would never know about.

Coop took a deep breath. "One problem at a time, Dix."

Dix slammed his hand on his table, making his glass jump and spilling just a bit of the whiskey. "I need to know, Coop. I need to know we're trying."

"Getting back to the Fleet and to our time period is an extreme long shot, Dix." Coop spoke softly. "And I'm not sure it's worth attempting. Because—the training, Dix. We're trained to make the most of the situation we're in, not to wish we were somewhere else."

The color fled Dix's face, leaving only two red spots on his cheeks, almost as if Coop had physically slapped him.

"I lost the love of my life," Dix said.

"Most likely," Coop said, and Yash tensed at the bluntness. Although she knew that was part of the training too. No use sugarcoating anything, because that didn't help anyone deal with change.

Better to face it straight on.

"But you would have lost her if her ship got damaged in some battle," Coop said. "You would have lost her if we remained stranded in foldspace. Hell, Dix, you would have lost her—or she would have lost you—at the end of your lives. One of you would have had to die first."

Dix pressed his lips together. His eyes had filled with tears. "You're a mean son of a bitch, you know that, Coop?"

Coop gave him a languid, sideways look. "I never pretended otherwise. You don't get to be the captain of a DV-Class vessel by being kind, Dix. I thought you knew that."

Dix ran a shaking hand over his face. "I didn't know anything."

Yash frowned at Dix in surprise. Of course he had known what it took to be captain. He had been on the captain track. There were personality tests, and stress tests, and a willingness to do exactly what Coop had done: disregard someone's feelings to get that someone back in line.

Had Dix forgotten that? *All* of it? Or had he tested well, only to perform poorly in the field?

Coop folded his hands together as if he had to hold them in place to prevent them from—what? Grabbing Dix and shaking him?

Because Yash wanted to do that.

"Remember who you are, Dix," Coop said. "Use your training. You're second in command on this ship."

"Not any more," Dix said bitterly. "You sidelined me."

"You need to face forward, Dix," Coop said, ignoring Dix's accusation. His *accurate* accusation. "We need you to work the problem."

"The problem, the problem," Dix snapped. "As if it's something minor."

Yash glanced at Coop. His expression was calm, but he was gripping his hands together so tightly that his knuckles had turned white.

"DV-Class ships never deal with something minor, Dix," Coop said. "You know that too."

"They don't deal with something like this, either," Dix said.

"How do you know?" Yash asked.

Both men looked at her with surprise. She shrugged. She had been thinking about this a lot.

"Dozens, maybe hundreds, of ships have disappeared forever, lost to foldspace. Those are the ones we know about, the ones that were actually observed entering foldspace. But we lose a lot of ships because they never return from some mission, and we can't track them down. We don't know how many other ships, how many other crews, how many other *captains* have dealt with this very thing."

Dix stared at her, his eyes tear-filled, his nose red. "And that's supposed to make me feel better?"

"We're not here to make you feel better," Coop said.

Dix turned that hideous gaze on Coop.

"None of us feel better," Coop said. "But most of us are working."

"Yeah," Dix said. "Working every angle. Sleeping with that woman who found us. Must be nice to have her to warm your bed."

Coop's impassive expression vanished. In its stead, he gazed at Dix with compassion.

"I know you lost Lenore," Coop said, clearly trying a different tack. "And I know you loved her more than anything."

"I won't replace her," Dix said. "I won't try."

"I'm not suggesting you do," Coop said.

"You have no idea how this feels," Dix said.

Coop nodded. "You're right," he said. "I don't."

Yash frowned. She hadn't expected him to say that. Was this another attempt at calming Dix? Or was this just Coop, tossing away any attempt at caution?

"I don't know if I ever will know what you felt for Lenore," Coop said. "They tested me. They test all candidates for captaincy. We're less likely than other members of the Fleet to have long-term romantic relationships. When have you ever heard a captain use the phrase, 'The love of my life'?"

"Are you saying I'm not captain material?" Dix asked.

Good God. Everything was about him. That wasn't the point, and if he had been listening—

"It would have depended on how you tested out on other things," Coop said. "But a willingness to sacrifice deep human connection in favor of the right decision for the ship, a certain bloodlessness, if you will, or, as you said, a willingness to be a mean son of a bitch, that's damn near the number one requirement."

"So you'd leave Boss for the Fleet?" Dix said.

"You're under a misapprehension," Coop said. "We're close, but we're not in a relationship."

Yet, Yash thought. But they would be.

"If you were." Dix's tone implied that he didn't believe Coop's denial. "Would you leave her to go home?"

Home was an interesting word choice. Although Yash empathized with it. That was the thing: the *Ivoire* felt like home, but this time period did not.

"Yes," Coop said. He relaxed his hands. They were still clasped together, but loosely. "Here's what you miss, Dix. I would leave a loved one for any mission, if ordered to do so by the Fleet. I would, and I have."

"Even someone you thought you could spend the rest of your life with?" Dix asked.

"Yes," Coop said.

"And never see them again?" Dix asked, voice trembling.

"That's the risk," Coop said. "That's what we all agreed to when we joined the crew of this vessel. I thought you understood that."

Dix blinked and looked away. A single tear hung on the lashes of his left eye. Yash stared at it, wondering if he knew it was there. Wondering if he cared.

"We lost everything," he whispered.

"Face forward," Coop said. The words were brutal. His *tone* was brutal. "That's what the Fleet does, Dix. Forever forward. You know that."

Dix nodded. The tear fell, landing on the edge of the table and falling out of Yash's line of sight.

"I forgot," he said, his voice thick with tears.

"I know," Coop said gently. He put a hand on Dix's shoulder. Dix jumped. "Drink with us. Yash and I have been talking about all of this since we got here. We'll catch you up on our plans."

Dix's Adam's apple bobbed—a nervous swallow.

For a moment, Yash thought he was going to stay. For a moment, she thought they would be able to reclaim the team that they had been just over a year ago.

Then Dix shook his head. "I have enough to think about for one night."

He stood, reached out one hand toward Coop.

Coop took it.

Dix shook.

"Thank you," Dix said. "You clarified things."

"Good," Coop said. But he didn't add, as Yash might have, *Glad I could help*. It was almost as if he didn't believe the conversation made any difference at all.

"Join us tomorrow?" Yash asked, partly because Coop didn't. Partly because it seemed like Dix expected it.

He smiled at her, and the smile was warm. "I've missed these moments," he said.

"Me, too," she said.

He picked up his whiskey, knocked it back, then carried the tumbler to the cleaner/recycler.

"I am sorry," Dix said.

She nodded. "We know."

Then he waved his fingers, a small goodbye. He left the bar.

Coop picked up his own drink, put his feet back on the table, and leaned back in the chair. He still didn't take a sip.

Yash watched until she was certain Dix was gone. Then she settled back into her spot although she didn't feel as relaxed.

"He did apologize," she said.

"He did," Coop said, as if it didn't matter.

They sat in silence for a long time. Then Yash said, "He's not the man you thought he was, is he?"

Coop finally picked up his glass. He peered into it, then—finally—took a sip.

"He's the man I feared he was," Coop said. It was, in its own way, the closest Coop had ever come to saying he had picked the wrong first officer.

Yash finished her drink, and thought about getting another. This night, it felt wrong to get drunk. Maybe she was past anesthetizing herself. Maybe she had moved to another stage.

"He's right, though," Coop said.

"About what?" Yash asked. She braced herself. She hadn't ever expected Jonathon "Coop" Cooper to talk about loss.

"I'll never know how he feels," Coop said, and finished his drink.

2

THE NEXT MORNING, Yash arrived on the *Ivoire* early to run the monthly systems checks. The *Ivoire* didn't need that many checks, but they made Yash feel better.

No one knew how often she came here, not even Coop.

She walked into the bridge, lights coming up as she entered. No matter how many times she had come here since they had arrived in this strange future, she still felt uncomfortable in the empty bridge. It had been built for activity, with dozens of work stations, and the captain's chair in the very center, waiting for someone to take command. A door to her right led into a small conference area, and a line of storage cabinets covered the wall beside that door.

She always glanced at them, afraid someone had tampered with them. She didn't trust everyone at Lost Souls, even though none of them should have had access to the *Ivoire's* bridge.

The bridge felt even more uncomfortable than usual this morning, and she couldn't quite put her finger on why. The hair on the back of her neck had gone up the moment she stepped into the main part of the bridge.

The only anomaly she could see were the screens. They had been shuttered, blocking the view of the docking bay she had seen just the night before.

She thought that odd; she liked having the portals open, liked seeing everything in real time. The shuttered portals were how she knew she hadn't been the last person up here. That too was odd, but she didn't think too much about it because Coop had been in the ship with her last night.

They no longer lived on the *Ivoire*, taking larger berths in the converted space station, but a handful of crew members still did. Coop did not discourage them. He wanted someone to continue manning the ship. He probably would have done it himself if no one else had volunteered to stay.

But he was gradually easing his grip on the past, and moving off the *Ivoire* had been one of those steps for him. Just like it had been for Yash.

She actually liked her new apartment. She liked the extra bedroom, which she had cluttered with equipment. She liked the large kitchen, and the bathroom was a religious experience.

She too, apparently, was easing her grip on the past.

The conversation last night, the apology from Dix, had buoyed her mood. Maybe others who were having trouble moving into the future would do so if Dix did.

She had gone to sleep hopeful, and had awakened with even more hope. She was humming as she went through some of the start-up routines.

As she saw it, one of her duties as chief engineer was to make sure each system activated and functioned. She had developed a cycle in the past year, a way of working through each system, checking it and its readings against the readings made before the *Ivoire* got trapped in foldspace, and also against the readings made after the *Ivoire* had come here.

The only system she hadn't worked on a lot was the *anacapa* drive. She had repaired it in foldspace, just like she had told Coop and Dix, but she hadn't cycled it on much here. They had used it when Coop had taken the *Ivoire* to Starbase Kappa, and they had used it again on a few "fact-finding missions" as Coop called them, searching for the Fleet.

But Yash had been tense each and every time. She used to trust the *anacapa* drive more than the rest of the crew did (which was to say, not that much), but she no longer trusted the *anacapa* drive at all.

If she was being honest with herself, she was a bit afraid of it now. The change had been large for her as well.

Still, on her monthly scans, she checked the *anacapa* drive's controls to make sure they functioned. She also checked the drive to make sure no one had snuck onto the ship and tampered with the drive or no one had activated it remotely.

Not that activating it remotely would have been easy, particularly since she did not have the drive in *assistance-needed* mode. But she worried about it.

Since arriving here, in this time period, she worried about everything.

She worked her way across control panels and through the bridge itself, checking each system just like she always did. There was an odd smell on the bridge, something coppery and slightly foul. She checked the environmental systems, and saw nothing amiss, although she didn't check all of the records to see if someone had spilled something. She would do that if the smell lingered after she had moved through the bridge.

The environmental system activated at different levels, depending on what was occurring on the bridge. Since nothing much had happened here in the last few weeks, the system had remained on low.

She rounded the corner of one of the stationary control panels, and stopped. Boots jutted out from under the console.

Boots, attached to legs, legs wearing an older dress uniform, black with silver piping.

That foul, coppery scent was stronger here.

She didn't even have to look to know what she would find. A body. The question was: Whose?

She moved to the side of the console, next to the large container protecting the *anacapa* drive.

Dix was wrapped around the container, clutching it like a lifeline. Blood had pooled near his head, and one of the bone knives he had received as a gift after successfully negotiating an agreement on Colashen was on the floor, not too far from his neck.

He had slit his own throat.

His hands gripped the container, though, palm prints everywhere, palm prints in blood.

He hadn't tried to clutch the wound closed. He hadn't sent for help. He had clearly intended to do this.

His face was whitish gray. She had always heard the term "bloodless," but she had never really seen it. Not like this.

His eyes were open and dull, his mouth slack.

He had done this deliberately. He had *planned* this, the bastard. He had known he was going to do this last night, and he had come to say goodbye.

That little finger-wave, that half smile. It wasn't because he was getting better. It was because he knew he was leaving.

He was getting out.

No. He was *quitting*.

She clenched her fist. She had this insane desire to kick him, to take his blood-covered hands off her *anacapa* container, and fling them away. To fling him away.

It took every ounce of control she had to remain still. The bastard. What did he think this would gain? This show he had put on. Had he expected the bridge to contact someone to help him, to prevent the actual death? If so, then why had he slit his own throat? He had cut the carotid artery, which was guaranteed to bleed him out in minutes, long before anyone could get to him.

Although there was equipment on the bridge that could be used in an emergency. Tools that would seal wounds, that would actually fly to the side of the injured and bind the wound until it could be repaired.

She glanced up, saw that nothing along the medical wall had been disturbed.

The fact that the medical wall was untouched meant he had actively shut off the assist controls before he had slit his own throat.

And he had called Coop cruel.

She took a deep breath, willing herself calm.

First she had to preserve the scene.

She leaned over the control panel, and made sure the information that the bridge recorded as a matter of course—who arrived, who left, the footage from the security cameras, the changes in environmental controls, and the record of the changes she had made since she arrived here—were archived.

She had brought a data strip and set it on the control panel. The strip copied data off the control panel, so she could remove that data from the *Ivoire*. The strip was unique to the Fleet, so that the control panel knew it could share the information. She would place that information in her second bedroom, with information she had taken off all of the Fleet ships that Lost Souls had found.

Then she froze.

Had Dix tampered with anything? More specifically, had he tampered with the *anacapa* drive?

He had tampered with the *anacapa* on Starbase Kappa, in a fruitless attempt to get back to their time period. What had stopped him from doing so here?

She swallowed hard, her heart hammering.

Nothing had happened yet. If he had done something, it would have to be on a timer, as something that would happen after he died.

She needed to contact Coop. Then she needed to look.

3

"I NEED YOU on the *Ivoire*." Yash sent through Coop's private command channel. "I need you on the bridge stat."

She hoped he was still hooked into the comm. So many members of the *Ivoire* crew had decided to go untethered—as they called it—removing the tiny communications devices that they normally wore when they left the ship.

"Problem?" Coop asked in that tone that told her he didn't want to be interrupted.

"I'm not saying any more," she said. "Get here. Now."

He was changing. The Coop of old would have been a lot more professional, less annoyed.

He probably thought there were no problems on the *Ivoire* that couldn't wait.

He was wrong.

She walked around the console, looking at the *anacapa* controls. It didn't seem like anyone had touched them, but she had to be sure.

She wiped her sweaty palms on the back of her shirt, then took a deep breath.

Before she did, she activated a voice log, giving the date in both the timeline of Lost Souls and also in the ship's time, as if the *Ivoire* had never left the past.

Then she said, "I am making this recording in case I find something else awry. For the record, I have found the body of former First Officer Dix Pompiono…" and she paused.

Coop hadn't officially removed Dix from duty. Coop had been following procedure, more or less. He had wanted to document everything that Dix had done wrong, and the medical attention Dix had probably needed.

If Coop had demoted Dix, Dix wouldn't have been able to access the bridge.

If only.

"Dix killed himself. At least as far as I can tell without touching or moving him. The medical team will have to confirm. The reasons I have activated a voice log are twofold: I am alone on the bridge, and will remain so for several minutes more as I wait for Captain Cooper to join me."

She let out a breath. She sounded calmer than she was. Not that she was panicked. The fury had her shaking. Goddamn it, Dix.

"The second reason is that I found Dix with his arms wrapped around the *anacapa* container. Dix had lost control of himself on a mission to Starbase Kappa five months ago, and had tampered with an active, if dying, *anacapa* drive. I am concerned he has done something similar here."

But why would he? He had planned to kill himself. And he wasn't so far gone that he would believe that the *anacapa* needed blood to activate.

She smiled grimly at the very thought.

"I do not know what I'm going to find. I have already set the bridge controls to record everything occurring on the bridge at full levels, but I still need to make sure that the record is clear. Which is why I'm going to narrate my investigation. I will not go into depth unless I need to."

She didn't want to go into depth, to think about the proper wording of every phrase. Not yet anyway.

"First," she said. "I need to check the *anacapa* controls."

She was not going to explain why. Nor was she going to mention how her right hand shook as it hovered over the section of the console that activated the controls quickly.

Sometimes she saw that section of the console in her nightmares, her fingers inputting codes, then her palm, slamming against the console, giving it permission to execute the commands she had just placed—commands that had sent the *Ivoire* into foldspace.

Commands that had led to the ship ending up here.

It didn't matter to her nightmares that at the very same moment, Quurzod ships had fired on the *Ivoire*, causing serious damage. It didn't matter to her, even though she knew that something in the Quurzod ships' weapons had interacted with the *anacapa* drive. The drive had been damaged: she had seen that in foldspace, and she had felt it that day.

She hadn't shut off the drive.

She probably should have shut off the drive.

Yash slowly brought her hand down on the smooth surface. The controls rose, responding to her touch.

The *anacapa* controls only worked for select personnel. She had no idea if Coop had restricted Dix's use of the *anacapa* drive. She would have. And she should have suggested it when they came back from Starbase Kappa, but she had been too busy, thinking about that mission. Too busy thinking about all the implications for their new future.

The controls looked normal.

Yash let out a small breath, then reminded herself that it didn't matter how the controls looked. They had looked normal after they had resumed their cycle, that day the *anacapa* drive had malfunctioned.

Still, she verbally noted that the controls seemed fine, and then discussed how she was going to dig further, to make sure that what *seemed* fine actually was fine.

First, she had the system show her any unusual activity, no matter how small.

What she found wasn't small at all. Dix had tried to access the *anacapa* drive, but he hadn't been able to.

Coop had done exactly what he should have done. He had removed Dix's access to sensitive systems.

Yash nodded as she saw that. Coop had figured Dix would test to see if he could still access the bridge, but had gambled that Dix wouldn't try to access sensitive systems—important systems.

Yash almost looked to see if Dix had tried to access other systems, but made herself stop. She needed to investigate the *anacapa* drive first. That was the one Dix was most focused on.

At Starbase Kappa, Dix thought he could recreate the circumstances that had sent the *Ivoire* into foldspace, and then five thousand years in the future. Dix had believed he could use that recreation to reverse what had happened.

Yash still had no idea how Dix believed that would happen. To her, that kind of thinking was as filled with magic as trying to active the *anacapa* drive using blood.

But Dix hadn't been in his right mind, no matter how he had seemed in the bar the night before.

The first hurdle crossed. Dix hadn't tampered with the *anacapa* drive controls. But she needed to examine more. Because of who Dix was, and how he had become First Officer.

Coop had always trusted Yash more than he trusted Dix. Coop had told Yash that more than once. But she had never been on the captain track as first officers usually were. She had been really honest with Coop from the beginning: she didn't want to become a captain. She loved the engineering work. She liked design and tech as well.

Being captain, being in charge of all these people, would have gotten in the way, even if she had been good at working with people, which she was not.

So she had been Coop's advisor on choosing among his first officer candidates. Coop had had reservations about all three candidates. Dix had been the most well rounded of all of them. He had known DV-Class vessels better than anyone. People liked him and, more importantly, they listened to him.

And, Coop had said—*Yash* had said—Dix had an uncanny ability to find the holes in a system. If there was a back door, even if it was unintentional—*especially* if it was unintentional—Dix would find it.

Yash was looking now to see if he had found anything here.

The unusual activity she had called up should have shown something like that, if he had done so. It would also have shown if he had tried and failed.

And he had.

He had spent hours after leaving Coop and Yash, searching for something, a way into the *anacapa* drive. But Dix hadn't found it, at least not from the console.

She looked down at Dix again, his hands on that container. The console should have showed if someone breached the container. Coop should have been notified if someone had.

But Dix, with that ability to find ways around systems, might have shut off the notifications.

She crouched, looked around the blood at the container's edges and the seals. They seemed normal, as normal as anything with blood smeared on it could be.

She couldn't entirely tell though. Not with a quick glance.

She stood up. She didn't want to open the container, not without Coop here. Not without help.

Dix could have set a trap. He might have set up something that would ensure the entire ship would blow up if she tried to open the container.

Her mouth had gone dry. She couldn't believe she was thinking of this, that she was mentally accusing Dix—someone she had known for years—of doing something so nasty.

Of course, this suicide was nasty, and she hadn't expected him to do that either.

But setting the *Ivoire*'s *anacapa* to blow, that required a special kind of nasty. Had he been crazy enough to believe that if he didn't want to live in this new time period, no one else did either?

And how would she know if that was the case without opening that container?

After voicing her suspicions for the recording she was making, she turned back to the console and made herself look at the notification system. She was looking to see if he had shut off the notifications that would have brought Coop here—or her, or someone else—if anyone touched the *anacapa* drive.

As far as she could tell, Dix hadn't touched the notification system. He hadn't touched any of it.

But did he need to? Would the system have notified her or Coop if Dix had touched it? Because he might have been authorized to do so.

Had she been careless enough to make it easy for the first officer to touch an *anacapa* drive, particularly a first officer like Dix, a man who had no real knowledge of the drives? She didn't know, and didn't remember what she had done. There were standard settings which allowed bridge officers access, and those were supposed to be altered once the main bridge crew was established.

The *Ivoire's* main bridge crew—the crew that had been on the bridge that horrid day over a year ago—had been together for years. She didn't remember everything she had done six months ago; she certainly couldn't remember what she had done more than a decade before.

She thought about accessing the notification records to see what she had set up, but she wasn't sure that was worthwhile. She usually did things properly. Should she trust in what she had usually done?

And did it matter?

Because Dix might have hidden what he touched.

Dix did have the ability to do something like that.

She closed her eyes. With all those paranoid thoughts, she was becoming as crazy as Dix. He was turning her into a crazy woman and he was dead.

One step at a time. Or, as Coop had said last night, one *problem* at a time.

Yash opened her eyes. She needed to find out exactly what Dix had accessed. As she did that, she needed to assess what that access meant. Then she would have to see if he had executed some inexplicable activity or performed activity he had tried to erase.

She didn't look at Dix's body. She couldn't. Not anymore.

She couldn't think about him. She decided to approach this like a math problem rather than an emotional problem. Tiny discovery after tiny discovery, keeping track in her head, making sure she understood whether or not the things she discovered could interact with each other in such a way as to make something new.

"I'm here. Now what?"

She jumped, her heart pounding. Coop had spoken from behind her. She had been expecting him, but she had gotten so deep into the work she hadn't thought of him in—however long.

She raised her head, turning until she could see him.

Coop stood near the entrance to the bridge. His hair was mussed as if he had been sleeping. He wore the same kind of black T-shirt and pants he had worn the night before, and she found herself wondering if he had even gone back to his rooms.

Not her business. What he did in his own time was personal. She didn't have a right to know.

He was scanning the entire bridge, probably seeing the empty work stations and the unattended captain's chair just like she had. He would note the changes since the last time he had been here, including the shuttered screens. He probably hadn't noticed the faint scent of death, though, since he stood just outside the entrance. He wasn't stepping into the bridge just in case the problem was internal and going inside would cause even more problems.

Procedure.

That calmed her. His presence calmed her.

She wasn't working this alone anymore.

She held up one finger, then explained her thinking in the recording, just so that she would remember.

Coop frowned as she spoke. She didn't mention Dix as she talked to the recording, didn't mention anything except her findings and her supposition on the ways those findings might work together.

When she finished, her gaze met Coop's. He looked both calm and serious, like he often did in the middle of a crisis.

He was someone she could rely on. She valued that more than she had realized.

She swallowed hard, gulping a little air as she did so. She had no idea how to tell Coop about Dix.

"Can I enter the bridge safely?" Coop asked.

"Yes," Yash said. "Come to me. You need to see this."

It was better to show him than to tell him.

At the same time, part of her didn't want him to know. She had no idea how Coop would react to this. They both had seen a lot of death among the crew—in battle, in the normal course of things like illness and aging. They had lost friends and colleagues from other ships. But they had never lost someone to suicide.

Coop walked slowly toward her, as if he was worried that something was going to go wrong near the other consoles. She directed him around the console she was working on, so he wouldn't get in her way.

Then she pointed at Dix's body, still wrapped around that *anacapa* drive.

Coop stared. His expression didn't change. Then he crouched, but didn't touch.

"The blood's tacky," he said.

"Yes," she said. "I think he's been here for hours."

"Have you called anyone from medical?"

"No," Yash said. "Not yet. I'm making sure Dix hasn't tampered with the *anacapa* drive."

Coop's head moved ever so slightly, as if he had started to shake it, and then stopped himself. He had placed his hands on his thighs, elbows out. Then he leaned forward just a little more.

"I don't see anything obvious," Coop said.

"Me either," Yash said. "But he chose to be here, and he touched that container in a variety of ways before dying."

Coop nodded, but didn't look at her. He was studying Dix's body and the container itself.

"I'm checking everything I can think of," Yash said.

Coop stood, glanced at the console she was working on, and frowned. He looked disturbed now.

"I revoked all Dix's clearances except the one that allowed him on the bridge," Coop said. "I should have revoked that one too."

A tiny thread of anger, barely discernable, in the deep timbre of his voice.

"No blaming," she said to him, like he had said to her when she discussed that *anacapa* freeze with him one of those drunken nights. "We get lost if we blame. It takes us in the wrong direction. Move forward."

Coop's lips twisted as if he had swallowed something sour.

"All right," he said. "Let's deal with what we have. What Dix presented us with."

The annoyance was clear in Coop's tone. His gaze met hers.

"Brief me," he said.

She did. She told him all she knew, and all she had done.

When she finished, she pointed at the container. The blood on its sides was turning black.

"The container concerns me," she said. "I have no idea if he breached it."

Coop followed her finger, staring at the container. "What could he have done if he had breached it?"

Coop made no secret of the fact that he was not an *anacapa* engineer. He had never wanted to learn how to do more than the basics on that drive.

Yash could think of a million things that anyone could do to tamper with the *anacapa*, but she knew that wasn't what Coop was asking.

"I mean," Coop said, still focused on the container—or maybe on the body beside it—"if he wanted to send us back into foldspace or into the past, wouldn't he have stuck around to see if it worked?"

That was when Yash knew that Coop still hadn't accepted how far Dix had deteriorated. Or maybe that kind of deterioration was unfathomable to Coop. It certainly didn't happen much among high-level DV-Class officers.

Yash wasn't sure it had ever happened before.

"At first, I too thought he was going to use his skills to send us back through time to our Fleet," she said. "Then I rejected the idea entirely."

Coop frowned at her. "But you still think he tampered with the *anacapa* drive."

She nodded, the movement small. "Suicides are angry people, Coop. Anger turned inward sometimes, but not always. Sometimes the suicide turns the anger outward as well."

Coop frowned at her as if he was trying to make sense of what she was saying. She didn't want to be more explicit, especially since she was still recording, but—

Coop cursed. "I almost said that Dix would never do anything like that, but I would have thought that Dix would never have done anything like *this* either."

He snapped his hand toward Dix's body, the movement revealing that Coop was as furious at Dix as Yash was.

"You think he tampered with the *anacapa* drive," Coop said.

"I don't know," Yash said. "He certainly tried, but I'm not sure how far he got or what his intentions were. I would have said that he killed himself after realizing he couldn't get into the system, but the bone knife belies that."

"Bone…oh." Coop crouched, and looked closely at the knife. Apparently he hadn't noticed it before. "That is part of a set."

"I know," she said.

"Those bone knives he got are the sharpest knives on the ship," Coop said.

"I know that too."

Coop looked up at her, then rose, slowly, his knees popping with the movement.

"You have a concern you haven't told me."

"I do," she said. "I'm afraid that he did something that would overload the *anacapa* drive."

"But nothing has happened yet, and he's clearly been dead for some time," Coop said.

Yash nodded. "I'm worried that he booby-trapped it."

"You think he would put this destruction on a timer of some kind?" Coop asked.

"That's one way." Yash peered at the body. She hated seeing Dix's hands still pressed against the container. "There are a lot of other ways to accomplish the same thing. Most of them use a trigger, not a timer, but they would have the same effect. They would overload the *anacapa* drive."

"From the tone of your voice," Coop said, "you have a specific vision of what an overloaded *anacapa* looks like. I understand it's bad. But either I don't know or never learned the details. Throughout my career, I was told that we needed to avoid it, and so we have. Except when we went into foldspace after the Quurzod weapons hit our ship."

Yash was shaking her head before he even finished. "What happened to us that day wasn't an *anacapa* overload. Those Quurzod weapons augmented the energy from the *anacapa* drive, altered it in some way, and that alteration destroyed a part of the *anacapa* as it was activating."

Coop was frowning. "So, what happened to us…that's not it. You mean something different when you say overload."

"I do," she said quietly. "I mean that everything explodes."

4

COOP TURNED AWAY from the *anacapa* container, away from Dix's body, away from Yash herself. He peered at the open portals.

Yash knew what he saw. The edge of the station. The other ships occasionally going by. The dots and light and blackness that all combined into this sector of space.

She also knew what he was doing as he looked away. He didn't want her to see his reaction.

But she had, already. He hadn't believed her when she said that everything would explode. He clearly needed a moment to think about what she had just said.

"Everything." He wasn't asking for clarification. He was repeating her word. Her unbelievable word.

"The *anacapa* has a lot of power, especially one this size—"

"You're talking overload." He spoke slowly. She recognized the tone. He was working it out for himself. "You mean one of those chain reactions, this *anacapa* drive will send the wrong kind of energy to the other *anacapa* drives nearby, triggering them, which will then cause this massive explosion, obliterating everything."

Technically, he was wrong. There was no "wrong kind of energy." But the effect was the same and the effect had been what she was talking about.

"If this *anacapa* drive overloads," she said, "then it could do many things. It could obliterate the ship. It could send us all back to foldspace, maybe in pieces. Or it could initiate those chain reactions you were talking about."

"Which would destroy the space station, the other ships, this ship, and everything in the vicinity," he said.

"Yes," she said quietly.

"Including every single human being."

She could only see the side of his face, but that impassive expression was back. The one that most people thought so calm, but which she knew was actually a cover for very deep emotions.

"You think Dix is trying to murder us all?" Coop asked.

"I think he was pretty angry about being here. I think he believed none of us belonged here. I also think he hated Lost Souls and what Boss is building." Yash swallowed hard again, wishing her mouth wasn't so dry. "So, yes. I think Dix might have been trying to destroy everything. I'm not sure he would think of it as murder. More as setting things right."

But what did she know? She wasn't a psychologist. She was an engineer.

Coop squared his shoulders, as if he was adjusting to a new weight that had just fallen on them. "How do we figure this out?"

"That's what I was doing when you arrived," Yash said.

"Do we touch the container?" Coop asked. "Do we remove it? Should we deactivate the *anacapa* remotely?"

Yash licked her lips. All of those things were possible, and all of them were predictable. If she could predict them, then Dix would have been able to.

"Should we bring others here to help you?" Coop asked, and something in his tone made her realize that her silence was frustrating him.

"No," she said. "Not yet. I worry that they'll trigger something. I won't be able to monitor them."

"I don't have the deep knowledge you have of the *anacapa* drive," Coop said. "I don't know how I can help you."

Yash nodded. Her heart, which had been pounding hard, had settled down. She felt calmer. Was it Coop's presence or was it because she had finally gotten a handle on what she feared?

"Dix picked this spot for a reason," she said. "He was sending us a message. He could have killed himself in his quarters. He could have fallen asleep and made sure he never woke up. There are a million ways he could have harmed himself, and none of them would have been this bloody or this obvious."

Coop turned, a slight frown between his eyebrows. Even though he was trying for the calm expression, he wasn't entirely managing it.

"I believe Dix wanted us to respond in a particular way." Yash took a deep breath. From this moment forward, clarity and honesty were the two most important parts of the conversation. "I believe he wanted *you* to respond in a particular way."

Coop nodded, and glanced at Dix's body. Then Coop nodded again.

"So, you need to imagine I didn't arrive first," Yash said. "You need to tell me what you would have done if you had been the person to discover Dix."

Coop folded his hands behind his back, head down, clearly contemplating. "And what if someone else had found him? Someone other than me? Wouldn't Dix have thought about that?"

"He would have," Yash said. "But he didn't know I visited the bridge a lot. I've never told him, and he wasn't usually here. So it didn't matter if someone else found Dix. Whoever it was—except for me—would have contacted you after making sure Dix was dead."

"But you did contact me," Coop said.

"After I ran through some diagnostics," Yash said. "Besides, if you didn't show up right away, I could take action. No one else could. Or rather, no one else would think to."

Coop's lips thinned. "All right," he said. "You want me to go through each step?"

"I need scenarios," she said. "If you found him, then what? If someone else did, then what? And work from there."

"You're betting that he used a trigger, not a timer," Coop said.

"Well, no," Yash said. "First, I'm going to go over everything he did on this panel. I'll find the timer if he placed one here. If I'm even right about the fact that he set a booby-trap at all."

35

"You are," Coop said. "You're right about the message. He and I argued endlessly about using the *anacapa* again, trying to get home. I finally told him I was never going to try."

"When did you say that?" Yash asked.

"I said it repeatedly," Coop said, "but he didn't hear me. Not until after the debacle on Starbase Kappa."

"He heard you then?" Yash asked.

"Not entirely," Coop said. "He kept trying, kept thinking I didn't understand what he meant, how we could recreate the circumstances that got us here, and that recreation would send us home."

"I never thought it would," Yash said.

"Neither did I," Coop said, "and that was what we argued first. Finally, I said I wasn't going to try. I was done trying. We weren't going home. Not ever. And nothing he could ever say would change my mind on that."

She could hear the forcefulness behind Coop's soft words. She could imagine how he had said that to Dix. Coop would have used that command voice of his. He would have spoken with hard and clipped authority, and he would have gotten through to Dix.

"When?" she asked. "When did you tell him that?"

Coop winced. "Last week."

Yash nodded, wanting to say she was unsurprised. But she wasn't. She was surprised that Coop was still taking Dix seriously as recently as one week ago. Dix had caused a serious crisis on Starbase Kappa, and Coop had still been trying to work with him?

Usually Yash didn't question Coop's judgment and she didn't say anything now. But Coop's refusal to accept Dix's mental failures was not like Coop. Had he been playing a longer game? Or had he seen something of himself in Dix? Had the Psychological and Emotional Stress Department been involved? Or had Coop simply been trying to talk Dix down on his own?

"The next time I saw him after that conversation," Coop said slowly, "was last night. And I thought—I guess I was hoping—with that apology, that the conversation last week worked."

"The discussion was tense," Yash said.

"It was," Coop said. "But he apologized. At the beginning, and at the end."

I owe you guys an apology. And *I'm sorry.*

He never said what he was sorry for.

"I thought—I hoped—he was going in a new direction." Coop shook his head. "I wanted to believe he would improve. I always wanted to believe he would improve. With logic, with time."

Yash nodded. Time. What had Dix said about time? He had looked out the window and had said, *There's the future. It's been there all along, hasn't it?*

Yash had thought he was looking forward, finally, taking those steps toward leaving their losses behind.

She had believed in Dix too. Maybe not as much as Coop had, but she had wanted Dix to rejoin them. The third leg in a once-sturdy stool.

"But Dix said 'this' had happened to all of us." Coop frowned at her. "Did that mean he thought we all were as despondent as him, unable to live in the moment? Didn't I disabuse him of that?"

Clearly, Coop hadn't disabused Dix of anything.

"He was apologizing in advance for what he was going to do here," Yash said. "Not for his behavior in the past. But for this."

Coop nodded.

"And now we need to figure out what he's done," Yash said. "I'm going to finish here. You're going to give me scenarios."

"Yeah, I will," Coop said. "But not yet."

He moved to a different console, then pressed his palm against it. The screen lit up. His fingers danced across it, but Yash couldn't see what he was doing.

She needed him to focus on the *anacapa* drive. She needed those scenarios if she was going to figure out how to use the data she was slowly deriving from Dix's actions.

A holographic screen popped up in front of Coop, and Yash recognized it. Communications.

"This is the captain," he said. "Evacuate the *Ivoire* immediately. Do not gather your things, do not search for a friend or family member. Proceed to the nearest exit and leave now."

The screen glowed red. He touched something on it, and the red blinked three times.

He wanted the message to repeat but only three times. Yash had no idea how long the people on board would have before there were more repeats.

"What're you doing?" she asked.

"Saving lives," he said.

5

WHILE HE WAITED FOR the thirty people on board to evacuate, Coop opened another screen and talked through all the scenarios he could think of.

Yash listened with half an ear. She was still pulling up more data. Dix had spent a lot of time on the bridge before he had killed himself.

She was becoming more and more convinced that her paranoia had been justified; Dix had done something.

She just hadn't figured out what yet.

The message repeated twice before Coop stopped talking. Yash looked up, startled. He hadn't finished the first scenario yet, let along getting to any others.

He was bent over the console, the screen in front of him still glowing red as the minutes ticked down before the announcement repeated.

A second half-screen floated over the console to his left, and she recognized that screen by color. It showed all the heat signatures of every living creature on board.

As she watched, five left the *Ivoire*. She scanned the entire map of the ship, just as she had been trained to do, and saw only two remaining heat signatures—hers and Coop's.

"Computer," he said, "check the entire ship for life signs."

His fingers brushed the side of the half-screen, creating yet another half-screen. That one showed the environmental system, calculating usage of air, based on human usage. She had taught Coop that trick years ago as a way of going outside the system to see if anyone hid on board.

She had learned that trick from Dix.

Bastard.

And then she made herself focus, and returned to work.

She got deep into the data, only dimly aware that Coop had moved away from the console to the main navigation console. Then the floor hummed beneath her feet, catching her in a familiar vibration.

He was starting up the ship. Of course he was. It was the only smart play.

If Dix had rigged the *anacapa* drive to overload and cause a cascade effect with the other *anacapa* drives nearby, then the best way to handle the crisis was to make sure only one *anacapa* drive exploded.

Theirs.

Coop didn't need the *anacapa* drive to move the ship. The standard engines would be able to get the *Ivoire* far away from the space station in a matter of minutes.

Yash tapped the console, making sure that there was no change in the *anacapa* drive as Coop started the ship. If the readings on the console were correct—and she had to assume they were—then the *anacapa* drive was just fine, at least at the moment.

She was banking a lot on the fact that Dix was using a trigger and not a timer. But to Dix, who wanted to make a point, a trigger made more sense.

A trigger guaranteed that someone found his body, saw his protest or whatever the hell this was, and had a chance of understanding his point.

A timer would make sure the *anacapa* explosion occurred, but if it occurred at the wrong moment and obliterated everything, then no one would ever know about Dix's suicide and his damn message.

She needed to concentrate. Because what she knew and what she guessed were two different things. There were no real studies on what happened to a ship when an *anacapa* overloaded. There were theories, not true knowledge.

The *Ivoire* would probably be destroyed, but there was a chance it would travel, damaged and unusable, into foldspace.

And then there was the chance that the *Ivoire* would explode, and all of its pieces, including its human crew, would be forced into foldspace. The crew would die, unprotected and alone, in the vastness of space.

Right now, its human crew numbered two—herself and Coop.

There was no way to protect her and Coop, except to find the problem and disarm it. She wasn't even going to put on an environmental suit. If the ship exploded and she and Coop were thrust into foldspace—alive—all an environmental suit would buy them was two or three days of agony, waiting for a rescue that would never come.

If Coop ordered her into an environmental suit, she would put it on. Otherwise, she was just going to continue working.

The air shifted, adding just a bit of oxygen like it always did when the ship was in motion, designed to keep the crew alert. The extra oxygen was a bit excessive, designed for a full crew compliment.

Instead, Coop was piloting the *Ivoire* alone. The ship was designed for that, but it wasn't recommended. And he almost always used a copilot.

Instead, he let Yash work.

So she did until he spoke up.

"We're clear of the space station and the shipping lanes," he said. "If we blow, we go alone."

In more ways than one. But she didn't say that. She didn't say anything.

Instead, she nodded.

"And," he said, "I don't know if you heard what I was doing, but I managed to finish the scenarios you asked for."

Perfect timing. She had done just about all she could with the bits of the data that Dix had touched. All she had been able to figure out was that he had come into this bridge with a clear plan. Dix might even have had a list—*do this to misdirect here; do that to misdirect there*—because none of what he had done, in the order he had done it, made sense otherwise.

Of course, she was following the trail of a crazy man who had ended up committing suicide. There was always the chance that he had done all of this out of order because he had been out of his mind.

She wasn't going to assume that. He had seemed rational enough the night before.

"All right," she said. "Let's give those scenarios a go."

She needed to listen first, see if there were similarities in the scenarios, things that Dix could have predicted. And then she had to correlate those similarities to whatever he had done—even though he had done those things out of order.

She nodded to Coop, and cleared a small screen before her, ready to listen.

6

SCENARIO ONE.

Coop's voice, rich and methodical, filled the bridge. Coop had a screen up as well, and he was making notes, just like Yash was. Only he was probably looking for different things.

After we left the bar last night, Yash, I went to the space station. I wouldn't have returned to the Ivoire *for two days or more. That's important. That's one of my patterns.*

She hadn't known that. Had Dix? Maybe. If he had been focused on Coop.

So I would have entered the bridge, and I would have assumed—and Dix probably assumed—that no one else had entered since he had.

After a minimum of two days, this bridge would stink. The environmental system would scrub the smell as much as it could, but a human body, particularly the size of Dix's, has an overpowering stench that challenges even the best environmental system.

It sounded like Coop was speaking from experience. Yash wasn't sure why he had that kind of experience. But she didn't know his entire history, any more than he knew all of hers.

The bridge environmental system is on minimal, so I'm sure I would have smelled him before I saw him. That would have immediately put me on alert. I would have known something was wrong, and I would have investigated—slowly.

I would have cursed myself for coming alone, for no longer wearing the standard uniform, for not carrying a weapon as a matter of routine. I've gotten pretty lax, Yash. I've become too comfortable in this place.

She hadn't expected Coop to be so honest. She glanced at him over the console. He shrugged, and toggled something, pausing his voice.

"I figured you needed to hear those things as well," he said. "Dix would know what I would be wearing. He would know what I am capable of."

She nodded. Coop was right. Dix would know all that. That was one reason Dix had become first officer—his ability to predict Coop's behavior.

Coop gave her a small smile, half sheepish, half rueful, and then he toggled his voice back on.

It doesn't take long to examine the bridge, and Dix's body is hard to miss. I would have found it fast.

By then it would have been in an obvious state of decay. I would scan the rest of the bridge, but I would assume, from what I saw of Dix's body, that there was no immediate threat, that the threat had been days ago, when Dix had died.

Coop's voice had gotten sad. There was an implication in his tone, something she felt as well: it was entirely plausible that Dix could have been dead for two days and no one would have noticed.

Dix had to know that as well. He'd been left alone a lot. That one detail alone made the trigger scenario the most plausible—that and the fact that nothing else had happened yet.

I would have gone to the body. I would have examined it the way I had done when you pointed the body out to me.

In other words, he would have crouched, looked, and examined.

I would not have touched him or anything near him, including that knife. I would have seen it. I would have assumed, from its presence, the fact that his carotid artery had been severed, and the way he was lying, that he had done this to himself.

I would have assumed that, as he died, he put his hands on the container, and I would have assumed he had done so for a reason. That reason would have been to send a message to me: that I should have listened to him about using the anacapa *drive to get us home, and since I refused him, he killed himself. Like a damn petulant child who wasn't getting his way.*

Yash smiled. Exactly.

I would have been angry first. I am angry. I suppose, even in that scenario, the one in which I did not suspect Dix of doing anything malicious, I would have been angry for days. Maybe afterward, I would have mourned. Maybe.

Coop's voice had trembled as he said that. There was more in his tone than he realized. A little devastation lurked beneath it.

Yash hadn't realized until today just how much Coop had cared about Dix.

The first thing I would have done, even as I crouched down to look at Dix, is contact the medical team. I wouldn't have asked for a specific person, because I have no idea who is on the ship at any given point. I do know that we always have a medical team on board.

Then he chuckled on the recording, which surprised her. She glanced over at him. Coop definitely was not chuckling now. He looked very serious.

Except right at the moment, I guess.

The scenario paused there, as if Coop had contemplated what he was going to say next. Or maybe he had been thinking about the risks he and Yash were taking.

Anyway...the medical team. I would have taken whoever was here. There would have been no reason to bring in a specialist that I would have seen, and Dix hadn't been close to anyone in the medical core. Or anywhere, for that matter. Which, I suppose, was part of the problem. His entire support system had been left in the past.

Yash started. She hadn't thought of that. She wondered how many others on the *Ivoire* crew had the same issue. She had never asked.

The medical team wouldn't have arrived immediately. I wouldn't have asked them to act like it was an emergency. So I would have had to wait, and while I waited, I would have tried to find out why the bridge itself hadn't notified me when Dix started bleeding. It should have.

Yash had looked for that as well. But she hadn't gone at it directly. She had cycled through the various systems, looking for something awry. She had found the command shutdowns that Dix had ordered, specifically the way he had shut off bridge notifications to senior staff members.

Dix hadn't tried to hide the shutdown commands, then. Because he expected Coop to look for them, and for nothing else?

I would have started with the environmental system, because it was the part of the bridge that would have noticed the blood first. If I didn't find anything there, I would have moved to the notification system itself, as well as the entire security system.

I have no idea how much I would have gotten done, because I can't factor in how long it would have taken the medical team to arrive. I also have no idea what I would have found.

But Yash did. She had found tampering in the *notification* system first, not the environmental system.

So Dix hadn't foreseen everything Coop would have done, in the order in which he would have done it.

Once the medical team arrived, I would have turned the investigation and the handling of Dix's body over to them. I would have supervised his removal from the area of the anacapa *container, making sure the team didn't touch anything they shouldn't have, but that would have been the extent of my focus.*

You'll have to look up what their procedures are for the dead body of a known bridge member, and with an easily discernable cause. I don't know that.

This time, Yash toggled the scenario playback off.

"What did you mean, 'a known bridge member'?" she asked Coop.

He frowned at her. He tilted his head, as if he couldn't quite believe the question. Clearly, whatever he was thinking about was fairly obvious, at least from his perspective.

"It's the 'easily discernable cause' that's the important part of the sentence," he said. "Not the known bridge member."

"Okay," Yash said. "Talk me through that. You clearly know more about it than I do."

He blinked in surprise, then nodded.

"We do a training exercise, several dozen of them, in fact, designed for all sorts of scenarios—"

"We who?" she asked.

"Anyone on the leadership track," he said. "When you make it to be considered as captain material, they run all kinds of holographic and hypothetical scenarios. Several of them have to do with a dead body on the bridge."

"Several of them," she repeated. She had never heard of this.

"Yes," he said. "If the ship has been breached by person or persons unknown who then murder a member of the bridge crew and leave the corpse on the bridge. Or an enemy, with malicious intent, leaves a body on the bridge."

"Malicious intent?" Yash asked. "What does that mean?"

Coop gave her a guarded look. "There are a lot of ways to destroy a ship, Yash. One way is to take out its command structure."

She nodded. She knew that.

"The body could be a Trojan horse. It could be filled with toxins or with a virus or some kind of plague. It could be rigged to explode—"

Coop stopped talking as Yash whirled, and looked down at Dix. She hadn't thought of that at all. Did he have explosives on him? Was *he* rigged to explode, not the *anacapa* drive?

Coop cursed. "That's what he did, isn't it?"

"It's certainly safer and easier than messing with the *anacapa* drive," she said. But it still bothered her that Dix had done a bunch of other things on the control panel.

Coop had already moved to the supplies locker. Inside that locker was containment clothing as well.

"What are you doing?" she asked.

"I'm going to check him out."

"He'll have set it up so that if you move him..." She stopped. She didn't know that either.

She picked up a hand scanner and took several small steps over to the body.

"Don't touch him," Coop said. "We don't know if he used the entire 'body on the bridge' playbook."

She turned the scanner on, keeping it as far from the *anacapa* container as possible. The scanner was useless to examine an *anacapa* drive, which was where her focus had been. She had figured the medical team would eventually examine the body.

But the scanner could interact with a damaged *anacapa* drive. Anything with energy could. She couldn't worry about that.

"Yash," Coop said. "Don't—"

"I'm not touching him," she said.

She held the scanner near his face, not sure what she was looking for. The scanner showed Dix was still in rigor. Then it delved into his entire bone structure, the soft tissues, all of the biological details. She moved the scanner slightly, saw that, indeed, the carotid had been cut all the way through. The artery looked flat and useless, probably because it wasn't filled with blood.

Information, flowing along the side of the scanner, actually listed the rate of decay and was pinpointing the time of death.

She didn't look. She roughly knew when that was.

Coop joined her, crouching beside her. He wore an environmental suit, which surprised her.

"You need to suit up," he said.

She nodded. He was right. If they touched the body and anything got released, they could die horribly.

She handed the scanner to Coop, stood, and headed around the other side of the console, to the supplies locker. Lots of weapons in there. Dix could have used any one of them to kill himself.

Instead he had used that bone knife.

Maybe he already knew he didn't have access to the locker.

But that hadn't stopped him from finding a back door into the console, and tampering there. He would have been able to tamper with the locker door as well. The lock there wasn't nearly as complicated as the system on the control panel.

She pulled out an environmental suit sized for her. Her regular suit was in her cabin on the lower deck. She hadn't even bothered to move that suit to her apartment on the space station, which said something about her attitude.

She slipped the suit on, and pulled up the hood. Then she glanced over her shoulder to see if Coop had done the same with his.

He was leaning over the body, the scanner just above it. She felt her breath catch. She hadn't warned him about staying away from the *anacapa* drive. He should have known that, of course, but still. She always preferred to err on the side of caution.

"Yash," Coop said. "There is something here."

She made her way back, feeling restricted in the suit. She usually didn't wear them. In fact, she couldn't remember the last time she had worn one.

"Come see this," Coop said. "Double-check me."

She crouched beside him, the material stretching over her clothes, pulling on it. She hated that feature of environmental suits in real gravity. The suits felt looser in zero-g, although it was arguable about whether or not they were.

She flicked on the suit's data stream, letting it run along one side of her clear hood. She also set the suit to alert her should anything toxic reveal itself in the atmosphere around her—toxic or potentially dangerous.

Then she took the scanner from Coop.

"His back and his left side," Coop said.

She brought the scanner as close as she dared, saw nothing obvious in the shape of his body, his clothing, or his skin. But the scanner read nanobit activity near the armpit and shoulder blade.

She enhanced the scanner, saw that the nanobits had become a coating over him. The chemical analysis made no sense to her, so she had the scanner explain it.

The scanner told her that the coating was made of a touch explosive developed in the same culture that had developed the bone knife.

"Did you see what that was?" she asked Coop, then thrust the scanner toward him.

49

She couldn't see Coop's expression through his hood. The light near the *anacapa* drive caused a weird reflection on the clear material.

But she didn't have to see Coop's face to know how he felt.

He felt like she did.

Dix had left the damn knife as something that would mislead them, and as a clue. Bastard. What had he been playing at?

She shook her head a little.

He hadn't been playing at all.

She moved the scanner across the rest of his body, looking for more coating or a variation on it. She found it near his left hip.

"Those are the places we would have used to leverage him off the floor," Coop said quietly.

"He was trying to take us all out," Yash said.

"But he wasn't," Coop said. "That container should have prevented any explosion from hitting the *anacapa* drive. Right?"

She was the one who had told Coop that. It was a great simplification. Various forms of energy could hit and interact with the *anacapa*. Most of them were rare, and often only occurred in strange circumstances.

Like an explosion. And not an explosion of the ship, where the energies and components were known. But an explosion using a different kind of device, like a touch explosive made of nanobits.

Still, that didn't answer her initial question: What had Dix been doing on the console?

She moved the scanner toward the container, following along Dix's arms to see if he had put more explosive on them.

No explosive, but the scanner lit up red when it got to his hands.

The word *breach* blinked, over and over again.

Breach.

Coop glanced over her shoulder. "The *container's* been breached?"

She nodded.

"But it's not obvious. It's not open," Coop said.

Exactly. She clicked through the scanner's readings. She let out a small breath.

"He used acid," she said, more to herself than Coop.

"For what?" Coop asked.

"On his hands." She winced. God, that would have been painful. And he would have had to do it before he slit his own throat.

She hadn't known this man. She had thought she had, but she hadn't. The determination he had shown, the level of destruction he was attempting.

She was appalled.

Coop stared at the scanner, then he looked at Dix's hands. "That's why they're attached to the container? They're not leaning on anything?"

She didn't move the scanner closer. She didn't dare.

"They're inside the container, just a little. The acid ate away his skin, but more importantly, it ate away the edges of the container."

"It looks solid," Coop said.

"If we touch it," she said, "it'll collapse."

Dix couldn't get into the system. That's what she had seen. He had gotten into the notification system, the environmental system—nominally anyway—but he couldn't find a back way into the *anacapa* drive. He had tried, which was why the readings she had initially gotten made no sense.

There was a logic to his early actions, but not his later ones—at least, not the kind of logic she had assumed. His early actions obfuscated what he was trying to do. His later ones showed his frustration as he searched for, but didn't find, a side way into the *anacapa* controls.

"Now what?" Coop asked.

Yash looked at him in surprise. She wasn't used to Coop asking for instructions from her.

But of course he was. They had to juggle two things: a body that could explode if they handled it wrong, and an exposed *anacapa* drive that could already be unstable.

One problem at a time.

First, the body. If it exploded, then anything else she had done up to that point would not matter.

She let out a small breath. The body was a two-pronged problem: the touch explosive and those hands.

"We need two different localized shields," she said to Coop. "First, one around the body—except the hands and arms. The other around the container."

The localized bridge shields protected crew members or bridge equipment in case of an attack, usually some kind of laser weapon or hand-to-hand combat. The bridge shields weren't very powerful, or else they would interfere with the operation of some of the equipment, but they would contain an explosion the size of the one that Dix tried to create—provided he hadn't done anything more, like swallow something explosive to enhance the magnitude of the bomb.

"We'll section the shields at the elbows, just in case." Coop said. He understood what she meant to do. The suggestion of sectioning made that clear.

The bridge shields were badly designed. Yash had always meant to fix them. Their energy could harm skin that came into long-term contact with them, so no one could—for example—stick an arm out, have the shield form around the arm, and then shoot an interloper. The burning on the skin would have been too painful, and the shot would end up being impossible.

But it didn't matter if Dix's arms burned at the point of contact with the shields. Still, she double-checked with the scanner, making sure no touch explosives—or even a handful of unbonded nanobits—coated his arms.

None did, not from the shoulder/armpit down.

She activated both shields, and watched them burn through the skin. For the first time since putting on the environmental suit, she was glad she wasn't breathing the air on the bridge. The stench had to be foul.

"Now what?" Coop asked.

She let out a small breath. "We unbond the nanobits. That should disassemble the touch explosive without setting it off. We isolate the component parts so they can't reassemble automatically, and then we remove the body from the bridge."

"All right," Coop said. "You handle the *anacapa* drive, and I'll deal with the body itself."

She glanced at him, about to protest, but then she stopped. He was right. If they worked in tandem, they might have a chance of getting out of here alive.

"Okay," she said. "I'll see what the damage is, and work from there. Tell me when or if you want to move the body."

Coop nodded. He moved to one of the consoles. He could activate all kinds of equipment inside the shield, using the right commands.

For a moment, she worried that he wouldn't know them, but of course he would. This was standard. Deactivating nanobit bonding was something that everyone learned. They just didn't learn how to do it with nanobits designed to explode.

Coop would know, though. That was the kind of thing that a captain could learn without becoming an expert.

It was the *anacapa* drive that was the main problem. She had to deal with that herself.

She made herself focus on the container. She stared at it, then had the computer analyze the container's solidity.

As she expected, the container was compromised.

She went to the console that housed the *anacapa* controls. She called up a holographic image of the *anacapa* itself.

The holographic image glowed golden, just like it was supposed to. She flipped it, changed it, moved it around, and examined it from all angles.

As far as she could tell, using just the equipment, the *anacapa* was fine. Whatever Dix had done to the container hadn't yet reached the drive.

She stopped, double-checked that assumption, gave it some extra thought. Nothing Dix had done could have altered the diagnostics for the *anacapa* drive. He hadn't tampered with those readings. She had a record of everything he touched, and he hadn't touched that.

Which meant she could trust the readings she was getting on the *anacapa* drive.

She needed to isolate the drive, and since it hadn't been harmed—yet—by that acid, she could do so.

She opened another screen, tapped it, and prepped another full bridge shield. She would put that shield around the *anacapa* drive.

The problem was that she had to do so in a perfectly timed manner. She had to open the container so that its lid wasn't inside that shield, and then she had to wrap the shield around the *anacapa* drive. The problem was that she would be jostling the container when she opened it, and that jostling might put the acid in touch with the *anacapa*.

And she couldn't even put anything in-between the drive and the container. There wasn't enough room.

She brought up one more small screen, and monitored Coop's work, as if he were a rookie engineer. He had pulled the nanobits off the body, and was separating them into component categories. He had created small shield bubbles so that the component parts of the nanobits would flow into the appropriate bubble, just like they were supposed to.

If he were one of her rookie engineers, he would have received a commendation from her.

She half smiled, hoping she would be able to do as well as Coop was.

She wasn't going to tell him what she was trying. Either it would work or it wouldn't. If it didn't work, then they were both screwed anyway.

She thought of automating the commands, letting the computer open the container and then send the shield down. Whatever she gained in split-second timing, she might lose if Dix had tampered with some of the automated command system.

Some of the automation lived in the environmental equipment. She didn't have time to check to see if Dix had tampered with any of that.

She needed to get the *anacapa* drive out of that container, and into a new one.

One step at a time. One problem at a time.

She was going to handle the movement herself. She had done tricky work on *anacapa* drives before. She could do it again.

She moved the holographic control screen with her, and walked to the front of the container. Dix had wrapped himself around three sides with his feet extended as close to the front of the container as possible.

He had clearly been thinking someone might try to break into the container. He figured they would have to maneuver around him.

Yash had to, because he was mostly covered in a shield. (*Which you hadn't expected, you bastard*, she thought at him, wishing he could actually hear that. He had always hated it when she yelled at him. She wanted him to hate this now. She certainly did.)

She had to take three-part action, not two-part action. She had to shut off the shield around the container, open the lid, and then put a shield around the *anacapa* drive.

She needed to do that in record time.

She wasn't going to think about being fast. She was going to concentrate on being precise.

"Okay," Coop said, startling her. "The body's ready to move, except for the hands."

She nodded. "You'll be able to move it in a minute or two. Call up a stretcher and a protective medical bubble. By the time it gets here, we'll be ready for it."

Everything in the medical bay was automated, so that someone trapped alone on the *Ivoire* could take care of themselves if need be. Hell, someone trapped alone on any of the Fleet's ships large enough to have a med bay could do that.

"Yes'm. I'll get right on that," Coop said. There was amusement in his tone, which meant that he had probably already done exactly what she asked.

Her cheeks heated. She had just given the captain orders. She really had moved far away from Fleet thinking in a lot of areas.

Then she put Coop out of her mind. She needed to fully concentrate to make sure she didn't miss a step of what she was going to do.

She set the commands on the screen before her, but didn't execute them. She kept them open, so that she could hit the commands in the proper sequence.

Step one: cancel the shield around the container.

Step two: open the container.

Step three: shield the *anacapa* drive itself.

Then she crouched near the container.

If she did this right, it would take less than thirty seconds to complete the entire task, maybe as few as ten seconds. If she did it wrong…

She took a deep breath, and started.

7

WITH THE TOUCH of a finger, Yash canceled the shield. It flared, then vanished, just like it was supposed to.

Then she commanded the *anacapa* container lid to open. This step made her the most nervous. She didn't know if the acid had destroyed any of the controls inside the container.

The container shuddered, then the lid floated back, hitting the shield around Dix's torso. The lid started to close again, but she activated the second shield, the one meant to surround the *anacapa* drive.

For a half second, she thought the lid would close before the shield activated, but the lid banged against the second shield, and flipped backward again. The lid hung between the two shields for a moment, then the entire container fell apart, leaving the *anacapa* drive to glow in the middle of the mess.

"Good job," Coop said. "We can get the body out of here now."

She nodded, feeling her heart race. It hadn't been racing earlier, but it was now—a reaction to getting this done.

The container's side was almost completely gone. She saw the bones and sinew in Dix's hands, looking half eaten away, like raw meat badly carved up.

He had done that to himself deliberately, probably as a last resort, after he couldn't break into the controls.

She shook her head. She wasn't going to think about him. He wasn't worth her time.

Instead, she stood and went to the equipment locker. There was a smaller container inside of it, a backup in case the *anacapa* drive's container got damaged.

At least, she hoped there was one, because that was the one thing she had forgotten to check.

She opened the door, and stared at everything for a moment, her heart still thudding hard.

There were more environmental suits, some smaller weapons, and a lot of parts of consoles, chairs, communications equipment. Finally, she saw the extra container, shoved toward the back.

She grabbed the container, slid it out, and turned.

The stretcher had lowered itself near Dix's body. Coop was supervising the transition. She hoped he had already wrapped the body in the protective medical bubble.

God, she was nervous. She didn't trust Coop—who probably knew more about this part of the plan than she ever would—to do his job properly.

At least the *make-sure* instructions hadn't come out of her mouth.

This time.

The stretcher floated upward, Dix's body flat on its back, the arms barely attached. The elbows were burned, the forearms hanging on only by bits of sinew. The hands didn't bleed or drip or anything, which surprised her, given how they looked. But they had been that way for more than twenty-four hours. There probably wasn't any fluid left.

Coop watched it, his expression grim. He had his arms crossed over his chest as the stretcher made its way toward the exit.

She didn't want to watch the stretcher leave. Instead, she went to the *anacapa* drive. She pushed the most damaged piece of the container away with her booted foot, and shoved the other pieces aside as well.

Then she set the backup container down in front of the drive on the one spot where Dix's body hadn't rested. She opened that container, made sure the interior had accumulated no dirt or grime, and left the lid tilted back.

She was nearly done.

Only a few more steps.

She shut off the shield around the *anacapa* drive, then gathered the drive in her arms. She hadn't held an *anacapa* drive in nearly five years. She could feel it pulsing through her environmental suit.

The drive was inactive, so she could move it without compromising its connection to the controls—provided she did so fast.

And she didn't want to hold this drive for very long.

Her teeth vibrated. The flowing energy actually made the bones in her body hum. She hated holding these drives. Holding it seemed easier with the suit on, but she still felt like she was holding something that could destroy her in a matter of seconds.

She put the drive in the new container.

With her gloved hands, she reached down and moved the bottom of the old container out of the way. Then, using her knuckles, she shoved the new container into place.

The bottom of the container would run through its diagnostics, making sure none of that acid had eaten its way to the controls. She didn't set the diagnostics to look for the acid, in case Dix had thought to tamper with that specific a command.

He hadn't. The diagnostic ran clean, and the system asked her if she wanted to establish contact with the *anacapa* drive through this new container.

She said yes.

The container and the *anacapa* flared orange as they hooked up, and then the lid came down on its own.

The system asked her if she wanted to engage the drive.

She declined.

Set up, ready to go. When—if—Coop decided to use the *Ivoire's* *anacapa* drive again, the system would remind whoever was in charge that the *anacapa* had been placed in a new container and would ask them to run the diagnostics again.

She let out a small sigh, stood, and stared at the pieces of the previous container, scattered across the floor.

Dix had tried to destroy everything.

Dix.

She shook her head, then set the thought aside.

She used another screen to access the cleaning equipment stored on the next deck down, in case Dix had messed with the bridge's cleaning protocols. She programmed the cleaners to come and remove the bits of the container and whatever else Dix had left around the bridge.

She marked the instruction *hazardous material*, so it would be dealt with properly.

Then she rocked back on her heels and closed her eyes.

"Done?" Coop asked.

She nodded without opening her eyes.

"We're safe?" he asked.

"As we can be." She opened her eyes and stood up. The cleaning equipment—some small robotic pieces and floating garbage dumps that looked oddly like that stretcher—were making their way onto the bridge.

"We have to dispose of the body," Coop said.

She nodded.

"I'd like to do it together," he said.

She wanted that, too. She wanted Dix gone. "You want me to join you in the med bay?"

"No," Coop said. "We can dispose of the body from here. I just want to watch it leave the ship."

He had moved to the captain's chair. He raised one of the portals, revealing the exterior of the ship. Then he tapped the controls, and a small pod jettisoned from the med bay side of the *Ivoire*.

The pod was small and white. Yash had seen more of them than she ever wanted to. A handful of the pods were designed to float to a particular planet or just travel through space, but they were golden, and often reflective. Usually, they were reserved for someone with clout.

Coop could probably ask for one of those at his funeral, but Yash couldn't. Or she couldn't *have*, if they were still with the Fleet.

But the white pods. They traveled a particular distance, and then burned from the inside out, scattering what little remained into whatever solar system the ship found itself in.

"I hope you sent him as far away as possible," Yash said.

"No. I want to see the destruction." Coop's voice was soft, but that didn't hide the emotion. The fury remained.

The pod glowed red for a moment, then appeared to melt. For a moment, the pod looked like it had become smoke, and then even that evaporated.

Yash let out a breath. Neither of them had said the customary words for a Fleet funeral. They hadn't even said words of honor for an enemy.

Instead, they stood, watching in silence.

"That's done," Coop said after a moment, then shut the portal.

Yash stared at it just a little longer.

"People are going to wonder what happened," she said. "Why we took the *Ivoire* out. What happened to Dix. They'll want to know."

Coop nodded. He shut down screens as well.

"Routine maintenance," he said. "We were just checking systems on the ship."

"That's not what the manifests will say," Yash said.

"You're going to clear all of that." Coop gave her a flat look. "We're not going to tell anyone what happened here."

Yash frowned. "But if they ask about Dix…?"

"We tell them he killed himself. We had to dispose of the body."

The words hung between them for a moment.

"Someone is going to want a service," she said.

"Yeah," Coop said dryly. "I'm sure they will."

"It'll be odd if we don't speak at it," she said.

"It'll be worse if we do." Coop's lips moved in a smile, but his eyes didn't change. They remained flat and calm. "He committed suicide. We're not up to talking about it. We won't have to either. Others will step in."

Yash nodded. Coop was right. The crew knew how he felt about suicides. He had no sympathy for them.

Yash had, until today.

Of course, Dix wasn't just a suicide. He had tried to take everyone with him.

And she would have to process that, apparently without the help of her comrades on the *Ivoire*.

Coop must have seen something on her face. He put a hand on her arm, his touch gentle.

"Dix was wrong," Coop said. "You have to remember that."

"I know," she said. "Killing himself, setting up this—"

"No," Coop said. "Saying that something bad had happened to all of us. He was wrong about that."

Yash frowned. Coop had been as upset about this move into the future as everyone else.

"The Fleet moves forward, Yash," Coop said. "We're as far forward as any ship has ever been. Not in space. In time. It's what we're designed for."

She swallowed. "Then why are you disbanding the crew?"

"I'm not," Coop said. "I'm letting them choose where they stand, just like I would have at any sector base stop."

Yash resisted the urge to look at the closed portal, at the new container on the floor.

"We learned a lot about Dix today," Coop said. "We've learned a bit about the others. We'll still have a crew years from now, but it'll be a different one. And we'll have figured out how to define our mission this far forward. We haven't figured that out yet."

She let out a small breath. He was right. That was the dislocated feeling she had had. It wasn't because they were here. That was almost theoretical. She hadn't tried to return to the past, and she had encountered many more unusual cultures than this one in the course of her career.

What they had lost was a sense of community, of the Fleet guiding them. They were on their own right now.

They needed a new mission.

"Do you know what that mission will be?" Yash asked.

"No," Coop said. "I think we keep searching for the Fleet, for what it has become in this time period. But if we don't find it, we have tools. We have resources. We can act as an adjunct to our Fleet, here and now."

"Boss won't like that," Yash said.

"In some ways," Coop said, "it dovetails with what she's trying to do with Lost Souls."

Finding the old tech. Revitalizing it. Making it work for them.

"You going to bring her in?" Yash asked.

"Only if it becomes necessary," Coop said. "Fleet business belongs to the Fleet."

"And the rest of the crew?" Yash asked.

"We'll let them settle. We have time. We need more information." Coop glanced at the closed portal. "I think, after today, the weak ones are gone."

Yash nodded, hoping he was right. Then she straightened her spine.

"You asked me to get rid of the information about what happened here," she said.

"Yes," Coop said.

"But if we stay Fleet, we follow Fleet procedure. I'll isolate all of the relevant information, and restrict access. Only you and I will be able to open anything to do with today."

Coop smiled at her, and this time, the smile reached his eyes. "Good call, Engineer Zarlengo. You are exactly right. We need to continue to follow procedure when we can. Which means, after we return to Lost Souls, I get to buy you a drink."

She smiled too. It felt weird to smile after all they'd been through. She still had a lot to process.

But the smile felt good, too.

"All right, Captain," she said. "Just you and me. One drink. Maybe a toast."

"To what?" he asked.

She shrugged one shoulder, pretending to be casual when she wasn't feeling casual at all.

"To the future," she said, "and moving forward. Just like we always have."

THE SEARCH
NOW

8

EVERYONE WANTED A PIECE of the runabout data. Yash wanted to hoard it.

She stood in the center of her lab on the space station the Lost Souls Corporation called home. Her lab was huge, more of a complex than a single area. She had chosen a suite with one big room in the exact middle of the lab, and several other smaller rooms around it. For the past several months, she had walked through the big room to get to one of the other smaller rooms, and otherwise didn't do much with the big room at all.

She kept the big room, though, hoping she would one day be able to get a small ship in there and do a lot of design work. Or do a lot of work on the ship to discover its secrets.

The ship she had hoped she would bring back had vanished a few weeks ago. It was a runabout that had clearly been built long after the *Ivoire* went into foldspace.

But the runabout's *anacapa* had activated when Yash and Boss were diving the ship, and they had barely escaped in time. Boss saw that as a near-miss.

Yash—well, Yash grinned every time she thought about it.

Somewhere, the Fleet still existed, and somehow, it had activated the runabout's *anacapa* from a distance, and brought it home.

Yash had managed to pull all of the runabout's data during that dive. She had just been turning her attention to the *anacapa* drive when it had activated.

She still wondered if she had somehow tripped something in the *anacapa* drive, and that had sent a message to the Fleet. She wished she knew. That piece of information didn't seem to be in the data she had pulled.

But she had a lot of other data, and she was accessing it in the big room of her lab. She didn't want to work on small screens. She wanted large holographic images, partly to make her work efficient, but also to inspire herself. She liked thinking about the runabout being back with the Fleet. She liked imagining what had happened when the ship returned.

She also liked walking inside the holographic image of the runabout's interior. She could imagine it as a state-of-the-art vessel, with additions she hadn't even imagined back in her day, and she saw it for what it had become—a ruin of a once-beautiful ship.

Both aspects of the runabout—the imagined glory days and the decay—excited her. They were both evidence of a Fleet that had existed long after she left.

They were evidence of the fact that she held data that would give her answers, answers she had been craving ever since she had arrived in this unfamiliar future.

She didn't understand all that she had pulled from the runabout—hell, she hadn't even accessed all of the information yet—but she knew that the ship had upgrades she had never seen before.

In fact, it wasn't even fair to call those things upgrades. They weren't tweaks to the runabouts she had worked with decades (centuries?) before this one was built. They were flat-out changes, things she wasn't entirely sure she understood.

She had finally found time to work on the runabout the way she wanted to. She had spent the last two weeks shedding most of her responsibilities at Lost Souls. And that was hard, because she had ended up with so many different jobs.

Some of that was the function of the corporation; it had been under-staffed from the beginning.

But some of it was because she was one of the few people with the knowledge to transform the broken-down, damaged, and dormant

DV-Class ships Lost Souls had found all over the sector into active, working vessels. Yash also helped develop tech—based on the Fleet's tech—for Lost Souls to sell.

Yash had arrived at the lab hours earlier than usual because she had been unable to sleep. Ilona Blake, who ran Lost Souls, had offered Yash as many assistants as she wanted to help her dig through the data, even the data on the Fleet.

Yash didn't want any assistants. She wanted to be alone with all of the information, and that caused problems, because Lost Souls had financed the trip to the Boneyard that resulted in this information. Ilona was the first person who wanted to mine the data of what she called "actionable items." She certainly wasn't the last.

Yash had done some of that, mostly to keep everyone off her back. She had thrown some tidbits to Ilona, tidbits that would keep staff busy for months.

But some of that had backfired on Yash.

Most of the people who worked in tech development were not part of the Fleet. Yash had more knowledge in her little finger than they had accumulated in a lifetime.

In the past, she had been readily available, answering questions, helping them structure their work so that they would learn which piece went where, and sometimes offering actual seminars on Fleet technology.

She hadn't minded doing any of that, because in her heart, she had believed the Fleet was gone. She would never find it again.

But she no longer believed that. She needed to focus on finding out how to contact the Fleet. And each moment that went by when she couldn't focus on finding the Fleet irritated the piss out of her.

She spent most of the morning establishing little holographic fiefdoms throughout the large room. The interior of the ruined runabout's cockpit faced the west wall. She left a space large enough for the interior of the cockpit when it was new. She couldn't set that up yet, because she hadn't found the specs.

Then she set up an area for the data sent by the two probes that had gone into the runabout. One probe had entered before any of the crew had, and the other before the second visit. Both had disappeared into foldspace when the runabout had.

Yash had hoped for more information to come filtering back to them through the probes, but that hadn't happened—yet.

Although she had set up a data capture device on the *Sove*, the DV-Class ship Boss was using again to dive the Boneyard.

The Boneyard was a ship graveyard, filled with Fleet vessels. It was in another sector, and unlike anything Yash had ever seen before. Early in her career, she had heard rumors of something the Fleet called a Scrapheap, but she hadn't connected that to a Boneyard until she saw mention of a Scrapheap in one of the DV-Class vessels that Boss had "liberated" from the Boneyard.

Boss had liberated the *Sove*, which was why (Yash believed) the *Sove* could go in and out of the Boneyard at will. The *Sove* was only slightly more advanced than the *Ivoire*, so the information on the *Sove* had not provided a lot of insight into what had become of the Fleet.

Plus, most of the *Sove's* data had been scrubbed from the ship. Yash had been able to find fragments of old data, and that had been the kind of data that did not compromise the Fleet itself.

Since the Fleet always scrubbed data from anything it abandoned, the fact that the *Sove* had been scrubbed led Yash to believe the Fleet had placed the *Sove* inside the Boneyard. Boss said the *Sove* might've been abandoned elsewhere and later brought to the Boneyard, but Coop hadn't liked that theory.

He didn't like most theories concerning the Boneyard, except his own. Coop worried that the Boneyard stored ships damaged in a major war involving the Fleet, although Yash had doubted that explanation from the moment she and Boss tried to access the Boneyard. The ships inside seemed to be Fleet vessels from different eras.

But so far, Lost Souls hadn't been able to pull any ships from the Boneyard that would help Yash in her search for the Fleet.

She half hoped that when the *Sove* returned to the Boneyard, the ship would pick up more data from the probes that had vanished with the runabout. That, of course, would require the runabout to be back in what they called "real space," as opposed to foldspace.

Yash hadn't told anyone of that particular hope, realizing it was closer to wish fulfillment than anything that could happen in reality.

And she worried about indulging in fantasies about ways to find the Fleet. She firmly believed that indulging fantasies like that had been part of what had driven Dix over the edge five years ago.

The probes had provided a lot of information before they vanished, however. Yash had gone through some of that information, but not all of it. And certainly not any of the data accumulated just before the probes vanished into foldspace.

So the probe data had its own little fiefdom. Next to it, she had set up a holographic representation of the runabout's engine. And next to that, several different representations of the runabout's *anacapa* drive.

She worried the most about those, because she wasn't sure the holographic representations were accurate. That *anacapa* drive, like all *anacapa* drives, lived in its container, and so wasn't subject to any recordings. The probes got readings from the drive, but not any visual contact with it, except when Yash herself had opened that container—and even then, her body had blocked most of the view.

For holographic representation of the *anacapa* drive, she was using the specs for the drive, as well as the information already logged into the runabout's databases. None of those databases had as much information on the *anacapa* drive as they did on the rest of the runabout.

That led Yash to believe whoever had been trapped in that runabout had known nothing about *anacapa* drives except how to use them.

That fact didn't surprise her, either, because most people in the Fleet didn't even know that much. The drives were so delicate, they took specialized training.

And that particular drive had had problems, because its strange signature had led Boss to dive the runabout in the first place. The energy coming off that drive had been dangerous. Yash believed then—and still believed now—that the drive had been malfunctioning.

It had mostly ceased to function by the time she and Boss had dived the runabout. In fact, when the runabout's *anacapa* had flared to life, Yash had been surprised, because she had thought the *anacapa* drive had already burned itself out.

Yash stepped back from her fiefdoms. The big room was only half full of holographic representations. They probably would have looked confusing to anyone else who came into the lab. A runabout cockpit, an empty space, a runabout's engine, data scrolling from the probes, and the *anacapa* drive, pulsing in the middle of the air as if *anacapas* normally floated off the ground, would probably seem like chaos to everyone else.

But to Yash, they were beautiful. She smiled whenever she looked at them.

She hadn't felt like this since she had come to this strange future. She couldn't remember just idly smiling at something before her. And she couldn't remember this level of excitement with such a workload ahead of her.

Her stomach rumbled. She was hungry. She had actually brought two meals to the lab, planning to lock herself in here for hours and hours. Ilona Blake wouldn't approve; she preferred the people at Lost Souls to eat regular meals outside of their workstations, but she would never know.

She would have to contact Yash to even get into the lab. The lab was as far from Ilona's office as possible.

When Yash had chosen her lab, it had been in a ring that she doubted Lost Souls would need for years. When Boss had purchased the space station, some of the team had chided her. The space station was huge, and seemed like it would be impossible to fill. The wasted space, half the team argued, would cost more money that Lost Souls would ever make, even if they kept the environmental systems off in the unused portions. And that didn't even count the condition the station had been in. The station had been left to sit empty, a casualty of another corporation's bankruptcy. Lost Souls had been repairing and augmenting the station section by section.

Yash had chosen a spot at the edge of the ring that people had to walk through abandoned and dilapidated corridors to get to. She had asked for and received that location partly because she had known some of her work would be dangerous, and partly because she didn't want constant visitors.

She wanted people to feel out of their depth when they approached her lab. She wanted them to feel a bit frightened as they traversed the emptiness. That way, she figured, anyone who came to her would think twice about a visit if they knew the effort they would have to put in to get to her.

Best laid plans. Those corridors were abandoned no longer. Lost Souls was growing faster than Yash had imagined the corporation could. At least, she had the distance from the main part of Lost Souls to keep people away.

And currently, she also had the lab locked down. If someone wanted to join her, they would have to contact her directly before getting inside.

She reluctantly pulled herself away from the setup and walked to the tiny closet-sized room she had allocated as a break room. She could chill or heat food here, but do little else.

As she pulled the door open, the smell of coffee overwhelmed her. She blinked, wondering what had happened, then remembered. When she arrived this morning, she had made coffee, but had gotten so involved in setting up the main part of the lab, she had forgotten about it. It was probably so strong that it would be barely drinkable—for anyone else.

She smiled to herself. She used to make coffee and forget about it when she was in school. She hadn't had the opportunity to do so on any ship, including the *Ivoire*. Instead, she would simply go to the cafeteria and get something.

But here—well, she was beginning to feel like a student again, in more ways than one.

The coffeepot sat on the small counter she had built against the wall when she set up the lab. She grabbed a white mug, poured herself a cup, and realized she couldn't even see the bottom of the mug through the liquid. Sludge. But she didn't care.

She pulled out her lunch—carrots, an apple, and a sandwich made with a cinnamon-raisin oat bread that one of the newer recruits baked.

Yash leaned against the wall, knowing she had to eat, but anxious to return to her work.

She was on the edge of being overwhelmed, even here. She had so much to do. Not just the setup, but sifting through the information, cross-checking it, and then examining it in comparison to the data from the other ships that Boss and her crew had pulled from the Boneyard.

And none of that included studying that little *anacapa* drive. Yash really wanted to dig into that, but was saving it until last, hoping she would find even more information about it before she got to it.

Not knowing exactly what she had here excited her, but also made her realize that her own private estimates of how long this work would take were probably wildly off.

She had no idea how she could keep Ilona from dragooning her into more work for Lost Souls, but she had to try. Technically, Yash didn't even work for Lost Souls. She was on loan from the *Ivoire*, something she could get Coop to revoke at a moment's notice.

If he was willing to do so.

She wasn't sure he was.

She had explained the runabout to him, but he wasn't as excited about it as she was.

You sure you didn't hit something yourself when you were opening that container? he asked after she had told him about the events in the runabout.

The thing was, she wasn't certain, and she couldn't lie to him. So ever since then, he had refused to believe the runabout's disappearance had anything to do with the Fleet. He preferred to think that Yash had somehow activated the runabout's system, and it had used old coordinates to send the runabout back where it came from.

Sometimes ships did operate like that, but not in this instance. The runabout's power was mostly drained. She had managed to power up the console briefly, but there wasn't enough power inside the runabout proper to allow the interface between the *anacapa* drive and the regular engine to power up, let alone send the runabout into foldspace.

Yash had given up trying to convince Coop of that.

She was beginning to think he didn't want to be convinced.

In spite of herself, she found Dix's words echoing in her head: *So you'd leave Boss for the Fleet?* he had asked Coop. And Coop had said he would leave anyone, that was part of the job.

But there was no Fleet, not anymore. Not in the way there had been when Coop had been trained.

Yash knew—Coop knew—that if they found the Fleet now, it wouldn't be their Fleet. She believed it would have similar attributes—thousands of ships, moving ever forward, changing the universe for the better as they went along.

But she wasn't sure that would be enough for Coop, not in this time period. Because if they rejoined the modern Fleet, Coop would not be a captain. He might not even be able to serve.

His knowledge would be too old, his habits something out of such a distant past that the modern Fleet wouldn't know what to do with him.

He would not command anyone in the Fleet, even if they had a record of the *Ivoire*, which Yash doubted they would.

But Yash, she would be able to survive in the new Fleet. Once they accepted her, she would go back to school, take classes in their tech, and start all over again as the lowest trainee if she had to.

She knew she could learn the new methods, as long as the Fleet had some of the same core values.

She wanted the mission. She wanted the regimentation. She wanted the attitude, focusing on the future, moving forever forward.

Coop probably didn't know that she was willing to leave though. Or maybe she was underestimating him.

Because Coop kept track of everything to do with the remaining *Ivoire* crew. He didn't want to be blindsided again by something going awry, the way it had with Dix.

Yash had finished the sandwich without tasting it. She put the carrots away untouched. She made herself eat the apple, and she still didn't drink the coffee. Not because it looked like it was made of nanobits, but because she was hyper enough.

The work itself—or rather, the thought of all that work—gave her energy. And she didn't want to waste a single minute thinking about Coop or dealing with what might happen instead of what already was happening.

Even before she realized she had done it, she had let herself out of the break room and back into the main part of the lab. She stopped, looking at her fiefdoms, and then grinned.

She was going to get answers—and unlike almost everyone else at Lost Souls—she didn't care where the answers would take her.

9

THE MESSAGE COOP GOT irritated the hell out of him.

I am working on a difficult project, Yash said in an automated audio-only file. *I will respond to emergencies only.*

Coop stood in the wide corridor outside the door to Yash's lab. He had wandered down here, ostensibly because he wanted to talk to her about some modifications he thought the DV-Class vessels needed to keep the Empire at the border between Empire Space and the Nine Planets Alliance—a border he had protected in some skirmishes almost a year ago.

There was some rumbling that Empire ships would come after Lost Souls, now that its tech was spreading into the Empire itself. He couldn't confirm the rumors, but he wouldn't put it past them.

Or maybe he was just itching for another fight. He had done a lot of work in the past ten months, but he hadn't done anything exciting.

He hovered outside the lab door. It was recessed into the wall, with a small shield in front of it, a shield he had activated when he tried to put his hand on the door's controls.

That was when Yash had spoken to him in that autocratic, auto-mated tone.

If he had thought of contacting her before he had walked all this way, he would have gotten the message back at his own quarters. Instead, he had decided to stretch his legs, and walked the nearly two miles inside the station just to get to the ring that housed Yash's lab.

He had no idea how far he had walked down the twisty corridors of this ring to get to the lab.

The problem was that when Yash said an emergency, she meant an emergency. She would be really mad at him if he interrupted her for any other reason.

But the fact that she had locked herself in her lab without telling him about it irritated him. Usually she gave him a heads-up when she was going to be unavailable.

He knew that part of the reason she had made the message was because of the data she had retrieved from that runabout. She had been different ever since she had returned from that trip to the Boneyard.

She was the old Yash these days. Her acerbic sense of humor had returned, and she laughed a lot. He had forgotten how lighthearted she could be.

The Yash whom he had seen for the past six years had been deadly serious about almost everything. That Yash had always appeared during stressful times on the *Ivoire*, but she used to vanish when the stress ended.

Apparently, the stress hadn't ended until Yash had gotten some answers from the runabout.

Or figured she would get answers.

Coop stepped back from her door, feeling indecisive. He was never indecisive, so that feeling irritated him as well.

And the corridor itself wasn't improving his mood.

Once he crossed into Yash's section of the ring, the corridor looked as dilapidated as it had when she decided to settle here. The garbage and the crumbling interior walls warned the casual visitors off, and made it uncomfortable to stand near the door.

The lighting was good right near her door, but the lighting malfunctioned in the rest of the corridor. Of course, Yash had the skills to fix something that simple, and of course she hadn't.

In fact, he suspected, she had made the entire corridor even more uncomfortable. The temperature was significantly lower than anywhere else in the station, and judging by the way he was breathing, the oxygen level of the air was just a bit too thin as well.

Yash hadn't wanted visitors from the start, but verbally excluding them hadn't worked as her duties for Lost Souls had increased. People felt as if their emergencies were her emergencies, something she complained about.

But these small changes, which affected the comfort level of anyone who came to this part of the ring, affected them on a subconscious level and probably had more effect than Yash's verbal warning.

On everyone except Coop.

He normally would have walked away. She was busy, but she was probably busy with that data from the runabout. She had, he discovered as he searched for her, quit most of the work she had been doing specifically for Lost Souls.

She had even stepped down from some commissions he wanted her to stay on, such as training the new recruits in the science, engineering, and technological aspects of Fleet vessels.

He needed Yash for a lot of things. She was his confidant on anything he couldn't share with Boss, anything to do with what the Fleet had been or might become in the future.

"Good Lord, you're lurking." Yash's voice filled the corridor. "You never lurk."

It was that second sentence that made Coop understand that Yash wasn't using a follow-up audio-only message, but was actually speaking to him.

"Technically," he said, "I don't have an emergency, but I would like to know what is going on with the runabout data."

There was a long moment of silence. He wondered if she actually heard him.

Then her voice echoed in the dingy space. "You're alone, right?"

He started to answer, but as he did, the small shield in front of the door sparkled, flared, and vanished. Then the door swished open.

Yash stood in front of the entry, blocking his way. Her hair, usually too short, had grown out a bit, uneven and ragged. Her eyes had deep circles underneath them, and her skin was the mottled gray that crew members who did not eat properly or exercise enough got on long voyages.

His heart ached at the sight of her. Was she going the way of Dix? That had become Coop's greatest fear, for all the members of the *Ivoire's* crew. Or at least the ones who had stayed with the *Ivoire* and come to Lost Souls.

He didn't dare ask if she was all right. She would snap at him. He was going to have to circle around the question.

"You have not cared about the runabout data at all," she snapped. So much for trying to prevent that reaction. "What's different today? Did Ilona send you?"

Coop had no idea why Ilona Blake would send him to talk with Yash about the runabout data.

"No," he said.

"Then what is it?" Yash stood with her arms at her sides as if she were about to go into battle.

The air coming out of her lab was warmer than the air in this corridor. And he thought he caught the scent of coffee.

"I've been paying attention, Yash," he said, which was as close as he was going to get to asking how she was. "You've been dropping a lot of your duties here at Lost Souls."

"And you've come to rope me back into them?" No one did defensive as well as Yash. She combined a bit of anger with even more bite. If he pushed too hard, she would find a way to lash into him, and it would be painful.

"No," he said, using the calmest voice he had. "What you do with your time is your business. You don't work for Lost Souls."

"Glad someone noticed," she said, but that statement didn't have the anger behind it that the other ones had.

"I heard you had locked yourself in your lab, and since I knew you'd been shedding Lost Souls duties, I figured it had something to do with the runabout data," he said.

She nodded, then put one hand on the side of the door, probably getting ready to close it.

"I'll let you know when I have something that might interest you." Her tone made it a rebuke.

"That's the thing, Yash," he said, balancing himself on the balls of his feet, ready to step forward quickly if she tried to close that door. "I know you. You're divorcing yourself from the data that Lost Souls wants, and you're focusing on Fleet data."

Her expression remained impassive. Her arm didn't move either.

"So?" she asked.

"So," he said. "I expect you found something. That's why you're doing this."

She gave him a wry half smile. "I haven't found a damn thing, Coop. I haven't had a chance to look. *That's* why I'm doing this."

She waited as if she wanted him to say something.

"You believe there's something there," he said.

"I *know* there's something in the data," she said. "We just need time to find it."

His entire body had grown tense. He nearly turned away, but he held himself in position.

"You don't want to believe that, do you?" she asked. "You don't want to find the Fleet."

He shook his head. "That's not it, Yash. I'm afraid if we go after the information assuming something is there, we'll find something, even if we make it up."

That wry half smile grew ever so slightly. "You're protecting yourself," she said.

His eyes narrowed. He didn't see himself as the kind of man who protected himself from information he didn't want.

"After that first year, you stopped going to places around the sector, trying to find the Fleet. You weren't even that excited about the Boneyard. Boss and I were, but you weren't." Yash tilted her head just a little. "You seemed to think all of those ships had been in some kind of war, and that's why they were there, unusable."

"It's a theory," he said, not willing to defend it.

"Yes, it's a theory," Yash said. "And it sounds made-up to me. The Boneyard has defensive capability. If those ships were abandoned because they had no value, then why defend it?"

"The defensive capability was automated," Coop said. "You do what you can to keep people from stealing ships."

"Like Boss has all these years?" Yash asked.

He rocked back on his heels. Normally, he would defend Boss, even to Yash. Coop and Boss had become a couple, if one could call two damaged people who were somewhat averse to sharing their lives with anyone a couple.

"Those ships Boss found were abandoned in the Empire," he said.

"As if that makes a difference," Yash said. "Some ships just become derelicts. I'm not sure the Fleet would care. We used to leave small ships behind. No one told us to retrieve them."

That was true. The only ships that Coop had orders to return to the Fleet were DV-Class vessels, and then, only when it was possible. The *anacapa* drives were to be shut down completely or brought back, again if possible.

But he knew from the long-abandoned ships Boss had found that the ship's crew hadn't always succeeded in shutting down the *anacapa* drive. Boss didn't keep records of her dives—at least not ones he could access—so he had no idea if the ships themselves had been destroyed so fast that the Fleet hadn't been able to find them.

But he had thought it suspicious that much of what Boss had found had been in the Empire's territory, and once she had moved into searching around the Nine Planets Alliance, there hadn't been any derelict ships at all.

"I know you think the Fleet still monitors that Boneyard," Coop said, "but it makes no sense to me, given the Fleet's mission."

"It makes sense to me," Yash said. "Now, if you don't mind, I have a lot of work to do."

She moved her right hand, apparently about to shut that door.

"I'd like to help," Coop said.

"Doing what?" she asked in a tone that would have gotten her called out for insubordination if she was still serving on the *Ivoire*.

"C'mon, Yash," he said, keeping his tone deliberately light. "I know how to search through data."

Her lips thinned. "It's going to be technical."

He resisted the urge to push past her. "Yes, it is. And I can handle all of the technical stuff, except the *anacapa* details. You know that."

"I also know you have had no interest in this," she said. "So what has changed?"

It was a good question, one he probably didn't have the best answer for. He needed a challenge. He needed something else to think about.

He needed a focus.

Boss was at the Boneyard, diving. He had no interest in accompanying her. He had already checked the ships patrolling the border, and nothing was happening on that front. The tentative truce was holding.

He was half tempted to take the *Ivoire* out with as full a crew complement as he could get, and just move forward, pretend they still had the Fleet's mission.

But eventually the *Ivoire* would run into trouble, and at some point, he would probably be coming back here, either to add more ships or to repair the *Ivoire*.

"There's enough data here that you've locked yourself away to go through it," he said. "Which means you believe that you'll find something worthwhile."

"Coop," Yash said. "You were hovering. There's something else going on."

He nodded. He didn't want to admit to himself what he'd been feeling, why he dithered here, why he had felt a little lost.

He finally understood part of Dix's impulse. Coop wanted the familiarity of the Fleet. He wanted a sense of home—even if he had to recreate it himself.

"I guess I'm ready for answers," he said.

Yash studied him for a moment, apparently trying to see if he was being sincere.

"You're going to do everything I tell you do to," she said after a minute.

"I know that," he said.

She took a deep breath, as if she was considering, and then she stepped aside.

"Welcome to my lair," she said. "Be prepared to work your ass off."

That last sentence reminded him of one of the first captains he had ever served under.

"Yes, ma'am," he said, resisting the urge to salute Yash. "Ass is ready to be sacrificed."

She laughed, the door swished closed, and the real work began.

LIEUTENANT TIGHTASS

OVER FIVE THOUSAND YEARS AGO
OR
THIRTY YEARS AGO
(DEPENDING ON WHO YOU ASK)

10

OVERDUE BY FIFTEEN HOURS. Too long, really. The *Voimakas* was in serious trouble. A ship lost in foldspace almost never came back, especially after the twenty-four-hour window.

Coop felt the urgency, but he was beginning to think no one else on the *Arama* did. Seven others worked on the *Arama's* bridge this afternoon, but none of them did their work with any kind of haste. They had even refused Coop's request to notify the captain of their new mission.

"Standard procedure," Lieutenant Leontyne Heyek said after Coop made his request. Even though he was a lieutenant too, he was the new guy on the ship. He had been told her experience made her outrank him. "We execute new orders and inform the captain when she returns to the bridge."

Which, he thought, was exactly backward of the way things ran in the Fleet. But he hadn't served on a foldspace search vessel before. He had been taught that time was of the essence in a foldspace grid search, so responding to commands from headquarters immediately made sense to him.

What didn't make sense was no one on the bridge crew wanted to let the captain know that new orders had arrived.

The *Arama* would meet four other foldspace search vessels at the exact point where the *Voimakas*, the ship they would be searching for, had entered foldspace. The search would commence according to procedures developed less than ten years ago.

Because the foldspace search program was so new, Coop had expected the *Arama* to be a much more sophisticated vessel, maybe something like the search-and-rescue ships he had worked on shortly after his graduation from officer training.

Instead, this ship was smaller than he had expected, and had a counterintuitive design that bothered him every time he reported for duty.

The bridge was circular, and the floor slanted downward. The command officers worked in the bottom of the circle, with their subordinates at stations on each level above.

There were no portals on this bridge, and the wall of screens that he had thought standard to all Fleet ships no matter the size did not exist here. Instead the circular walls of this bridge were covered with equipment, much of it lashed down. There were no lockers on this bridge either, no real storage.

His first thought when he had received his tour of the *Arama* was that the bridge was the most dangerous space on the ship. If something went awry and loosened all that equipment, the bridge crew would be in danger of injury just from flying debris.

Had he been running this ship—and of course he wasn't—he would have requested a bridge redesign at the next sector base stop. The designers there wouldn't have been able to put in portals because this bridge was in the exact center of the *Arama*, but the designers would have been able to build better storage.

And that alone would have made him more comfortable here.

Although he doubted anything could have made him completely comfortable here.

Usually he worked at the back of the bridge near the entrance, but this afternoon, he stood in the bridge's exact center, six screens floating around him. He had set them up like a barrier, even though it was an ineffective barrier at best. He could see the other seven crew members only because they stood higher than he did. They could see him as well, but they couldn't see what was on the screens he was monitoring.

He was capturing all the information coming from headquarters, from other ships that had served in the area near the *Voimakas,* and the last information from the *Voimakas* itself. He was trying to reconstruct the *Voimakas's* last hour or so.

Heyek had told him that a reconstruction was a waste of time: the *Arama* had never found a ship in foldspace because of a reconstruction. He would have listened to her had the *Arama* already been onsite and ready to start the search—time was of the essence, after all—but the *Arama* had to get to the location, and while they were speeding toward those coordinates, he saw no harm in following procedure.

Or rather, he felt compelled to follow procedure.

He was beginning to think he was the only one here who was.

He stood slightly to the right of the tattered captain's chair. The *Arama's* captain, Debbie Nisen, refused to let the chair be replaced or recovered, claiming that it fit her the way that it was. The cushions did retain the shape of her body because she wouldn't allow anyone to change them out.

Nor did she allow anyone else to sit in that chair. Not even someone who had to command the *Arama* when she wasn't on the bridge. It made for an awkward work environment. Coop had had the comm more than once since he arrived, and each time, he had stood behind the chair and worked the controls on its arms while standing up.

He hadn't wanted to sit in the thing—he thought he detected the faint smell of ancient sweat and unwashed bodies—but he did wish that Captain Nisen followed at least some of the procedures mandated by headquarters. Especially the ones concerning bridge and day-to-day operations.

Someone, probably Coop's predecessor, had built a small console to the right of the captain's chair. Coop knew that a crew member had built that console because it didn't conform to modern regulations. It had more flaws than anything he had ever worked on.

Rather like the *Arama.*

He didn't complain, though. He had learned at previous postings to remain silent about the different ways that different captains ran their ships. As his advisor on the officer training track had told him more than once, Coop would be learning from example—and sometimes those examples wouldn't be pretty.

The *Arama* wasn't pretty at all. It didn't even feel like a Fleet ship, not in design and certainly not in crew behavior. The crew had a startling lack of discipline, which made him as (or maybe more) uncomfortable than the bridge's strange design.

He was disciplined and focused, which was why he stood down here now, coordinating all of the information. Lieutenant Heyek, who was nominally in charge this afternoon, hadn't even assigned him the work; she had simply assumed he would do it.

Or perhaps she assumed he would do something else, and the fact that he hadn't intuited what that something else was would get him a reprimand on the record.

He didn't know, and at the moment, he didn't care. His focus was on the rescue of the *Voimakas*. The *Arama* had failed to rescue the last nine ships it had gone after in foldspace, something he had learned before he came here.

He had been told that it was pretty common to fail at foldspace search and rescue. One of his instructors had told him that foldspace search and rescue was a fool's mission, but that someone important in Command Operations had lost family to foldspace and felt the new procedures were worth the investment in time, ships, and personnel.

Another former instructor had smiled when she learned that Coop was joining the crew of the *Arama*. *Someone thinks you need to learn humility*, she had said with a chuckle.

Maybe Coop needed to learn humility or maybe the crew of the *Arama* needed to remember the importance of procedure.

Or maybe it was just a random assignment. Those happened as well.

All that really mattered was that Coop was the new guy, automatically transferred because he had done so well on his previous assignment. When he arrived on the *Arama*, he learned that he had supplanted a popular officer who had been transferred too, which would have made the crew irritated at him no matter what, but Captain Nisen had compounded his unpopularity right from the start.

She had announced that Coop was on a captain's trajectory and wouldn't be with the ship that long. Her introduction to the officer core on the *Arama* made him sound like a grasping opportunist, rather than a man who wanted to work and learn how to command.

Coop hadn't understood why she had done that to him on the very first day. She had to know that the introduction would hurt his chances of working well with the crew. But she hadn't seemed to care about crew relations.

When he had asked her why she had informed the crew about his career trajectory in his introduction, trying as hard as he could to keep his tone neutral, she had squinted up at him, and said, *Better they know now you're a short-timer*, and then had walked away.

Her response had startled him. He had no idea if he was a short-timer or not. Officers on his career path often served for years on the same vessel.

Besides, his projected tenure on this vessel shouldn't have mattered. Crews were supposed to work together whether they knew each other well or not.

For a week or two, he wondered if the captain had made that introduction in that manner because he was married, and she was warning off anyone interested in some kind of hook-up. He'd had captains do that before when he'd come onboard a ship, but usually during leisure hours, and always with a joking tone.

He would have understood that admonition; some married officers had trouble maintaining their vows after months (or years) apart from their spouses.

But Coop followed regulation and procedure assiduously, and that meant with his marriage as well. He and Mae had discussed their continual separations before they decided to marry, debating whether the marriage was necessary while they were both building their careers.

Ultimately, they decided it was. The Fleet gave preferences to spouses who indicated the desire to start a family. If those spouses could share a ship or a mission, then they would. Mae was a linguist, and once Coop became captain, he could request her presence on any ship he commanded.

He missed her more than he wanted to contemplate, particularly while he was on this ship. He couldn't complain about his treatment here when he contacted her; he knew that there was a distinct possibility that his communications were monitored. He figured they could talk freely when they got together on leave.

He wished he had leave now. He didn't want to perform another foldspace grid search. The first two he had participated in had been cleanup efforts, mapping a part of foldspace with no real hope of finding the missing vessels.

He had no idea if this mission would be the same, but given Heyek's lack of interest in following procedure, he had a hunch she believed that the *Voimakas* was already lost.

That defeatist attitude was the thing he hated the most about serving on the *Arama*. They were supposed to be a search-and-rescue vehicle. Instead, they were more of a cover-your-ass vehicle—at least that was how it seemed to him.

Which was why he was personally reviewing every bit of information on the *Voimakas* that he could find.

The *Voimakas* was a new DV-Class vessel with an upgraded *anacapa* drive. The *anacapa* drive had, in theory, some extra features. He had no idea what those were.

He didn't know much about the *anacapa* drive or about foldspace, although he figured he would learn while he was here.

He had thought of it all as theory until he had joined the crew of the *Arama*. At that moment, foldspace ceased to be a tool that a starship sometimes used to travel long distances, and became an actual place where ships disappeared, never to be seen again.

Like the *Voimakas*. It was one of three DV-Class vessels assigned to a new sector. They were to travel to that new sector to search for the best location for a new sector base.

The *Voimakas* had gone into foldspace first. The other two ships had followed. When they had arrived in the new sector, they hadn't seen the *Voimakas*. It should have arrived before them.

But foldspace could be tricky. A minute in foldspace might actually be an hour in what the Fleet called "real space." It wasn't unusual for three ships to go into foldspace at roughly the same time and arrive at the new coordinates half an hour apart.

The other two ships waited the requisite hour. Then two. And after that, they had to contact the Fleet to let them know that the *Voimakas* might be trapped in foldspace.

At that point, the Fleet sent another ship to the coordinates where the *Voimakas* had gone into foldspace. Sometimes ships rebounded out of foldspace, unable to travel the distance across the fold.

But the *Voimakas* wasn't there either. It didn't respond to hails. Seven hours in, the Fleet declared the *Voimakas* missing. If the Fleet waited longer than that to declare a ship missing, the Fleet would miss the best rescue window.

That early declaration meant that the missing ships might appear just as the investigation got started. That had happened on Coop's first mission with the *Arama*. The so-called missing ship hadn't been missing at all. It had arrived at the coordinates on the other side of the sector ten hours after the ship had entered foldspace.

When the news of the ship's appearance hit, Kyle Rettig, one of the engineers who had been manning the bridge alongside Coop, had leaned over and said, *Get used to this. We get sent back all the time. Sometimes I think all we do is criss-cross the sector on made-up assignments.*

Coop hadn't known how to respond to that, so he hadn't. But he hadn't forgotten it. He had no idea if Rettig had been goading him or had been simply being kind, and Coop had no way to find out.

But so far, Coop's experience on the *Arama* had been arriving at coordinates, doing a grid search inside foldspace, and then giving up much too early, declaring the ship lost.

This time he was determined that the *Arama* wouldn't lose the *Voimakas*. If the ship still existed, the *Arama* would find it.

The bridge doors hissed open, and Captain Nisen entered. She was a short, square woman with spiky blonde hair and a muscular frame. Her black-and-gray uniform was rumpled as if she had slept in it or stored it in a ball at the foot of her bed. Her boots were dull and stained.

She certainly wasn't setting an example for her crew—or rather, she was setting the wrong kind of example. Coop only gave her a quick glance, because if he looked longer, his disapproving expression would become obvious.

"Brief me," she said to Heyek as she passed.

Heyek gave a succinct timeline of the notification of the missing *Voimakas*, and then let Nisen know they were less than thirty minutes from the coordinates where the ship was last seen.

"And what's the new guy doing?" Nisen asked, as if Coop wasn't there—or couldn't hear her.

"He seems to think we should review all the information the Fleet sent," Heyek said. "As if the four other ships aren't doing the same thing."

Maybe they're blowing off procedure too, Coop wanted to say but didn't. *Maybe your laziness in relying on your colleagues is what ensured that the other ships we searched for never got found.*

He bit the inside of his lower lip so that he wouldn't speak up. His mouth tasted faintly of blood. He had bit down too hard.

"Rookie moves," Nisen said with a laugh. "But we'll put it in the report anyway. The Fleet'll think we actually followed procedure for once in our lives."

Coop filtered the information into one screen, so that he had an accurate map of the *Voimakas's* last journey. He had the coordinates where the ship entered foldspace down to the most precise measurement possible.

Nisen tripped over nothing as she reached the command circle, grabbing the edge of her chair and chuckling to herself. The sour smell of last night's brandy mixed with old sweat rose off her like a cloud.

Coop kept his head down, and started breathing through his mouth, making a mental note of the time. He would write her behavior into a mission report, which he would file when the *Arama* reached the next sector base.

He would report that Nisen was still drunk from the night before. The senior staff had found a table in the *Arama*'s only bar, grabbed two bottles of whiskey, and proceeded to drink hard. When Nisen arrived, she had grabbed a bottle of brandy from the stash under one of the counters and had finished it all herself.

Coop had sat at the edge of the group, nursing a single glass of whiskey while the rest of the senior staff polished off the bottles. Heyek hadn't gotten drunk, as far as he could tell, but Nisen had become embarrassing. She grew louder with each glass, laughing so hard that at one point Coop thought she was going to laugh herself sick.

She had staggered out of the bar around midnight, taking a second bottle of brandy with her back to the captain's quarters.

He must have had a disapproving expression on his face as he watched her go, because Heyek had said, "We drink here, Cooper. Nothing in regulations prevents it. So stop being so damned straight-laced and join the party."

After that, he hadn't been able to leave. He stayed for a half hour before he felt comfortable enough to slip away. He hadn't even finished his first glass of whiskey, let alone the five or six the rest of the senior staff had downed.

He had gotten to his quarters, a tiny single room with a bed that folded out of the wall, and had laid awake for nearly an hour, wondering what he had gotten himself into.

He had seen the crew drink before, but he hadn't paid attention to the amount until last night.

And he hadn't liked what he saw.

"How you doing, Lieutenant Tightass?" Nisen asked him as she flopped into the captain's chair.

Coop didn't acknowledge her at all. He wasn't going to start answering to insults, because if he did, the name would stick, not just on this ship, but on future assignments as well.

"Underwear's too tight for the second day in a row," she muttered, leaning back in the ruined chair. "We need to get you one size up, Lieutenant Tightass. The pressure on your balls is making you rigid everywhere."

He tapped one of the screens, working hard to concentrate on the numbers before him.

She chuckled. "Okay," she said, "probably not *everywhere*…"

He kept his head bent downward, and closed his eyes for a brief second, hoping no one else could see his response. He had to learn how to train his face to remain impassive while his emotions whipsawed inside of him. He usually managed impassive when there was a crisis, but he hadn't quite hit impassive when he was feeling humiliated.

"Good God, Lieutenant Cooper, you really are a tightass," Nisen said. "I always find it suspicious when a man can't laugh at himself."

And I always find it difficult to laugh when someone confuses bullying with humor, he nearly said. He had to bite the inside of his lip again, so that the words wouldn't leave.

"All right," she said in a slightly different tone. "Report to me, Lieutenant Cooper. What are you finding in all your research?"

He raised his head. His gaze met hers. Her eyes were bloodshot.

"I'm finding nothing unusual, sir," he said in his most formal voice.

"Told you it was a waste of time," Heyek said from behind him.

Nisen grinned, then put her hand on the edge of the control arm of the captain's chair.

"I don't agree with Lieutenant Heyek," Coop said. "I don't believe that looking at the data was a waste of time in this instance."

Nisen leaned her head back, then tilted it toward him, clearly surprised. "Even though you found nothing different?"

"Especially because I found nothing different." He lowered the screen between him and her. That single movement made it feel like he had taken a step closer to her when he hadn't.

"Intriguing, Lieutenant," Nisen said. "You want to explain that logic?"

"I compared the *Voimakas's* actions with her sister ships. The

Voimakas performed the exact same calculations as the other ships. The *Voimakas* followed procedure to the letter."

"Foldspace is a crapshoot, Lieutenant," Heyek said. "Hasn't anyone told you that?"

Is that why you all drink to excess? he thought but did not say. *Because your job entails entering foldspace dozens of times searching for someone who got lost by entering it once?*

"The only differences are slight." Coop continued as if Heyek hadn't spoken at all. "The other two ships entered foldspace from slightly different grid coordinates. They weren't at the same coordinates at all, nor did they move to those coordinates."

"Close enough, though," said Heyek. Apparently Nisen was letting the lieutenant do her dirty work for her.

This time, Coop looked directly at Heyek. She, at least, didn't look like she had slept in her uniform. It was crisp and clean, just like she was. Her dark hair was pulled back tightly from her face. There was no sign that she had been drinking the night before with Nisen.

"Close enough," he repeated, letting just a hint of sarcasm into his voice. "Apparently, they were not 'close enough,' Lieutenant. They entered foldspace and then exited with no problem at all. The *Voimakas* did not."

Heyek had her arms crossed. She was looking down on him from her perch three rows up. "And you think it was because of the entry point?"

"I am looking for anomalies," he said.

"It's not an anomaly for a ship to enter foldspace from a slightly different coordinate than her sister ships," Heyek said. "That's how we do it when more than one ship enters foldspace at the same time."

"That's right," Coop said, making sure his voice held no irritation at the fact that she had just explained procedure to him as if he were an ensign on his first assignment.

Heyek frowned at him. "We—and the experts back on the *Pasteur*—don't think the *anacapa* drives of the ships interact when they all head to foldspace at the same time. We've run experiments—"

"I know," Coop said, cutting her off. "I've studied them."

"Then you're wasting all of our time," Heyek said.

Coop exhaled through his teeth, making sure there was no sound of irritation.

"Ships vanish into foldspace when no other ship surrounds them," Heyek said, as if she couldn't let it go. "We don't always get close-up information from nearby ships. That's a luxury in this case. And it proves nothing."

"I agree," Coop said. "It *proves* nothing. But—"

"But nothing." Heyek glanced at Nisen, and said to her, "I told you, we don't need to do this kind of fussy—"

"Actually, Captain, we do," Coop said.

Nisen raised her eyebrows at him. "You have a theory, Lieutenant Tightass?"

She was trying to shut him up.

"Lieutenant Cooper, sir," he said. "In case you'd forgotten."

Isaak Li, the comm officer just inside Coop's line of sight behind the captain, snickered, and ducked behind a nearby console. Li was a small man, so he could hide easily.

"Lieutenant *Cooper*," Nisen said. "You have a theory?"

Every word dripped with sarcasm, with a lack of respect that he found breathtaking. If he ever became lucky enough to run his own ship, this kind of treatment would not happen—especially from a superior officer to a subordinate.

"I do, Captain," Coop said. "I think those slightly different coordinates make all of the difference. The ships are not entering foldspace from the same point. They're entering at different points. Foldspace is tricky, particularly when it comes to time. Perhaps it is just as tricky with its entry points."

"You don't think the experts have been studying that?" Heyek snapped.

Coop gave her a slow, measured look. "I suspect they have," he said, "and I suspect that's why they're always asking us for more information. Have you ever thought that the procedure might not be about *our* search, but about future searches?"

Heyek's eyes narrowed. Two of the bridge officers behind her grinned openly as if they were pleased that Coop had taken her on.

Nisen hadn't noticed any of that. Instead, she pursed her lips and nodded.

"Lieutenant Tightass might have a point," she said.

Coop felt a surge of irritation, which he kept off his face. He didn't correct her this time because correcting her again would show her that she was getting under his skin.

"I don't think they take any of that into account," Heyek said, "any more than they look at the build and design of the ship. Every ship is different, even if it is the same class of vessel as the other ships that didn't get lost. *Anacapa* drives have anomalies, command structures vary—"

"Information is information, Lieutenant," Nisen snapped, "and the scientists probably use all of it. Sometimes we cut too many corners. I think Lieutenant Tightass is right: we shouldn't cut any on these rescues."

Heyek opened her mouth to argue, then seemed to think the better of it, and closed her mouth again.

"I want to give some thought to the entry point thing," Nisen said. "Who are we working with at the site?"

"The *Soeker,* the *Tragač,* the *Iarrthóir,* and the *Ofuna,*" Li said. He had spoken up quickly as if he wanted a change of subject. Until he snickered at the interchange, Coop hadn't paid a lot of attention to him, thinking him just another of the bridge officers who marched in lock-step with Nisen.

But Li looked over a nearby console at Coop, and gave him a thumbs-up so quick that Coop barely had time to register it.

Heyek shot Li a dirty look. "They were close to the coordinates, just like we were," she said, taking over the narrative again. "That's why they were chosen to work with us."

"We'll arrive first," Li said, head down. Coop wondered if Li was smiling. He seemed to be enjoying poking at Heyek.

"We're about ten minutes out," Heyek said.

"Good," Nisen said. "Because I want to look at Lieutenant Tightass's findings."

She propelled herself out of her chair as if it had an eject button.

She stood just outside Coop's screen barrier, looked at all of them which were, for her, eye-height, grinned, and said, "Tightass, permission to come aboard."

The phrase sounded vaguely dirty, which she probably intended. It also acknowledged the separation he had built from the rest of the crew. And then there was that nickname again. He was going to be stuck with it, no matter what he did.

"Permission granted, Captain," Coop said as formally as he could. He stepped away from the jury-rigged console so that she could enter his little protected space.

As she did, he bowed ever so slightly.

"Welcome aboard," he said, and set to work.

11

THE MATH WAS COMPLICATED, but the information it communicated wasn't. The *Voimakas* entered foldspace one-point-two seconds ahead of the *Mandela,* one of its sister ships, and two-point-five seconds ahead of the other ship, the *Krachtige.* The *Mandela* arrived at the new coordinates seventeen minutes later, the *Krachtige* five minutes after that. They waited, as per procedure, for the *Voimakas,* which never arrived.

The *Krachtige* did the first round of investigation, checking to see if the *Voimakas* ended up at a starbase or a sector base. Sometimes, a malfunctioning *anacapa* drive sent a ship back to the place where the drive had last been repaired or replaced.

None of the nearby bases reported anything. Once the Fleet got involved, they double-checked that same information, and did not find the *Voimakas.* Nor was it near any coordinates where it had entered or exited foldspace before.

The one thing none of these reports addressed, the one thing Coop didn't know how to address either, was the fact that sometimes foldspace sent a ship to a different time period. Usually the differences were small—a few hours, maybe a few days. But sometimes they were vast, ten, twenty, thirty years into the future.

If the *Voimakas* ended up a few days in its future, everyone would know soon enough. It would arrive on some future date, and let the entire Fleet know about the return. But if the *Voimakas* ended up years in the future—or, God forbid—in the past, then there was no way to know without a records search.

And records searches in Fleet records were difficult at best. The Fleet didn't keep a lot of information about its past. Only the history ships attached to the various universities even had the capability for such storage, and their storage facilities were haphazard. The active sector bases also kept information—or they were supposed to. Whether or not that information got moved when the sector bases shut down was something no one seemed to know.

After Coop made his small presentation to Nisen, as quietly as he could even though he knew the rest of the bridge listened in, he said, "Let me ask one question. You have done many foldspace grid searches involving multiple ships just like we're going to do here."

Nisen raised her head and looked up at him. She was nearly a foot shorter than he was, something he only noticed at moments like this. Her outsized personality made her seem much taller.

"When ships coordinate pieces of the grid, there's overlap in the map, right?" he asked.

She frowned, then blinked, as if she didn't know how to answer him. Coop found that interesting all by itself.

"Yes." Rettig walked down the aisle from his perch near the exit. He had kept a low profile in the discussions until now. "Usually, there's a lot of overlap."

Rettig was the one person on the bridge crew that Coop liked. Rettig was a wiry man with arms like sticks, the kind that training hard in zero-g often gave an athlete. Coop had no idea what (if anything) Rettig trained for, but Coop suspected it was some kind of intership competition.

"Usually?" Coop asked.

"Sometimes there isn't." Rettig stepped into the same protected space that Coop and Nisen were in, as if it were a separate conference room and he had been invited to join them. "If there is no overlap, we abort the mission."

"That's not protocol," Coop said.

Nisen straightened, as if his words irritated her, but Rettig nodded.

"We developed it," he said. "Or rather, I did, and the captain agreed. What freaks us all out is that the star maps don't coordinate."

Coop looked from him to Nisen. Her entire demeanor had changed. She seemed larger, stronger, more in control than she had just five minutes before.

"We never find the ship we're looking for if the star maps don't coordinate," she said softly.

"The ship you're looking for," Coop repeated. "You find ships though."

Rettig nodded. "That's what freaked me out. All of us, really."

"The ships we find are old." Nisen's voice was very soft now. Coop doubted anyone else could hear this. "Fifty, sixty, seventy years old."

A chill ran through him. "Abandoned?"

"Not always," Rettig said. "You wish they were, though."

"Before you ask," Nisen said, "no one's alive on them either."

The words hung in the air around them.

Then Nisen turned, and tapped one of the holoscreens. It winked out and returned, looking exactly the same.

"We usually do twenty, twenty-five trips into foldspace during a grid search," she said in a louder voice.

"Sometimes as many as fifty." Rettig was looking at Coop, as if Coop should understand.

He finally did. They were losing their nerve. All of them. They were diving into and out of foldspace like it was regular space, aware that each trip, no matter how short, might trap them there.

"We're going to arrive first," Nisen said, more to the screen than to Coop or Rettig. "We should go in first."

Coop nearly blurted, *That's not procedure*, but of course, she knew that.

"What are you thinking, Captain?" Heyek had come down another aisle and was peering over one of the screens. Apparently she didn't like being left out of the discussions either.

"I'd like to see if Lieutenant Cooper's hypothesis is correct. If we enter foldspace at the *exact* coordinates that the *Voimakas* used, then maybe we'll see the ship." Nisen wasn't looking at any of them, which was probably good, because Rettig paled, and Heyek winced.

Coop froze ever so slightly. He was aware that the captain had just used his real name, as a sign of respect. He was probably going to lose that respect with his next question. He tried to keep his tone nonconfrontational. "I thought when the grid search started, it always started from the entry point."

"We go in and out at the same spot as four other ships, we'll pile on top of each other," Heyek said, treating him as if this were his first time into foldspace ever. Apparently, she *had* heard the question as confrontational.

Coop gave her a withering glance. "I would have thought at least one ship went in at the precise coordinates."

"We never have," Rettig said. "I think the fear is we'd appear in foldspace on top of the ship we're looking for."

"Unstated fear," Nisen said. "Not in the manuals, of course. But the thought is there."

"We're always close," Heyek said, as if she had come up with the grid search method herself.

"But not precise," Rettig said, "not down to the fifteenth decimal, like you found, Coop."

Coop. Was that the first time someone on this ship had deliberately used his nickname? He suspected it was.

"How far out are we from the others?" Nisen wasn't talking to the three inside Coop's little protective barrier. She was looking at Li.

"The first ship will join us about fifteen minutes after we arrive," Li said.

Nisen braced her hands on the jury-rigged console. "Fifteen minutes. We can try your method, then, Lieutenant."

Coop wanted to say it wasn't his method. But he didn't. Let her blame him if something went wrong.

"We'll let the other ships know that we're going in before they get here," Nisen said. "We'll do what we can, then we'll be the ones in charge of organizing the grid search after the others turn up. I'll argue that the *Arama* go in at those coordinates every time we have a turn."

"Unless the star maps don't match." Heyek said that softly, her gaze on Nisen.

Nisen looked over at her, as if they shared a secret. Then Nisen nodded. She didn't say yes, though. She didn't go on the record, which Coop found interesting.

He found the entire discussion interesting. He had thought this was a shoddy crew, lax and undisciplined. He hadn't realized that this was a terrified crew, determined to do their jobs despite the fear they had for their own lives.

That put all of the behavior he had seen into a different context, including the captain's bullying. She wanted to make it unpleasant for him to stay, maybe even request a transfer before the time was right. Had she forced other candidates on the captain track off the ship in the past?

Nisen had moved closer to him. She was so close, in fact, that it took all of his personal strength not to step backward.

"If your theory is correct," she said, "we're taking a large risk going in at those exact coordinates. We might end up as lost as the *Voimakas*."

"Isn't that always the risk?" Coop asked.

Nisen's expression hardened. "Spoken like someone who doesn't understand the risk," she said, and pushed past Rettig to leave the little protected area.

She flopped back into her captain's chair.

Heyek shook her head and went back to her station. Only Rettig remained.

"You stay onboard long enough," he said quietly, "and you'll understand why that was probably not the most politic response you could have made."

"It's that bad?" Coop asked, speaking as softly as Rettig had.

"No," Rettig said. "It's worse."

12

THE *ARAMA* ARRIVED AT the area of space where the *Voimakas* entered foldspace at the exact moment Heyek said they would. This was one of those regions of space that felt far away from anything. A star glimmered in the distance, with a dozen planets in its habitable zone. But those were all far enough away to make them points of light on the small two-dimensional holoscreen he kept open below one of the larger screens.

He hated not having portals on the bridge, so he created his own. He felt vaguely insubordinate doing so, but no one had told him not to. In fact, he doubted that anyone had even noticed.

The crew had gone from the slapdash organization that Coop had seen on the previous missions to a focused, if slightly uncomfortable, group.

They seemed ready to take on the challenges the change in procedure presented.

Nisen sat upright in her chair, a holoscreen floating in front of her. Coop couldn't see what was on that screen.

She had asked him to double-check his coordinates, and then had Rettig monitor them as well. She told the other ships that the *Arama* would go in first, then cut off the protests she got in response.

She did not tell Command Operations her plans.

"I am changing our procedure inside foldspace slightly," she said to the bridge crew. She had her back to them, which Coop thought odd, but she was staring at that screen as if it held the secrets of the universe.

Maybe it did.

"We will enter and remain for three minutes, rather than the usual one. We will conduct a normal high-speed scan along with mapping, but we will take a little extra time." Her voice was flat and unemotional. "If all goes well, we should emerge from foldspace around the time that the other ships arrive."

She didn't have to say what might happen if things did not go well.

Coop's mouth had gone dry. Fear, apparently, was contagious, and there was a lot of fear on this bridge. He was used to ignoring his emotions as he worked, concentrating on getting the job done.

But the worry around him made him question his own plan. Perhaps he was going to get the *Arama* lost in foldspace.

Then he forced himself to take a deep breath. The risk of getting lost in foldspace did not change just because of the entry coordinates. The entire ship might get lost anyway. Or it might not. The odds remained the same each time a ship traveled into or out of foldspace.

He had seen nothing in the research that suggested otherwise. And, he had to believe, if there was research that showed an increased danger when a ship executed certain actions, the Fleet would issue a caution or would prevent ships from taking those actions.

It was expensive to lose ships, both in materials and in personnel.

"We will gather as much information as we can as rapidly as we can," Nisen said. "Then we will return. The only change will be the time limit. Is that clear?"

"Yes, sir," said Heyek, apparently speaking for all of them.

No one else looked ready. Li actually grabbed the edges of his console. Rettig stood stiffly behind his workstation. One of the officers closest to the exit actually looked at it as if it might provide an escape.

Coop opened three small screens—one that read heat signatures, one that would give a three-D rendering of whatever was outside the ship, and one that ran every bit of telemetry coming into his console. On any other ship, he would have assumed that someone else was running the same kind of three-screen scan, but he wasn't going to assume anything here—even though the crew had shaped up, just a little.

It really irritated him that the captain did not monitor all of the information she had available. She was unlike any other captain he had ever served with. That alone made him continually feel uneasy.

Nisen opened the left arm of her chair, revealing a small command module. She pressed two fingers on the tiny screen.

The *Arama* stuttered and bumped as if it were a ground vehicle that had hit holes in a road. The *anacapa* drive had been engaged.

Coop should have been used to that stutter-bump feeling by now—he had gone in and out of foldspace enough with the *Arama*—but he wasn't. The *Arama*'s entry into foldspace always felt a little too hard, as if something had gone vaguely wrong.

The shift into foldspace took only a few seconds, and then the stutter-bump stopped. The *Arama* eased into position. Another ship loomed much too close to starboard. So close, in fact, that it was pretty clear the *Arama* had just barely missed hitting it.

"The hell," Nisen said as Heyek said, "Good God."

Coop bit back a curse as well. Everyone else looked at the captain and her second in command as if they had done something wrong.

Which meant that only three people on the bridge even knew how close they had come to hitting that other ship.

Using his right hand, Coop adjusted his two-dimensional screen so that the image zoomed outward. He wished it were as easy to adjust his heart. It was pounding, hard.

"That's the *Voimakas*," he said, relieved that his voice sounded calm.

"If that's true," Heyek said, annoying him, "then this will be the easiest rescue we've ever had."

"You haven't looked at her clearly, then, have you, Lieutenant?" Nisen asked. The lieutenant she referred to was Heyek, not Coop.

Coop hadn't looked at the ship clearly either. He had simply found her ship's signature, and compared it to the *Voimakas*. Now, he looked.

She listed, as if her attitude controls weren't working. Her escape pods were gone, leaving small holes in her side. The holes would have looked like part of the design to anyone who had never seen a DV-Class ship before, but to someone like Coop who studied the ships continually, the *Voimakas* looked denuded.

There were no other ships nearby. Stars winked in the distance, and a milky white smudge appeared to port. Coop didn't even investigate what that smudge was. It was too far away to consider as anything more than a point on a grid map.

That thought made him realize everyone was focused on the *Voimakas*, and not on the grid map they usually did. He hit three controls and had three different systems map the area. He also recorded as much of the information he had taken from the *Voimakas* as he could.

"We've got life signs," said Li. "But not a lot of them."

"And weirdly," Rettig said, "it looks like all the ship bays are empty."

Nisen stood, then looked at Coop. Her glance was measuring, and for one brief, insecure moment, he thought she was blaming him for something. Then he realized she was looking to see if he understood what had happened here.

He did not. He could guess, but he didn't believe in guessing. He shrugged ever so slightly.

She sighed, and turned away from him. Then she raised her single holoscreen, glanced at it, and shook her head.

"Hail them," she said to the screen as if it were part of her bridge crew.

"Already have, sir," Li said. "There's an open channel, but I'm not getting any response."

Coop found that surprising. He would have responded immediately.

"No one is on their bridge, sir," Rettig said.

Nisen nodded as if she expected that. "Can you access their system enough to open a ship-wide channel?" she asked Li.

The timer in front of Coop said that a minute had gone by. If they continued to follow the original plan, they only had two more minutes before they had to jump back to regular space.

"Yes, sir, I can," Li said. "It's done. Go ahead."

Coop looked at him in surprise. On other ships, the captain usually had to tell the communications officer her exact plan. Apparently not here. Li had known what she planned.

Maybe Coop had too, but he wouldn't have presumed.

"This is the *Arama*," Nisen said, in a somewhat louder and more formal voice than she usually used. "We are part of a five-ship rescue team sent to pull you out of foldspace. I would like to speak to Captain Golan."

There was a pause that ran seconds too long for Coop's taste. Nisen didn't move, but Rettig shifted, as if the silence made him nervous.

"This is Captain Golan," said a tired female voice. "Who am I speaking to?"

"Captain Debbie Nisen of the *Arama*."

"That's not possible," Golan said. "Please leave. We will defend this ship if need be."

Coop glanced at Rettig, who shrugged. Li's head was bent over the console, as if he were working at something.

Coop went back to his screens, looking for a way to penetrate the *Voimakas's* hull, to see if he could identify the two heat signatures.

"Why is that not possible?" Nisen asked.

"Just leave," the female voice said.

"We can't," Nisen said. "We're here to bring you back to real space. Where's the rest of your crew?"

Golan let out a bitter laugh. "I gave them permission to leave the ship five years ago."

Rettig raised his head, looking startled.

"Captain," Heyek said, speaking softly, "we only have thirty seconds."

"We're staying a moment longer, Lieutenant."

Not, Coop noted, an exact time. A vague time. The nerves he had felt earlier rose again.

"Can you recall your crew quickly?" Nisen asked.

"I have no fucking idea where they ended up." Golan let out another half laugh. "You really are Debbie Nisen, aren't you?"

"I am." Nisen sounded surprisingly calm, even after the mention of five years and Golan's earlier disbelief.

"Goddammit," Golan said. "God-fucking-dammit."

"I need you to activate your *anacapa* drive," Nisen said.

Coop looked at her in surprise. He hadn't realized the *Voimakas's anacapa* drive wasn't operational. But Nisen had clearly checked.

"We're going to hook to it and pull you back through foldspace," Nisen said.

"There's only two of us left," Golan said. "It's not worth it. Go back before you can't."

"I don't have time to argue with you, Captain," Nisen said. "Activate the drive."

"We think it malfunctioned," Golan said.

"You don't know?" Heyek asked. Nisen whipped her head around and glared at Heyek, but the damage was done.

Coop folded his hands behind his back, watching and listening.

"We inspected it several times," Golan said. "It seemed fine, but something wasn't engaging."

Past tense. They hadn't tried for a long time.

"Captain." Rettig spoke softly to Nisen. "If I may…?"

She nodded at him.

"Captain Golan." Rettig spoke louder this time. "I'm Kyle Rettig, chief engineer on the *Arama*. You don't have to fully activate the *anacapa*. Just toggle it to rest mode. Can you do that?"

"It might blow us all to hell, but I can try," she said.

"Please do," he said, *and hurry*, he mouthed.

The bridge crew watched each other as if they were the ones taking action. All except Nisen, who stared at her screen.

Coop looked back at his. He shifted the telemetry to focus on readings from the *Voimakas*. He saw the exact moment they activated their *anacapa*.

Apparently, so did Nisen.

"*Now!*" she ordered.

The *Arama* shuddered and bumped. A light glowed from the *anacapa* drive half hidden under a panel in the wall directly across from Coop. He'd never seen a drive do that.

His heart rate increased, and he forced himself to look away. The bumping and shuddering felt stronger than it had when the *Arama* had left real space. The bumping and shuddering also went on longer.

Now, no one made eye contact. Everyone was either studying their consoles or had their eyes completely closed.

Coop had the odd sense that some of them were praying. The nerves on the bridge were palpable. He made himself focus on the telemetry screen. The numbers helped him focus and stay calm. Even when the screen blanked for five seconds, he remained calm.

That data stream blank was normal. It happened whenever a ship traveled into or out of foldspace. *Normal,* he repeated to himself, so that he wouldn't focus on what could go wrong. Or what had gone wrong for the *Voimakas.*

Five years in foldspace. The crew gone. The captain and one other person remaining.

The shuddering eased. The *Arama* bumped two more times, then the telemetry reappeared on Coop's screen. As did all the other images on his other screens.

The bridge crew burst into spontaneous applause, although Coop didn't join in. Neither did Nisen. She remained standing, head bent toward her screen.

Coop examined the two-dimensional images, and saw the *Voimakas* appear beside the *Arama.* They were surrounded by four other ships: The *Soeker,* the *Tragač,* the *Iarrthóir,* and the *Ofuna.*

Either they had arrived at record speed, or the *Arama* had been inside foldspace longer than anticipated.

"Captain," Li said, "you're getting congratulations from the other ships. Would you like me to put those on speaker?"

"Nice of them to show up," Nisen said. "And no, I don't want to hear it. I'm heading to my quarters. I'll deal with this mess there."

Then she shut down the screen in front of her, whirled, and marched up the aisle. She had nearly reached the exit when Heyek said, "Captain? What would you like from us?"

"Fifteen minutes of peace," Nisen said, and left the bridge.

The rest of the bridge crew stood very still, as if she had told them not to move a muscle. The euphoria from a few minutes ago had completely disappeared.

They had completed a successful mission—they had brought the *Voimakas* out of foldspace—but not in the way anyone anticipated. It would be impossible to call this a victory, really. The entire crew, minus two people, was lost.

"Li," Heyek said. "Coordinate with the *Tragač*. Find out how long we were in foldspace."

"Already done, Lieutenant," Li said. His voice sounded thin and reedy. "We've been gone for two hours."

Two hours. Coop gripped the edge of the makeshift console. Time really had operated differently in that part of foldspace.

"Why hadn't they started the search, then?" Heyek said. "That's procedure. If the other ship—"

"They had, Lieutenant." Li spoke softly. "They started mapping the grid ninety minutes ago."

"But they didn't see us?" Heyek asked.

"No, sir," Li said.

"Tell them I have a grid map and imagery of where we ended up," Coop said. "I also have coordinates from inside foldspace."

"So do I," Rettig said. "I would like to compare our grid map with theirs."

"I'm sure the captain is working all of that out," someone from the back said, somewhat primly.

"I'm sure she hasn't gotten to that yet," Heyek said. "They're going to have to figure out what to do with the *Voimakas*."

Her words resounded in the bridge. What to do with a ship that had been missing only a day, but whose crew was gone—five years gone—and whose captain and someone else had remained on board to…what? Guard the ship?

Coop couldn't imagine what they were feeling at the moment. Elation to be back? The pressure of the loss and lost time? Something else, something he couldn't even understand?

He supposed he would find out eventually. He was feeling a little unnerved having lost hours.

The *Voimakas* had lost *years*.

"So share the information," Heyek said. "It's something we all need to know, after all."

Coop glanced at her over the screens. She looked no different than she always had—except for her eyes. They seemed smaller, as if she was trying to keep them open somehow.

Her gaze met his and, for the first time, he felt no hostility from her. Then she looked away.

He gathered the information, and forwarded it to Li in a form someone else could easily understand. As he did that, a grid map arrived on one of his screens. He didn't recognize it.

"Is that the grid map from the *Tragač?*" he asked.

"Compiled by them, the *Soeker*, the *Iarrthóir*, and the *Ofuna*," Li said. "They were in and out of foldspace nearly twenty times before we came back."

Twenty times. Coop didn't want to consider that. It did mean that his theory was right, though. The *Arama* had gone into foldspace at the exact coordinates the *Voimakas* had. Not close to the same coordinates. The same ones.

And had ended up nearly on top of the *Voimakas*. But not anywhere near the other ships.

At least their maps would be extensive. Maybe they had entered that part of foldspace some distance from the *Voimakas*.

He was breathing shallowly, working on the information in front of him. He couldn't stop himself from thinking about the fact that the *Arama* had come close to getting lost as well.

The *Arama* hadn't been in foldspace long—maybe five minutes—and had lost two hours. Yet the ship managed to bring itself back and the *Voimakas* back as well.

The *Arama* had a functioning *anacapa* drive; Captain Golan believed that the *Voimakas's* drive had malfunctioned.

Not believed. If she had been in foldspace for more than five years, then she would have known that the drive wasn't functioning properly.

She had been worried that activating it, even minimally, would damage both ships.

It hadn't, though.

The *Voimakas* was just fine—or as fine as a ship could be, considering.

Coop swallowed hard, and focused on the maps before him. He took the grid map from the four sister ships, and overlaid it on the grid map he had made.

He wished he had more than a grid map from the other ships. He'd like to see what features the space around that area had. The other ships' grid map didn't seem to extend far enough.

He hadn't had time when he'd been in foldspace to find what was unique about that nearby planet. But he had seen that milky white smudge. He hadn't identified that either. From his perspective in space, without focusing any telescopes or other scanning equipment on that area, he had no idea if he was looking at a distant galaxy, a dense asteroid belt, the remains of a planet, or something else entirely.

If he had known exactly what that milky white smudge was, he would have been able to look for it with more precision. But he didn't know, and he wasn't sure what he was seeing.

That's why comprehensive mapping was important to finding lost ships in foldspace. Most rescue ships didn't stumble on their targets. Most rescue ships found the lost ship through thorough and detailed mapping, covering vast areas of foldspace small sections at a time.

The other ships' map had a lot more detail than his did. His was a one-time capture, the beginning of a search—and not a very good beginning at that.

Theirs followed procedure; the map was precise, accurate, and clear. Still, he should have been able to find something. That planet, *something*.

"I'm not working with a lot of data here," Coop said, "but I'm not finding any points in common."

"Me, either," Rettig said. Apparently, he had been working on this as well.

Of course he had. He was clearly as curious about these things as Coop was.

The entire bridge was silent. Then Heyek cleared her throat.

"We'll deal with that later," she said. "I'm sure the *Voimakas* has extensive maps of that sector of foldspace. We'll get better answers when they're ready to work with us."

Answers. No one had actually spoken the question out loud. That question was: Had the *Arama* and the *Voimakas* been in a completely different sector of foldspace than the four other rescue ships?

Based on what he was seeing right now, Coop would have said yes. But he had more than enough science training to know that he didn't have enough data to make that determination with any kind of accuracy.

Just a gut sense.

A gut sense he didn't entirely like.

13

FOR THE REST OF THE DAY, senior officials went in and out of the captain's quarters. Even though Coop's rank placed him higher than some of the people Nisen was talking with, Coop had not been invited.

When his duty shift ended, he headed to the mess for a meal. He wanted information, but he couldn't get any more than he already had.

It wasn't that the senior staff had locked him out; it was simply that he wasn't entitled to know more than he already did.

Usually, he didn't mind the segregation of information. He understood the chain of command and the need-to-know basis of all information that came through a ship daily.

But this experience had been so unusual that he was curious about what had happened to the *Voimakas* and what would happen next. If he had made any close friends among the crew, he would have asked if they had lost time in foldspace before, but he didn't know anyone well enough.

He supposed he could go through the records, but that felt like he was taking the wrong matters into his own hands. He would learn what he needed to learn when he needed to learn it.

As frustrating as that was.

His stomach growled as he arrived on the recreation deck. He passed the empty recreation room. The smell of seared beef, peppers, and onion came out of the mess and made him even hungrier. He would indulge in a high-calorie meal, just because he had nothing better to do.

He passed the ship's only bar as he headed toward the mess's open doors. The bar was a large room with no windows. It had an actual bar in the center of the room. The bar itself, which had a shiny black surface, ran in an oval, with only one way to get behind it. Whoever stepped into that oval and got caught became bartender for the night.

Someone always had to step inside, too, because all of the alcohol was stored in cases below the bar's surface. Coop had learned that the hard way on his first visit to the bar on his second night. He had wanted a drink, and he had not received it because he had spent the entire night making drinks for everyone else.

He glanced inside as he walked past, and was startled to see the captain sitting near the door, her feet up on a black table, an overflowing pilsner glass in her hand.

"Lieutenant Tightass!" she shouted. "Come in here."

She'd shouted at him as he walked by the bar in the past, usually telling him to join the group or to have a drink. Answering her summons had been how he'd gotten trapped behind the bar on that second night.

"Thank you, Captain. May I have my dinner first?" he said, stopping.

"This is not a request, Tightass. I need your shapely buns in this chair across from me right now." She set the pilsner glass down and did not signal for a drink for him, also a change from the other times she had brought him inside.

He let out a sigh that he knew she couldn't hear. A dozen people were scattered at various tables around the bar, and Li stood behind the bar, mixing a bright blue concoction that fizzed and popped.

Coop stepped inside, pulled back the molded black chair, and sat down. Heyek came over, holding a glass half full of the blue fizzy stuff.

"I gotta have a private conversation with Tightass," Nisen said to Heyek. "Make sure no one gets close for the next ten minutes, all right?"

Heyek nodded, then clapped her hands together, getting the patrons' attention. "Door's off limits for the next ten," she said. "You gotta leave, do so in the next thirty seconds."

Rettig sprinted from the far side of the room to the corridor. He gave Coop a thumb's up as he went by. No one else left.

In fact, the remaining patrons moved as far from the captain's table as they could get. Coop had seen this before. The captain liked to have private meetings here, no matter who it inconvenienced.

Heyek sauntered to the edge of the actual bar, and sat on a stool, far enough away that she couldn't hear the conversation, but not so far away that she couldn't get up and block anyone who came too close.

Nisen swung her feet off the tabletop. She leaned forward, close enough to Coop that he could see her eyes. They were no longer red. She might've been drinking, but she wasn't drunk.

"You think I've been picking on you, don't you, Lieutenant Cooper?" she asked.

"What I think is immaterial, Captain," he said.

"From anyone else, I'd call that a 'yes.' But you're one cautious man, aren't you, Lieutenant?" She shoved the pilsner glass out of her way. "You keep all of your opinions to yourself."

When he didn't know anyone well, he did. And he knew no one well enough to trust them on this vessel.

"You performed amazingly well today," Nisen said. "I was impressed."

He hadn't expected her to say that. "Thank you, ma'am."

She nodded. "You beginning to understand what it's like to serve on a foldspace rescue vehicle?"

"I think so, ma'am."

"Because it's not all fun and games and high-level math."

"Clearly, ma'am."

Her eyes narrowed. "Today was a victory. We found two people alive. We lost over five hundred, but we got two. By their reckoning, they've been gone six years. The captain and her first officer remained to protect the ship and guard the *anacapa*. They weren't trying to get back. They'd given up on that. But they knew someone would be searching for them. As soon as their supplies ran out—and they had another six months—they would have destroyed the ship. That's why we find so many exploded ships in foldspace. It's procedure after it looks like no rescue will come. Did you know that, Lieutenant?"

He felt cold. "No," he said.

"Yeah, you probably haven't hit that level of command training. And so what you probably don't know is that we rarely find ships with living crews. Sometimes they die before they can blow the ship. Sometimes, I think, they refuse to do so."

He didn't know how to respond to that. This entire conversation was making him feel off balance.

"Our mission really isn't rescue. It's recovery. We're supposed to pull vessels out of foldspace and return them to the main part of the Fleet for scrubbing. We also use any information gathered to learn more about foldspace." Her hand moved to the pilsner glass, then moved away as if she had thought the better of it.

Heyek was watching from the stool, her eyes glittering. Coop couldn't tell if she knew what Nisen was talking to him about.

The remaining crew was talking and laughing in their corner, thumping fists on tables, and occasionally shouting insults. Everyone seemed to be working hard at ignoring this conversation he was having with Nisen. Everyone except Heyek.

"Working these ships is life-threatening and ugly," Nisen said. Then she leaned back in her chair and folded her hands across her stomach. "This is where anyone else would ask me why we do it. But you're not going to, are you, Coop?"

He started. She had used his nickname. She had never done that before.

"You really are a tightass. One of those regulations-are-regulations guys." She made that sound like a fault.

He had no idea how to respond. He had never had a conversation like this in his career.

"I know you think I'm a drunk and a fuck-up," she said. "You also probably assume I've been assigned here, and I'm just waiting until my retirement."

He had to hold himself very still so that he wouldn't nod.

"I volunteered for this assignment," she said.

"Ma'am?" He couldn't prevent the word from escaping. He was surprised.

"Not this rescue of the *Voimakas*," she said, as if that was the question he was asking. He wasn't sure if it was or not. "I volunteered to captain a foldspace rescue vehicle. And your poker face isn't as good as you think, you know. You're wondering why anyone would volunteer."

He had been wondering that.

"I volunteered because I was waiting for you, Tightass," she said.

He didn't move. She wasn't hitting on him, was she? Because it sounded like she was, but it didn't feel like she was.

"I knew you were coming," she said.

"Me, ma'am?" he asked. This wasn't making sense. She had been captain of the *Arama* for eight years. He had checked the ship's records before he had come on board. He had done that on every vessel he'd been assigned to.

"Not you, exactly," Nisen said, sliding down in her chair. "But someone like you. I was beginning to think that I wouldn't find you."

"I'm afraid I don't understand, ma'am," Coop said.

"No, I don't suppose you do," she said. "You're a natural leader, Lieutenant. On top of that, you're bright and you're an original thinker when you let yourself relax. You could be one of the great captains of the Fleet. Don't let them promote you higher."

He frowned, not sure what she was telling him.

"But your regulations-are-regulations attitudes are going to get in the way of you doing your job," she said. "You couldn't run this ship."

"I'd like to think I can, ma'am," he said.

"I know you'd like to think that," she said. "And maybe, ten or fifteen years from now, if your ass loosens up, you'll be able to. But now? You'd have a ship full of failed officers, or suicides, or you'd face a mutiny. Running a foldspace rescue vehicle is a delicate balance. Your crew will see everything and anything. They'll have to be reckless enough to enter foldspace repeatedly without freezing up, and they'll have to be compassionate enough to handle people like Captain Golan and her first officer upon the return from hell, and they'll have to be willing to fail almost continually."

Coop wished now he'd gotten a drink before this conversation started. He at least wanted something to do with his hands. Instead, he folded them together.

"They can't be the brightest officers in the Fleet, but they have to be creative enough to take whatever is thrown at them. They need to be a good crew, but not a great crew. You understand?"

He was beginning to think he did.

Nisen leaned forward and put an elbow on the table. "I've processed a lot of captain candidates through here. I was starting to think that I had made up this idea that there were great captains in waiting. I was starting to think that there were good candidates and horseshit candidates and nothing beyond that and nothing in between."

Coop frowned.

She nodded toward the crew in the corner. "They're going to get drunk tonight. And tomorrow night. And the night after that, if we don't get a new assignment. And the other shifts, they'll get drunk in their off-duty hours or they'll screw like insane teenagers. I'd like to say I don't care, but I do. I picked them because they can blow off steam, and I let them do it. They're not going anywhere. This is their past, present, and future. When they leave the *Arama*, they'll retire. If experience is a judge, they'll retire as far from *anacapa* drives as they can get."

Coop resisted the urge to glance at the crew. Some of the people at the far end of the room were still in their twenties. And she had already written them off.

"This job ruins you for extended time in foldspace," she said. "And yet we require all of our captain candidates to serve on a foldspace rescue vehicle."

"To understand what happens in foldspace," he said.

She shook her head. "To see if it breaks them. Half the candidates we get here leave the career captain track when they leave the *Arama*. If they leave. Heyek didn't."

Coop's gaze flicked toward Heyek, and then he silently cursed himself. He was usually better than that.

"Why did she stay?" he asked.

"Because she realized she had only a few years to spend around fold-space. She decided she would be useful instead of fearing the jump every time. She's almost at the end of her service, and she knows it. I know it too."

Coop swallowed. "But you're not?"

Nisen's mouth twisted in a bitter smile. "Foldspace already destroyed my life. I lost everyone I cared about decades ago, and it wasn't even my fault. I wasn't on that ship. I was heading home from another assignment."

He waited, immobile, trying to see what else she would say.

"I insisted on doing the grid search," she said. "I found the ship. And I'm not going to describe to you what I found inside—what *we* found inside. But I will tell you that the captain's chair you look at with barely concealed contempt came off that ship. It's my reminder of the stakes here."

"The stakes," he repeated, not quite a question, but not quite a statement either.

"Yeah." Her voice took on an edge he had never heard before. "Everyone on that ship died because their captain followed regulation to the letter. The original tightass, unwilling to bend a regulation to save three hundred lives."

Coop opened his mouth to respond, then realize he had no idea what to say.

"So I monitor captain candidates. I wash out the ones who would strand their crews in foldspace because the rules are too important." She was staring at him.

"And that's what you think I am," he said.

"Hell, no," she said. "You could be, if you don't fix that ass of yours. But you're also bright, and you'll listen. You know how to conquer your fear—don't think I didn't see it in your face this afternoon—and get the job done. And you only question your assumptions when it's worthwhile to do so, not in the middle of the work."

He sat stiffly.

"Which makes you," she said, "the first captain candidate in eight years that I didn't send back for more training, keep on this ship in a different capacity, or wash out entirely. I'm transferring you out of here, Lieutenant, and I'm sending you with a commendation."

He frowned. "Not to sound ungrateful, ma'am," he said, "but I didn't do anything worthy of a recommendation."

She laughed. The laugh was big and brash and it filled the room. The laugh also stopped all conversation, and everyone looked at their table, which made it clear the laugh was as unusual as Coop thought it was.

Nisen waved her hand dismissively, and Heyek turned to the crew. They turned away, without Heyek having to say anything.

Nisen said, "You found us a ship that we wouldn't have found without you. You didn't balk when you realized you were sending us into a dangerous situation, and you didn't apologize when you realized you nearly got us trapped as well. You reminded me that I needed to follow some regulations, not because of my ship, but because the Fleet might need those regulations followed for other reasons. You changed a lot of things today, Lieutenant, and you did so as a matter of course, not because you were gunning for a promotion."

He didn't gun for promotions. He never had. But he didn't say that. He had a hunch she already knew it.

"I am going to recommend one thing, though," she said, her eyes glinting with humor. It transformed her. She looked younger when she smiled, even when the smile was a bit feral. "I'm going to send a request with your transfer. For the first month in your new posting, I'm going to demand as a condition of your service that your C.O. call you Lieutenant Tightass."

His cheeks heated.

"It sounds frivolous," she said. "But it's not. Because if that nickname sticks after that month, then you're going to end up being a danger to whatever crew you lead. But if the nickname vanishes within six months because it no longer applies, then you'll be as good a captain as I think you can be."

He stared at her, feeling like he was in between foldspace and real space, stuttering along, hoping he'd get by.

"Now," she said, "get the hell out of here. You look like a man who needs a meal."

"I actually think I'm a man who needs a drink," he said.

She grinned. "Amateurs who drink on an empty stomach get drunk."

He grinned back. "But I'm no amateur."

Although he might be, compared to her. And compared to the rest of the crew of the *Arama*. He only drank when he was on leave.

He let his grin fade. "Thank you, ma'am," he said.

"Don't thank me," she said. "You just make sure that when something goes horribly, terribly wrong in your command—and it will, you'll walk into one of those impossible situations where there are no good results—you'll do the best you can by your crew, even if it means breaking all the rules. Can you promise me that, Tightass?"

He thought about it for a moment, thought about being trapped for years in foldspace, about staying on the ship even though it meant sacrificing his life, his future, while the rest of the crew went to places unknown to start again.

That probably broke some rules. Just like bringing a ratty captain's chair into a pristine new vessel probably broke rules.

He needed to pay more attention. He needed to see what leaders were doing, when they chose to follow regulations and when they chose not to. He needed to figure out whether a break with regulation meant something good for the crew or not.

Nisen tilted her head. He had been silent long enough to catch her attention.

"I can make you that promise, Captain," he said. "Even though at this moment, I'm not sure I understand all the implications of it."

She smiled and grabbed her beer.

"That's spot on, Coop," she said. "You don't understand the implications of it. You won't, until the day comes. I'd like to say you'll think about me in that moment, but you won't. I'll be a distant memory, if you think of me at all. I want this all to be second nature to you."

She raised her glass to him.

"And I'm pretty sure it will," she said. Then she downed the contents. "You're one behind, Tightass. I'm buying. Catch up."

Then she signaled Heyek, who went behind the bar and poured Coop a pale ale. Not his usual drink of choice, but he didn't say anything.

Heyek brought the drink over and handed it to him without a change in expression, leading him to believe this was how the meetings with the captain candidates and Nisen always ended.

Heyek went back to the bar, and Coop raised his glass to Nisen.

"To you, Captain," he said, "and your crew."

She grinned at him. "For God's sake, Tightass. Let's just drink."

And so they did.

THE SEARCH
NOW

14

AT FIRST, YASH THOUGHT she had seen the flashing light because she needed to sleep.

She had gotten only four hours of sleep per night since she had started work on the runabout data. Much of that sleep had been in a small suite she had set aside for rest during long projects.

That suite had actually been someone's quarters when the station had been functional. The bathroom had needed repair, but it had a good-sized working shower, a sink that functioned well enough, and the second toilet in the lab. The main room wasn't much bigger than a closet, but it was the right size for sleeping.

Until she started this project, she hadn't needed the sleeping suite. She would work here, then traipse back to her apartment, which had more room than she had ever needed.

She wasn't sure Ilona would approve of a sleep suite in a lab. Some kind of order had gone out early, designating sections throughout the station—some sections set aside for offices, others for scientific projects, and still others for work with the various ships. There were the hopeful sections set aside for restaurants and shops. While a couple of bars with food had shown up, no real restaurants had yet.

And then, of course, there were the living quarters, off in their own section, with a myriad of rules governing behavior so that people who lived in each other's pockets didn't get on each other's nerves.

Yash had never told anyone about this particular suite. She had even brought in the bed herself so that no one would know about it. She didn't want to go through the permission cycle to do unusual things. While Yash mostly liked the fact that Ilona had moved Lost Souls from a haphazard management system to a business-oriented one, Yash had hated all the procedures that had come along with it.

She found her own behavior a bit surprising for a woman who had been raised in the Fleet's strict regimentation. When it suited her, she claimed she didn't work for Lost Souls because she was on loan from the Fleet. And when it suited her, she reminded herself that the Fleet that she knew didn't exist anymore, so she could behave as she pleased.

She had never been that woman before. Even if she found the Fleet, she wondered if she would be able to return to the woman she had been.

She kept secrets now, which she had never done before—not like this. And even about smaller things, like this suite.

Although the suite wasn't as much of a secret as it had been. Coop had just learned about it because he had been working alongside her. Although he had kept sensible hours. He didn't seem as eager to work his way through the data as she did.

In an unspoken agreement, he worked while she slept, although from his attitude, she wondered if he was doing that as a favor for her so that she felt the research could continue even though she was forced to take time away from it all.

Still, she was finding it impossible to shut off her mind. She could only sleep when exhausted, and it seemed to take a lot to exhaust her.

She hadn't been this focused since the *Ivoire* was stuck in foldspace, nearly six years ago.

This time, she had only had three hours' sleep before she staggered into one of the side labs. She had to check one thing her brain had given her during its brief rest: it had wondered what all of the probe imagery showed at that moment the *anacapa* drive activated.

Her brain seemed to remember a flash that had appeared on the probe imagery. But now that she was awake, she worried that she had imagined it.

She needed to check it out before she got distracted by other things.

The side lab had been set up for a small tech crew: three work stations along three sides. All of the workstations were networked with each other, but not with any other part of the lab or of the station.

She had several small labs set up like this around that big room. That way, she felt secure doing research with old, rundown data from ships that had either been damaged or destroyed. She didn't want the old data to contaminate anything in her lab.

This side lab was cold and smelled faintly of stale air. She hadn't been in here since she had loaded the probe telemetry into the workstation nearest the door. The center of this room was empty—no table, no chairs, nothing to make anyone comfortable.

When she had set it up, she had imagined this room would be used for the kind of holographic projection she was now doing in that large central room.

The floor beneath her bare feet was cold as well. As she activated the nearest workstation, she realized she was wearing only the T-shirt and loose pants she'd taken to sleeping in. She couldn't remember the last time she'd showered.

She ran a hand over her face. If she couldn't sleep, then she had to eat. If she failed at both, she would collapse on the floor of the lab, and Coop would shut down the research until she was on her feet, and she didn't want that.

At that thought, her stomach growled. She needed to get the food soon. But she just wanted to move to the *anacapa* drive activation, to quiet her mind.

She shivered a little in the room's chill, using the flat screen in front of her to set the data to the precise time stamp she needed.

She knew that the imagery from the probe would show a golden light that emanated from the *anacapa* itself. When she had been in the runabout's cockpit, that light had tipped her off to the fact that the *anacapa* drive had come alive.

Then that light had nearly blinded her, and adrenalin had shot through her. Just thinking about that moment made adrenalin shoot through her again. If she could have, she would have thrown her arms around the *anacapa* drive. Her first thought in that moment had been that someone had activated the *anacapa* drive, and she wanted to find that someone.

Yash took a deep breath, making herself feel the cold of the room, her bare feet on the floor. She needed to focus on the memory without the emotion. Reviewing how the drive had activated, that moment of joy and then fear that the malfunctioning drive might trap her and Boss in foldspace. Yash had shouted a warning, galvanized into action by her own concerns, and then forced Boss out of that cockpit.

It had all seemed surreal, the way the nanobits floating around them had glowed in the light, the last-second grab of the data stick that Yash had somehow managed, and the fast, panicky escape through zero-g. (Okay, she had panicked a little; Boss had not.)

They had gotten out, and Yash always felt relieved about that.

From the moment she had escaped the runabout, she had felt different—lighter, excited about the future, feeling as if she had a future for the first time in years.

But from that moment, she had focused on the data she had retrieved from the console, not on the data from the probes.

Now, she licked her lips. They were dry. The room felt a little arid. Maybe she had the environmental controls set on some kind of default. If she remembered when she left, she would check that.

She ran a hand through her hair, feeling it spike upward. All she wanted to do right now was see the probe imagery before she grabbed something out of that small break room. Something edible, plus coffee.

She smiled a little at that thought. The coffee she made, which had been getting systematically worse as time went on, had been the one thing sustaining her. She sometimes forgot to eat, but she hadn't forgotten to make coffee.

It wasn't even leaving her jittery.

Or maybe she just didn't notice anymore.

She did notice not having any. She had been studying data these past few days while clutching a mug in one hand. The mug almost felt like a necessary tool.

She rubbed her hands against the loose pants, feeling them slide along her thighs, and forced herself to concentrate.

In their escape from the runabout, Yash and Boss hadn't been able to remove the probes. There hadn't been time for one thing, and Yash doubted they would have tried even if they could.

During that crisis, she hadn't even given the probes any thought. They became an issue later, when someone—and she couldn't remember who—realized the probes were still inside the runabout.

At that moment, the diving crew had believed (hoped) that they could get data from the runabout after it had ended up elsewhere. But they hadn't been able to—although the data streamed to the *Sove* until the probes disappeared with the runabout.

That was a lot of data. The files were huge and complex. The probes that the *Sove* had sent into the runabout had been the most sophisticated that Lost Souls had. Boss liked a lot of data before she dived anything.

She always wanted her divers to be safe.

Yash had been planning to review the probe data, but not yet. The instant she had realized that the probes didn't provide data about where the runabout had ended up, she had dismissed them. They were not relevant to her or any of the work she was doing.

She had hoped to review their data later, to see if there were any surprises, but there was so much other work to be done first that they had slipped her mind.

Or rather, they had slipped her conscious mind. Her subconscious was after something.

Yash had been running the probe imagery in their own holographic projection in the large room while she worked on the *anacapa* itself. Sometimes she would glance at the projection, so perhaps that was how she had seen the flash.

And if that were the case, then that flash might have been less significant than she thought when she woke up this morning.

She rubbed a hand over her face. She was kinda sorta waking up—waking up enough, anyway, to start feeling annoyed at herself.

She had developed a system so that she could study all of the data in what she had thought would be the right order—for her. Not for Lost Souls. But to find the Fleet.

If the Fleet still existed. With that thought, she made a mental bow toward Coop. He was insisting that she add that phrase to everything she thought, said, and did.

It was his insistence on that phrase that made her decide to study the *anacapa* drive first. She realized she had been assuming that the small drive in the runabout acted like the drives in the DV-Class vessels.

She was usually smart enough to know that any equipment, modified to fit a slightly different purpose, would probably have quirks the original piece of equipment did not have.

But she had been so excited about the runabout disappearing into foldspace that she had automatically assumed its *anacapa* worked the way the *Ivoire's anacapa* worked. And that would have meant that something activated the *anacapa* from elsewhere.

She had started work on the *anacapa* because she was becoming afraid she had made what she privately called a Dix Assumption. A Dix Assumption was an assumption based on the desire to return to the Fleet, not based on evidence at all. Everyone from the *Ivoire* had Dix Assumptions. Everyone, even Coop. Most of the Dix Assumptions were harmless, but some of them could be deadly.

And she didn't want to make one of the deadly Dix Assumptions.

Yash hadn't told Coop about her own suspicions because she needed him to work beside her. He had been looking up information on where the runabout had been built, what ship it had been assigned to, and where it had vanished from.

So far, he hadn't told her anything, but to be fair, she hadn't asked. She had been focused too deeply on the drives themselves.

She had started with the specs of the *anacapa* drives for runabouts, buried in the runabout's Fleet materials. She had planned to move to that specific runabout's *anacapa* within a few hours of examining the specs, but the specs had proven so interesting, she had stuck with them longer than expected.

She had found some small differences between the drives already, just from the specs. If she had to guess about those differences, and apparently she did because there was no one to consult, she would say that the differences had been built in to stabilize the drive.

Not that it had worked. The drive's malfunction was what had led Boss into that runabout in the first place.

What Yash did not know was if the drive's malfunction was unique to that particular runabout or if all of the small *anacapa* drives could malfunction like that.

Yash wasn't sure she would be able to find that information, either. If something had gone wrong on the runabout and the person piloting the runabout had not been an engineer or *anacapa* expert, then the information Yash needed might not be in the records.

She had a small nagging fear that she would never find the answers in the records, just because whoever had piloted the runabout hadn't known anything technical at all.

Yash shook off that thought. The reason she had been working in a particular order was so that she wouldn't be distracted by other research. She needed to focus, and this morning—if, indeed, it was morning—she had violated one of her hard-and-fast rules, just by being here, in this room, to look at the probe data, not the runabout data.

But that sense that the flash was something important had been impossible to shake.

She needed to see the data that she had watched on a continual loop in the big room. And she didn't want to see the data in a modified three-dimensional projection.

She wanted to see the data as the data was designed to be viewed, exactly as the probes had sent it to the *Sove* in real time. That data would consist of flat, gray, two-dimensional imagery, plus all kinds of telemetry. All of that could be (and was) modified to create the three-dimensional image she had been using, but the key here was the word *modified*. She had changed a few things, which might have caused the flash that had gotten the attention of her sleeping mind.

She opened four flat screens—two for each probe—and set them to float in front of her. She made them solid, not clear, because she didn't want to see any part of this small lab through the data.

She wanted the data to appear as pure as it possibly could. That way she could concentrate on it fully.

Then the lab door opened. Of course it did. She had just gotten ready to focus, and someone interrupted her. That was becoming the norm for her these days.

It was all she could do not to snap at the person. Because only one person could be opening that door.

She whirled, nearly lost her balance, and had that momentary thought of *Whoops. I really do need sleep* before catching herself on the side of a console.

Coop watched her with a slightly bemused expression on his face. He hadn't lost himself to the research. He wore his usual black T-shirt and black pants. His hair, which was longer than he used to wear it on the *Ivoire*, glistened in the artificial light. He looked like he was about to go on his usual business, as if nothing could make him deviate from his usual routines.

Of course, he had looked this put together when the *Ivoire* had been trapped in foldspace, and even more put together in the six months after the *Ivoire* had arrived in this time period.

Coop seemed to get tidier as he became more focused, not a wreck like she was.

"I have breakfast in the break room," he said.

"In a minute." Yash turned away from him, making sure that she had all of the data in this room.

"Now," he said. "You're insisting on staying awake, so I'm insisting on feeding you."

"Yeah," she said, not looking at him. "I'll be there."

"The food's warm," he said, "the coffee's hot, and I'm not taking no for an answer."

"I'm not giving you no," she said. "I'm telling you to wait a minute."

"I'm not going to wait," he said. "You're coming with me now."

She looked up, saw the determined look on his face, and knew she no longer had a choice about what she would do next. The man leaning in the doorway wasn't Coop, her partner in research. It was Captain Cooper of the *Ivoire* at his most demanding, the man who would take matters into his own hands when he needed to.

Her lips thinned. She was too tired to argue with Coop. That was her excuse and she was holding to it.

"Okay, Captain." She shut down the screens. She didn't want the data to start scrolling before she came back. She wanted to be in control of all of it.

She sauntered past him, pretending she wasn't as annoyed as she actually was.

He made a show of sniffing the air as she walked by.

"After you eat," he said, "you will shower."

"That can wait," she said, stepping into the main lab. She didn't have time to shower. She needed to get to work.

"No," he said. "It really can't wait. It's been waiting too long already."

There was no humor in his tone. She glanced at him. He raised his eyebrows, and she flushed.

She hadn't realized it had gotten that bad.

He was probably worried. Bad hygiene was often a sign of someone who no longer cared about himself. Dix had gone through a phase like that early on, as had some of the others who hadn't coped well with the loss of the Fleet.

But she had coped well. And she often went without showering when she was deep into a project.

Of course, Coop didn't normally know that, because he hadn't worked in engineering. Everyone in the engineering section had worked for days without showering, shorting sleep, and barely managing to eat enough during those days in foldspace. The entire crew of engineers had done the same thing to get themselves through school, through any major crisis.

Engineers didn't care.

Apparently, captains did.

She let herself into the break room and stopped, startled, as the peppery scent of her favorite breakfast soup filled the room. Coop hadn't cobbled something together from the food stuffs she kept here; he had actually brought a vat of the soup she had introduced him to when she had first joined the *Ivoire*. Either he had made it or he had gotten someone to do it for him.

It was simmering on its own heat source, enough food here to last a few days. Beside it, a paler coffee than she usually made steamed from its own pot. And a large loaf of sourdough bread sat on its own plate. Coop took a cup of chopped hardboiled eggs out of the cooler and set them down, then handed her an empty bowl.

She was hungrier than she remembered being in years. She grabbed the ladle and made sure she got some of the tomatoes, bell peppers, chard, and chickpeas before she took a slice of the bread, placed it on top of the broth, and added some eggs.

Then she sat down in her usual chair.

"Thank you," she said, feeling moved that he had done this. She was so hungry she hadn't even poured the coffee first.

He served himself as well, then sat across from her. She noted that he was sitting in the steam coming off the soup. Apparently the scent of garlic and spicy red pepper was preferable to the stench of Yash.

She half smiled, then spooned up some of the soup. It was as good as it smelled.

"To what do I owe this?" she asked, before breaking off some bread and eggs with her spoon.

"I was hoping to get a bit more work done before you woke up," he said. "I thought this would simmer longer."

"It doesn't need to," she said. She was eating faster than she probably should have. "You have news though."

"I have near news," he said.

She paused, and looked up at him. She had been wrong: he wasn't quite as put together as she had thought he was. He had shadows under his eyes, and his face seemed thinner than it had before.

Or maybe she was just imagining that. Lord knows, her brain was taking her to unusual places on this day.

"Near news?" she said. "What the heck is that?"

"Something that has little meaning out of context," he said. "I had hoped to have context for you when you woke up."

She frowned, intrigued now. She paused, giving the food time to settle as she watched him.

"This model of runabout was designed and first created at Sector Base D-2," Coop said quietly.

Yash had to set her bowl down. She didn't trust herself to keep her hands steady.

"D-2," she said. "Do you know where that is?"

"I have coordinates, but I don't know what to make of them," he said. "In the records, it appears that the runabout's last journey might have been out of a different sector base. I was going to confirm that before you woke up."

"You make it sound like I committed a crime, getting up early," she said.

"I'm beginning to think so," he said. "I worry about you."

Then he paused, stirring his bread and eggs into the reddish broth.

"This runabout is probably three thousand years old," he said. "I expected more of a reaction from you about that."

She shrugged. She had discovered its age when she looked up the *anacapa* specs. "I expected it to be old," she said. "It was in the Boneyard."

"But the runabout activated," he said. "You thought the activation came from the Fleet."

She nodded, not quite able to explain how she felt. "The runabout had been ransacked," she said. "There was a possibility that someone had stolen from it and was pulling it out of the Boneyard for their own use."

"But you don't think so," Coop said.

She got up, mostly because she couldn't sit with this, and poured herself her first coffee of the morning.

"The *Ivoire* was pulled out of foldspace by a Fleet facility," she said. "In fact, it was pulled back to the last base that we had visited before we went into foldspace."

"That was a fluke," Coop said.

"Was it?" she asked, then turned. "Someone had to put that runabout into the Boneyard. We've been moving ancient ships around. Boss had been doing that before she met us. And the Empire moves ships too. Why wouldn't a modern version of the Fleet? I'm sure some of the equipment still has its uses or they would have destroyed the ships by now."

Coop made a soft snorting sound. His spoon clanged against the side of the bowl. "You're making a lot of assumptions there."

"Yes, I am." She brought her coffee back to her spot, feeling a bit self-conscious now about her lack of shower. "I have even more assumptions. I seem to come up with some every single day, which isn't good. That's why I set aside this time to delve into the data from the runabout. Better to work from facts and see where they lead us."

"That was the general idea behind this project," Coop said. "But it sounds like—"

"I'm tired," she said, not wanting to argue with him. "I want to work even faster, but I can't. I need to go over what the computers find. I need to trust the data. I need to make sure that whatever I find can be backed up by a thousand pieces of evidence."

"What do you expect to find?" Coop asked.

"What I *hope* to find," she said, "is a way to get to the Fleet. What I *fear* we will find are the scavengers who pulled most of the materials from the interior of that runabout. What I *suspect* we'll find is just enough information to irritate me."

Coop didn't smile like she had hoped he would. Instead, he frowned at her. She couldn't read him. She wasn't sure if that was because she was exhausted, or because her brain was busy with all the research, or because he was in that Captain Cooper space he entered, the one where he kept his emotions walled off from everyone.

"Were you disappointed that the runabout is so old?" she asked him.

"Surprised," he said, which was often Coop-speak for a deeper emotion. She would wait to see if he told her what that emotion was. "The data we have says the runabout is not old."

"Not as much nanobit decay," she said, "not like you would expect from a three-thousand-year-old ship. But the *Ivoire* seems brand-new, and she's more than five thousand years old."

He nodded, that frown remaining on his face. "The equipment is different," he said. "Newer. I had thought…"

Then he let his voice trail off.

So Coop had hopes too, he just didn't voice them the way that Yash had. The way that Dix had.

Yash figured that anything which had been in that Boneyard was ancient. "The Boneyard is old," she said.

"That means nothing," Coop said. "It was built for storage. I would have expected that the Fleet used the Boneyard for storage until the Boneyard was filled up."

There was no way to fill the Boneyard. There was enough room to keep adding ships for centuries or more. But Yash didn't say that to Coop. Coop had been working off a Dix Assumption.

When Dix Assumptions burst, it was painful.

"I figure the Fleet used that Boneyard until they moved too far away from it to make it viable," Yash said. "Like sector bases."

Coop's frown deepened. He dipped a piece of bread in his soup, then ate the piece, his hand cupped beneath it to catch the drips.

"That suggests there are a lot of Boneyards," he said.

"The Fleet went through a lot of ships during our lifetimes. We're talking about thousands of years worth of ships," Yash said.

"We're trained to take parts and use them in new ships," he said, almost at a mumble.

"When the parts are viable," Yash said.

"So if these ships are just junked," Coop said, "why are you so excited about the loss of that runabout?"

"It's not a loss," Yash said. "Something activated that *anacapa*."

She paused, thought about it, realized that the flash and the activation were linked. She was standing before she even realized it. She grabbed the mug of coffee and another slice of bread, and started out of the room.

Then Coop stood. "Shower," he said.

"Coop, this is—"

"Shower," he repeated. He walked to the door and held it open.

She rolled her eyes at him, then set the food and coffee down. "I can get there on my own," she said, realizing his intention.

"And yet you haven't, for days," he said.

She shook her head, and walked to her small cabin. "You going to watch?" she asked.

"I'm going to wait until you get into the shower, yes," he said.

She smiled at him, about to tell him that engineers worked like this all the time, but realized it would make no impact. He was worried about her; she was worried about him.

The runabout and its disappearance had brought a new element into the relationship they had maintained for the past six years.

The runabout had reintroduced hope.

She wondered if Coop thought it was the wrong kind of hope—the kind that led people to make stupid decisions, the way Dix had.

Perhaps that was why Coop was hovering.

Or perhaps he was infected with hope as she was.

She decided not to clutter her brain with that kind of speculation. The faster she took a shower, the sooner she would be able to return to work.

She walked into the suite, which was in as bad shape as she was. She didn't want Coop to see it—or, more accurately, smell it. But she apparently had no choice.

He looked at the room with that unsmiling face he'd been wearing since breakfast.

"You're going to start taking care of yourself," he said.

She opened her mouth to protest, but he raised one hand.

"This is not the request of a friend," he said. "This is an order, one I should have given you when you came back. You're the only one we have now who can figure out some of this stuff. I can't lose you, Yash."

She wondered if he knew that he was still crossing the lines between personal and professional. *He* couldn't lose her. Not the Fleet wherever it was. Not the crew of the *Ivoire*. Not Lost Souls.

Coop himself.

Whether he knew it or not, he was moving into a different place in his head. That insidious hope had changed his priorities.

Just like it had changed hers.

15

COOP WAITED UNTIL HE HEARD the shower start. Then he cleaned up Yash's bedroom. He pulled the filthy sheets and piled the dirty clothes into the suite's only closet. He put new sheets on the bed, set the environmental controls on *cleanse*, and had one of the small robots that had come with the starbase to clean up the main floor.

The room smelled better by the time he had finished those things.

He felt like he had done something, but he also felt like it hadn't been enough.

Yash was obsessed. Dix had been obsessed. Some of the others—the ones who had died—had been obsessed.

Obsession was dangerous.

And Coop felt it lurking in his own subconscious.

He made himself return to the break room. The soup remained on simmer. He had made enough of it to last the day, figuring neither of them would care that it was (in theory) a breakfast soup. He also left the coffee on. He would make more later, since Yash was so bad at making good coffee.

But he cleaned up the room, forcing himself to take the time. He couldn't go after Yash for failing to take care of herself if he failed to take care of himself.

He could feel that same urge to work and work and work that she had, hoping to find answers to questions he had buried years ago.

He had already found a few, startled at how disappointed he had been by the age of that runabout.

He finished cleaning up, then grabbed one more slice of bread, and filled his mug with coffee. Then he left the break room, and headed to the workstation he had chosen from all of the little areas that Yash had constructed in this large space.

The work area he had chosen had five different easily accessible screens, a flat monitor along the front with more controls than he felt like using, a few actual tables on each side, and an adjustable chair, should he decide to sit while working.

He didn't let himself do that. Whenever his legs got fatigued, he would take that as a sign he needed to move around. He pulled up the screens, making a barrier out of them like he used to do when he was a mere lieutenant on the various ships he had cycled through.

He had no idea why he believed he needed a barrier here; he trusted Yash. But at the same time, he felt strangely vulnerable, something he hadn't acknowledged about himself for years.

He needed to review all of the information that Yash had assigned him, but he didn't feel like being methodical this morning. He had reviewed enough data off the runabout to find that it had been built on Sector Base D-2. The sector base that he had visited last in his own time-line had been Sector Base V.

The *Ivoire* had returned to Sector Base V five thousand years in the *Ivoire's* future, only to discover that the base had been decommissioned, and was in ruins. The base was deep in the Empire, far from Lost Souls, but not so far that it took an *anacapa* drive to get there.

If Coop wanted to, he could travel back to Vaycehn, where Sector Base V was buried, on a regular ship without an *anacapa* drive. It would take time—weeks, maybe, depending on the ship. But not the years it would take to go to the sector base where he had received his commission. To return to that base—which had been decommissioned in his own timeline—he would have to use the *Ivoire* or some other ship that had an *anacapa* drive.

Not that he wanted to go that far back.

The Fleet would have built eight sector bases between Sector Base V and Sector Base D-2. He now had the coordinates for Sector Base D-2, so he knew what direction the Fleet had moved in.

If he dug through the records, he would also be able to find the coordinates for those eight sector bases.

Part of him wasn't sure he wanted to; they would be closed and abandoned as well. But part of him knew they would have information that he wouldn't get off one small ship.

Still, following the trajectory of a ship that was three thousand years old wouldn't put him in contact with the Fleet. They could have veered off in a completely different direction at Sector Base G-2 or continued on the same path. He had no way of knowing.

But he wanted to learn.

He had just set up the middle screen to map the trajectory of the Fleet between Sector Base V and Sector Base D-2 when Yash came out of her small suite. Her hair was still wet, plastered to her head, but she was wearing a black shirt that didn't look slept in and black pants that weren't covered with dust or dirt or whatever the last pair of pants had been covered in.

With her hair wet, she looked younger and more vulnerable, the shadows under her eyes prominent. Then she grinned at him.

"Just so you know," she said, "I'm going to have more soup before I go back to work. And then I don't want to be interrupted. I have an idea. I want to follow it through."

He nodded, made himself smile, and didn't allow himself to say that he was following through on an idea as well. He sipped his own coffee, pleased it tasted rich and warm instead of like burned wires, and looked at the screen before him.

Sector Base D-2 was so far from here that Boss's equipment did not have any accurate maps for that region of space. The Fleet maps that Coop was also working off of were three thousand years old, and probably no longer accurate.

But that was all he had.

He isolated the Fleet information, then put it on a separate screen. He took the coordinates for the other eight bases, and had the computers translate those coordinates to Boss's maps. Three of those bases disappeared into the unmapped section of Boss's maps as well.

He felt a surge of frustration. If he needed any kind of visual representation of how far away the Fleet was, he had it now. Because, if his math was correct, the Fleet (if it still existed) was building Sector Base L-2. That meant the only active bases—depending on the place the Fleet would be in the cycle of base building and base closures—were Sector Bases J-2 and K-2, and maybe, just maybe, Sector Base I-2 was still in the process of being shut down.

Usually he was very good at imagining broad expanses of distances, but the problems with the star maps frustrated him. The old technology here at Lost Souls frustrated him. The fact that he couldn't find the Fleet frustrated him.

He pressed his fists knuckle-side-down on the edge of the large console, bent his head, closed his eyes, and made himself take very deep breaths.

He had to remind himself that what he was looking for were answers—not a resumption of his old life with the Fleet. Even if he found the Fleet, that life was five thousand years gone.

He had built a life here, and he was building a future here. The life he had envisioned for himself as a young man, the life he had pursued with great vigor, was no longer possible. It would never be possible again.

A small involuntary smile crossed his face. He opened his eyes.

He had given that speech to dozens of *Ivoire* crew members over the years. He had believed it when he had given it to them.

He had also believed he had not been in need of that speech. He had thought all of his years of experience, training to become a captain, dealing with foldspace—its good sides and its bad—had immunized him against any kind of problem with the loss of that kind of dream.

Clearly, his beliefs had been wrong.

The irony was that he and Yash weren't even close to finding the Fleet. All they had found was confirmation that the Fleet had existed for two thousand years after the *Ivoire* had disappeared.

He made himself stand up straight. He opened his fists, shook out his shoulders, and took one last deep breath.

The one thing that was becoming clear to him, though, was something that had been clear to Yash from the start. The Boneyard was not a graveyard of vessels that had survived some great war. The Boneyard was something else.

He still firmly believed that the Fleet—at least the Fleet as he had known it—would not waste resources maintaining an active defensive system around a bunch of ruined ships.

Unless that defensive system was no longer state of the art. Unless it was the kind of thing that the Fleet had felt it could put into place and abandon at will.

The Fleet abandoned a lot of things in its constant movement forward. It abandoned sector bases and starbases. It abandoned people who no longer wanted to travel regardless of their level of training and value to the Fleet. It even abandoned ships. The smaller ships, like the runabout, didn't have an internal destruct protocol. The DV-Class vessels did.

He picked up his coffee mug and sipped. The liquid was tepid.

Then he sat down. The chair he pulled over squeaked under his weight. He stretched his legs under the console, staring at the information on the screens before him but not really seeing any of it.

Every DV-Class vessel they had found in that Boneyard had been stripped of proprietary Fleet information. The movement of ships, the names of crew members, the history of the Fleet itself, was mostly gone. Sometimes procedures remained. Sometimes information on how to repair certain systems.

Once, Yash had found information on Sector Base V's shutdown, but not anything about Sector Base W. A few times, Yash had pulled some of the deleted information back.

But usually, the DV-Class vessels that Lost Souls was taking from the Boneyard were of an era not too far off of Coop's. Those ships were in worse shape than the *Ivoire* as well, which was why Lost Souls had to use so many of those ships for parts.

The later ships didn't seem to have as much fragmentary information on them or, as Yash had said more than once in great frustration, she did not know how to even recognize the files that had held the deleted information.

Coop, she had said to him one afternoon, *at some point, we'll encounter ships that will be so far beyond my technical expertise that I won't even recognize that there's fragments of information available.*

He had tried to soothe her. Once he had reminded her that the technological growth in this region of space had peaked and then fallen backward.

She hadn't believed that the Fleet would lose its technological edge, and now, given that he had coordinates for the Fleet that took it far beyond this sector of space—so far beyond that the cultures around this sector had never gone in that direction—he was beginning to think that Yash was right.

The Fleet's technology had continued moving forward.

Perhaps that was why they had placed defenses around these old ships. Perhaps it would take no effort at all for someone from the Fleet to return and take what they needed from those ships.

Coop frowned. That hypothesis made no sense, given what he knew of the Fleet's culture. The Fleet would never come backward, not for old ships, not for anything that he was aware of.

Although he didn't know that for a fact. And the runabout itself might provide answers he couldn't get from DV-Class vessels.

He'd been so worried about Yash that he hadn't thought about the differences between the smaller ships and the larger ones. He had looked at the data files, had seen that they were large, and had immediately triaged.

He had tried to find information he thought relevant to the search for the Fleet, rather than information that would give him answers to questions he wasn't even certain he had thought of yet.

All of the data files in that runabout should have been intact. *All* of them.

No wonder Yash was so excited.

No wonder she had asked for help—*his* help, not the help that Lost Souls could provide.

Lost Souls would want all the technological specs—and they were going to get more specs than they had planned for.

But Yash and Coop, and many of the survivors of the *Ivoire*, they wanted to know about the Fleet. What had happened, what they had missed.

He might be able to find that.

He might be able to find a lot of things.

If he went slowly and methodically.

He finished his cold coffee. He felt better than he had in days. Maybe weeks.

He had a mission. He didn't have to tell anyone about it.

He just had to complete it, one little bit of data at a time.

16

COOP HAD CLEANED UP AFTER HER. When she had stepped out of the shower and seen that Coop had actually straightened her suite, her face had heated. Instead of feeling annoyance at his lack of understanding of her process, she felt embarrassed that she had let everything go that far.

Or maybe she was embarrassed that a captain of the Fleet had actually cleaned her rooms for her. The training of how people behaved in the Fleet was deep, and it was old, and it was engrained.

She put the sheets into the built-in cleaner, then headed back into the lab itself. It still smelled of garlic and spicy red pepper, mixed with coffee. She wasn't hungry, but the smell could tempt her toward more food. After she finished some of her work.

That flash needed her attention.

She padded, no longer barefoot, past Coop. He was working behind several screens, a look of fierce concentration on his face. He hadn't seemed disappointed that the runabout had been built thousands of years before, which surprised her.

She had been thinking about that in the shower, not certain how a ship that old could have been called back to the Fleet. Her disappointment had grown the more she thought about it, worried that the runabout had been plucked out of time by a random occurrence at a closed sector or star base, just like the *Ivoire* had.

With Coop's news, she was less certain that the Fleet still existed than she had been when she woke up.

She didn't say anything, though. She was still going to focus on extracting as much information from those probes as she could.

Coop raised his head as she passed by. He acknowledged her with a preoccupied smile that she recognized from serving beside him for years. It meant that he saw her but he was too busy to talk.

Not that she wanted to either.

She stepped into the break room, which had also been cleaned up. The flush returned to her cheeks. If she was going to continue to work with Coop at her side, she was going to have to dump some old habits. She couldn't be completely obsessed with work at the expense of everything else.

She grabbed a mug of Coop's really good coffee, then let herself out of the break room again.

This time, Coop didn't acknowledge her. He seemed lost in the work he was doing.

She walked past as quietly as she could, heading into her side lab.

It was colder than the rest of the lab, and the air still smelled stale. When Coop had dragged her out for breakfast, she had frozen the information coming off the imagery from the probes. The screens remained frozen on the two-dimensional grainy images. The interior of the runabout was barely visible, the console and the captain's chair looking more like gray lumps than anything recognizable.

Which, at the moment, was all right with her. The one image that still haunted her from that dive was the woman who had mummified in that captain's chair. She had lashed herself to the console so that she could work, a movement that Yash didn't entirely understand.

Sometimes her mind played with that image, running over it the way that the tongue ran over a bit of food caught in a tooth.

Yash stepped into the workspace, called up the environmental controls, and set the temperature a few degrees warmer. She also had the air recycle, to get rid of the stale smell—and didn't let herself wonder if part of that smell had lingered from her and her lack of showers.

She reset all the probe data, leaving two screens with the two-dimensional imagery right in front of her. The telemetry from the first probe ran to her left, and the second on the farthest screen to her right. Directly in front of her was the probe that showed the cockpit door. Slightly off center was the probe that had come in later. It had pointed toward the area that had held the *anacapa* drive.

She synched all four screens to the moment that the second probe arrived, then hurried through the data to find the beginning of her dive with Boss. That dive had seemed like it lasted forever, but it really hadn't—maybe half an hour at most, at least in the cockpit itself.

The trip to the airlock to escape the runabout after the *anacapa* drive activated had seemed like it had taken hours, but that had probably been the fastest part of the entire dive.

Fortunately, Yash didn't have to watch that again.

All she wanted to see were the events in the cockpit, from the moment she and Boss touched any equipment until the *anacapa* drive had activated.

Yash watched that in the flat black, gray, and white imagery. Boss's movements held a lot of confidence. Strangely, Yash's had too, even though Yash had been scared spitless throughout the entire dive.

At the beginning of the dive, Yash had put the data recorder on the console. Now, she watched the imagery slowly. As far as she could tell, she had not activated anything when she put that recorder on the console. Boss had gone to work on the console, while Yash had moved closer to the *anacapa* drive.

There the helpful imagery only appeared from the second probe. Yash, negotiating the floating nanobits (which made the imagery even blurrier), touching the case, then easing it open, using all of her training to avoid touching anything important.

What she couldn't tell from this imagery or from any other imagery was whether or not this *anacapa* drive had other triggers, ones that did not exist on the *anacapa* drives she was familiar with.

But from this vantage now, it seemed like she had not activated anything on the *anacapa* drive as she examined it. The probes recorded no fluctuation in energy level—not on the visual spectrum or any other spectrum. And the one thing that Lost Souls' high-end probes specialized in was varying energy readings, particularly from *anacapa* drives.

Boss had lost too many divers to malfunctioning *anacapa* fields. She was highly sensitive to changes in those energy readings and had calibrated every probe owned by Lost Souls to account for all of the possible readings.

Yash trusted the probe readings on energy levels as if she had programmed those probes herself.

Yash watched the imagery until the light from the *anacapa* appeared, illuminating everything. There had been no flash there, nothing that even resembled a strobing that her brain recalled from the imagery she saw in the other, larger lab.

That meant that the flash she had seen—if it hadn't been a trick of the modified files—hadn't come from the *anacapa*'s activation. It had come later.

She crossed her arms, watching very carefully. The light as the *anacapa* activated, her silent response, Boss's snap into action—all of that so familiar Yash could recite what happened second by second.

Yash's diving self grabbed the data recorder off the console as Boss hustled her out of the cockpit, the nanobits floating around them in the disturbance and the bright glare of the light from the *anacapa* drive.

Outside of that cockpit, she and Boss had scurried, moving as fast as they could to escape.

Inside that cockpit, the nanobits settled just a bit, no longer disturbed by the two women. The cockpit probably looked like it had before they arrived—except for the glowing *anacapa* drive.

Yash glanced at the mummified woman, wondering if she had hoped for the *anacapa* to light up like that, if she would have seen it as a good thing—a rescue, something she had been waiting for.

Then Yash shook off the image of that long-dead woman, although it haunted her. That woman showed Yash yet another future, one everyone on the *Ivoire* could have experienced had they remained stuck in foldspace. Coop would probably have sent the crew to any livable planet nearby when it looked like they wouldn't get out of foldspace, but not everyone would have left.

Yash would not have left.

She shook off the thought and focused on the imagery. The glow from the *anacapa* drive grew so intense that it outlined everything in that cockpit.

Yash sipped her coffee. She had never seen an *anacapa* glow like that, because every time she had seen one activate, it had been in a closed container.

She had left that container open. Maybe that had something to do with the flash; maybe that light, plus the nanobits, plus the two-dimensional rendering had created an illusion of some kind of flare. Maybe—

Then a gigantic flash of light appeared. That flash showed up on the imagery of both probes. The probe that faced the entry into the cockpit caught the edge of the flash, while the probe that focused on the *anacapa* itself caught all of it.

The flash seemed to obliterate the entire wall of the cockpit—just for a second—and then the wall reappeared. But something opened along the edge, some kind of darkness, a bit of gloom, followed by—equipment? She couldn't tell.

She stopped all of the imagery there—not just the visual imagery but the telemetry as well. She didn't look at the telemetry. She would save that for later.

First she wanted to see if what she was looking at was an optical illusion or something real.

The hair stood up on the back of her neck, leading her to believe that her subconscious—which had started all of this—thought the opening was real. But she was a data-driven woman. She wasn't going to believe anything until she had numbers to back it all up.

She took one more sip from her coffee mug—not because she wanted coffee at this moment (she didn't) but because she wanted to do something normal, something to keep her grounded in the present while she looked at her own past.

Then she isolated the imagery from the probe facing the exit. First she watched that more closely, saw that the whiteness from the flash made everything vanish there too.

She was beginning to think that was a flaw in the visual recording equipment—something had happened in that cockpit that the probe's cameras didn't have the range to capture.

Then that flash vanished, and the cockpit exit reappeared. Shadows— or some illusion from the nanobits?—swept across the exit, like a hand moving in front of a light. The shadows continued for nearly thirty seconds, before the imagery completely ended.

She backed that imagery up to the place where the flash began, then froze it. She turned her attention to the other probe's imagery. This time, she went through it bit by bit.

The *anacapa* glow, then the flare of light, appearing, growing slowly, and then obliterating every image coming out of the probe. She had been right. The equipment—at least the probe's cameras—couldn't adequately record whatever had happened, so it defaulted to some kind of whiteness.

The whiteness gradually faded, replaced by an actual opening near the *anacapa* drive. Again, the camera didn't have the capacity to show whatever was in that darkness, although it did show the darkness changing color—going from black to gray to dark gray to black. And then, for a half second, shelves, wall screens, a console…?

She blinked, thinking those images weren't possible. She reversed the imagery from the probe, and looked again.

Perhaps the probe recorded over old imagery or substituted images of things it knew for the data that had been coming through the camera.

Still, she froze those images, went through them one by one, and thought that yes, she was seeing through foldspace, into something else—a destination, perhaps?

That wasn't possible. Was it?

She had never seen it before. She had used *anacapa* drives to go into foldspace her entire life, but her eyes had never registered anything like this.

But she had never watched a ship enter foldspace with the *anacapa* container open. She also had never used a probe like these two to record the entry into foldspace.

She had traveled in, with equipment that had traveled in.

She felt a momentary giddiness, followed by a great sense of impossibility, followed by a curiosity she hadn't felt in a long time.

Had the Fleet ever had any outside equipment monitoring the entry into foldspace? Had there ever been this kind of analysis?

She couldn't remember seeing any. She wouldn't have even thought of it on her own. Entering foldspace was difficult, uncomfortable, and nerve-wracking, but it was something the ships of the Fleet did every day.

It was something she had done so often that she had only noticed it after an *anacapa* (the *Ivoire's anacapa*) had malfunctioned.

"Fascinating," she said to herself, as she dug into the work. "Absolutely fascinating."

17

COOP STILL STOOD IN THE CENTER of a screen barrier, but he had the visuals shut off on four of those screens. He was deep in his work now, figuring out exactly what he needed to do.

The lab he was working in felt warm, and his stomach growled. It had been a long time since that breakfast he had forced into Yash. At some point, he would have to find her and drag her in for another meal.

But he was finally beginning to understand her obsession. There was more information here than he could go through easily—and he wanted it all in his head. *Right now.* Although he knew that wasn't possible.

He felt a little internal push that lied to him and told him that he could get through everything if he just worked harder. If he skipped meals. If he slept less.

He usually wasn't a researcher. He had done research on his various jobs as he worked his way up to captain, but he hadn't enjoyed it. Of course, he hadn't done the work because he wanted to do it. He had done the work because it was assigned.

And now, recognizing that he was on the knife's edge of losing himself to the same obsession that was gripping Yash, he forced himself to get more coffee and another slice of bread.

Besides, those moments away were good for him. They helped his eyes rest and his brain consider other things.

On one of his walks to the break room, he had decided not to have the computers search for the information he believed he needed. Having the computers search would have been his old method—the one he had done on his various jobs. And he still might do that.

But, right now, he wanted to see the data himself, wanted to get as close to it as he could, follow the trails he hadn't known existed, trails he wouldn't even see if he let the computers do the searching.

On this short walk to the break room, he realized that searching for data this way was akin to doing some of the work in a starship himself. When he trained, he insisted on shadowing every job at least once. He needed to know what his people were doing.

He needed to know how to do almost everything—or have an idea of how that work was structured, so he could bring in the right person. He was still using those skills here at Lost Souls. That enabled him to bring in a few people from outside the *Ivoire* crew to work the various DV-Class ships, people he believed had the skill set, if not currently the ability, to handle one of the ships in the future.

He slipped into the break room. The soup smelled even better, the odors blending together. He couldn't separate out the garlic from the other spices anymore.

He thought of getting a bowl, but he wanted to wait until he had a bit of news so he could grab Yash and pull her into the room again. He believed—he hoped—he would have something to report shortly.

He poured himself another cup of coffee, grabbed the heel of the bread, and then let himself out of the break room, thinking over the work he had already done.

The runabout's data files were segmented, just like Coop had hoped they would be. Apparently this "newer" runabout's information systems were designed just like the information systems onboard a runabout on the *Ivoire*.

The runabout had its basic controls, with the basic instructions, in the most easily accessible files. Some of the controls even had additional explanations in case whoever was piloting the runabout did not know the intricacies of the runabout's internal systems.

Then, the next segment held the basic information on the Fleet itself—not quite what it was, because anyone flying the runabout would know that—but how to locate help from the Fleet if the runabout went off course. That information, which Coop had looked at first, wasn't very different from the information Coop had seen in his own day.

That information followed the basic protocols—how to contact a Fleet vessel, how to approach one if the runabout's identification system no longer worked, how to communicate what the runabout's crew needed should that not be immediately obvious.

The next segment contained Fleet history and background, much of it designed as entertainment for long voyages. Again, basic, but there would be a lot of information in that segment that Coop did not know. Two thousand years of information, minimum.

He had flagged that file but hadn't thought it worth examining first.

The data files that had initially intrigued him the most were the logs. There were two sets. There was the permanent log, the one that covered every mission the runabout had gone on, who had piloted it, the point of the mission, where it had started and where it had ended.

That permanent log was automatically generated and, he had noted as he set it aside to work on, it had larger data files attached. Most of those were also automatically generated—minute-by-minute records of what happened to the runabout and her equipment.

That secondary permanent log was designed to be removed at a sector base when the runabout went in for its regular service. In Coop's day, that regular service happened every five years or so on smaller ships. If the ships aged out or if they had taken on too much wear and tear, they were then replaced with a newer model.

He hadn't usually paid much attention to that procedure unless there were small ships that he favored—and there had been damn few of those. So he let the experts at the sector bases handle the upgrades of the smaller ships.

He assumed that the size of that permanent log was large because the runabout had gotten lost/stranded/abandoned. It was still doing its job, even though there was no one to download the data.

He figured that log would be helpful, not just to him but to Yash. She might be able to pinpoint what had gone wrong with the *anacapa* drive. He knew that she normally dove right into those permanent logs, and he suspected she had already downloaded a copy of these for herself.

For all he knew, those were what she had been working on so diligently since she got the runabout data.

In the logs, he also found the mission logs. Anyone who piloted a small ship was required to keep one, and it appeared that whoever this last pilot had been on the runabout had done so as well.

He suspected the mission log had morphed into something larger, maybe a journal of sorts, for the sole survivor—that mummified woman who seemed to haunt Yash so.

Provided that mummified woman had been a registered Fleet pilot, and not the person who had scavenged half the equipment out of that runabout.

He stepped back into his circle of screens, the bread already gone. He set the coffee down, then brushed his hands on his pants.

What he had decided to work on was the last mission: he wanted to know where the runabout's journey originated and where the runabout had been going. He also wanted to know where it had run into trouble, and what kind of trouble that was.

He suspected Yash knew what kind of trouble the runabout had had with its equipment, but he wasn't about to interrupt her over that. He would interrupt her over food after he felt he had finished enough work.

He dug into the mission data and did not find any assignment for the runabout's last trip. No one had logged in a course, no one had set coordinates, no one had listed the names of the passengers and crew. Not, of course, that the runabout needed a large crew—a single person could operate it if need be. The runabouts were designed for short trips only—or had been in his day, which was why he was startled that this particular runabout had had an *anacapa* drive.

As he stumbled through the data on the way to something else, he noted that the name of the model was unusual. It had an FS-Prime designation. He had never seen a runabout with an FS designation. And "prime," at least in his day, had meant the first model of its type.

He left his search of the internal mission logs and moved to a separate screen. He dug into the basic information about the runabout and felt relief when he discovered that the "prime" designation hadn't changed in two thousand years.

Then he stopped work for a moment, and mentally chastised himself for feeling that relief. Things would change; his assumptions wouldn't work. Neither of those two things should reflect on him or his knowledge. Nor did finding that something hadn't changed in two thousand years mean he should trust his gut on any of the information he found.

He ran a hand over his face, realizing he had been spending the last few days giving himself the speeches he sometimes gave the *Ivoire* crew. It seemed so easy when he said these things to them. It felt hard when he had to apply them to himself.

FS-Prime. He dug deeper into the basic ship information and nearly gave up when he finally found what the FS meant.

Foldspace. Apparently, this was the first iteration of runabout models that had *anacapa* drives built in.

And something had clearly malfunctioned. He smiled grimly as he looked at the reason for the name. Yash had fought strenuously to keep *anacapa* drives out of small ships. It looked like the Fleet had finally decided to give that design a try, and it looked like—in this one case, anyway—the design had caused problems.

She would probably be very happy to hear that her fight against *anacapa* drives in small ships had been on target.

He left the screen open to the basic information on the runabout, but returned to the mission logs.

It seemed odd that there was no filing, no information about this journey. Even top-secret journeys using small ships had some kind of internal method of tracking—or at least they had…

"In my day," he whispered, and then cursed. He was suddenly feeling old and useless. He'd only heard retired officers use that phrase, and he'd always felt for them.

That phrase, at least to him, had meant that their best days were behind them.

"But that's not how I mean it," he said aloud. His voice echoed in the large space. He wondered if Yash had heard him.

Probably not. She seemed incredibly focused on what she was doing. Yash often didn't hear anyone yelling in her ear when she was focused.

He went back to the internal data from the previous mission. It had taken place nearly a year before the final liftoff, and that data tracking had all of the correct information.

The runabout had left the DV-Class vessel, the *Ijo*, and had gone to a moon at coordinates that Coop did not recognize. The mission was a diplomatic one, judging by the ranks of two of the passengers. A single pilot handled the trip. The other two passengers had been security.

The *anacapa* drive had not been used on that trip.

He had the computer search the logs, looking for the last time the *anacapa* drive had been used. It had been nearly two decades since the *anacapa* drive had been used on a mission.

But he found one other listing, which brought itself to his attention.

The *anacapa* drive had been used on a short hop, taking the runabout from one of the ship bays on the *Ijo* to a location deep inside Sector Base E-2.

He followed the information trail, and saw that the drive's use had happened only a short time before the runabout's final mission. Which seemed even odder to him.

He dug even more, and found that the runabout had been scheduled for repairs. A woman named Bristol Iannazzi had flagged a note in the file. She had made a video, audio, and documentary record of that note.

He clicked the video file and was startled to see a short-haired, middle-aged woman glaring at him from his screen.

I am protesting the work that Captain Harriet Virji of the Ijo *has assigned to me. Like so many captains, she believes she knows best when*

163

it comes to what she needs for her ship. She does not. The FS-Prime runabouts are dangerous. They should have been retired decades ago. I have made this complaint up the chain of command, but the orders have come through that as long as captains want to keep their FS-Prime runabouts, they can.

I have made dozens of reports, as have my colleagues. The anacapa drive on a small ship like the FS-Prime runabout does not have the redundant safety controls that exist in larger vessels. There simply is not room for more than one backup safety control.

I will work on this runabout under protest. Should it malfunction, I will not take the blame. I want my objections on the record before I even examine this runabout. I will also place these objections in the runabout itself. If you have accessed these files through the runabout's control panel, then God help you. If you are having troubles, I'm afraid I can offer you no solace. Any troubles you have were foreseeable and were ignored by Captain Virji, the Fleet, and my superiors.

Then the file faded.

Coop let out a small breath. He wondered if the mummified woman had seen this or read something in the files. It certainly wouldn't have brought anyone comfort. It would have frightened them.

It certainly unnerved him.

Almost as much as the captain's name. Harriet Virji. Coop had worked with a Miguel Virji when Coop was a lowly ensign. Miguel had been the chief engineer on the first full DV-Class vessel that Coop had worked on, and the man had been tough. Coop had worked harder on other assignments, but he had never worked with as much fear of his superior before or after.

Apparently, the Virji family remained in the Fleet in one capacity or another.

Coop flagged that part of the file. Yash needed to see it, if she hadn't already. He suspected she hadn't, or she would have mentioned it to him.

Maybe. If she remembered. She had worked herself past the point of exhaustion.

That thought made him grab his coffee mug. The liquid was luke-warm now, but still good. He sipped, studied the dark screen, wondered at the depth of frustration it took for someone to make a report like that.

He hoped he had never driven his crew to make those kinds of reports. He wondered if he would have known.

He set the coffee mug down, and tapped his thumbnail against his teeth, thinking. The runabout was at least three thousand years old, the first of its design, and long past retirement when it had shown up in Bristol Iannazzi's part of her sector base.

Which meant that the runabout had been in use less than three thousand years ago.

But he still didn't have a date.

He went back into the file. Bristol Iannazzi had time stamped her video. She had used a calendar system unfamiliar to Coop.

He cursed. Of all the things that had to change. The calendar?

He scrolled through the protest file, and looked to see if there was a different date on the document.

There was. She had used a standard time code, one he still found familiar. She had protested twenty-four hundred years ago.

He wondered if she had gotten the chance to fix the runabout—at least as best she could. He wondered if it had been in use long after that final repair.

If not—and the data he had suggested hers were the last experienced hands to touch that *anacapa* drive—he wondered why someone or something would remove the runabout from the Boneyard. What would be desirable about that ship?

Or was there something desirable *on* that ship?

Whatever it was, it wouldn't have remained. The runabout's interior had been torn apart, and the only person who had been on board was dead.

Depending, of course, on the mission.

He dove back into the data, looking to see where this Bristol Iannazzi worked. Sector base? Starbase? It was clearly somewhere that Captain

Virji had to bring her DV-Class vessel. And if it was a routine repair, then it was most likely a sector base.

It took longer than he expected to find the information he was searching for. Bristol Iannazzi might have been good at her engineering and repair work, but she was haphazard when it came to writing down dates, times, and locations.

Sometimes, it appeared, she used local time, dates, and names of areas. And sometimes, she followed Fleet protocol.

She had been working "in her lab," on various things. Her lab was deep inside the base in Sandoveil, wherever that was. Once she'd mentioned the Payyer Mountain Range. Another time, she had muttered something about visiting Fiskett Falls.

Finally, when he was just about to give up on Iannazzi telling him the information he really wanted to know, he found out that she had worked on Sector Base E-2—just like he would have guessed.

Sector Base E-2, according to the basic data on the Fleet he found in the runabout's files, had been built on a planet named Nindowne. The coordinates placed it on a path that angled away from the trajectory he had seen with the previous eight sector bases.

He leaned back, closed his eyes, thought for a moment, remembering all the arguments he had had with his crew about those sector bases. His main crew had always believed they could chart where the Fleet had gone simply by looking for habitable planets in the sectors on the direct path.

But Coop remembered studying the way that the Fleet had built its bases. Occasionally, the advance team warned the Fleet that certain sectors were filled with bellicose societies—rather like the Empire was now—and that those regions were best to be avoided.

And once, if his memory served, the Fleet had avoided an entire sector because a star had recently exploded. The Fleet had not studied what happened to that star—if the destruction was a natural event or caused by one of the nearby cultures. All the Fleet had done was mark that sector off its exploration grid and moved in a different direction.

Which they had apparently done with Sector Base E-2.

He would never have found those coordinates on his own without this information from the runabout.

He clenched one fist, forcing himself to keep his emotions in check. He had not yet found the base or the Fleet. He just had another piece of the puzzle.

And maybe, he would be able to find out about Sector Bases F-2, G-2, and H-2 if he dug deep enough in this data stream.

"Coop, I have a question for you."

He started, knocking his mug off the table. He caught the mug, not even letting it spill a drop, and looked up to see Yash grinning at him.

The old Yash, the one who did not look as tired as she had just that morning.

"Lost in research, I see," she said.

"I found the sector bases through E-2," he said, unable to keep that news to himself for even a moment.

"E-2," she said. "Wow." And then she frowned. "E-2. I saw something about E-2."

"In the runabout materials?" he asked.

She shook her head. "When we were working on one of the DV-Class ships we brought back from the Boneyard. I was able to recover some information off it, although not as much as I wanted. I remembered the mention of Sector Base E-2, because I was hoping I could find the coordinates. I didn't, of course. Good work."

"That's it?" he asked. "You remember it because of a passing mention?"

"And the frustration of not finding the coordinates," she said. "It was more than a year ago. And I…"

Her voice trailed off, and her eyes got a faraway look. Then she focused on him. Her expression was serious.

"Coop, there was something about Sector Base E-2. Something weird and unusual."

"It was near a mountain range," he said.

"Most sector bases are near mountain ranges," she said with just a bit of contempt. "There was something else. Some mystery or some nastiness or something. God, I can't remember because I didn't think it was important."

Her gaze was darting all over his screens as if they held the answer.

"God, Coop, it was some kind of scandal." She finally stopped looking around. Her eyes met his directly, and he felt the shock of her entire personality behind them.

Her personality and an uncertainty that wasn't normal for her.

"What would a two-thousand-year-old scandal matter?" he asked.

"It wouldn't," she said. "That was why I ignored it, more or less. But I think…"

She stopped, shook her head, and then sighed.

"Yash, just tell me," he said.

"I might be misremembering," she said.

"Noted," he said, using his most formal tone.

"But I think," she said. "I think that the scandal…involved a runabout."

He glanced at her, allowing his skepticism to show on his face.

"I know, I know," she said. "That's why I think I'm misremembering it. But there was something, a scandal with a small ship, and I remember thinking that was weird, and then not doing anything about it because we have so much other work."

He held his mug tightly, afraid he was going to drop it on the equipment. When had he become that guy, the one who set his food and drink on the same surface as his work? He used to ban liquids and food in the bridge, except during long, long missions, and then he required everyone to keep their beverages on a secondary surface, one far from the equipment.

"It was memorable," she said into his silence. "Whatever it was. And I know it was about Sector Base E-2."

"That base," he said, "isn't on the same trajectory as the other bases."

He set his mug on the floor, and then tapped one of the commands for the screen with the Fleet's coordinates for the sector bases on it. That screen spun so that Yash could see it as well.

"Wow," she said. "Like a finger, broken at the tip. I wouldn't have expected that."

Coop nodded. "And there's no concurrent map in our current archives for the sectors from Sector Base Z to E-2."

"The numbering's weird," Yash said. "There's no A-1 through Z-1?"

"No," Coop said. "That tripped me up at first as well. They went from A-Z to A-2 to Z-2, although if my math is right, they should be building L-2 right about now."

"If everything's the same," Yash said. And then she grinned, catching him by surprise. "And of course, it's not the same, because I never would have allowed A-1 to disappear."

He smiled back at her. "You wouldn't have lived long enough to plan it. Even if we had stayed in our own timeline."

She gave him a withering glance, but her eyes twinkled. "I would have insisted on living long enough. I would have planned it before I died."

He loved seeing her improved mood. They were moving forward on something that had stalled them for six years. It had lightened his mood as well.

"Do you recall where you saw the mention of E-2?" he asked. "Which ship?"

"I didn't see any coordinates for that base or for any other sector base that we were looking for." Her smile had faded. "I did search for that. Almost obsessively."

He wondered if the word "almost" had been added for his benefit.

"Every ship we got," he said, in acknowledgement. Because he had done that as well, probably not in the same depth that she had, though. He hadn't seen a mention of E-2 or any sector base past V when he had gone through the records.

She dipped her head toward him in acknowledgement. "Yeah," she said. Then sighed. "That Boneyard—I keep looking at it, and thinking the answers we need are in there."

"There are thousands upon thousands of ships there," he said.

She nodded. "And I want to go into every one of them, access their control panels, download the information, and bring it back here."

"I want to bring all of the ships here," he said before he could stop himself.

Her gaze met his, sharp and penetrating. "You don't want to go back to the Fleet."

"We can't go back," he said, letting the frustration color his words. "We had that discussion with Dix. It's not possible."

She shook her head, waving a hand dismissively. "I said that wrong. You're not interested in finding the modern Fleet. You want to build one."

He held her gaze, steady. "It's ridiculous, isn't it?" he said after a moment.

"I thought you were building a fleet of ships for Boss," Yash said.

"Boss isn't interested in anything military. She wants the Nine Planets Alliance protected. She wants the Empire to stay away. But she doesn't care about anything besides diving and exploring ships. She's not even that interested in the new technology that Lost Souls is marketing, except that it is making money to fund her dives."

He said all of that as dispassionately as he could. He had never talked with Boss about this dream—if dream were the correct word. He had helped her build what she wanted and he had helped her maintain the tenuous border with the Empire.

But the little tastes he'd had of combat, the tastes he'd had of exploration, the tastes he'd had of the old days of the Fleet, leading the *Ivoire* into places it had never been before, those galvanized him, made him remember the man he had been, the man he was afraid he was losing.

Yash was frowning at him. "Rebuilding would take so many people. Skilled people. We're not going to find them in this place."

"I know," he said quietly.

She glanced at the sector base maps. "You think we'll find the people we need at the abandoned sector bases? Coop, they've been abandoned for centuries. You remember Vaycehn."

The people there had completely forgotten that a sector base even existed below ground. They had lived with the consequences of malfunctioning *anacapa* drives for generations because they had no ability to fix the problem.

"I haven't forgotten," he said quietly. "But every culture is different."

"You actually believe we'll find some culture whose tech moved forward after the Fleet left? Not backward?"

He shrugged one shoulder. "I haven't thought that far ahead. I want some questions answered first."

"Like what happened to the Fleet," Yash said. "You don't want to go head-to-head with them if they still exist."

He didn't know how to address that. He hadn't given that any thought at all. The Fleet didn't fight unless it had a reason to. He couldn't imagine ever giving them any reason to.

"I do want to know what happened to the Fleet," he said slowly, as if acknowledging all of this for the first time. "But I think it's because I'm feeling the gap between our past and our present. I want to fill in those five thousand years. It's more than idle curiosity. It's a way to move forward, I guess. So that I'm not mired in the past."

She stared at him. "Moving forward," she said quietly.

He nodded.

"We've been flailing," she said.

"We've been stuck in the present," he said. "And we don't even recognize the present we're in."

"Huh," she said softly. "I had never thought of it that way."

"I've been dancing around it for quite some time," he said, "letting Lost Souls take the lead, point us in the direction we needed to go."

Letting Boss take the lead. Standing back because Coop hadn't understood this place, this sector, this *now*. But he'd been here for years. He understood this little sector. He needed to move away from it, somehow. But in a way that made sense for him.

"I'm hungry," Yash said. "You hungry?"

He shook his head. He had been hungry, but he wasn't any longer. He needed to dig deeper in the work.

"Just tell me which ship you found that information on," he said.

She smiled. "I can do better than that," she said. "I can give you the information right now."

171

18

YASH LED COOP INTO a different side lab. At the moment, she had the luxury of too much space. She had spread her research into a variety of labs, one lab per ship. She had figured over time she would consolidate, or maybe bring someone else in to help her with the lab work.

She hadn't expected to bring in Coop.

He looked around at the computers, the work consoles that resembled consoles on Fleet ships, and the equipment lining the walls.

"I had no idea you had this much space," he said after a minute, but she knew that wasn't what he had originally been about to say.

The side lab she had initially placed him in had been makeshift, the kind of lab that was all over Lost Souls. These side labs, toward the back of the gigantic space she had commandeered, deliberately contained Fleet-based equipment.

If she couldn't find it from the various ships that Lost Souls had taken for their parts, she had built it—primarily by herself, with some robotic help. She had also brought in a few people she trusted from the design labs, but never the same people for the same project.

Coop glanced at her and raised his eyebrows. "Almost looks like a small area on a sector base."

"Starbase, actually," Yash said.

He nodded, then stepped farther inside. He ran his fingers along the edge of the nearest console, and shook his head.

She slipped past him and went to the farthest console. She had pulled information off one of the derelict DV vessels. That ship had looked like it had been used by a variety of non-Fleet pilots, and she worried that all the information on that vessel had been corrupted.

She also worried that it would harm anything she put it in contact with, unleashing some kind of virus or some kind of location beacon, or something that Lost Souls didn't want.

She hadn't had the time to scrub everything she had brought into this lab. Which wasn't entirely true. She hadn't *taken* the time. It was easier to isolate the data than it was to carefully scrub it, making certain that she didn't remove any of the Fleet tags as she did so.

"Keep this information isolated," she said to Coop. "This ship was one of those derelicts that we believe had squatters."

He nodded.

"The database is pretty corrupted," she added. "Someone had tried to recover the Fleet's data. The captain had done their duty and deleted everything important, but not all that well. So what we have is what we have."

He took his place behind the console, with the frozen data stream visible.

But he wasn't looking at the information she had called up. Instead, he was looking at her with such concentration that it made her feel vaguely uncomfortable.

"How much information have you squirreled away?" he asked.

The term *squirreled* would have offended her, if it weren't so very accurate.

She caressed the console's edge, keeping her head down. She didn't want to see his reaction.

"Every bit of data from every Fleet ship that Lost Souls has ever found or touched, I have somewhere in this lab." She swallowed, then shrugged one shoulder. "If the only thing we found was a console or a ruined back section to a fighter, I pulled that too. I really hadn't had the time to go through any of it. I was too busy training new recruits for Lost Souls and figuring out how to make their backward and stupid systems work with ours."

But that was different now. She didn't say it because he was aware of the change.

"And to answer the questions you haven't asked yet," she said, still running her fingertips along that very smooth edge, "I haven't found any coordinates for anything useful. Most of what I found didn't even have Sector Base V's location. Mostly, I was finding ships that had last rendezvoused with Sector Base U."

She had found that curious too, and she half expected Coop to say so. He didn't. He probably hadn't thought it through.

She had. Most of the ships that Lost Souls had found in the Empire or around this area of the Nine Planets Alliance had been older than the *Ivoire*, and abandoned here.

She had assumed they drifted here from somewhere else, but she hadn't done any mapping. She hadn't had time.

The lack of time was beginning to frustrate her more than she could say.

She finally raised her head. He wasn't watching her at all. He had already started to dig into the information on the console.

She hadn't seen him this engaged in a long time.

"The information on Sector Base E-2 is scattered throughout," she said. "I didn't try to organize anything. But the largest file had to do with that scandal. There's a lot of data in it, most of which I ignored."

He nodded, still not looking at her. He added, "Thank you," in a tone that completely dismissed her.

She smiled. She suddenly felt less alone in her searching—and in her focus.

She hovered for a minute, wanting to see what he found. He straightened a little, and she knew the next step would be him turning to her, meeting her gaze, and repeating *Thank you* pointedly.

For a moment, she felt like she had lost control of her lab. Then she smiled at herself. She had been wanting help for a long time. She had the best help she could possibly get.

She was still tired, and still distractible—not that she expected to be anything else right now.

She slipped out of the side lab, and that was when she realized she hadn't told him about the strangeness she had found in that probe imagery.

The strange imagery had been the reason she sought him out in the first place.

She toyed with walking back in, letting him know what she had found, and then decided that was a bad idea.

He was focused on Sector Base E-2 right now, and the lost information. Anything she told him might get set aside because of that focus.

She would wait for a few hours, then come back with a bowl of that soup he had made for her. He would need to eat then.

He had convinced her to take care of herself while she worked; she needed to remind him to do the same.

She looked around the main lab, her fiefdoms still established, but neglected since this morning's revelation.

She was so overwhelmed by how much data she had found, how much she needed to do, and how it all tied in with all of the information that both she had Coop wanted, that she felt as if her narrow focus for a few hours today had jeopardized the work she'd been doing.

"A little paranoid, aren't we?" she muttered to herself.

Paranoid, overwhelmed, frightened, and lost.

She shook her head ever so slightly. She had felt lost ever since the *Ivoire* had arrived here. She just hadn't acknowledged it much—because, she was afraid, to do so might be the first step down a steep slide that would lead to Dix kind of crazy.

Or she had felt that way until today.

Now, she felt like she was moving forward again, by teeny tiny increments. Where she was moving forward to, however, she had no idea. And she had a hunch she wouldn't know that for a long, long time.

19

YASH WASN'T IN THE SIDE LAB she had been working in all day. Coop peered through the door, saw imagery of something gray and black on two flat screens, saw telemetry frozen in place on two other screens, and an unmoving holographic image of Yash herself.

He left the door slightly ajar, and began a search for her. He didn't want to use the comm system she had installed here, just in case she was deep in her work, wherever that was. He would make the decision on whether or not to interrupt her when he found her.

Turned out, there was no decision to make. He pushed open the break room door, only to see Yash sound asleep on the small table, an empty bowl and spoon to one side.

The coffee was nearly empty. She had ground some beans, but she hadn't put the grounds in a filter. A ladle remained in the soup, the bread was more than half gone, and Yash herself was making little snoring sounds.

He needed to wake her, but the spicy garlic scent of the soup reminded him that he hadn't eaten in hours.

He grabbed a bowl, served himself, and then put a lid back on the soup. He didn't make more coffee, although he did dump out the remains of the batch he had made more than eight hours before.

The snoring stopped. He turned as he was getting himself a piece of bread to see Yash sitting up and running her hand through her hair. Her hair stood up in tufts. He finally understood why it looked spiky after she had been working for a while.

"What the…?" she asked, not finishing the sentence.

"I think you fell asleep." He set his bowl in front of her and took her bowl away. He did not comment on how exhausted she had to be to fall asleep that fast.

He got himself another bowl of soup, and sat across from her.

"I was looking for you," he said.

She blinked hard, then wiped her eyes. "God," she said. "I haven't done that in years."

He assumed she meant falling asleep after eating, but he didn't ask and she didn't explain further.

"I found that file," he said as he stirred his soup. "It is *fascinating*."

She slid her own bowl of soup in front of her, then stood up and grabbed some bread. She ripped it into small pieces and put those pieces on top of the broth, the way that the soup had been designed.

He had been too hungry to do so.

"I have something to tell you too," she said as she sat back down. "I forgot earlier. How long was I asleep?"

"Long enough for me to go through that file," he said, being deliberately unclear. He wanted her to focus on what he was telling her, not on the fact that she had fallen asleep without planning to.

She stirred her soup, then took a bite, not saying anything.

He made himself eat a few bites first, before he started talking. He wasn't sure he'd be able to stop once he started.

"You going to keep me in suspense?" she asked.

"Didn't mean to, sorry," he said. "I haven't eaten much since this morning."

He set the spoon against the edge of the bowl so that he wouldn't tap the spoon nervously against the bowl's side.

"There was a huge scandal at E-2," he said. "It was so bad that they actually closed the base earlier than planned."

"What?" She sounded surprised. He had been. He knew of no base that had closed early like that—not that he knew the history of all of the sector bases. "What happened?"

"Sandoveil, the town built around that sector base, was a tourist town. There were a lot of natural wonders in the area, and a lot of beauty. Some very rustic aspects to the entire region, things that people loved."

She waved a hand at him to get to the point. But the history of the region was part of the point.

"Even members of the Fleet vacationed there, sometimes taking weeks in cabins near a river and a massive waterfall, enjoying the quiet."

She frowned at him.

"This information is important," he said. "Because the area was considered quite dangerous."

"And it wasn't dangerous?" she asked.

"Oh, it was," he said. "Lots of people died there or got injured because of the natural terrain. Not as many from the Fleet as you'd think. More local tourists from other parts of Nindowne, which was what the planet was called."

"So?" Yash asked.

"So, apparently, not all of those people died of natural causes," he said.

She took another bite of soup, frowning. "Someone was killing them?" she asked.

"Yeah," he said. "For years. And she was connected to the Sector Base in a way that I couldn't find."

"She...?" Yash asked.

He nodded.

"She was part of the Fleet?" Yash asked.

"Apparently," he said. "I didn't get much of her history."

"And she's important why?" Yash asked.

"She stole the runabout," he said.

"*Our* runabout?" Yash asked.

It wasn't theirs. It had never been theirs. And he hadn't even been in it, but he didn't correct her.

"Yes," he said. "The runabout you found in the Boneyard."

"She flew *back* here from Sector Base E-2?" Yash asked. She set her spoon down. She had finished her second bowl of soup quickly. "That doesn't make sense."

"It doesn't make sense for a reason," Coop said. "Because she stole the runabout from *inside* the sector base."

Yash let out a small breath, her eyes widening. "Using the *anacapa* drive."

"Yeah," he said. "And the runabout returned not too long afterwards, in terrible shape, with a mummified corpse inside."

"Was she the dead woman?" Yash asked.

"Yes," Coop said, feeling the excitement he had felt as he had found out this information return.

Yash opened her mouth slightly, then let out a small breath, almost a huh. She seemed more affected by this news than Coop expected.

Or rather, affected in a very different way.

"She got lost in foldspace," Yash said softly.

Coop shrugged. He hadn't seen evidence of that. There was nothing in the file he had found. He wasn't even sure why that file had been in one of the ships that Lost Souls had found.

Actually, Yash had taken him almost directly to the information. Coop really wasn't certain which ship held the information or what that ship had been doing.

Or if the information had come from only one part of one ship.

Yash looked lost in thought. Or maybe lost in the memory of what it had been like to be trapped in foldspace.

Coop put out a hand, and gently touched her arm. "She was a murderer, Yash. Fleeing justice."

Yash's gaze focused on him. "We know that for sure?"

"Whoever put that file together seemed pretty certain," Coop said.

"Fleeing justice," Yash said. "Alone in a runabout. With an *anacapa* drive. Do you think she knew where she was going?"

Coop squeezed Yash's arm ever so gently. "I don't think it matters much anymore. What she did, how they meant to punish her. Which actually ended up happening to her."

"What happened to her does matter to us," Yash said. "She ended up here, for a long long time."

"In the Boneyard," Coop said. "She ended up in the Boneyard."

Yash's frown grew. "If they knew she had stolen the runabout, they would have been pinging that *anacapa* drive, searching for it."

"Probably," Coop said. "I didn't see the technical details in the file I was reading."

Yash picked up her spoon, and scraped the last of the soup out of her bowl. The movement was methodical, not about the soup per se. She was clearly thinking, and clearly needed to keep her hands busy.

"The point that caught me," Coop said, releasing her arm, "was that this woman and this runabout were not in foldspace when you found them."

Yash raised her head and let the spoon, filled with the remnants of the soup, fall against the bowl.

"So it didn't matter if they pinged the *anacapa*. They couldn't find her. Do you think she was here, in this part of space, for all that time?"

"I don't know, not without more study," Coop said.

"From what you said, Sector Base E-2 is very far from here. Their signal shouldn't have reached that *anacapa* drive." Yash was speaking quietly, almost speaking to herself.

Then her gaze met Coop's.

"Let's be clear," Yash said. "The runabout—the one that we found—made it back to E-2 with a mummified corpse inside."

"Yes," Coop said.

"Anything else to identify the time period?" Yash asked.

"Which time period?" Coop asked.

"That the runabout came from?" Yash asked, a bit of impatience in her voice.

"I saw images of the interior," Coop said. "It matched the images I've seen from you and Boss."

He had one more piece of information, but he wasn't sure he wanted to share it with her.

"That doesn't mean anything. The runabout could have gone back into foldspace, and then stayed there for some time. And then the signal from E-2 pulled it back." Yash tapped her spoon on the side of the bowl. The sound was irritating.

Coop took the spoon from her as if she was a child.

She didn't even seem to notice.

"The runabout might not have gone from the Boneyard to E-2," Yash said. "It might have—"

"I think it did," Coop said. He picked up all the empty bowls and put them in the cleaner. Then he started to make coffee. He needed to keep his hands busy.

"Why?" Yash asked.

"Because," he said, "they had images of you."

20

YASH SAT VERY STILL. She wanted to think she hadn't heard Coop correctly, but she knew she had.

They had images of you.

She couldn't quite wrap her brain around that, and for once, Coop wasn't watching her intently. He apparently did not want to see the effect his words had on her. Instead, he had gotten up and was cleaning up the break room. He left the soup alone, but he was putting the remains of the bread into a container.

He had already done something with the coffee beans she had ground. Normally, she would have loved the fact that he was making more coffee, but at the moment, she was annoyed.

She wanted to see his face, and she knew he was deliberately not watching her. It was one of his tricks, so that someone could take hard information and absorb it better.

"Me? They have images of me?" she asked after a moment. "Alone?"

"No," he said. "You and Boss. It's fleeting. I saw it. You are doing some work around that console. And then the imagery goes away."

Fleeting images. She thought back to those moments in the runabout's cockpit. For a brief moment, the runabout's systems had come to life. That had surprised both Yash and Boss. The runabout hadn't had a lot of energy left in its systems, but apparently it had had enough to not only startle them, but record them in the system.

"And," Coop was saying, "they found the labels you had put on the exterior door, the airlock door, and the *anacapa* drive."

"Labels?" Yash didn't know what he was referring to.

"The warning stickers, the danger ones? The ones that you and Boss fought about all those years ago?"

Yash half smiled. Coop remembered the argument, not the procedure. But then, he hadn't gone diving with Boss, at least that Yash remembered, so he wouldn't know how the procedure worked in practice.

Boss had insisted on placing warning signs on everything she found that had a small whiff of danger. She didn't want someone to die accidentally in a wave of malfunctioning *anacapa* energy.

The fight, which Yash had forgotten until now, was not about placing the warning signs, but about how the signs should be designed for maximum effect, and where, when, and how they should get placed on anything. She and Boss had argued about which language to use, they had argued about placement, and they had argued about how best to protect anyone going into a derelict vessel.

In the end, Yash had the designers at Lost Souls make warnings that were primarily directed at anyone connected to Lost Souls.

She and Boss had placed a number of those warnings on the runabout. The final one Yash had slapped into place had been on the *anacapa* drive container.

Her brain caught on that moment, turned it over in her head. She hadn't touched anything but the container when she slapped that warning on it.

"Still," she said, "that image, those warnings, they could have been there after years."

Coop was shaking his head. He finished assembling the coffee, and it started to brew, filling the small room with the scent of a lighter roast than she usually chose. Maybe he hadn't used the beans she had set aside after all.

He sat down across from her, his expression serious. "I believe that the runabout went from the Boneyard back to E-2."

"Based on what evidence?" she asked.

He gave her a look she recognized. It was one of his *did you really say that?* looks. And it was tinged with disappointment. Or maybe she had imagined that part.

"Based on everything you said, Yash." His tone was gentle. "You said the runabout hadn't had a lot of energy. You said the *anacapa* drive was activated from somewhere else. You were perfectly willing to believe that the drive was activated by the Fleet here and now. Why aren't you willing to believe that the drive was activated from E-2 three thousand years ago?"

"Because that's not how it works," she said. "The runabout wasn't trapped in foldspace. The *Ivoire* was trapped in foldspace."

He remained motionless for a long moment. Behind him, the coffee darkened. He had used a drip method to make it. The slow way, not the instant way she used.

His silence bothered her.

"When Boss and her crew accidentally activated the beacon on Sector Base V," Yash said, "the *anacapa* reached into foldspace, and pulled us out."

"I know," Coop said quietly. Clearly, she had insulted him by over explaining. But he hadn't responded.

"Then I don't see how you believe that it happened this time," Yash said.

"The only thing that's different between your scenario and mine," Coop said, "is that Sector Base E-2 pulled the runabout into the past. You initially believed that a current version of the Fleet had pulled the runabout somewhere else."

"Yes," Yash said.

"So you think the time jumps only happen when the ship is stranded in foldspace," he said.

Now he was asking for something she wasn't sure of. She hesitated. "We don't understand foldspace," she said.

"That's right," he said. "We don't. Nor do we fully understand the *anacapa* drive."

She sat very still.

"Even if the modern Fleet had pulled the runabout out of the Boneyard, they would have had to pull it through foldspace, Yash."

She knew that. Now, she was the one who felt talked down to.

"You said there was some kind of strange energy field in the Boneyard," Coop said.

"Most of it caused by the runabout," Yash said.

"But not all of it," he said.

She had to concede that point. "Not all of it, no."

"Then maybe some strange circumstances happened with the runabout. You activated it, and somehow, it triggered the beacon from E-2," Coop said.

"That's backwards from what happened to us," Yash said. "The beacon on Sector Base V had been shut down. Boss activated it."

"She did," Coop said. "But I'm sure it had been activated more than once in five thousand years. Something brought us forward in time, some vagary that we don't understand. And it might have been something in foldspace, something we did that interacted with what they did, something that we had in common with the runabout, maybe. Some kind of reading…?"

"Some kind of telemetry," she said, more to herself than to him. "Oh, my goodness, Coop. You need to come with me."

He frowned at her. "What?"

She had to show him the telemetry, the images from that probe.

"You have to come with me," she repeated. "Right now."

21

THE LIGHT HAD RETURNED to Yash's eyes. For a moment, Coop had been worried. She had seemed very upset that the runabout had gone from the Boneyard to the past, and he hadn't been able to pinpoint the exact cause of her upset.

He wasn't sure if she had been upset because the runabout going directly from the Boneyard back to Sector Base E-2 thousands of years ago meant that—in Yash's mind—the Fleet did not exist now. Or if she had been upset because she and Boss had somehow tampered with the runabout. Or if Yash had been upset because she didn't understand the mechanism that sent the runabout back.

But he had said something to trigger an idea, something that got her powerful mind working in a different direction.

She was already on her feet. He shot a wistful glance at the coffee, wishing he had time to pour a mug, but he clearly didn't.

"Come *on*," she said.

He stood. By the time he was out of his chair, she was out of the break room, and heading back to her side lab. He had to hurry to follow.

She was inside before he was even halfway there. He sped up, and got inside just as she shut down the holographic image of herself. Otherwise, she hadn't touched anything.

"See this?" she asked, tapping one of the two-dimensional images.

He could answer that as if she were referring to the screen or as if she was referring to something in the image.

He chose neither. "I'm seeing blurs of gray and black."

"Come closer," she said and stepped aside.

He stepped into the ring of screens, startlingly like his ring in his side lab, and frowned at the image in front of him. He saw vague shapes, but nothing that resolved itself into something he understood.

"I'm sorry," he said. "I'm not sure what I'm looking at."

"Watch." She backed up the image, then replayed it. He saw a bright light obliterate most of the screen, and then something opening where the wall had been.

"What is this, the runabout?" he asked.

"More than that," she said. "It's imagery from one of the probes. According to the telemetry, that opening appeared just as the runabout went into fold-space. Have we ever had an outside image of a ship entering foldspace?"

He wasn't at all sure what she meant by her question. He was about to say so, when she clarified.

"I don't mean an image from another ship watching a ship go into foldspace or images from a vessel's own internal systems as it entered foldspace. I mean, from some other kind of equipment with a focus on the *anacapa* drive, showing the foldspace opening from inside the ship."

He didn't answer immediately, because he couldn't think of anything, which meant nothing. He didn't know the technological history of the Fleet. He had no idea what existed and what hadn't.

"I haven't seen anything like that," he said. "But I've never seen that kind of light flare when an *anacapa* activated, either."

"I forgot to tell you," she said. "The container was open. So everything was exaggerated."

He blinked. He couldn't remember the last time he had actually looked at the *anacapa* drive as it initiated.

He wasn't sure he had *ever* looked at an *anacapa* drive when it initiated. Part of him actually believed that looking at a drive when it activated was bad for his health or his eyes or something.

He would have to pinpoint that memory later.

"What has this to do with the runabout's return to E-2?" he asked.

"This." She froze the image again and tapped it. "*Look.*"

She was no longer questioning the runabout's return to E-2. Or, maybe, she was ignoring that part of what he said.

She tapped that blur of images.

He looked, saw…an opening? Shelves? Equipment? A door? He wasn't sure.

"I don't know what you're showing me," he said, not wanting to guess.

"I think we were looking through the fold in space," she said. "Just for a moment. The telemetry said the runabout was already in fold-space when this happened. And we got images—the last images—from that probe."

He frowned. He would need to see it again.

"That doesn't look like the runabout went to a DV-Class vessel," Coop said. "If that's a room, then the runabout went to a sector base."

"I think that's probably the case," she said.

"You just spent fifteen minutes arguing that the runabout couldn't have gone to Sector Base E-2," Coop said.

"In the past," she said. "I was protesting the *in the past* part."

She wasn't looking at him. She was studying the data she had frozen on one of the screens.

"And you're not protesting that now?" he asked.

"I have a working theory," she said.

"A working theory." He had no idea how she had gone from arguing with him to having a theory in the space of a few minutes.

She nodded. "You said what does the *Ivoire* have in common with the runabout?"

"Besides a long trip through time," he said.

"Besides that," she said, as if it were nothing.

He had no idea what the two ships had in common. The ships were different sizes. They had gone to different places. They were from different timelines.

But Yash's brain was clearly making connections, and they seemed so obvious to her that she believed they would be obvious to him. They weren't obvious at all.

"You'll have to tell me," he said.

She leaned back just a little. From that position, he realized, she could see both him and one of the screens.

"The *Ivoire* had just been to Sector Base V," Yash said. "We had taken a little time there, and then we activated our *anacapa* drive to get out of there. We had gone on the mission, and the Quurzod shot at us, harming the drive."

He bit his tongue, not wanting to remind her that he had been there, that he remembered all of these details. But he didn't interrupt her because he recognized this mode of hers.

She was laying the groundwork for her assumptions, picking the details that helped her make those connections that he hadn't been able to see.

"The shots damaged the *anacapa*," she said. They both knew that. They had seen it happen, *felt* it happen. The *anacapa* had actually frozen—stopped—as it activated. Then it rebooted. At least, that was how Yash explained it at the time.

He hadn't asked her since. Dix had, and Dix hadn't liked her responses.

But Coop had continued to move forward, blaming the Quurzod, thinking the event was a one-time occurrence—at least when it came to traveling that far through time.

"I think," Yash said, "Maybe, the hits to the *anacapa* drive interfered with the way that we went into foldspace."

She had never quite expressed it that way before. She had talked about the damage, and had hypothesized, when they were trapped in foldspace, that the drive had been so badly damaged that it couldn't reactivate.

But she hadn't said that the damage to the *anacapa* drive had affected the manner in which they entered foldspace.

"What I'm thinking now," she said, "what might be plausible, given what happened to the runabout, is this. That last memory in the *anacapa* drive, the last normal trip that we took—"

"Was out of Sector Base V," he said quietly, finally getting the connections she was making.

"And the last place the runabout had been," she said, "was in Sector Base E-2. When the damaged *anacapa* finally activated, it took the runabout back to the place it had left."

"The failsafe," he said. "Of course."

It seemed so simple, and yet he hadn't thought of it. Yash hadn't either.

Probably because they believed what happened to the *Ivoire* was unique. And considering the evidence he had just pulled about the runabout, that belief was probably false.

Other ships had had similar problems. Getting lost in time through foldspace might have been unusual, but what happened to the *Ivoire* had not been unique.

And because he had assumed that what happened to the *Ivoire* was unique, he had never even considered the simplest reason that the *Ivoire* had gone to Sector Base V.

The failsafe that all *anacapa* drives had.

The failsafe existed in case the *anacapa* drive couldn't be programmed, but could be activated. In those circumstances, which were a lot more common than the one the *Ivoire* and that runabout had found themselves in, the failsafe enabled the drive to send the ship back to the place where it had entered foldspace.

Coop had never used that failsafe in his years with the Fleet, but apparently, the *Ivoire* had activated the failsafe on its own. If Yash was right.

"Did you activate that *anacapa* drive on that runabout?" he asked. Because if she had, then that *anacapa* drive's failsafe might have activated as well.

"I don't know if I activated it," she said. "Possibly, although I'm not sure how. But the interior of that runabout was badly damaged. Someone might have jury-rigged some of the controls, and when the runabout came to life, ever so briefly, it might have activated more than we realized."

It took a lot of power to activate an *anacapa* that wasn't working. He had struggled with that problem on several missions, in a variety of different ways.

The idea that the momentary activation that Boss and Yash had made of the runabout made the *anacapa* drive work properly didn't seem likely to him.

But if he were considering simple solutions he hadn't contemplated before, there was one other that he needed to mention.

"That moment on the runabout might just have provided enough energy to send out a distress beacon," he said. "We were constantly sending distress beacons. The entire time we were trapped in foldspace. We sent out distress beacons in every format we could think of."

Her gaze met his. That energy gleamed in her eyes as if she hadn't gotten tired, as if she hadn't nearly worked herself to death the last few days.

"The *Ivoire* was constantly sending distress beacons," she said, "and those beacons were *only* going to Sector Base V."

"You know that for a fact?" he asked.

"No," she said. "But I could look. Distress beacons can be localized. It might have had something to do with the default, with the failsafe. I never checked the distress beacon. All the work I had done to figure out why we came here, and I had never done that."

There were other simple things Coop hadn't considered. He would review protocols and see what (if anything) he had missed.

Because as excited as Yash seemed to be now about these new paths, Coop still had some doubts.

And he felt out of his depth. She knew more about the systems than he did. He was good, but she was the expert.

"A number of things bother me," he said, "especially if we consider that the *Ivoire's* distress beacon sent messages back to Sector Base V. Sector Base V was new when we vanished. It existed for another three to four hundred years. It should have picked up our signal some other way—and sooner. Shortly after we left, in fact."

"Should have," Yash said. "But we were in foldspace, and foldspace sometimes does strange things with time."

He knew that. He had known that for his entire career. Years after he helped rescue the captain of the *Voimakas*, he had met her. She had retired right after the incident and had moved planetside, working outside, handling gardening for an apartment complex near Sector Base U.

She hadn't thanked him for saving her life. Instead, she had said, *The best thing about being outside is that it feels timeless.* And then she had smiled at him. *Isn't it ironic? I find gardening timeless, when it is based on seasons and the passage of time. Heh.*

And then she had walked away from him.

Strange things with time. Lost time. Lost ships.

"But," he said, trying to shake off that memory. It was as disturbing now as it had been the day it happened. "As you were reminding me earlier, the runabout wasn't in foldspace when it was pulled back to E-2."

"Your theory, not mine," Yash said. "We don't know that for sure. But let's go with your theory for a moment, shall we?"

He tensed, waiting. He always found it intriguing when she did this, because her mind worked so differently than his. He never knew what direction she would take his ideas to.

"That runabout had had some kind of massive power failure," she said. "It couldn't send out a distress beacon. Not until we activated it ever so briefly."

He glanced at the flat imagery, at the grays and blacks and the suggestion of shelves in the blur.

"But," Yash said, "if this woman had stolen the runabout, then the sector base or the ship or wherever she stole the runabout from would have a procedure for recovering it."

"The sector base," he said. "She stole it from the base."

Yash nodded. "But the ship the runabout came from might have procedures as well."

"True," Coop said. He hated guessing about procedures developed in a future the two of them did not know.

"In our time," Yash said, "the procedure was to constantly ping the runabout. We would have had a way to contact it, and we would have been using a very powerful beacon to pull it back to Sector Base E-2."

Coop looked at her.

"And if this woman knew that," Yash said, "then she would have not activated the distress signal, ever. No matter what happened to her. She would not have allowed anything to come her way from any Fleet ship or base."

That made sense to Coop. If he were running from the Fleet in a Fleet vessel, he would have made sure that the vessel was not in touch with the Fleet in any way.

"But," he said, "when you activated the runabout briefly, you must have activated everything, including the signals back to the Fleet."

"Maybe," Yash said. "It might have been the only time that the distress signal went back to Sector Base E-2."

He let out an involuntary *huh* of surprise. That made sense. But they were guessing. And if the last few years had done anything for him, they had given him a hatred of guessing.

"Is there any way to check that assumption?" he asked.

"Yes," she said. "We can check all of these assumptions. We have the runabout's data files. We can see if this woman ever activated a distress signal, if she cut off contact to the Fleet, what exactly happened to that runabout."

He felt a bit of tension leave him. He liked that, much better than speculating.

"We can also check the runabout's files against the files on the *Ivoire* to see if there were any similarities in procedure, particularly around the time that the *anacapa* drives pulled the ships into another time period."

She sounded excited about all of this. Coop was as well.

They had a focus, a way to solve one of the mysteries that had been bothering him since he got to this time period.

She was smiling as she contemplated all of that work. Then her smile faded.

"You know," she said, "Dix would have seen this as the beginning of a map that might take us back to our own time."

She was right; Dix would have seen that. He would have urged them to replicate whatever they found so that the *Ivoire* could return to its own time.

"Do you see it that way?" Coop asked, feeling a little breathless. He didn't want to lose Yash to a Dix kind of crazy.

"No," Yash said. "But it's intriguing, isn't it?"

It was intriguing and beguiling. Coop didn't like the things he was seeing in himself these past few days. The tendency toward obsession hadn't been like him, and now he was feeling beguiled by figuring out exactly what had brought the *Ivoire* here.

"What's really fascinating to me," Yash said, as if she hadn't noticed his concern, "is peering into foldspace like that."

He hadn't thought of it. He still hadn't accepted it. But she was clearly excited about it. She had dragged him into this side lab just to see those images.

"If that's what we're seeing," Coop said.

She nodded, a bit preoccupied. "If we can do that, if we can see into foldspace, we might make travel through foldspace safer."

He frowned. He wanted to make foldspace travel safer. But right now, that felt like a side branch off what they had been working on.

Everything they had discussed, looking at the ways the ships got compromised, investigating the *anacapa* drives, looking into foldspace, would increase their knowledge and would probably make Lost Souls money as Yash helped them develop changes to the technology.

But it didn't help them resolve the mysteries that had dogged him for years.

And now, he was ready to have them solved.

He was about to say so when Yash's gaze met his. She had been puzzling something.

"None of this explains how that runabout got into the Boneyard in the first place," she said.

"Your theory actually does," he said.

She shook her head slightly, the small frown between her eyes asking him to clarify without her voicing the question at all.

"If that woman did not want contact with the Fleet," Coop said, "she might have left foldspace—not where she intended to be, but somewhere else. Maybe back in what we now call Empire space. She might have gone backward, thinking the Fleet would never look for her in a sector they had long abandoned. In doing so, she would have avoided the Fleet, but she might have had other issues, issues that compromised the runabout."

"Like running into a culture that didn't want her in their region of space," Yash said. "And if they fired on her like the Quurzod had with us...."

Coop nodded. "Or," he said, "she might have emerged from foldspace only to have some kind of cascade failure with the runabout, something that prevented her from going planetside somewhere and seeking help. She might not have been stranded in foldspace at all."

"Stranded in regular space," Yash said.

"That seems likely," Coop said. "The runabout was being upgraded and repaired at the sector base."

He thought of the protest from the long-dead *anacapa* engineer, her complaints about working on the smaller *anacapa* drives. He would have to share that with Yash.

"And if the work wasn't complete," Yash said, "it could have caused a serious malfunction in the runabout, something that an amateur couldn't have fixed."

"Or even someone with a bit of knowledge about systems," Coop said. "At a certain point, you do need an expert."

"If she couldn't contact the Fleet," Yash said, "then she couldn't have gone to starbases or sector bases or any place where someone connected to the Fleet might have been. She might not have been able to find the right kind of help."

"If she could find any help at all," Coop said.

"It looked like she had been in there a long time," Yash said.

"To mummify, yes," Coop said. "It—"

"No," Yash said quietly. "Some of the things we found in the cabins. It just seemed like she had been trapped, alone, in that runabout for more than a few weeks."

"I thought everything was torn up," Coop said.

"Not everything," Yash said.

"So she tried to fix the ship," Coop said, "and failed."

"Then she ran out of food or water or something happened to her physically."

Coop nodded. "And then she died."

Yash's lips thinned. She turned away from the images on the screens, almost as if they reminded her of that body, of the months (or years) of desperation that the woman had suffered through.

That a murderer had suffered through.

Coop had to remind himself of that.

"Then," Yash said after a moment, "the ship got torn up for useful parts by person or persons unknown."

"Yeah," Coop said. "Then, whoever put the Boneyard together—"

"The Fleet?" Yash asked.

Coop shrugged. "We don't know that. We're using Fleet technology. Someone else might have as well."

"Whoever," Yash said.

"Whoever," Coop said, in agreement, "they scooped up the runabout and put it in the Boneyard."

"Not caring there was a body inside," Yash said. That had bothered her from the beginning. She had believed the Fleet would have not allowed a dead body to remain in a derelict ship.

Coop hadn't been so certain, and he wasn't going to argue that point now, either.

"I'm not sure anyone knew there was a body inside," he said. "I'm not sure they even knew *what* was inside. I suspect the runabout was scanned and then stored in that Boneyard, maybe kept for parts."

"Like we're keeping some of the ships we find," she said.

"Exactly," he said.

"A ship graveyard," she said, using the phrase they had used from the beginning. "And it wasn't until we went into that runabout that the little ship even managed to contact E-2."

"Or, more accurately," Coop said, "receive all the signals coming from E-2."

"Maybe that power, those pings, coming from E-2 through foldspace had accumulated. Amplified their reach somehow." Yash sighed, then shook her head. "You know, it's really stupid that we don't understand foldspace better. We use it all the damn time."

Coop understood the "we." It meant the Fleet. And they had had this discussion dozens of times over their careers.

"Foldspace revealed itself over decades," he said.

"Yeah, yeah, I know the excuse," she said.

"And if we stopped using it," he said, referring to Fleet, "we would have had to change our entire culture."

"It's a fine risk to take every day," Yash said, "until it bites you in the ass."

Like it had bitten them. Like it had bitten that woman in the runabout.

He wondered if he would trade it, though. He had always been conscious of the risk. Maybe not the risk as he had experienced it—the risk of losing everything familiar in a leap to a different part of space—but he had known he could lose time. Or friends. Or loved ones.

And, if he was being honest with himself, he liked the challenge of it. He wouldn't have gone on the captain track if he hadn't. And, after he had become captain, he would have resigned if he felt he couldn't handle the duties.

"Makes you not want to enter foldspace ever again, doesn't it?" Yash asked.

He blinked at her, startled by the question. Not enter foldspace? Not have the opportunity to travel great distances in short periods of time? Piloting a starship through entire galaxies, star system by star system? Never leaving one or two sectors of space? Never experiencing all the different cultures? All the different lives? All the different ways humans conducted themselves in all their infinite variety?

Never enter foldspace again? Never move forward? Never live life to the fullest ever again? He couldn't comprehend it.

And yet he had been on the verge of it.

197

"I think we've been too timid about foldspace these last six years," he said.

"What?" It was clearly Yash's turn to be surprised. "You're joking, right? We finally understand how dangerous it is."

He shook his head. "We've always known. We just thought we were immune."

"We're not immune," she said. "No one is."

"Exactly," he said. "Kinda mirrors life, doesn't it? We never know what's around the next corner. We can be afraid of it, or we can keep going."

Yash stared at him as if she couldn't believe what he was saying.

"You know there are other options, right?" she asked. "Investigate. See what we can learn before we go around that corner."

"And no matter how much we prepare," Coop said, "we never prepare enough. We're always surprised by something."

"I think I'd rather go through life with fewer surprises, thank you," she said.

"That's not true and you know it," he said. "Or you wouldn't have been excited about *that*."

He pointed at the image of what Yash was calling the entry into foldspace. The image, with all its blurred mystery.

She glanced at it, her cheeks growing red. Then she sighed.

"I guess I don't want to go through something like this ever again," she said.

He assumed that what she meant by *like this* was the entire adventure they found themselves on, living in a future they hadn't even been able to imagine ten years before. Back in their own timeline, back before the Quurzod had fired on the *Ivoire*.

"You won't go through anything like this ever again," he said.

"You can't promise that," Yash said.

He smiled at her. "Oh, but I can. Each event is different, Yash. And even if we end up traveling long distances through time again, it'll never be the same as this."

She studied him for a moment, the red in her cheeks fading.

"That doesn't bother you?" she asked. "Losing everything all over again?"

"What do we have to lose from here?" he asked.

"We're building a life," she said. "*You're* building a life. You have Boss."

He nodded. "And Lost Souls and some plans that might or might not work out. We're building a life, Yash, and if we lose it, we'll build another one. We're not like Dix. We don't give up."

She pursed her lips, frowned, then shrugged.

"You want to travel a long distance through foldspace again, don't you?" she asked.

He nodded. "I want to go to Sector Base E-2."

"It's gone, Coop. It's been gone for centuries."

"And they closed it fast," he said. "We might learn something."

"I thought you don't want to find the modern Fleet," she said.

"I don't think I do," he said. "But I want answers. I want to know what happened. I want to know where they went."

"To join them?" Yash asked.

To avoid them, he almost said, but didn't. He was surprised at the thought. Then he half smiled. Two Fleets—his and theirs.

And an entire universe to explore.

He felt a flutter of excitement, something he hadn't felt in years.

Six years, maybe more.

"What are you thinking?" Yash asked, clearly seeing the moods change on his face.

"About the future," he said, letting that half smile become a full smile. "I'm thinking about the future."

And it felt really, really good.

ADVANCED ANACAPA THEORY

OVER FIVE THOUSAND YEARS AGO
OR
THIRTY YEARS AGO
(DEPENDING ON WHO YOU ASK)

22

THE SMALL LAB WAS COLD. Yash had not worn a heavy enough shirt to comfortably make it through the day-long class. She didn't even have a sweater or a jacket or anything else to layer over her clothes.

Just her work pants and her normal work shirt, along with the lunch that Professor Helga Bellier had told the students to bring. The lunches in their little prep containers were stored on the large runabout that had brought the class to this weird lab, built on the side of a crater deep in an unpopulated moon halfway across the sector from the main part of the Fleet.

Just the day before, one of Bellier's teaching assistants had made some snide comment about the dangerous part of the class would begin now. Bellier hadn't simply shushed the TA; she had removed the TA from any duties to do with this class.

Yash had been too busy with homework to check to see if the TA had been demoted permanently. It wouldn't surprise Yash. Bellier was known for her no-nonsense, no-mistakes policies.

Mistakes get people killed, Professor Bellier had said that first day on the *Brazza*. The Advanced *Anacapa* Theory class had met on the *Brazza* only once, in a borrowed classroom, since Professor Bellier preferred to conduct class on ancient security vessels, science vessels, runabouts, and orbiters. Sometimes she took the class to starbases and sector bases.

Mostly, though, she drilled the students, tested them over and over again, lectured them damn near to death, gave them homework that seemed utterly impossible, and worked harder than any professor Yash had ever had at trying to get all of the students—every single one of them—to drop out of class.

When Yash had signed up for this course, her advisor had warned her that there were semesters in which no one made it past week six of Bellier's course, semesters in which Bellier had flunked everyone, and semesters in which no one even signed up.

But Yash also knew that anyone who survived Bellier's Advanced *Anacapa* Theory course got accepted into the Dignity Vessel Engineering program, and often was fast-tracked for service on a DV-Class ship. Apparently, anyone who could handle whatever Bellier dished out could also handle what the universe dished out.

Yash just hadn't been expecting the cold.

Bellier had told them that from this day forward, the class would be hands-on. Bellier had informed them yesterday that the title of the class was a lie.

I don't believe in theories, Bellier had said. *I believe in engineers. If you're going to be an expert in something, then you need to be an expert in all aspects of it. From what makes it work to what makes it desirable to what makes it flawed.*

And then she had said something that made two people drop out that very day. She had scanned the class, made eye contact with each and every student, then said,

We will be working with anacapa *drives. The drives are dangerous. They will be live. One mistake could obliterate all of us. I know some of you took this class because it was labeled* theory, *and so you believed you could gain an understanding of these complex drives without getting your hands dirty.*

Then she paused, tilted her head, and laser-focused her gaze on one student in particular.

You can't understand these drives without touching them and working with them. There is no theory of the anacapa *drive. There is only the practicality of them. If that scares you, drop this class, and any idea you have of being an engineer, ship designer, or a scientist on board any kind of vessel that carries an* anacapa *drive.*

The speech had excited Yash, which was probably the opposite reaction she should have had, given the way the rest of the class had responded. A few got together over beers to discuss what they wanted to do. The two whom Professor Bellier had laser-eyed had left the class and immediately found their way back to the *Brazza* to drop out of the program entirely.

Yash hadn't expected to work on *anacapa* drives for another year or two. The very idea had excited her. These drives were the heart and soul of the Fleet. But they were also, as one of her professors had put it years ago, as unknowable as the human heart and soul. The mechanics of the heart seemed obvious, but to this day, no one knew why every culture the Fleet had come into contact with believed the heart to be the center of love, and why most believed that human beings were more than a collection of physical parts.

Unknowable, mysterious, and more important than anything else.

Yash shivered, but resisted the urge to put her arms around her torso to keep warm. A few of the other students had done that, and Professor Bellier had given them the same sort of laser-eyed stare she had given the two dropouts the day before.

Professor Bellier was not dressed any warmer than they were. She was a tiny woman, with fierce black eyes, nut-brown skin decorated with very fine age lines, and gray hair cut so close to her scalp that from a distance it looked like she was wearing a gray skullcap.

She was small, but her entire body radiated a kind of power that Yash had never seen in a human being before. Every movement suggested confidence. Every action seemed deliberate.

Professor Helga Bellier was the most in-control human being that Yash had ever met, bar none.

And part of Yash wanted to grow up to be just like her.

The runabout had docked on top of the lab. The moon had no atmosphere, which made Yash a bit nervous. Professor Bellier hadn't told them to bring their personal environmental suits.

Unless there was one on the skip, Professor Bellier hadn't brought one either.

But the pilot and the cockpit crew all wore theirs as if they antici-pated going out onto the moon.

Yash had noted all of that as the runabout had traveled the short distance to this moon and settled in one of its larger craters. Half of her fellow students had taken the trip lightly, talking about the future of the class or what they had to drink the night before.

A handful of others had sat in their seats, tensely watching the scen-ery change outside the portals. Only three—Yash included—had taken the name of the moon, looked up its specs, and then investigated the small lab itself.

The lab had been built into the crater's side to protect the moon's surface from any possible damage should there be a massive explosion. Apparently other labs on other moons and asteroids had exploded over the years that Bellier had taught this course. Some of those labs had been in different sectors. Some of them had exploded decades ago.

Yet Bellier had never been disciplined, nor had she been written up. In fact, the Fleet considered her classes primary requirements for anyone who wanted a permanent engineering assignment on a DV-Class vessel.

Yash wanted that permanent assignment. She wanted to travel with the Fleet whenever the Fleet moved forward. Her parents lagged behind the Fleet. Their specialty was closing sector bases and starbases, examining closed bases to make certain that protocols were followed, and doing all kinds of maintenance on planetside support systems for the Fleet itself.

Yash had lived on three different planets in her childhood, always envying the kids who were raised on ships. She had traveled a lot on ships, often on DV-Class ships, and she wanted to stay on them. But her father in particular had a great dislike for enclosed environments. He loved to go outside in atmosphere. He adored weather and seasons and the ways that planets went through their own personal cycles. He loved learning those cycles.

He always felt that he had been born into the wrong culture, hating the constant moving. If he hadn't married Yash's mother, he probably would have remained behind after closing some sector base, figuring that he could live inside half the day and outside for the other half.

Yash's mother had loved her work, though, and couldn't do any of it if the Fleet left whatever sector she was working in. Yash's mother was a research scientist of a kind that Yash never really bothered to understand. Her mother could work anywhere that there was a Fleet lab, and hadn't cared one way or another if she traveled with the Fleet or remained at a sector base.

She had raised four children with Yash's father and claimed to love him as much as she loved her work. She hadn't been willing to sacrifice either, so he had to give up his idea of a permanent home to have a family.

He hadn't seemed to mind.

But Yash had. As soon as she qualified, she applied to boarding school on the Fleet's squadron of school ships. She had been thirteen when she left home for good, traveling back only three times a year for vacations.

Then she skipped several levels, her scientific and engineering skills considered exceptional, and she no longer had time to travel. The engineering school was the most competitive school in the Fleet. Everyone wanted a DV-Class assignment, and there were very few to go around.

Yash apologized to her parents, told them that they could visit her if they needed to see her, and then set to work.

That work—and her stellar grades—had brought her here. She couldn't imagine walking away like those two students had done, just because the *anacapa* work would be hands-on earlier than they expected.

Yash figured if the Fleet had managed to live with the drives for tens of thousands of years, she could live with the drives as well.

Besides, she was deeply curious about them.

The lab had the same structure as the previous labs that the Fleet had built for Professor Bellier. Six rooms, one of which was exceptionally large. The others were smaller, with an eating area, a bunk room with enough sleeping capacity for sixteen, one bathroom, and some research labs. There was also a maintenance room which, if the specs were to be believed, contained not only redundant environmental controls, but some controls that would seal off the top of the crater so that nothing could get in—and nothing could get out.

Yash hadn't mentioned that to any of her fellow students. She hadn't discussed any of this. She liked several of them, but she didn't feel close to them.

She kept expecting them to drop out at any moment.

Professor Bellier stood in front of a wide door. They had initially gone into one of the side labs, where Yash had expected class to begin. But it hadn't. Instead, Professor Bellier had insisted that they all prepare themselves for a long class with no breaks. That meant using the bathroom and making certain they divested themselves of everything except one multipurpose tool—if they owned one (Yash did)—and the clothes on their backs.

A couple of the other students had grumbled about this, which also caught the professor's attention. Yash had simply followed instructions, wondering what was in the lab beyond.

She had waited as patiently as she could, expecting that this too was a test.

And sure enough. Once Professor Bellier opened the door, she paused in front of it.

"I can only take nine students with me inside this room," she said.

Yash's stomach lurched. Suddenly all of the self-confidence she had felt earlier vanished.

"Six of you will remain out here. And those six are…" She named names, much too slowly for Yash's taste. Eventually, though, Bellier got through the names.

She did not say Yash's name. Yash wasn't certain if she should be tense or not. So she waited.

Then Bellier looked at the students excluded from this part of the trip. They included some of the gossips and complainers, but not all of them, which surprised Yash. If she were weeding out the group, she would have weeded out everyone who fit in those two categories.

Also, one of the men designated to stay out of the lab had been one of the three researchers. So doing due diligence wasn't the key to accompanying the professor either.

"What would you like us to work on while you're gone, Professor?" he asked.

Her dark eyes snapped with, it seemed to Yash, annoyance.

"Initiative," she said to him. Then she looked at the nine students she had chosen. "Come with me."

Yash followed the other students inside.

This room was five times larger than the room they had just left. It was as cold as that room though, so frosty that she could almost see her breath.

The air had a charge to it as well, an aliveness. Her father would have said it felt like a storm was on the horizon, but to Yash it felt like the air right after a powerful (and nearby) lightning strike.

There was some kind of energy in here, energy she recognized only in comparing it to something else.

The room was long and wide. One other door stood on the same wall as the door Yash had just come through. That door surprised her. She couldn't quite square it with the map of the lab she had seen.

In front of her were gigantic reinforced windows that overlooked the crater. An ambient blue light rose out of the crater, illuminating some of the rocks.

Yash didn't know if the light came from some human-developed source below, or if the light arose from something in the rocks themselves.

She wouldn't be able to find out, at least not right now.

The room itself was lit the way the labs back on the *Brazza* were lit—lighting at every available angle, including lighting pods along the floor. There was no other equipment, though. No consoles attached to any walls, no chairs for the group to sit on, just a wide-open space filled with black boxes and large rocks.

The boxes were almost the size of Yash's bed back on the *Brazza*. They stood as high as her knees and had no obvious locks or control mechanisms.

Beside each one was a rock. The rocks were different sizes, but none was smaller than Yash's head. They had pits and grooves, rather like the rocks in the crater outside, but they were an odd gray color.

If someone asked her what that color was, she would have said that it was the color of death.

She shivered involuntarily, then looked down. The hair on her arms had risen. She would have said it had risen with the cold, but that wasn't accurate. That reaction on her skin was caused by the energy field.

Professor Bellier waited until all nine students crowded into the room. Five women, four men. No one moved away from the door because they had no idea where to stand.

Yash didn't like being clustered with the group, so she moved off to one side, nearest the right wall. It was colder over here, if that was possible, but the energy field didn't feel quite as strong.

She licked her lips, realizing for the first time that near the door, even her teeth had vibrated slightly with the field. She had, at first, thought the inside of her mouth felt strange because she had been nervously grinding her teeth. But that wasn't true.

Something in that field was vibrating her bones.

Bellier's gaze raked over Yash. Yash's cheeks heated. Was she supposed to stick with the group? Was she supposed to cluster like a frightened child, waiting for an invitation to go deeper into the room?

She didn't ask, though, just met Bellier's gaze until it slid away from her.

"Welcome to the hands-on *anacapa* lab," Bellier said as the door closed behind the group. "We will be spending the next week or two here, provided all of you make it through the training. You will learn how the drives work, how to repair them on a minimal level, and how to set one up—again, at the beginning level."

Yash felt her heart leap. She wanted to do work like this. She loved getting her hands on equipment.

"If you make so much as one error," Bellier said, "you could compromise your drive. If you make a large enough error, you could send us all into foldspace, unprotected. If you end up doing that, you will probably activate some of the other drives, and that will send this entire lab into foldspace, along with the runabout attached to the surface of the lab. And before someone asks the most stupid question of all—*has this happened?*—it has happened, just not in my class. I had two predecessors on this part of the job. One survived."

Her expression wasn't as grim as Yash would have thought it needed to be, given what she was saying. Sometimes, Yash had a sense that the professors in hands-on engineering school liked to scare the students with apocryphal tales of disaster.

"Now," Bellier said, "you will each take a place near one of the containers. That will be your workspace for the duration of this lesson."

The students glanced at each other. It seemed to be an involuntary reaction, waiting to see who would go first. Yash did it as well, then realized she was doing so, and barely prevented herself from rolling her eyes at her own behavior.

She left the side of the room, walked between the boxes and the windows, which took her directly in front of Professor Bellier.

Up close the rocks looked less like rocks and more like something made from nanobits and then destroyed by time and decay. The rocks weren't black, which they would have been if they were made of new nanobits, but the rocks had that gray color that nanobits sometimes got when they were unbonding from each other.

Some of the rocks had gold and white threads running through them, but again, on a more uniform level than one might find outside, on a moon, for example.

The largest rock that she had seen was only two feet away from Bellier. But if they were going to learn how to work on these drives, and the rocks were somehow important, then Yash wanted one large enough to enable her to see everything clearly.

She knew she needed to face the professor, so Yash threaded her way between the large rock and one of the containers, stopping behind the rock, and standing very still, her hands clasped behind her back.

Professor Bellier gave her a hooded look, then nodded ever so slightly. Yash had a sense that Bellier had expected her to go first.

Yash's movements freed the other students. They still milled just a bit, then started toward the containers, most moving in a clump.

No one seemed to want to walk past Yash to take the containers beyond her, but two of the women and one man ended up with no choice. They walked behind her, making her just a bit nervous. The woman who led that small group took the container as far from Yash as possible. The man took the next container, leaving the container beside Yash open.

She frowned, then realized the container on the other side was open as well. No one took that. The remaining woman took the container to Yash's left.

No one stood directly in front of Professor Bellier. Who had apparently lied in the other room. She had said she could only take nine, but there were ten rocks and containers. Was she going to use one? She hadn't said so.

Or had she decided that only nine students were worthy?

Yash decided that conundrum had nothing to do with her. She would simply take each moment as it came.

"That was a bit more work than expected," Professor Bellier said drily. "You'll need to make decisions quickly if you ever want to work on a DV-Class ship. Zarlengo is the only one who seems to have confidence in her abilities. Or perhaps she is the only one of you who is not scared of me."

Oh, Yash was scared of Bellier. Not of Bellier as a person so much as scared of what Bellier could do to her and her dreams. Perhaps that was what tripped up the other students as well.

"All right," Bellier said. "Before you, you see an inactive *anacapa* drive. These drives are old and have been decommissioned. When you are working in a normal *anacapa* lab, you will be working with newly developed drives. They're much more dangerous than the older drives. We have tested these drives and believe they can do no harm."

"Believe," muttered Flavia Latour, the woman beside Yash. Latour was tall and thin, red-haired, with skin so pale it seemed translucent.

"Yes, Latour," Bellier said. "'Believe.' You will learn that with the *anacapa* drives, we cannot be certain of everything."

"That's why they're dangerous to work with," said Lionel Crenshaw. He stood three containers down from Yash. She was glad he hadn't chosen to stand beside her. She had found him to be a hard-edged know-it-all who loved to curry favor from the professor.

Which, apparently, he was trying to do now.

"Are you teaching this class, Crenshaw?" Bellier snapped.

He straightened, not that it did much good. He was one of the shortest students in the class, with just a bit of extra weight around his waist. Yash always wondered how someone so clearly inactive had managed to qualify for a program that had more physical requirements than most.

But he was part of the Crenshaw family, which had at least one Admiral in its ranks. He had probably gotten this far because no one wanted to say no to him.

"No, ma'am," Crenshaw said to Bellier. "I'm sorry, ma'am."

"If you were sorry, Crenshaw," Bellier said, "you would stop offering unsubstantiated opinions."

He nodded, almost desperately, but Bellier didn't seem to notice that. She scanned the rest of the class, making eye contact with each and every one of them as if she were making certain that they were all paying attention.

"The *anacapa* drive is dangerous because of the amount of energy it contains," she said, "not because we do not know everything about them. There is much we don't know about many things that we use almost daily, and yet we use them with great enthusiasm and do not think about what we don't know."

Yash resisted the urge to glance at Crenshaw. He had annoyed her from the day they had started the class together, and she loved hearing him get set-down. So much so that she wanted to see him react.

"The fear of the *anacapa* drive," Bellier said, "comes because of its power. The myth of the *anacapa* drive is that it is unknowable. The truth of the *anacapa* drive is that we are still learning—even after millennia of use—its capacity. We have only used small parts of this drive to fuel our trips into foldspace. There is much more that the drive can do, if we can figure out how to harness its power."

Yash had never heard Bellier sound passionate about anything before. Until this point, being in Bellier's class had been a marathon of dry lectures and even drier information, none of it presented in an entertaining manner, the way information in the other classes in the section had been.

Sometimes Yash had wondered if Bellier had done that on purpose, trying to weed out the members of the class by boring them to death.

But Yash never asked. She just endured.

"No two drives are the same," Bellier said. "They have similar capacities and similar structures, but they differ. Some of my colleagues believe *anacapa* drives are living things, rather than simple tools that enable the Fleet to travel as well as it does. I do not believe that. I believe that whenever you try to harness power this great, you will find variations in it, and that is what we have experienced so far. Variation."

Yash took in the information, and mentally set her questions aside. She knew better than to interrupt Bellier's flow, no matter how many questions the lecture raised.

"The drive before you is your drive," Bellier said. "You will learn all of its components. Then you will learn how to activate it. You will learn how to attach that drive to a small system, and if any of you make it past those lessons, you will learn how to install that drive into a replica of a DV-Class ship. Now, are there questions?"

No one moved. Yash had learned through the course of the class to only ask questions she felt might not be answered otherwise.

And Yash had one of those.

"Um, Professor?" Yash said, wishing she didn't sound as uncertain as she felt. "I had always heard that it was dangerous to have more than one *anacapa* drive in the same area. In fact, one of my other professors had said the reason small ships did not have *anacapa* drives was so that the drives wouldn't interact or interfere with the drive on board a DV-Class vessel."

"And who is the idiot who told you that?" Bellier asked.

Yash hadn't meant to call out one of her professors. She had simply discovered that the best way to approach Bellier was to have some kind of source to back up an assumption.

"Professor Temin," said Crenshaw, clearly trying to suck up to Bellier all over again.

Bellier sighed. "Some people truly do not belong in this department," she said. She didn't even look at Crenshaw. Instead, her gaze was still on Yash.

Yash did not move, even though she felt the urge to swallow hard. Nerves. None of her other professors intimidated her the way that Bellier did.

"Let me unpack your questions," Bellier said, surprisingly with no contempt at all. "First, it is dangerous to have many *anacapa* drives in the same area, but it is also inevitable. If it were dangerous to have too many *anacapa* drives in the same area, then the *anacapa* research stations inside the sector bases would not be bundled close together. Sometimes there are as many as fifty *anacapa* drives, in one form or another of activation, in less space than we have right now."

Yash nodded. She had known that, and yet hadn't put it together with the admonitions she had heard. Clearly, Professor Bellier was right; there was a lot of misinformation about *anacapa* drives floating around the Fleet.

"Which brings us to Professor Temin's stupidity," Professor Bellier said. "There are many reasons we do not have *anacapa* drives in small ships. The main reason, and the only one that needs to concern you at the moment, is because the ships need a smaller version of the drive, and we have not yet found one that meets all of our very rigorous standards."

She glanced at Crenshaw, and the look didn't seem friendly.

"Even if we did," Bellier said, "there are many other problems with sending small ships into foldspace. Problems outside of our purview here. However, I suggest you ask Professor Temin about the potential problems of small ships in foldspace and see what kind of idiotic answer he gives you."

Then Bellier returned her gaze to Yash. Yash felt her cheeks heat, even though she had willed them not to.

"To address the underlying question behind your artful and somewhat manipulative initial question," Bellier said. "Is it dangerous to be in this room with all of the *anacapa* drives? Of course. And it is more dangerous than you realize. There are not simply ten inactive drives in this small space. There are ten active drives in the containers."

She gave them all a slight smile.

"And you thought you were nervous before," she said. Then she laughed.

Yash did not like the sound of that laugh at all. Neither, it seemed, did her fellow students. They shifted slightly, almost as if the laugh had shoved them somehow.

"On top of each container," Bellier said, "you will find a pair of gloves. Put them on, then adjust them to your hand-size. You will need those to work with the drives."

Yash hadn't seen gloves on top of the containers, but she had been preoccupied with what she had thought were rocks, and which had turned out to be *anacapa* drives. Inactive ones, but still.

She had seen a few of the drives during her studies, but all had been active, all pulsed with life and color. They had seemed so much smoother than these drives, which were pitted and dark.

She walked to her container. The other students followed suit, and she felt a surge of annoyance. She was not their leader. She was learning just like they were. Didn't they have any self-confidence? Didn't they have initiative?

She scanned the top of the container, and still didn't see the gloves. Then she realized they were recessed inside a small depression on the top of the container.

Before she grabbed them, though, she paused: If Bellier wanted them to have gloves, why hadn't she told them to bring their normal pair? Either these gloves were special or it was common to keep an additional pair on or near one of the containers.

Yash would reserve judgment about whether the gloves were special until she touched them.

But she approached the gloves with caution, examining the depression before touching it.

Then something snapped, and Latour cried out in pain.

Startled, Yash looked over at Latour. Latour was standing beside her container, cradling her right hand in her left, tears in her eyes. Blood dripped down her right arm.

"Looks like you need medical attention, Latour." Bellier didn't quite sound the same as she usually did. Nor did she sound concerned. She almost sounded pleased, which annoyed Yash. "There is a door to your left. It will take you to the infirmary. We have medical technicians standing by."

Latour sniffed. "I'm fine. It's just a cut. I can work."

"You probably could," Bellier said. "But you won't. You did not examine the area around the gloves before grabbing your pair. You were reckless, and we can't have recklessness around an *anacapa* drive."

"I-I didn't mean it," Latour said. "You said to get the gloves, and I was getting the gloves. I was completing the instructions as you gave them."

Yash glanced at Bellier. Bellier's eyes had narrowed.

"So," Bellier said, "you're saying it's my fault that you got injured."

"No, I mean, the instructions could have been clearer," Latour said. She glanced at Yash, as if expecting Yash—of all people—to back her up. "You were grabbing for the gloves, right?"

Yash didn't answer her. No one answered her.

"You're dismissed, Latour," Bellier said.

"I can come back though, right?" Latour asked. She sounded desperate. Yash didn't blame her. If Yash had been in her situation, Yash would have felt desperate.

Right now, though, Yash was working very hard at keeping her own emotions in check.

She didn't want to feel desperate before she needed to.

"No, you may not come back," Bellier said. She stared at Latour.

Latour still clutched her injured hand, pivoting slightly, looking at the other students as if she thought they would defend her.

"You're getting blood on the floor, Latour," Bellier said. "You need to tend to that wound."

"I'll be *fine*," Latour said. Apparently she associated leaving with failure, not the ill-considered grab for the glove.

"I don't care," Bellier said. "You have failed my class. Get out."

Latour made a small sound, almost like a sob, and then fled to that rear door. It slid open. She paused in front of it as if hoping someone would call her back.

No one did. No one was looking at her at all, except Yash and Bellier.

Then a shadow appeared on the edge of the door as someone arrived there. There was a murmur of voices, something Yash couldn't hear clearly.

Latour either stepped through or was yanked through that door and then it swished closed.

A small trail of blood led from the door back to the now abandoned container. Yash's gaze followed it, then returned to Bellier, whose lips thinned.

"Have I told you all to stop working?" Her voice snapped like that container had snapped at Latour. "I have told you in the past that work on an *anacapa* drive requires complete focus. *None* of you has focused on the work before you. Not a single one."

Yash's heart started pounding. Could she lose her opportunity because she had watched Latour lose hers? Yash would never forgive herself if that were the case.

She crouched beside the case and looked at the depression where the gloves were, hoping that by immediately getting to work, Bellier would forget Yash's lack of focus.

But even that hope showed a lack of focus. Yash made herself take a deep breath and shut out everything around her—the cold, the strange energy in the room, the rustle of the other students—and examine the container before her.

The top appeared smooth until she looked closely. There were several depressions, each holding different items, each difficult to see without knowing they were there.

She had never seen a container like this one before, and she had examined the *anacapa* containers on the bridges of various DV-Class vessels. They seemed a lot simpler than the container before her.

Simpler, and smaller. The containers on the DV-Class ships were about half the size of this container. The *anacapa* drive before her, the dead one, would have easily fit in something smaller.

So one of the many questions before her was why was this container so much larger?

She didn't touch it, not yet. She looked at it, took a deep breath through her nose to see if the container had an odor (it didn't that she could find), and guessed that it was all made of nanobits. The shiny black surface certainly suggested it, but she'd have to touch to find out.

She wasn't ready to touch.

The gloves were in the depression in the exact center of the container's top. The other depressions—five of them in all—were scattered across the surface.

Some were larger than the glove depression, some were deeper, and one looked less like a depression and more like a button, waiting to be pushed.

She wasn't going to do that either.

The depressions were odd in and of themselves. They looked like drawers built into the container—drawers without lids.

Or did they have lids? Clear lids? Or maybe some of the lids had recessed into the container and other lids had not.

A snap resounded so loudly in the quiet of the room that Yash jumped. Someone whimpered. A male whimper.

"You know what to do, Hettinger," Bellier said. "At least, now you do, since Latour showed you the way. And for your future career, do pay attention to what others do wrong so that you don't have to replicate their unfortunate actions."

The whimpering continued, but Hettinger, at least, did not protest his expulsion. His shoes squeaked as he walked behind Yash, who didn't even spare him a look.

She did hear the second door open and swish closed. Then she mentally reminded herself to focus. Focus was gravely important.

Lids. The depressions had to have lids, maybe even a series of them.

The depression closest to her appeared to contain an array of very small tools, barely the size of her little finger, none of which she recognized. A depression a bit father away occasionally blinked red, but not warning red. More like something was reminding anyone who looked at it that something else had been activated.

The button was the most tempting, but it was far enough away from her that she wasn't even going to give it much thought, not until she was ready.

"If you are going to spend the next hour staring at the damn gloves," Bellier said, "then I will flunk all of you. Get the gloves. We need to start."

She was egging them on, forcing them to move faster than they normally would have, given the injuries that had happened to two of their number.

Injuries to the hand. Latour's injury had been to her right hand, the hand she reached with. It had looked like a cut, something that had sliced the skin quickly and efficiently, but with a snap.

Yash let out a small breath. She slid her hand into her right pocket and pulled out the multipurpose tool. She did not look up to see if Bellier approved or disapproved.

Then Yash flipped through the tiny controls on the side of the slender tool until she found the penlight. She flicked it on and pointed it at the edges of the depression around the gloves.

The gloves themselves glowed in the light, revealing dozens of reflectors built into the surface. Yash ignored that (although she did find it fascinating). Instead she looked for the edges of a fast-closing lid, and found it—a third lip between two edges.

But she didn't touch that either. Clearly the lid was on a spring of some kind and it caught anything in its path.

If she were going for the gloves without paying attention to any of the warnings she had already received, she would have reached into the middle of the depression without touching the edges, gripped the gloves in her hand, and pulled them free.

So, instead of doing that, she peered at the sides of that depression right at the center where her hand would have gone in.

And recognized two tiny motion detectors, so small she wouldn't have been able to see them if she hadn't been looking. They reflected the light from her multipurpose tool.

Now, she had to find a way to deactivate the motion sensors. Or to activate them and find a way to open the lid.

There had to be easily accessible controls nearby.

She ran the light around the outside edge of the depression and saw nothing. Then she leaned back, examined the side of the container, and saw a very thin line that indicated a small door. The door was also on a spring, the kind that sprang open with nothing more than a push.

She wasn't sure she dared touch it. But she also felt the ticking clock.

"Shit," one of the women said. "Shit, shit, shit, shit."

Yash wondered what went wrong this time. She wasn't going to look, even though Bellier had urged them all to learn from each other's mistakes.

"Thank you for the commentary, Darlington," Bellier said, her voice tinged with amusement. "Continue your work without the scatology, if you please."

"Continue?" Darlington sounded as surprised as Yash felt. Whatever Darlington had done, it hadn't risen to the level of error that Latour's work had.

"Continue," Bellier said, as if she were a queen granting an audience.

"Oh, wow. Good," Darlington said, and then said nothing else.

Yash almost hazarded a look, but stopped herself just in time. Darlington had done something, and Bellier had approved of the fact that Darlington had taken action, at least.

Yash took a deep breath. She needed to do the same. What would she do if she wasn't so damn terrified of losing her position with Bellier?

Yash turned the multipurpose tool around to its rounded edge, the one that usually belonged in her hand. She elongated the tool's body, swallowed hard, hoped her nervousness didn't show, and then pressed the rounded edge against the middle of that side door.

The door sprang open, revealing a control panel.

Nothing else happened. No snapping lids, no unexpected trap. Just the blinking of a standard panel that would allow her to handle the container's controls.

Still, she took an extra minute with the interior of the panel, making certain that she saw every part of those controls before she touched them.

Then she put the multipurpose tool back in her pocket. Her heart was pounding and her hands were sweating. She rubbed them on her shirt, then found the controls that handled the motion detectors. She shut those off.

She still wasn't going to reach inside the depression. Someone had set this container on the highest level of security so that any touch to one of the systems marked critical would get some kind of reaction.

Gloves in a little storage depression weren't a critical system—normally. But clearly this was some kind of evil test that Bellier had designed.

Yash was not going to assume that anything about this exercise was normal.

She shut off the security protocols—all of them—and then closed the lids of the small storage depressions, hoping that would reset to standard protocols. She did not do an entire reboot of the container because she had no idea what was inside.

Someone made a small sound of distress.

"A near miss, Crenshaw. Perhaps if you paid attention to your own container instead of peering at all the others, you would get this one small task done." Bellier's voice held a lot of contempt.

Yash swallowed, hard, trying to shut out all of the distraction.

"If no one has those gloves on in five minutes," Bellier said, "then we will forgo this exercise, and I will leave here with high hopes for next year's class."

She's trying to rattle you, Yash thought, deliberately forming the words in her mind to keep herself calm.

She's succeeding, her brain shoved back at her somewhat defiantly, making her smile.

Then Yash let the smile fade. But it had helped. It had calmed her a great deal.

She rose up slightly, and looked at the surface of the container. It looked smooth, as if there were no storage sections on that surface at all.

To her right, she could see Bellier staring at her. And if Yash peered ever so slightly over the container at the other containers that the remaining students on that side of the room were working on, she saw all of them still had the glove depression open.

No one, as far as she could tell, had found the controls.

She focused on her own work again.

It was time to take a risk.

23

YASH LET OUT A SMALL BREATH, her heart pounding. So far, two students had failed, and the class had just started the first exercise.

She had wanted hands-on. She hadn't expected to be leaning in front of a coffin-size container, a dead *anacapa* drive at her feet, with Bellier watching closely, hoping everyone would fail.

Yash ran her fingers along the top of the container. She felt tiny differences in the surface where the storage lids had closed, but those differences were not visible to the naked eye.

The top of the container was surprisingly warm, which made her heart rate increase. She wasn't sure what she would find inside if the exterior was that warm.

But she wasn't to that stage yet. She just needed the damn gloves.

She swallowed compulsively again, wished she had some water to get rid of the sour taste in her mouth, and then squatted down again, peering at the controls.

They claimed that everything inside the container was normal, including, she assumed, the gloves.

The controls also claimed that the advanced security measures had been shut down.

She was going to have to trust that, going to have to believe that no other traps awaited her.

She used the tip of her right index finger to activate the control that opened the storage lid over the gloves. The lid slid back.

She removed the multipurpose tool from her pants, turned on its penlight function, and peered at the motion sensors.

They were dark. So were some of the other chips nearby, chips she hadn't even seen when she had looked the first time.

She shivered. So if she had deactivated the motion sensors but left the other security measures on, she would have tripped some other kind of alarm.

Out of the corner of her eye, she saw Bellier shift slightly. Bellier was still watching her, maybe even watching more closely than she had a few moments ago.

Yash tried to ignore that. She had to wipe her sweating palms on her pants again. Even though the room was cold, she wasn't anymore. A thin layer of sweat covered her everywhere.

She wasn't sure she had been this nervous since she had gone through her initial testing for engineering school.

She started to reach for the gloves, stopped, wiped off her sweaty palm again, and cursed silently. If she failed, she failed.

If she failed now, then she deserved to fail.

Yash eased her hand over the top of the container until her palm was above the gloves themselves. Then she lowered her hand, expecting something to snap closed or some alarm to go off.

But nothing happened. Her hand sank into the depression and brushed the surface of the gloves. They were rough, as if they were made of scales rather than fabric.

Her fingers closed around the gloves, and she pulled them free.

"Well, brava, Zarlengo. You are the first. It only took you ten minutes to do such a simple task, but you managed it."

Yash expected the sarcasm, but that didn't make it sting less. She had just completed a not-so-simple task.

She did not put on the gloves because she was afraid they were booby-trapped as well. But she took a deep breath and felt a little bit of the tension leave.

Bellier's eyes were twinkling as they met Yash's. Then Bellier clapped her hands.

Something snapped and someone cursed. This time, Yash looked. One of the women clutched her right hand, tears streaming down her face.

"Oh, for God's sake," Bellier said. "You're doing delicate work, Palfrey. You shouldn't let a simple sound derail you. Remember that in whatever assignment they give you that is much more suited to your…talents."

Palfrey kept her hand clutched to her chest and made her way around the back of the containers. As she passed Yash, Palfrey sniffed audibly.

"By the way," Bellier said as Palfrey continued past, "tears are unprofessional. Everyone fails. One should learn to take failures in stride."

Palfrey stopped and turned, her face red, her lower lip trembling.

Yash tried to make herself as small as possible. She had a hunch she knew what was coming.

"There's no reason to be this level of mean," Palfrey said. "I've put up with your nastiness all semester. You're unreasonable, and I will report you."

Bellier smiled. "You won't be the first. Go ahead. But I will warn you, because—although you do not believe it—I am not mean. I am difficult and tough and I push you on purpose. My superiors know this, and know my practices. They also know that my work weeds out the unprepared. I should have weeded you out sooner, Palfrey. The emotional response here isn't just undignified, it's dangerous."

"It is not!" Palfrey said. "You're being unfair."

"And you may leave now," Bellier said.

Palfrey stared at her, and Bellier met that stare with one that seemed deadly. In front of Yash, two of the remaining students grabbed gloves. She smiled, impressed in spite of herself.

She wasn't sure if she could have remained focused with this fight going on.

Finally, Palfrey stomped to the door and let herself out of the room.

"Two more in the middle of all of that commotion," Bellier said. "Bravo, you two. Excellent work. Zarlengo gets a commendation for arriving at the solution first. You both will also get a commendation" for completing the work in the midst of someone's unnecessary emotional crisis."

Behind Yash, a woman made a small sound of satisfaction.

"And another," Bellier said. "Excellent. The rest of you, you only have one minute before I ask you to leave as well."

Yash opened her left hand and set the gloves on the palm. She examined the material they were made out of and realized she had never seen it before.

The top of the glove had small chips or something like chips. There was a technological layer over a secure layer and then, on the interior, some kind of fabric.

She still didn't put them on. She was supposed to, but she wasn't ready to, afraid they too might be laced with traps.

"Emotions," Bellier said, "have no place in a workspace as serious as one involving *anacapa* drives. Nor does desire or ambition or some sense of fairness. If you graduate from this program, and that's still up for debate, you will someday find yourself in a difficult situation, time of the essence, a crisis happening around you—Ah, well done."

She nodded toward the students. Yash did not look in either direction to see who they were.

"Well done. Six of you. That's the best score we've had in more than eight classes. We'll see if you can move on from here. But know I am well pleased."

Bellier didn't smile—it would probably take an order from the Fleet to make her smile—but she appeared a lot lighter than she had a few moments ago.

"You'll note that they finished with only ten seconds to spare," she said. "That is just fine. The key is to get the job done within the time limit provided. If you can complete the job quickly and accurately, then all the better, but if you cannot, it is better to finish."

Yash closed her left hand around the gloves. Receiving praise from Bellier felt even more uncomfortable than listening to the woman yell.

"Now," Bellier said, "your instructions were to put on the gloves, but none of you have done that. I understand the reluctance, after the trial you just went through. I also know that if I reassure you all is fine, you will still not feel comfortable."

Yash smiled. That was true. She no longer trusted Bellier to do anything in a straightforward manner.

"The gloves, as Zarlengo has noted because I saw her investigate them closely, are unlike any you've seen before."

Yash saw a couple of heads bob downward, obviously looking more closely at the gloves.

"These gloves are specially designed for work on inactive and dead *anacapa* drives," Bellier said. "They will absorb small amounts of energy, should something in the drive accidentally activate. Should something like that happen to you today, you must set the drive down and back away. In theory, the gloves will protect you long enough to stop touching that drive."

"In theory?" Darlington asked.

Yash admired her courage. After nearly screwing up the first part of this test, Darlington still felt confident enough to ask a question like that.

Or maybe she was too stupid to realize that she should just keep her mouth shut, like Yash was doing. Even though those two words had caught her as well.

Bellier made a grim little face, but her eyes were twinkling again. She was enjoying this day—maybe the first time since the semester began that Bellier seemed to enjoy anything.

"In theory," Bellier repeated. "So far, the gloves have worked. I have no idea what will happen should someone hang on to one of the *anacapa* drives too long or if more power runs through a drive than we expect. So I hedge, because I cannot predict what will happen with perfect accuracy."

The way she said that last part made another shiver run down Yash's back. Bellier had said that bit about prediction on purpose—not just to make them uneasy, but to teach them that nothing was certain in this lab.

Except maybe the subtle parts of Bellier's teaching methods.

If browbeating the students could be called subtle.

"Gloves on," Bellier said.

Yash took one glove and slid it over her left hand first. She was right-handed. If the glove had some nasty bite to it, she wanted to avoid having that bite on her dominant hand.

The glove's interior felt smooth and cool, almost as cool as the inside of the room. The fabric was soft and thin and incredibly responsive. She twitched a finger, and the glove felt as if it were a part of her hand.

The glove's exterior clicked as it moved. The parts on it—the scales, for lack of a better word—were hard enough to make that sound as they brushed against each other.

She had never worn a glove like this before, but, if she survived this course, she might wear gloves like this all the time.

There seemed to be no ill effects from the glove, so she slipped on the other one. It too was cool and supple. She moved her fingers in a modified wave. The more she moved, the more it felt like the glove had become part of her hand.

"The specs for these gloves exist in every DV-Class ship," Bellier said. "Should your *anacapa* drive on that ship become inactive or die, and you feel the need to interact with it using your hands, I urge you to make a copy of these gloves before you do so."

"I take it they're made of nanobits?" Crenshaw asked.

Yash couldn't quite suppress a surge of irritation. Couldn't he ask a question in a normal way, one that made him sound less like a know-it-all?

"Answer your own question, Crenshaw," Bellier said. "And think about it for a moment before you do."

This time, Yash looked. A red flush was climbing up his neck. It reached his chin, then his cheeks, and then his ears. He actually looked terrified.

She felt no compassion for him, though. His mouth kept getting him into these strange situations. He would have to learn to shut up or some-one would pull him out of the program, no matter how smart he was.

"Apparently, Crenshaw here has declined to guess," Bellier said. "Perhaps he really did need that question answered. Can you answer it, Zarlengo?"

Yash's mouth went instantly dry. "I can't answer with accuracy," she said. "But I can answer with a supposition that I'm reasonably satisfied with."

Bellier's eyebrows went up in amusement. "Let's hear your supposition."

Yash took an ever-so-quiet breath to steady herself.

"You said that the gloves' template exists in each DV-Class ship, and that we can make the gloves if we need them. DV-Class ships do not carry a wide variety of materials with them, especially if they're going long distances without backup. However, DV-Class vessels carry a large supply of nanobits for repair, for emergency, and for other uses around the ship. So, based on what you said, I'm guessing—and it truly is a guess, since I did not have time to test this—that the gloves are made up of nanobits."

"You seem to be on a roll today, Zarlengo," Bellier said. "Good time to put in your best performance of the class so far."

A few of the students were frowning at Bellier. Did they truly not understand that Bellier had just confirmed what Yash had said?

"Yes, indeed," Bellier said, that edge of contempt back in her voice as she looked at the other five students. "Zarlengo's supposition is correct. The gloves are made of nanobits, which is both good and bad. Before Crenshaw can ask another stupid question, let me say that I will get to the 'good and bad' part in a moment. I do want to comment on Zarlengo's ability to take disparate pieces of evidence and put them into a logical whole. It's a skill you all should cultivate. I'm assuming you used that to figure out what was going on with the container?"

Going on with the container. The question was vague, maybe deliberately so. But Yash had to answer.

"Um," she said, annoyed that the single word showed just how nervous she was, "if you're asking how I figured out there was a control panel, yeah, I saw what happened to the others, figured out that they probably hadn't touched anything, and that meant that they had activated something else. If you wanted us to have the gloves, then there had to be a way to deactivate whatever that something else was."

"Excellent," Bellier said. "That is the kind of reasoning you all practice. You will need the ability to leap across certain pieces of evidence to arrive at conclusions that will enable you to make snap decisions. You will not always have time to test your hypothesis, so you must learn to trust your instincts on some matters."

"I don't get it," Crenshaw said, and Yash wasn't alone in cringing. She saw Vincent Mercer, standing beside the very last container, shake his head slightly as if to say, *Don't do it, Lionel.*

Bellier turned toward Crenshaw, her face almost expressionless.

Crenshaw clearly didn't take that expressionless face as a warning. "First, you make us go through this elaborate scenario without telling us that there were security protocols and you put some pressure on us, and you punish the people who act quickly, and then you tell us that acting quickly is what we need to do. I don't get it. What are you trying to teach us? How to be uncomfortable?"

"Are you angry, Crenshaw?" Bellier asked.

"I'm not happy," he said.

She nodded once. "Did you fail to hear my comment on emotion?"

"I was finishing the task you assigned," Crenshaw snapped. "You told us to ignore everything around us until we were done."

So he was one of the last two. That had to grate on Mr. Know-It-All.

"And yet, you know when I made that statement," Bellier said, "so you were paying attention. You simply were not absorbing the lesson."

"I was trying to get to the damn gloves inside your time limit," Crenshaw said.

"Which you succeeded at doing. Let me ask you again, Crenshaw. Are you angry right now?"

"I'm going to give you the same answer," he said. "I'm not happy."

"Why do you expect to be happy?" Bellier asked. "This class does not exist to make you happy. It exists to teach the best engineers from this year's class how to work with *anacapa* drives. Do you recall what I said about emotions?"

"I recall that you pontificated on emotions," Crenshaw said. "I don't know the exact language."

Yash winced at the word "pontificated." Her gaze met Abby Darlington's. Darlington's dark skin looked pale in this light, or maybe she had simply gone pale with panic.

Darlington actually liked Crenshaw. They often left class together, talking and comparing notes. She clearly knew that Crenshaw was blowing up his entire future, right now, with this single conversation.

"I said that emotions have no place here," Bellier said.

"And yet you let Zarlengo make some kind of leap of faith and then tell us how impressive that is," Crenshaw said.

"Taking pieces of information and compiling them into a working hypothesis is not a leap of faith, Crenshaw. It is essential to this job." Bellier's tone hadn't changed at all. She didn't even seem surprised that she was having this argument.

Yash was. Yash couldn't believe anyone would challenge Bellier like this.

"It upsets you that you are not the star pupil in this afternoon's class, doesn't it, Crenshaw?" Bellier asked.

"I'm not that petty," he said a bit too quickly.

Bellier's eyes narrowed. "But you are angry—oh, excuse me. You are not happy. You want me to give you rules, don't you, Crenshaw?"

"It would certainly help," he said. "Because this poking around in the dark is just plain stupid."

"And yet it is the essence of the job, should you end up on a DV-Class ship. Nothing will follow rules."

"That can't be true," Crenshaw said. "We've been spending years studying systems and how they're compiled, how they work. Systems exist for a reason, and that reason translates into rules. Saying that nothing will follow rules is something you're doing to mess with us."

"I am?" Bellier almost smiled, but seemed to catch herself before she did.

"Yeah," Crenshaw said. "This whole thing. It's just mind games. You're messing with us on purpose for some sadistic reason of your own."

Yash wondered if he wanted out of the program or if he was always like this. She had never been in a class with him before this one. She had found him deeply annoying all semester, and now she found him both annoying and worrisome. She hated that she was worried about him losing his place in class, but she also knew that she would rather have someone leave class because they had made a technical mistake rather than some kind of emotional blowup.

"Tell me, Crenshaw," Bellier said, "did you have Professor Alsworth's class on Unusual Technologies?"

Yash had loved that class. It had been very similar to this afternoon; find something unusual, examine it, see if it was useful, dangerous, or harmless, see if it could be co-opted into something for the Fleet. She had applied to be in Alsworth's upper level programs, should Yash survive this particular course.

"No," Crenshaw said. "I tested out of it. I spent three years interning in one of the labs on Sector Base T."

Yash let out a small breath. The fact that he had not taken that class explained a lot. Professor Alsworth had had a large waiting list, three times the size of the class. Why she did had become clear in the first week, when she had flunked six students, one each on six separate days, and six others took their place. By the end of the first month, nearly twenty students had washed out of the engineering program thanks to Professor Alsworth.

Once they were gone, the class moved forward with energy and curiosity and a sense of fun. But that first month had been brutal.

Bellier nodded. "I shall discuss this with my superiors," she said, "because Unusual Technologies is a class one should not test out of."

"Well, I did test out of it," Crenshaw said. "Your bosses determined that I didn't need something like that. I had enough experience."

"And yet you do not," Bellier said. "Because you are challenging me right now."

"You don't like someone pushing back?" Crenshaw asked.

"I don't have any emotional entanglement here at all," Bellier said. "I simply do not like wasting a slot in my class on someone who is terribly unprepared for it."

Someone near Yash gasped. It wasn't Crenshaw, though. His entire face was red. He was finally beginning to understand that he was in some kind of trouble.

"You are a bright man, Crenshaw. You have tested well in my class. You have done the work. You're often ahead of the curve on anything to do with logical systems and following instructions point by point."

His shoulders relaxed ever so slightly, but Yash thought that they shouldn't. Because there was a "but" lurking in Bellier's sentence.

Crenshaw didn't seem to be able to feel it coming. Yash suddenly wondered if he was unable to understand some of the nuances of human interaction, particularly when it was as controlled as Bellier's had been all semester.

"Unfortunately, you have an arrogance that gets in the way of learning, and even more unfortunately, the system has encouraged that arrogance by letting you test out of essential classes." Bellier walked until she stood in front of the container that Crenshaw had chosen.

He remained motionless, but his flush got even deeper.

"You have performed well today on the technical aspects," Bellier said, "but you have made unwise choices since you entered this room. Actually, those choices began when you sat down in my class and felt that you could comment on every small part of—"

"You don't like being questioned, do you?" he blurted. "You think you're better than all of us. You like going after us, like picking on us. You could teach this class in a kinder way, you know."

Bellier did not move. She barely seemed to breathe. Yash was having trouble breathing as well.

Yash had seen other students break down in other classes, but she had never seen anyone lose it in front of Bellier. Bellier usually dismissed them long before the emotions got heated. Or rather, the student's emotions got heated. Bellier seemed to have a preternatural calm that emanated from her no matter what she did.

"If you were to graduate from this program," Bellier said to Crenshaw, "you would then have to enter a military program that would train you in the Fleet's military protocols. All engineers end up with officer-level credentials."

Bellier paused as if she expected Crenshaw to say something snide. When he didn't, Yash glanced at him. He was sweating visibly now. If he didn't know where this conversation was going, he was dumber than he looked.

"Superior officers do not like being challenged without cause," Bellier said. "I—"

"I have cause." Crenshaw said. And there it was, Crenshaw having trouble being disciplined. Or Crenshaw having trouble with impulse control.

Or both.

Yash wished she could step out of the room. Or that Crenshaw would leave the room. Because this wasn't going to end well.

"You know I have cause," Crenshaw was saying to Bellier. "You're just being unfair."

Bellier waited again until he was done speaking. When it was clear to the entire class that he was not going to say anything else, she said, "Superior officers also do not like to be interrupted. You should know that as well, Crenshaw. You grew up in the Fleet. You've watched the military protocols—"

"They didn't apply to me," he said.

Bellier paused, as if she was editing her words before speaking them. Then she spoke very calmly. "As I said, Crenshaw, you have an ability in this area. It will be sad to lose you from this program."

"Will be...?" he said, sounding stunned. Apparently it was taking him a moment to process her words. "You're getting rid of me? You just said I'm doing well."

"At the technical aspects," she said.

"Those are the *important* aspects," he said.

"And because you believe that," she said, "I am letting you go, with great reluctance."

Yash wasn't feeling reluctant. The sooner he left, the happier she would feel.

"I'm going to protest your treatment," he said.

"That is your choice." Bellier waited, as if she expected something more from him. Maybe she wanted him to back down? Apologize?

Yash could sense Bellier wanted something, but Crenshaw didn't seem to notice.

"Just get rid of me then," he said.

"All right, Crenshaw," Bellier said. "Please leave by the door through which you entered."

He glanced at the other door, as if he had expected to go that way. Then he threw the gloves onto the floor next to the dead *anacapa* drive he had been assigned to, and stomped back toward the original door.

He yanked it open, paused as if he was going to say something, then shook his head as if he had changed his mind. He left, slamming the door behind him.

Bellier hadn't moved. She had watched him leave.

"If he hadn't continually interrupted me," she said to the class, "I would have sent him back for retraining. He would have had another chance two years from now. But his temperament has shown me he is not the kind of man who can do this job."

She walked back to the center of the room, her slight form reflected in the windows. It looked like she was etched against the rock of the crater.

"You should be learning that this job is about how well you handle a crisis emotionally. You might be technically proficient, but if you cannot handle the pressure of a classroom setting where there are no real stakes, then you will not be able to perform on a bridge, in the middle of a life-or-death emergency, while everyone around you is dealing with their own version of the crisis."

Yash had never seen a crisis like that, but she knew they existed. She'd heard stories. She'd studied some of the best and most creative solutions that had come out of those crises.

She wanted to believe that she could handle all those situations. At least she knew better than Crenshaw. Yash would never have picked this kind of fight, not with Bellier, not with any of her instructors.

"Well," Bellier said, "since none of you feel the need to interject yourself personally into the drama that we have had this afternoon, we can turn to the reason for our class—the *anacapa* drive. Are you ready to learn how it works?"

Yash almost said yes. She had a hunch the other four also would have said yes if it hadn't been for that showdown with Crenshaw.

"Good," Bellier said, apparently taking their silence for assent. "Then let us begin."

24

YASH SAT CROSS-LEGGED on the floor of the lab, her hands the only warm thing about her. The floor had a chill that made the chill in the air seem balmy.

She could barely see Bellier, who now paced back and forth across the front of the lab, moving from student to student. Only five remained, and they were scattered between the ten containers.

Bellier had not asked anyone to get closer to anyone else. She had kept them in the spots they had initially chosen.

Back at the start of this session, Yash had thought that she had been wise to take the largest dead drive, but now she wasn't so certain. The instructions Bellier had given them sounded simple (why did Bellier's instructions always sound simple?)—take a hard, close look at the dead *anacapa* drive without touching it.

But the students did have to keep their gloves on. Yash wasn't sure about the whys and wherefores of that either, and after the problems with Crenshaw, she was even more reluctant to ask questions than she had been when the session started.

The dead *anacapa* drive really did look like a rock, at least from far away. Up close, she could see some gray nanobits flaking off its edges. However, not every part of the *anacapa* drive had nanobits on it.

It actually looked like the drive had been covered with a nanobit coating and the coating was coming off in chunks.

Underneath those chunks, she saw more brown than gray. The drives in all the learning materials were round or oblong or imperfectly rectangular. The drive before her looked like a pillow that was trying to regain its form after someone had punched it repeatedly and in different places.

Only that pillow had sharp edges, small craters, and the same kind of tiny, tiny scales that the gloves had. Those scales were not on the parts of the drive that had the nanobit coating—or rather, the scales were not visible on the parts of the drive that had the nanobit coating.

Bits of gold threaded through the entire drive, disappearing under the nanobit coating wherever there was some, and reappearing in the brown materials. Black lines also threaded through the drive, only those black lines looked more like something burned into the drive than something intentional.

Yash crawled around to the other side of the drive, following the instructions not to touch it, and saw more of the same. Only on the side closest to the window, she did see a hole that led all the way into the drive.

She removed her penlight and used it to illuminate that hole. Bellier hadn't forbidden the use of tools, after all, provided that they did not touch the exterior of the drive.

Not that Bellier had said anything at all about the use of tools, but that was how Yash took the instructions.

Inside that hole, she saw something dull silver that didn't look like a rock or like it had been made of nanobits. In fact, it didn't look like anything she recognized.

She frowned, examined the sides of the drive—using the multipurpose tool's light and then without it—but seeing nothing unusual. Or rather, nothing she hadn't seen on the front and back.

She returned to her original spot, her body aching from the chill of the floor. Her stomach growled as well. This class had gone on longer than the three hours that Bellier had initially predicted it would take before lunch, probably because of Crenshaw and the others.

"All right," Bellier said. "Stop staring at the drive. I will answer five questions, one from each of you. Then we will break for lunch, and you will make notes in your class file about what you have seen."

Bellier had let them know that the notes would be important to their grade. The system they used uploaded their notes to Bellier's teaching accounts. So far, half a semester in, Bellier had not responded to a single note, nor had she acknowledged receiving them.

However, Yash always felt Bellier's presence as she made the notes, hoping that Bellier would not think everything Yash had to say was stupid.

"Zarlengo."

Yash jumped as Bellier said her name.

"You're on a roll today. Ask me a question about the drive."

Great. Yash was going first. She had a million questions. She had hoped someone else would weed through them so that she could focus on the best question to ask.

She mentally skipped the obvious questions about the nanobit covering and the black threads. She wasn't sure that everyone got a glimpse of that silver thing inside the center of the drive.

"I have never seen images of drives that are being retired," Yash said, "only the structure of a new and/or functioning drive."

Bellier tilted her head just a little, signaling impatience.

"I saw a lot of materials I expected, but one thing I did not. In the center of the drive, there's something silver, and it looks like it was made of a material that I haven't seen before. I'm assuming it's something important. What is it, exactly?"

Bellier's eyebrows went up. Then she walked to Yash's drive.

"Where is it?" Bellier asked.

Yash scooted over and pointed to the hole that went all the way in. Then Yash used her multipurpose light to illuminate the silver thing.

Bellier crouched and peered inside.

"Hmph," Bellier said, and then she nodded. She seemed a bit surprised to see that, but Yash might've been reading more into that reaction than there actually was.

Bellier put her hands on her thighs, and stood up.

"Good question, Zarlengo," Bellier said. "I decline to answer it at this time."

Yash frowned, not expecting that at all.

Bellier had already turned away from her. "Darlington, your question?"

"Um, there appears to be a nanobit coating on mine, and it's either come off in parts or it never covered the entire drive. Yash mentioned the specs, and I was thinking about them too. I don't recall a mention of a nanobit coating. Is that coating unusual or isn't it listed in the materials?"

Yash couldn't see Darlington, who was probably sitting on the floor just like Yash had been. But she could see Bellier.

Bellier's face was a lot more expressive than it had been a few hours ago. Apparently, she enjoyed this give-and-take.

"The coating is a repair technique that has fallen into disfavor," Bellier said, "for precisely the reason you cited. It doesn't stick to the drive well enough to make the drives safe to use. Over time, nanobits unbond. Sometimes nanobit coatings unbond, just like you'd expect, but more often than not, they slough off. Next question. Mercer?"

Mercer cleared his throat. Yash couldn't see him either. She couldn't see any of the others, and that felt a bit odd. She usually looked at her fellow students when they had the floor.

"The drives in the specs," he said slowly, "and the drives I've seen when someone opened a container, always look symmetrical. Mine does not. It's pitted and filled with holes. It looks like parts have broken off. Is this what dead or dying *anacapa* drives look like or is this the result of some kind of trauma that this class is as yet unfamiliar with?"

"Neither, Mercer," said Bellier. "There is no standard look for a retired *anacapa* drive. Next question. Triplett?"

Yash wished Bellier hadn't called on Dilys Triplett so quickly because Bellier had done something in her answer that surprised Yash. Bellier had changed words.

Mercer had asked about dead or dying *anacapa* drives. Bellier had responded discussing retired *anacapa* drives. Yash wasn't sure those were the same thing.

But she didn't ask about it. Bellier had said five questions, and each student would get to ask one. Yash wasn't going against those orders.

Fortunately, Triplett had taken a moment as well to ask her question.

"My drive is really tiny compared to the others," Triplett finally said. "Was it this tiny when it was in use, and if so, did that have an impact on how it worked or where it was used?"

"Yes, it was that small," Bellier said, "and no, the size had no impact on how it was used. Final question. Gallatin?"

"Ah." Rex Gallatin sounded nervous, but then he always sounded nervous. "I called up the specs and images of working drives. You didn't say we couldn't."

"That is correct," Bellier said. "I didn't restrict that."

Yash silently cursed at herself. She hadn't even thought of that. She had been too focused on the drive in front of her.

"In my quick review of those images," he said, "I noted that there were no thin black lines threading through any of those drives. Yet mine has a lot of black threading through it. Is that sign of use or are there variations or is it something else I should note?"

"Good question, Gallatin," Bellier said. "I will, as with Zarlengo's question, decline to answer at the moment. I do want to commend you, however, on the initiative. When dealing with an unfamiliar system, always look at the specs if you have access to them."

Yash felt her own cheeks heat. She knew that. She had forgotten it as, apparently, had everyone except Gallatin.

"You have fifteen minutes for lunch and for taking notes. Replace your gloves into their storage spot before you go. I expect you back here after you've eaten, but do not touch anything. You are free to go."

Yash peeled off her gloves. They made a grating noise as they rubbed against each other, and that made the hair on the back of her neck rise. She would have to get used to that sound or she would have to suffer through it every time she used the gloves.

She was willing to, though. She wanted this more than she realized. Every time someone got dismissed, her desire to work in this field grew exponentially.

She double-checked the controls on the side of the container before she returned the gloves to their little storage area. Then she hit the controls, making sure the gloves were hidden from view.

Her stomach growled again as she headed toward the door. She would have to take time to eat, even though she didn't want to. It was going to be a push to finish her notes in the time allotted, which, she was sure, was the point.

She was the first one through the door. She hurried through the main entry, then climbed up the ramp to the runabout. She would get her lunch, shove as much of it into her mouth as she could, and then return to the entry below, where she might get some privacy from the other students.

The runabout door slid open, and she stepped inside—and immediately wished she had skipped lunch altogether.

The six students whom Bellier wouldn't even take into the lab were seated in the large cabin adjacent to the cockpit. And adjacent to the tiny galley kitchen where everyone had left their food.

She gave them all a nervous smile, then pushed past them into the galley kitchen, and immediately wished she hadn't. Crenshaw stood near the packets of food. He was eating a carrot out of a pink bowl, which probably meant that the carrot wasn't from his lunch.

She couldn't imagine any other reason the runabout had pink dishware. The bowl certainly didn't look spaceworthy. It looked like some kind of container that had some kind of lid.

"She finally boot you out?" he asked.

Yash wasn't going to answer that. She wasn't going to get into any kind of conversation with Crenshaw.

"Excuse me," she said.

He leaned against the cabinet where the lunches were stored. "I asked you a question."

"I know," Yash said. "I'd like to grab my lunch."

"You can have it when you answer me," he said.

She didn't have time for a conversation, but she recognized his mood. If she told him that, he would continue to engage. He probably had a sense that she was on the clock and he would continue to engage anyway.

So she walked over to him, grabbed his arm, and pulled him away from the cabinet.

"Hey," he said. "You can't do that."

Just did, asshole, she thought, but didn't say. She didn't want to engage him any more than she already had.

She opened the cabinet, grabbed the bright green packet with her lunch inside, and decided to change her plan. She certainly couldn't eat on the runabout.

She turned, hoping she could eat in that outer area in the lab, only to see Mercer and Triplett enter.

"Oh," Crenshaw said. "Must be lunch time. Unless you all got dismissed."

Mercer and Triplett glanced at Yash, who shook her head just a little. She held the cabinet door open for them. They pushed past Crenshaw.

Yash did too, trying to leave. Gallatin had stopped to talk to one of the six who'd been stuck on the runabout all day. Darlington stood outside the kitchen, looking a little uneasy.

"I think he's eating your lunch," Yash said. "You want to share mine?"

To Yash's surprise, Darlington teared up. Then she nodded.

"I'm leaving the runabout," Yash said.

"Okay," Darlington said softly. She gave the kitchen one last look over her shoulder, then followed Yash out of the runabout and back into the lab building.

She didn't see Bellier. In fact, she didn't see anyone else.

Several chairs lined the wall closest to the door. Yash indicated those, and Darlington came with her.

"I—we were—I'm—he's going to hate me," Darlington said.

Yash nodded. Darlington wanted to talk about Crenshaw and Yash didn't. Normally, she would be polite.

"We don't have time to have this discussion right now," Yash said, handing her half of a sandwich made with turkey, some kind of yellow cheese, and a piece of lettuce that was almost bigger than the bread.

Yash ate the half sandwich faster than she had ever eaten anything in her life, saw that she only had seven minutes left to make her notes, and shoved the remaining lunch at Darlington.

"If you need to talk later…" Yash said, deliberately leaving that sentence unfinished.

She grabbed the pack that Bellier had made them bring wherever they went, but which Bellier had not allowed inside the lab with the *anacapa* drives, and hurried to the other side of the lab. Inside the pack, Yash found her tablet, deciding to make her notes there. She hoped that the tablet would back everything up.

Yash set a timer on the edge of the tablet, and then described what she had seen as quickly as she could. She noted that all the drives were a different size, that they seemed to have different characteristics. She didn't spare herself in her analysis, mentioning that Gallatin had been the most brilliant one in the *anacapa* investigation because he had been sensible enough to compare everything to the specs in real time.

At that moment, her timer went off. She had one last observation, which she added hastily. *I always thought that* anacapa *drives had controls on the drive itself. I didn't see any on the drive I was dealing with. I can't imagine that the controls would have been on the bottom of the drive, but I've seen a lot that I hadn't been able to imagine before today.*

Then she closed the notes, set the tablet to back everything up and send an extra copy to Bellier, put the tablet into her pack, and put the pack back where she had found it.

She didn't see Darlington anywhere, but the remains of lunch sat on the chair Darlington had been using. Yash grabbed the lunch remains and shoved them into her pack before she hurried back to class.

Bellier stood alone in front of the bank of windows, her back to all the containers. Her face was visible, though, because it was reflected in the odd lighting. Her gaze met Yash's.

Yash gave her a nervous smile and returned to her place near what she was now thinking of as her *anacapa* drive.

She was the first back into the room, but only by a few seconds. Mercer came in next, followed by Gallatin and Triplett. Yash hoped that Darlington hadn't given up and gone back to talk with Crenshaw.

But Yash had barely had that thought when Darlington hurried through the door.

Bellier hadn't turned around, but she clearly watched everyone come in, reflected in the glass.

"Close the door," she said.

Since Darlington was the last in, she was the one who had that unenviable task. The controls weren't obvious. Of course, nothing in this lab was obvious, and that was probably by design.

It took her a full minute to find the controls, and by then her hands were shaking. Darlington was clearly trying to hide the emotions that had swept over her at lunch.

Bellier turned around.

"Take your places," she said.

Everyone did. This time, Yash made note of where they were. Ironically, no one ended up right next to anyone else. The gaps left by the students who had failed were obvious.

It wasn't until that moment that Yash realized that the three students who had been injured weren't on the runabout—or, at least, weren't near the other students on the runabout.

Oh, the ride back was going to be ugly.

"On the top of your containers," Bellier said, "you will find several sets of tools. You've probably already noticed them. Put your gloves on and find the small red-laser blade. It looks like this."

She held up a six-inch-long black tube.

"The cutting edge itself is clearly marked. And before you ask, there are no more tricks with the tools or the gloves. Now I would like you to focus on other aspects of learning, so get your equipment as quickly as possible."

Yash wished she hadn't eaten the sandwich. She hadn't tasted it as she crammed it into her mouth, but she was tasting it now. Nerves made it feel like she hadn't even swallowed the sandwich, although she had.

She used the controls on the panel, opening the lids on all of the storage units on top of the container. She took the gloves first, moving faster than she wanted to and praying that Bellier hadn't lied to the class.

She hadn't—at least with the gloves. Then Yash scouted for the right tool, seeing several different laser blades. It took a minute, but she finally found it.

She didn't grab it right away, though. First she put on the gloves. This time they almost seemed to slide on without her help. Then she reached for the tool.

The scales on her right glove caught on the lip of the storage area. She wanted to pull away, but she didn't. She didn't want to rip those gloves— not that she was sure whether or not they could be ripped.

She peered over the side and carefully unhooked the trapped glove without removing it.

Then she grabbed the tool.

It glowed a slight orange at her touch. She didn't like that. She hadn't activated the tool. She didn't want it to have a mind of its own.

She set it back into the compartment and was about to look for a way to shut it off when Bellier spoke.

"For those of you who are trying to shut off the orange light flowing through the tool, please stop worrying." Bellier's tone this afternoon was kinder than it had been in the morning. Much kinder, in fact. There was no contempt at all. "Your gloves activated the power switch automatically."

Yash didn't like that feature at all, but she didn't say so. She just removed the tool and held it at her side, careful that the laser blade's edge didn't point at anything.

Bellier looked a little amused. She made a point of making eye contact with all five students.

"You are now going to cut off the nanobit coating. You may take bits of the surface beneath it along with the coating." Then Bellier glanced at Yash. "Zarlengo, avoid the hole that you showed me earlier."

Yash's stomach clenched. "Yes, professor," she said.

Yash sat down beside the drive and methodically trimmed the nanobit layer off the surface, setting the nanobits aside. It took less than two minutes.

Apparently everyone else finished in an equally short period of time because Bellier said, "Well done," and she clearly meant that for the class. "Questions?"

No one spoke for a moment. Yash's heart rate pounded. She didn't want to ask, didn't want to seem stupid, but she did have questions.

So, she figured, no risk no reward.

"I'm assuming that we didn't simply unbond the nanobits for some reason to do with the *anacapa* drive," she said. She didn't add that unbonding the bits was the normal way to clear off a layer of nanobits.

"That is correct," Bellier said. "All of these drives are different. Your drive would have held up to the unbonding. Mercer's would not have. Best to learn that there is more than one method of handling a task at hand."

Yash nodded. The lesson, then, wasn't that there was one prescribed way to handle all of this, but that there were several, and each was unique to the circumstance.

"It would seem to me," Gallatin said, "that a laser would be more dangerous than unbonding."

"A laser is surgical," Bellier said. "The unbonding is not. You can make a mistake with the laser, for the most part. One small error with the unbonding, and we would lose this lab."

As well as their own lives. But she didn't have to add that, because everyone in the room knew it.

"You've all examined the exterior of your drive," Bellier said. "Set down your laser blade, and pick up the *anacapa* drive. Examine its underside, and then set it down exactly as you found it."

Yash replaced the blade in its holder on the top of the container, careful to avoid the lip with her gloves. Then she placed her hands on the sides of the *anacapa* drive and lifted it.

She grunted at the weight. The drive was heavier than she expected. She held it up, which was easier than she would have thought, only because the gloves adhered to the sides.

Underneath, the drive was completely flat and clear, with a door carved into the material. Above that door was a small ring that could be pulled.

If Yash had to guess, she would guess that was where the *anacapa* drive's controls were. She found it very odd that they were underneath some kind of clear covering. It would take work to get to the controls, which seemed impractical to her.

"All right," Bellier said, "if you haven't done so already, please set the drive back the way you found it."

Yash did so. It took a little extra work to get her gloves off the sides of the drive. She didn't like the gloves. They seemed unnecessarily complex.

"This next instruction," Bellier said, "is for everyone except Zarlengo."

Yash felt a little uneasy being singled out. She waited, motionless, while Bellier gave that instruction.

"Take the deepest hole on your drive," she said, "and deepen it until you see some silver. The moment you see the silver color, stop."

And that was why Yash hadn't been included. She let out a breath she hadn't even realized she had been holding.

She heard rustling as the others did their task. Then little by little, the rustling eased.

Bellier walked the room, stepping into each area to examine what the others had done. She seemed unusually cautious about this procedure.

When she finished examining, she returned to her spot in front of the windows.

"Well done," she said. "Your first delicate task on an *anacapa* drive. You've all managed to carve into the mass before you, and you managed to find the drive itself."

Yash frowned, surprised. She thought the entire thing before her was the drive. She knew from the questions that the others had too.

"Two of you asked in a sideways fashion, and one of you in a straight-forward manner, why these drives do not look like the drives you've seen in the specs or in existing containers. The short answer is that these drives *do* look like the specs, only you can't see the drives themselves."

Yash's frown grew deeper, and then she understood. The clue was the nanobit coating.

Apparently, Bellier saw Yash's change of expression. "Would you like to answer your own question now, Zarlengo?"

"The silver thing," Yash said. "That's the actual *anacapa* drive."

Bellier actually smiled. Yash hadn't been sure that was possible, but it had just happened. "Exactly, Zarlengo. You asked if that silver thing was important. It is extremely important."

"What the heck is all that stuff then?" Darlington asked, or rather, blurted. Because Yash doubted anyone would simply ask a question in a normal give-and-take fashion, given their day so far. "Coating?"

"Yes, Darlington," Bellier said. "You've just encountered layers and layers of protective coating. The containers we use now came into common use only one hundred years ago. Until that point, the look of the *anacapa* drive depended on the engineer. Some used a protective coating. Some used several protective coatings. All then put the drive into a container of some kind, but often that container was open on the side. You'll find all of these variations throughout your career. Many of the older drives are not yet retired, and rather than tamper with the layers of coating, we have learned that it's safer to leave the layers alone, and work with the drive as it is."

Yash tilted her head at her drive, looking at it in a whole new light. She had seen the different surfaces, but she had figured they had something to do with the age of the *anacapa* drive, not some kind of covering on the drive itself.

Bellier paced slowly in front of the students, in lecture mode now.

"I deliberately chose the messiest drives for this class. These drives are retired. They have no power through them, although they can be revived. That will be tomorrow's task, if you make it through the rest of the day."

Yash tensed. For a moment, she had forgotten the elimination aspect of today's work. Because that was what this had boiled down to. Some kind of elimination work.

"The gold threads you've seen are power conductors into the drives. We don't use that kind of conductor any longer," Bellier said, "but you will find drives with those conductors. And to answer your question, Gallatin, the black threads you see are burned-out or blown-out conductors. These drives have been through a lot. That does make them a tad unstable, but not so unstable that we can't work with them."

Oh, great, Yash thought but somehow managed to keep to herself. She was nervous again. She had gone from being frightened to nervous to worried to enjoying the tasks to worried to nervous again.

And Bellier had told them to keep their emotions out of the lab. As if that were possible.

"All right," Bellier said. "I would like you all to replace your laser tool, and remove your gloves. Seal the storage units on the top of the container."

Yash did all of those things in the exact order that Bellier told her to. The job was easier than Yash expected. She was getting this part at least.

"Now," Bellier said, "open your container."

Yash's stomach clenched. The sandwich had traveled down there, obviously, because she was no longer burping it, but it sure felt heavy down there.

The nerves. The nerves were getting to her.

She examined the container's lid, saw nothing that would make her uneasy, and then checked the controls. They were still set at normal, whatever that was, but she remembered hearing that all *anacapa* containers had redundant security so that someone couldn't accidentally open one on the bridge, hit the wrong *anacapa* control, and destabilize the entire thing.

Not that Yash knew whether or not an *anacapa* drive could be destabilized. The secrets of the drive—hell, the basic workings of the drive—were kept from the entire Fleet. No one except the engineers and maybe the upper level brass knew how to mess with, disable, or weaponize an *anacapa* drive.

Which, Yash was beginning to realize, was just as well.

She studied the container's controls for a moment, looking to see if she needed to change anything.

As she did, she heard one of the men curse. Something clicked, clicked again, and then hummed.

"Well, Mercer," Bellier said, "the container thinks you're breaking into it. You'll have to wait three minutes and try again."

"Three minutes isn't a lot of protection," he said.

"That's because these containers are generally on the bridge, and someone might have a legitimate reason for trying to open it. Not everyone knows how to open the container, as you can tell." Bellier sounded amused rather than angry. Which was good.

And that interaction told Yash a lot about the standard settings. Because Mercer was good at what he did. So he had probably checked the controls and then tried to open the container. He hadn't realized that standard was still secure.

She peered deeper in the controls and finally found what she was looking for. It wasn't labeled anything obvious like *open* or *release* but *examine*. At least, she hoped *examine* was the setting she needed. She couldn't see anything else that worked.

Her heart pounded. Such internal drama for activating a control. She had to work on her own emotional control or she really wouldn't be up for this job.

She activated the control and heard something snick inside the container. Then the edges were limned with a faint light.

Her cheeks warmed. She hoped that light wasn't coming from the *anacapa* drive. She hoped she hadn't activated anything accidentally.

She leaned up just a bit, looked at the container's edges again, and saw that the seal had been broken. The light did come from inside.

With a shaking hand, she grabbed the edge of the container and pushed it back.

No alarm went off, no sirens blared, she didn't get injured. All well and good. Her sweating hand simply held the smooth, cool edge of the container.

She had to lean forward to peer inside.

The *anacapa* drive was symmetrical. It was round and sat in a box of its own, only that box didn't have a lid. The drive glowed a soft whitish gold and pulsed just a little.

The other side of the container held another, similar box. At the bottom of it, she saw a place to snap in controls like the ones she had seen on the bottom of the retired drive. Some kind of raised metal (or nano-bits or something) ran between the two boxes.

Her teeth were on edge again. They almost felt like they were vibrating. Her entire skull itched, and the itch seemed to come from the bones themselves.

That feeling slowly worked its way down her entire body.

She could guess what it was—it was the energy from the drive, released. She suspected it would get worse as four other containers opened.

With that thought, she saw another container open in her peripheral vision, and Triplett leaning over the edge. Then there was a bang behind Yash, which got a "Be more careful!" from Bellier. A creak, a metallic groan, and silence.

Yash's hair floated around her face. She hadn't double-checked the clasp holding her hair back since that morning. The floating strands decided her: she was cutting it all off. Long hair was impractical for this work. She had known it, but her vanity had gotten to her until this point.

If she was going to work on these drives, though, in this kind of energy, she wouldn't be able to keep her hair long at all.

"Very good," Bellier said. "Now, I need you all to stand and look at me."

Yash stood, and out of the corner of her eye, she noted movement as Darlington, Mercer, Triplett, and Gallatin stood as well. They glowed in the light coming out of the containers.

Yash could no longer see the crater through the windows. The windows reflected light and nothing else except what was going on inside the lab.

The jittery feeling continued. Her entire body felt like it moved involuntarily. Not big movements—small ones. Twitches, shaking, some kind of vibration.

It made her uncomfortable, but she didn't mind it. She simply accepted it.

Gallatin had moved away from his container. His entire body was rigid. He stared at the container as if something was going to come out of it and attack him.

Triplett was rubbing her forefinger against her mouth, a nervous habit that Yash had seen from her a few times before, mostly when faced with something she felt uncertain of.

Mercer was leaning in, like Yash had, investigating every part of the container. She hadn't done that yet, but she had seen enough to know that there was more to the interior than she could understand with a single glance.

And Darlington had both hands on the side of her container as if she was trying to keep herself from floating away in zero-g. The light had paled her face but accented the circles under her eyes from the tears she'd shed at lunch.

Bellier looked at all of them as if she were unsurprised by what she saw.

"All right," she said after a moment. "We are going to do one thing, something you might have to do many times in your career. You need to reach in, and lift the *anacapa* drive from its moorings. Be very careful."

Yash's mouth went completely dry. *Touch* an active *anacapa* drive. She didn't know people could do that.

"A few things," Bellier said. "You will not be able to disengage the controls, so don't even try. The *anacapa* drives are functioning at the moment, even though they are not attached to any navigation system. We have programmed the drives so that they cannot be turned off without a code. I have that code should something go wrong."

Should something go wrong. Oh, crap. Yash squared her shoulders. This was what she had signed on for. If someone had asked her that morning what she had hoped would happen, she would have said she wanted to be hands-on with an *anacapa* drive.

Well, this was as hands-on as it got.

"Secondly, you will touch the drives with your bare hands. The gloves you found in this container cannot and should not *ever* touch an actual *anacapa* drive."

Great, Yash thought. She had come close to touching hers. Really close. *It would have been nice to have that warning earlier,* she thought at Bellier, but did not allow herself to say that out loud.

If she had, she would have been just as bad as Crenshaw.

Yash had to remind herself: working with *anacapa* drives was dangerous. Everyone who took this class knew that up front. There were dozens of warnings and alerts and tests that occurred before anyone could sign up for the class.

She had almost forgotten about the danger until today. Today was all about the danger.

"You will hold the drive until I tell you to set it down," Bellier said. "This is the first step toward moving the drive to another container. You will not do that today, although I might have you do so tomorrow. That's a two-person job, however, and we might not have two people to do the job by tomorrow's class."

Tomorrow's class? Yash frowned. That seemed very far in the future.

"I would suggest that you do not bend at the waist to do this," Bellier said. "I would suggest that you kneel beside the container, and lean into it, bracing your arms on the container's lip, and using its strength to help you. You'll see why once you're underway."

Yash knelt down. Her knees complained. She had already been on them more today than she had in months. She might even end up with bruises.

"Ready?" Bellier asked. She paused for a moment, probably watching the others get into position. And then she said, "Go ahead. The timer starts…now."

Timer. Okay. That was how Bellier was going to keep track of them.

Yash lowered her hands. At least they weren't shaking. And she didn't think her palms were sweating, although she found it hard to tell because her entire body was still vibrating. So in that sense, she *was* shaking.

She could see through her skin, the bones, sinew, and blood vessels etched like a painting on the back of her hand. She swallowed against the dryness in her mouth. If she could see through her hands, what was happening to her eyes? That light was really, really powerful.

So was the energy coming off the *anacapa* drive. She could almost feel the waves—or maybe she could feel the waves. If she let her hands hang, they moved ever so subtly up and down.

But she was on some kind of clock. What kind, she did not know. So she needed to continue downward.

The area near the *anacapa* drive was warmer than the area at the top of the container, warmer than the lab. Apparently the drive gave off heat—or the light did—or the work the container did in…well, containing…the energy created its own little heat bubble.

Not enough to rise to her face or her upper arms, but enough that she could feel the temperature differential as she moved her hands downward.

Finally, her fingers brushed the edges. The vibration grew so bad that her teeth chattered as if she were cold. The sides were smooth and not warm at all. It felt like touching the sides of a gigantic egg—albeit an egg that vibrated with so much energy that it felt like it was going to blow at any moment.

That was the most difficult part—that the *anacapa* drive felt unstable. Or rather, it made her feel like she was unstable, as if she would topple off her knees.

She was glad for Bellier's recommendation to lean on the container. Otherwise, Yash might actually have fallen over.

Her hands didn't slip, though, despite the vibration. If anything, it felt like her hands had adhered to the sides of the *anacapa* drive, as if the entire thing had commandeered her skin to its own purposes.

Her heart pounded. Or maybe that was just the vibration echoing all the way through her.

She couldn't tell where her skin began. She felt fused to the drive. It should have alarmed her, but it didn't. It made her feel…"excited" wasn't the word. "Alive" was more like it, as if she hadn't ever been attached to anything before.

That thought alarmed her and made her wonder if the drive could co-opt her brain.

Maybe it already had. She had forgotten that she was supposed to lift the damn thing and hold it for a few minutes.

She wasn't sure she could lift it. She leaned on the side of the container, her torso sliding ever so slightly with the vibration. It didn't matter how hard she pressed against the container, she couldn't stop the movement.

So she stopped trying, and the feeling of slipping eased. She braced her toes against the floor, pushing her against that container as best as possible. The container bit into her armpits.

She focused on that sharp feeling under her arms, then leaned ever so slightly more and lifted.

The *anacapa* drive was lighter than she expected. She had thought it would weigh fifty, a hundred pounds. It barely weighed ten. But if her hands hadn't been fused to it (or felt like they were fused to it), she wouldn't have been able to keep it steady.

Its interior pulsed with a golden light, but the pulsing wasn't constant. Not like the vibration.

The vibration was almost alive. She could feel it in her skull, making her bones thrum. It raised a slight sound, almost musical in its intensity. Not a whistle, not a hum, more like a very faint chorus of voices…

"All right," Bellier said from very far away. "Put your drives down."

Yash didn't want to. She wanted to listen to those voices, see what they said.

She had to will her arms downward. They moved, but slowly, as if she didn't have full control over them.

She set the drive down.

The vibration almost felt normal now, as if it had become a part of her. She let it continue, not quite willing to let go.

"Release the drive," Bellier said, sounding even farther away, "and stand up."

Yash wanted to close her eyes as she pulled her hands away, but something told her that would be a bad idea.

She unhooked her right hand, and then her left. The palms felt—scratchy. Not quite hot, but not the same temperature as the rest of her hands.

She could still see the bones and sinew and blood vessels, but not as brightly now.

Slowly, carefully, she raised her arms and—

Someone screamed.

25

"I can't! I can't! I can't!"

The screams got louder with each word.

"I can't! I can't! I can't!"

And another voice joined the first, deeper, more intense.

"Get it off me! Get it off me now! Help! Get it off me!"

Yash made herself sit on her haunches, her knees complaining. The vibration in her teeth and bones was easing, but it took all of her strength to look at Bellier.

Bellier was not helping the two yellers. She was staring at them though.

"I'm stuck!" That voice—the *I-can't* voice—was female.

"So am I!" The other voice, male, sounded even more panicked. "Someone help me."

"Help *us*!" the woman yelled.

Yash put her hands on her thighs. Normally, someone yelling like that would make her adrenaline spike, but she had a hunch her adrenaline was already spiked.

Bellier was still watching the students, doing nothing.

Yash wondered if this was a test.

"Heeeeeeelp!" the woman screamed.

Yash couldn't deal with that anymore. She used her hands on her thighs to push herself upward. Standing was harder than she expected. She almost toppled again and had to catch herself on the lip of her container.

The yellers were apart from each other—Triplett and Gallatin—with Mercer between them. Mercer looked stunned.

Triplett had tears running down her face, her body bent over her container. Gallatin was bent over his as well, his face so red it looked like the top of his head would blow off.

Yash wiped her hands on her pants, feeling the vibration ease. She glanced at her own container, the *anacapa* drive still glowing.

Instructions, from day one, were that anyone who revealed a drive couldn't leave it unattended. She bent over, used the controls to close the container's lid, and then she secured it.

Mercer was doing the same.

Triplett had stopped screaming words. She was making a long, almost voiceless scream. Gallatin was yanking his torso backward, but not loosening his arms, grunting with panic.

Yash glared at Bellier, who just watched.

This was another one of those damn tests, and Yash didn't care. If she was supposed to ignore these people, she couldn't. They were colleagues, even if she didn't like them much or interact with them at all.

She sprinted across the room, her feet sliding, her knees aching, the lower part of her legs feeling as if they were being poked with sharp needles.

She reached Gallatin first. His fingers were clenched into his drive, his body rigid with panic.

There appeared to be nothing different about his drive than hers, but she checked the controls anyway and saw nothing. The drive itself was the same size, just as golden, pulsing in the same way.

He looked up at her, sweat dripping down his face. "Help me," he said. "Please."

Behind her, Mercer was getting up. And Darlington was running from across the room as well.

It was as if Yash's burst of energy had inspired them too.

Mercer passed her and went to Triplett. "I got you," he said, but that didn't stop her from making that horrible noise.

Somehow, Yash had to separate Gallatin from the drive. If she closed the lid, it might actually hurt him. And yanking one arm might not work at all.

Instead, she got behind him, and poked him in his sides so hard that his breath left in a giant gasp. His entire body jerked, including his arms.

At that moment, she grabbed his armpits and dragged him backward.

He fell on top of her, knocking the wind out of her. Her entire body ached. And she couldn't catch her breath for a long, hard minute.

But the sound behind her, that weird noise that Triplett had been making, stopped. Supplanted by huge, gasping sobs, and Darlington, speaking calmly, repeating that stupidest of phrases, *It'll be all right. It's okay. It'll be all right.*

Gallatin remained on top of Yash. He clearly wasn't going to move on his own. She shoved at him, but he didn't move. Dead weight. Had he passed out?

She had no idea. So she scooched out from underneath him, toppling him to one side as she did so.

He caught himself as he fell, but that seemed reflexive. He looked terrified.

"Thank you," he said, his voice nearly gone. "Yash, thank you."

She nodded, then climbed away from him. She felt bruised and exhausted, her body aching not just from the fall and the kneeling, but from the vibrating too.

The light coming out of Gallatin's container continued to glow a bright white. She couldn't just leave it like that. Against regulation. Or something.

Who cared?

Bellier probably cared, but she was going to flunk them all now. So what did it matter that Yash followed procedure?

Except that it would have bothered Yash if she didn't.

She got on her sore knees, examined the controls again, saw that they were the same as hers, and pressed the right combination to close and seal the container.

The lid came down, the seals engaged, and she leaned against the container, relieved that it wasn't vibrating.

Mercer was bent over the other container. Triplett was clinging to Darlington and sobbing. Darlington, who looked like she wanted to be somewhere—anywhere—else.

Their gazes met. Yash nodded at her but was too tired to go help. Or maybe Yash was just tired of all the raw emotion in this room today.

Class was supposed to be facts and figures and thinking and logic, not tears and anger and complete panic.

Yash ran a hand over her face. Gallatin remained on the floor, the back of his hand on his forehead, his other hand across his stomach. His skin was a weird pasty color that made Yash think he was queasy.

The lid on the other container rose up, then settled into place, and finally snicked closed. She couldn't see how it came up, what made that happen. She suspected Mercer did it.

"Return to your places," Bellier said.

Yash wasn't even sure that was possible. She certainly didn't want to go back to her container.

But she knew she had no choice. Time to take the reprimand, in whatever form Bellier decided to dish it up.

Yash sighed, feeling a little hollow. Even her teeth ached, remnants of that damn vibration.

She brought her legs up, then leaned forward, and used the side of the container to help herself stand.

She felt a little more sturdy than she had a few moments ago. But her chest ached from having the wind knocked out of it, and she just realized that she had a similar ache on the back of her head.

Dammit, Gallatin had knocked her back hard. But Yash didn't say anything. Her legs felt more like they normally did. No little needles, even though the knees really hurt.

She limped back to her spot, then stood behind the retired *anacapa* drive, wishing she would make it to tomorrow, sorry she wasn't going to learn whatever weird and violent lesson that Bellier had been going to teach them but wouldn't now, now that they had all broken rank and screwed up the instructions and hadn't focused on the task at hand.

"Sit up, Gallatin," Bellier said. Her voice sounded sharper, crisper. Or maybe Yash's ears had become her own again.

"And you," Bellier said to Triplett, "let go of Darlington so that she can return to her place."

Yash looked—there was no percentage in failing to look. Triplett was nodding, still crying (not as loudly now), and still clinging to Darlington. Darlington was trying to free herself.

She disentangled one of Triplett's hands, then the other, and scooted backward, before standing, and running back to her place, as if she expected Triplett to follow and tackle her.

Mercer stood and calmly walked back to his spot, careful to stay away from Triplett's grasp.

Neither Triplett nor Gallatin stood up. But Bellier didn't seem to notice.

Instead she tilted her head, that somewhat amused motion she sometimes made.

"Well," she said. "This was quite a revelation."

No kidding, Yash thought. An ugly, horrible, terrible revelation, the kind of revelation Yash could have lived without experiencing. Ever.

"There are people," Bellier said, "who cannot deal with the energy coming out of an *anacapa* drive. It doesn't matter how strong they are, how smart, how gifted. Something in that energy spikes their fight-or-flight response, and makes it worse as time goes on."

Yash frowned. She glanced toward Gallatin and Triplett, but didn't see them. Still.

"The only way to test that," Bellier said, "is to have them touch an *anacapa* drive with their bare hands in a closed environment. Like this lab."

"You could've done it first." Triplett's voice wobbled, filled with tears. "We didn't need to go through everything else. If you wanted to know who could work on an *anacapa* drive, then the fairest thing to do was do that first."

"Yes, we used to bring the students in and have them touch an *anacapa* drive on the first day of class." Bellier glanced at Yash, then Mercer, and then Darlington, apparently unconcerned about Triplett and Gallatin.

"You shouldn't have changed." Triplett's voice was almost a wail. Yash wanted to step over to Triplett and shake her, wanted to tell her to get herself together and to stop crying.

The emotion was bothering Yash after all. Bellier was right: there was no place in this lab for emotion. It got in the way.

"We made the policy change accidentally," Bellier said. "One of our instructors forgot to start with the drives, and we learned something."

Bellier continued to make eye contact with Yash, Mercer, and Darlington. She wasn't talking to Triplett at all. She was talking to the three students who were still standing.

That meant something, right? It had to mean something.

"We learned that 'everything else,' as you called it, Triplett, isn't for you or anyone like you. It's for the others, the ones who can touch *anacapa* drives with their bare hands."

Yash and Mercer and Darlington. Who also failed this experiment.

Yash looked in Triplett's direction, but still couldn't see her. She didn't respond to Bellier, though, which was a mercy.

When Yash looked back at Bellier, she realized that Bellier was watching her. A slight chill ran through Yash, the cool air coating her sweat. Her adrenaline levels were going back down.

"We needed to see how the others responded to an extreme emergency." It seemed like Bellier was talking directly to Yash. She resisted the urge to cross her arms and rub her hands on her bare skin. She was cold again, but the chill went deeper than the physical. It also came from the absolute calm in Bellier's tone.

"The experience you just had," Bellier was saying, "qualifies as an extreme emergency. As far as you three knew, the energy from the drives was harming the other two, and you needed to stop that harm."

Yash hadn't thought about harm, at least explicitly. She hadn't gotten to the idea of harm. She had simply seen two people in distress, and knew that something had gone wrong. She needed to make matters right before she could ever assess whether or not the other two were harmed.

"The drives were harming us," Gallatin said, his voice muffled. He remained on the floor. "And you didn't warn us."

A small smile crossed Bellier's lips. "Nice try, Gallatin," she said. "But you were warned dozens of times. From the moment you started into the engineering program to the day you signed up for the *anacapa* track, you were always warned that working with the *anacapa* drives was dangerous. In fact, you even signed waivers, stating that you knew the work in this class might kill you or cause permanent damage."

"You should bring in doctors," Gallatin said, "because I don't feel right."

Neither did Yash, but she wasn't complaining. However, her experience hadn't been nearly as bad as Gallatin's. Her experience hadn't been bad at all.

"You will go through a medical exam," Bellier said. "All of you will. We will be looking for certain things, things that don't show up in such dramatic form as we saw today."

Yash did rub her hands on her arms, feeling the pebbling of gooseflesh. She was going to start shivering soon. She could feel it as deep in her bones as she felt that vibration.

"I can tell you, though, that none of you—not even Gallatin and Triplett—suffered permanent damage." Bellier did not sound reassuring. "I have seen others get seriously injured from *anacapa* drives, and you have none of the symptoms."

"That's supposed to reassure us?" Triplett asked, her voice still thick with tears.

"I'm not here to reassure you," Bellier said.

Besides, Yash suspected, Bellier was no longer talking to those two. Bellier was probably no longer even thinking much about them.

But Yash had no sense of how Bellier was going to treat her, Mercer, and Darlington. Maybe they would get a chance to reapply to the program. Because Bellier wasn't dismissing the entire group out of hand, no matter what had happened here.

"Triplett and Gallatin," Bellier said, her tone suddenly more official. "Can you stand?"

Rather than respond, Triplett started to put her hand on the dead *anacapa* drive before her to brace herself as she stood. She stopped, midway, and closed her fist as if she never wanted to touch anything like that again.

Instead, she braced herself on the floor and awkwardly got to her feet.

Gallatin was using the container to help himself up. He was still that strange gray color and his eyes looked bruised.

"You two did very well in this class," Bellier said. "Unfortunately, your reaction to the *anacapa* drives is not a one-time thing. Nor is it something you can overcome with sheer will. We've had students try that as well, in the dark recesses of this course's history. It doesn't work and, for those students, it does eventually lead to permanent damage."

Yash stopped rubbing her hands on her arms. The gooseflesh was receding, as was the deepest chill. Now she only felt the cold in the room and little more.

"What you're feeling right now," Bellier said to them, "is a panic that is leftover from your contact with the *anacapa* drive. Should you continue to touch *anacapa* drives through the course of your work, that panic will become permanent. You will respond to everything with a measure of fear. We have treatments for that, but the best is to avoid the condition altogether."

Triplett let out a shivery sob. Gallatin still braced himself on the container.

Yash did a mental check. Was she panicked and so detached that she wasn't allowing herself to actually feel it?

The check reassured her: she wasn't panicked or detached. But she was remarkably calm.

"I am sorry to dismiss you from this class," Bellier was saying to Triplett and Gallatin. "I am sorry to dismiss you from the *anacapa* program. You will both be excellent engineers. You're bright and intuitive and learn well. But you cannot work in an *anacapa* field. You will have to work in ships that do not have *anacapa* drives. Or you will need to work in a capacity other than engineering if you wish to serve on a DV-Class ship. Do you understand?"

Triplett sniffed, then wiped a hand underneath her nose. She nodded.

"You're sure about this?" Gallatin asked, his voice small.

"I am afraid I am," Bellier said. "You may talk to counselors if you wish, and the chair of the department. But your reactions pretty much sealed your fate here. And again, I am sorry."

Bellier apologizing. Yash wouldn't have thought it possible.

"You're dismissed," Bellier said to them. "Do you need assistance leaving the room?"

"No," Gallatin said. Yash recognized his expression. She would have had the same one. She would have left on her own power no matter what had happened to her.

Because this was a pretty big personal setback for them. She had no idea how she would feel in their shoes—how she might actually feel in a few minutes after Bellier finished with her and the other two.

Gallatin pushed himself away from the container and wobbled toward the door. Triplett reached his side and slipped her arm around him. He put one of his arms around her, and together they made their way out of the lab.

Yash, Darlington, and Mercer watched. So did Bellier. She waited until the lab door closed before she spoke again.

"Well," she said. "And now, the three of you. I can see from your faces that you're worried."

Do you blame us? Yash wanted to ask, but didn't. She didn't even glance at the other two survivors either.

"You shouldn't be worried at all," Bellier said. "I am well pleased."

Yash blinked, not sure she heard that correctly. *Pleased?* Bellier? Really? Why?

"You all showed incredible presence of mind," Bellier said. "Zarlengo, Mercer, before rushing to the emergency, you closed your containers. That is correct, and had there been some kind of *anacapa* overload that could have triggered other problems, that maneuver right there might have prevented the situation from escalating."

Yash was holding her breath. The praise was hard to hear. It was so very unexpected.

"Darlington, you did not close your container immediately, but when you saw the other two do so, you did as well, displaying a capacity to think even in an extreme and unusual circumstance. Well done."

Yash risked a glance at Darlington, whose cheeks had gone dusky, either from nerves or from being singled out.

"The three of you handled the emergency swiftly and with great thought. You also showed compassion, especially you, Darlington. That is a rare trait among the leadership positions in the Fleet. It will be an asset if you use it correctly. We will work on that."

Yash frowned. *We will work...?* Did she dare hope?

Bellier actually smiled. "I said I was well pleased, and I am. I have three students who will now proceed with the *anacapa* program. Some years, I initiate the work in this lab and by the end of the day, I have no students left. I don't recall a year where I have had three."

Yash glanced at Mercer. He smiled just a little, not joyfully—Yash wasn't feeling joyful either—but with some kind of relief.

"Don't worry," Bellier said, "the elimination portion of this class—and your future classes in this curriculum—are over. You will make mistakes. You will make many mistakes. We can only hope that the mistakes will be good ones, ones we can learn from."

Yash frowned. She still wasn't following. "We?" She had no idea why Bellier would say *we.* "You're the experts, right? How can you learn from our mistakes?"

"Ah, Zarlengo. You are the first student I've had who has picked up on that phraseology. You are more detail oriented than any who have come before, including me. Combine that with the creative side of your mind, and you are exactly what this program needs."

Now, Yash felt her own skin heat up. Bellier's switch to extreme praise was very strange. Yash felt more off her game than she had felt during the so-called extreme emergency.

"To answer your question, Zarlengo," Bellier said. "We are not experts. We simply know more about the *anacapa* drive than the three of you do. But not as much more as you probably think."

266

Both Mercer and Darlington glanced at Yash, as if the question had made them uncomfortable, not Bellier's answer.

"Isn't the essence of being an expert knowing more than a beginner?" Yash asked.

"On all the other systems in the Fleet," Bellier said, "we have actual experts, people who can build those systems from scratch, people who know more than the specs ever explain, people who know the limits and the capabilities of those systems so deeply that they can use the systems in ways the rest of us cannot."

Yash did not like how this answer was going. She was beginning to regret asking the question.

"With the *anacapa* drive, however," Bellier said, "no one knows its limits or its capabilities. We believe we only understand a small fraction of what the drive can do."

"But we build them from scratch," Mercer said.

"Yes," Bellier said. "We do, replicating the original drive exactly every single time."

"The original drive?" Darlington asked.

Bellier nodded. "We started with one drive, thousands of years ago," she said. "It was not created by the Fleet. It took more than a decade to recreate the drive, and once that happened, everything the Fleet was started to develop."

"Not created by the Fleet?" Yash asked. "What do you mean?"

"Must I spell this out exactly for you, Zarlengo?" Bellier asked, but she didn't sound sarcastic or disappointed. Just slightly amused. "We didn't invent the *anacapa* drive. We stole it."

THE SEARCH
NOW

26

THE *IVOIRE* ORBITED A MOON one planet away from the coordinates that Coop had discovered back at Lost Souls. The planet that, in theory, once housed Sector Base E-2 looked like a gray, blue, and white ball on the holographic map that he had called up of this solar system.

He didn't know the name of the solar system, not even something given to him from the incomplete Fleet files. He had researchers digging through all of the data Yash and her team had pulled from the ships that Boss had found or pulled from the Boneyard.

Unfortunately, for the most part, the Fleet captains had done their duty and destroyed all of the sensitive data. What Coop had were fragments, maddening fragments—and the coordinates of Sector Base E-2.

It had taken a longer trip through foldspace than he liked to get here. Everyone had been nervous, especially the *Ivoire's* crew. He'd managed to bring back almost the original crew. Only a few dozen who had made lives away from Lost Souls or who couldn't face foldspace again had stayed behind.

And of course, then there were a handful who had died, a few of them by their own hand. Like Dix.

For the first time in years, the bridge had a full crew compliment. Lynda Rooney once again acted as his first officer. Usually she helmed the *Shadow*, but when he had sent out the call to the entire crew of the *Ivoire*, saying he wanted to go to a newly discovered site of a sector base, they had all signed on.

He hadn't even felt bad that he was leaving Lost Souls in the lurch. He and his people had trained a lot of staff over the past year, enough that they could run a DV-Class vessel and continue the patrol of the border between the Empire and the Nine Planets Alliance.

Ilona Blake had argued with him when he told her he was taking the *Ivoire* on this mission, especially when she found out how far he was going, but he hadn't even let her finish before he reminded her that no one in the Fleet belonged to Lost Souls. Yes, some of them were employed by Lost Souls, but they were Fleet first. The Fleet, wherever and whenever it was, would always hold their allegiance.

She had no argument against that, especially since the crew of the *Ivoire* had given Lost Souls so much. As he argued with Blake, he knew Yash was meeting with several of Lost Soul's techs, briefing them on some of the new things she had discovered about *anacapa* drives, runabouts, and smaller ships.

After the *Ivoire* set out on this, its first mission in more than a year, Yash had told him with a smile that in the last week she had given Lost Souls enough work—and enough new tech—to last them three decades. No one could argue with that.

The only person that Coop hadn't told was Boss. She was on a long mission to the Boneyard, recovering ships and sending them back to Lost Souls with surprising regularity. It was as if her injury on the previous trip with Yash had whipped Boss into some kind of frenzy, making her want to dive and recover every single ship in the Boneyard.

She should have come back two months before Coop left, but she hadn't, sending message after message delaying her return. When she had sent her first message, he and Yash had just discovered the location of Sector Base E-2. He had promised himself he would tell Boss about the base when she returned.

Then she delayed her return three more times. Each time, he nearly told her about the mission to the base, and each time he backed away.

He had no idea if Blake had mentioned it to her. It would probably come out while he was gone—and he wasn't sure he cared. Boss might end up angry at him, but she of all people should understand why he had to do this.

And why he had to do it with as many of his own people as possible.

Still, he had taken a few of hers—on loan, as he said to Blake, who hadn't objected as much as he expected. Two of the loaned crew sat on the bridge now, in front of consoles that were powered up but not in use.

The first, Lucretia Stone, was an archeologist who had helped Coop and Yash search for sector bases in the past. She had tangled with Coop, particularly at the site of Sector Base W, but she was exceptionally good at her job.

She had brought an entire team with her, mostly archeologists, many of whom had continued to work at the site of Sector Base W after Coop had abandoned it, looking for the next sector base.

Yash had convinced him that their experiences with old closed sector bases would make them invaluable on this mission.

Stone had also insisted on McAllister Bridge, a scientist whose specialty Coop didn't entirely understand. He had been on Boss's team when the *Ivoire* first showed up in this time period. At that point, Bridge was one of the only people from this time who had an even slight grasp of nanobit technology.

He had learned more in the intervening years, or so Stone said. She also claimed that he had made a point of studying nanobit decay as well as the way that closed sector bases changed over time.

Coop didn't care about what happened to the bases as much as he cared about how to use that information to find another sector base.

McAllister Bridge was monitoring his console, already examining information that was coming from the planet that the Fleet had called Nindowne. It had ten continents and the base had been located in the most environmentally hostile, least populated of the continents—but that had been more than 2,000 years before.

The archeologists would study what had changed in 2,000 years. They could figure out how the lay of the land would alter, what to look for, and how the natural environment would destroy anything manmade in easily discernable ways.

Provided, of course, that nothing else was built over the old base, or if the base wasn't repurposed, or if it was destroyed.

"There's a lot of junk in orbit around Nindowne," said Kjersti Perkins. Coop loved having her on his bridge. She was always no-nonsense. She knew more about the systems than anyone on the ship except Yash. "I don't like it."

"I don't either," said Anita Tren. She was the tiniest officer on the *Ivoire*, but one of the most talented. In the intervening years, she had altered her console on the bridge to accommodate her height—once the *Ivoire* no longer had to answer to the Fleet and its sometimes ridiculously rigid regulations.

"That stuff really is junk," said Lynda Rooney. She had a holographic screen floating above her console showing Nindowne in three dimensions. She had enlarged the image so much that Coop could see all kinds of details. "Old satellites that are no longer active, the remains of some kind of space station, some ships that don't seem to have any power, and lots of floating debris."

Coop tapped his fingers on the arm of his command chair, calling up some screens on his own. He peered at the telemetry pouring at him from Nindowne.

They were right: the junk floating around the planet seemed to be uniformly inactive. And old.

"I've never seen anything like it," Coop said. "What do you think is going on here? Was there a war? Some kind of invasion force?"

"I think it's too soon to tell." Jason Xilvii stood at the farthest console from Coop's command chair. Xilvii had been a junior officer when the *Ivoire* was actually with the Fleet. Once Xilvii had arrived at Lost Souls, he left the Fleet to work weapons and tactical and research at the corporation, thinking it would be easier on him to embrace his new life completely rather than try to continue a career that no longer truly existed.

He had been invaluable in Coop's skirmishes with the Empire on the border of the Nine Planets a year ago, and Coop had personally asked him on this mission.

Even so, Xilvii seemed to feel like he didn't belong with the bridge crew. He kept himself as far from the main crew as possible. In off hours, he didn't socialize with the main bridge crew, keeping with some of his old friends—still junior officers, if ranking meant anything anymore.

Coop wasn't sure it did.

"You have some kind of theory, Xilvii," Coop said. "Share it."

"No theory, really." Xilvii sounded nervous. "More like an observation. I've been drilling past the junk to look at the surface itself. Nine of the ten continents are populated. From the numbers we sort of had from the data Engineer Zarlengo provided us, it seems that the population of those nine continents has grown exponentially in the past two thousand years."

Coop tried not to let his amusement show at Xilvii's formality. *Engineer Zarlengo* indeed. If Yash were on the bridge instead of coordinating things in engineering, she would have been amused at the designation, spoken with such stiff formality.

"But the population of that tenth continent hasn't grown like the other places," Coop said. He saw the numbers as well. He just didn't know what they meant. "It's still populated, though."

"By a fraction of the people who had lived there when the sector base was open," Xilvii said.

"That's not unusual," Rooney said, sounding dismissive. "Most of the Fleet moves on when a sector base is closed. Even the land-based. They often go to other sector bases and start over."

"But not all of them," Anita said softly, as if she didn't want to completely disagree with Rooney.

"True," Rooney said. "Not all of them. But we don't always find thriving communities around a sector base."

Coop was watching Xilvii. The man was moving slightly, as if he was shifting back and forth on his feet. As if he couldn't contain his nervousness.

"That's not what you're getting at, is it, Xilvii?" Coop had forgotten this element of command—seeing his people and figuring out what they were actually trying to communicate to him.

"No, sir," Xilvii said. "This planet, whatever they call it now—"

"We're still calling it Nindowne," Stone said.

Coop glared at her. She wasn't part of the bridge crew. He had warned her that she wouldn't be able to participate in a free discussion like she usually did at Lost Souls.

But she had always been difficult. It shouldn't have surprised him that she would ignore his warnings.

And, in truth, he wasn't sure if it mattered that she had. He was feeling a lot less rigid than he used to feel, as if the full force of the Fleet no longer held him in check and made him follow certain regulations that now seemed stringent to him.

Maybe Boss had had more of an effect on him than he realized.

"Nindowne," Xilvii repeated softly. "Right. Anyway. This planet, *Nindowne*, it um, it's in rough shape, sir."

"Meaning what?" Coop asked.

"The largest continent has five different cities and their air quality is exceptionally poor. If we were going to the largest continent, I would have to recommend oxygen masks. The air quality is that bad."

"Wow," Bridge said. Coop glanced at him. Bridge seemed surprised that Coop had heard him. Bridge hadn't moved from his previous position, meaning he hadn't done anything to double-check the air quality; he had just seemed stunned by what Xilvii had to say.

"But," Xilvii said, "Judging by the air quality over the tenth continent, we should have no trouble down there. It's oxygen rich, has a nutrient mix that's very familiar to Fleet-friendly planets, and is very human-friendly. I can see why the Fleet chose this place as the home of a sector base. But if I were to establish a base now, I might have passed it over. The planet's atmosphere isn't toxic, exactly, but it's heading that way. A superficial scan doesn't match what the Fleet usually looks for in a sector base planet."

Xilvii said all of this as if it had import. But half the bridge crew was frowning at him, clearly not following the logic. Coop wasn't sure he did either.

"What has this to do with the space junk?" Coop asked.

"May I, Captain?" Bridge asked. Coop shot him another glance, surprised that he had spoken up.

"If it's all right with Xilvii," Coop said, and looked at him to confirm. Xilvii was watching Bridge with something like relief. "Please," Xilvii said.

Bridge nodded and then stood up. He clearly wasn't used to Fleet procedures. He wasn't giving a speech; he was just going to make a comment.

Coop felt his lips twitch with a potential smile. He didn't allow it. He didn't want Bridge to feel as if Coop was making fun of him.

"I think the relevant point here," Bridge said, "is that the people of this planet are treating, and have treated, their home with great disregard. They've polluted the atmosphere in the most populated areas, and, from my scans, it looks like they've made some other bad choices for the health of the planet as well."

Fair point. But they were two thousand years in the future. The sector base closing had occurred a long time ago. What the people of this planet had or had not done since really didn't matter to Coop.

What mattered to him was finding the coordinates for the next sector base in the sequence, Sector Base F-2.

"It does not surprise me," Bridge said, "or, I would hazard a guess, surprise Xilvii, that the people of this planet are now polluting the space around it."

Ah, that was the point. In other words, they both believed that the materials in orbit around Nindowne were not defensive or offensive weapons. That made quite a difference in how the *Ivoire* would approach the base.

"You think the space junk is just litter?" Perkins asked, as if she couldn't believe that.

"I do," Xilvii said as Bridge said, "I do."

"One of the things that backs this up, I think," Bridge continued, "is that there is neither rhyme nor reason to that space junk. The material seems to be of different ages and different types."

"And some of it," Xilvii said, "is really garbage, like food waste and human waste and other stuff. It's disgusting."

Coop grimaced. He couldn't help himself.

"I'm not seeing much evidence that they're particularly advanced, either," said Anita. "It's not that they're backwards. It's just that they don't seem to have modified any Fleet technology into their own. No matter what culture I'm looking at."

"And what I'm finding on that tenth continent," Xilvii said, "shows some kind of regression. The people who live there don't live in large communities. I'm finding clusters of ten and twenty, a small village of maybe a hundred people, and not much more."

"I thought the planet's climate was hospitable," Rooney said.

"It is. It's a bit warmer than we usually like, but it's not out of the norm for a place that would house a Fleet's sector base," said Xilvii.

Coop wasn't that interested in the speculation. He wanted to send a ship to Nindowne and get the task of exploring that sector base—or the remains of it—underway.

If there was one at all.

"If I'm understanding you correctly," he said, "you're telling me that the space junk is a hazard only if we enter orbit or try to land on Nindowne."

"Yes, that's right," Xilvii said. "The junk is not warships, it's not anything that could hurt us, except if we hit it. And there's a lot to hit."

"There's more stuff per square inch than we find in even the most dense asteroid belts," said Anita.

Great. If Coop did want to go down there, he would have to send the right ship. All the small ships had shields, but some were stronger and more effective than others.

"Any sign of the base?" he asked Stone.

"Not from this distance, no," she said. "But there are the remnants of an old settlement exactly where we'd expect to find the City of Sandoveil."

According to the records, Sandoveil was where the base had been located.

"All right," Coop said. "That's good enough for me."

Everyone looked at him. There must have been something in his tone...hell, of course there was something in his tone. He was excited about a mission for the first time in years.

"Here's what we're going to do," he said. "The *Ivoire* will remain here, far enough away that it won't appear on the most sophisticated sensors we've found in this time period. I'm going to take one of our skips with a small crew, and we're going to see what we can find. Until I return, Rooney, you'll be in charge."

Her lips thinned and her eyes narrowed. He recognized the look. He was sure he'd had it on his own face a few times. She was used to being in command now, so taking orders was hard.

Especially orders she clearly disagreed with.

"Captain, if I may…?" Rooney's question was barely one. It had the full force of her command voice.

He could ignore it, or he could listen and see if she could change his mind.

He knew what a good commander would do. He just wasn't sure he wanted to be a good commander anymore.

At least, not of the Fleet.

He gave her one curt nod, because he didn't trust his voice. He didn't want to sound sarcastic or judgmental before she even had a chance to make her case.

"I think we should send several ships closer, including a small fighter, just in case we're not reading that junk correctly," Rooney said. "The *Ivoire* isn't close enough to immediately come to the defense of the skip that you send, should you need defending."

And they all knew—except maybe Bridge and Stone—that skips of the *Ivoire's* era did not have *anacapa* drives to help them escape quickly, nor did they have weaponry so that they could fight back against any kind of attack.

"Also," Rooney said, sounding just a bit more hesitant, "I think we should do some more reconnaissance before sending anyone to the planet, especially someone as valuable as you, sir."

Coop smiled. He had expected that objection right from the start.

"Finished, Rooney?" he asked.

"No, sir," she said. "I think it would be prudent to have the linguists capture transmissions from this Nindowne, if that's what the locals call it, to see what languages are spoken there. It would be nice to have at least a rudimentary knowledge of the most common language before we send anyone down. That will only take a day or so."

He knew how long it would take. He had been married to a linguist once. But he didn't say that. He realized at that moment that Rooney wasn't over-explaining for him; she was doing it for the newbies on the crew.

She stopped, her gaze meeting his—not quite defiantly. She didn't need to be defiant. She had nothing she had to prove, to him or to anyone else.

"You're right, Rooney," he said.

Her eyes widened ever so slightly. He had surprised her. She clearly had expected him to disagree with her on every point.

"We do need a few fighters positioned around Nindowne," he said, "just in case we're misreading what we're seeing or in case there's some kind of system in one of those cities that has long-range weapons capabilities and perceives us as a threat."

A slight frown creased her forehead. Had he been so unreasonable lately that being reasonable was unusual? Or did she simply understand the depth of his interest in finding the base? (Or, if he were being honest with himself, the depth of his obsession, not his interest.)

He continued, "I think we should send two smaller vessels, whichever ones we have that are best equipped for a scientific mission, to orbit—if we can do that easily—or at least get close enough to probe two things: that area on the tenth continent where a city used to be, and also the main cities on Nindowne."

Everyone was staring at him. Did they really expect him to be so unreasonable that he wouldn't be able to see the wisdom in what she had been saying? Or was he just unused to being the center of attention, after all this time?

"I think we should also figure out the languages," he said. "We'll bring a linguist with us, as well as the best equipment we have in case we run into some locals."

Rooney's expression fell for only a moment. She clearly had hoped he would abandon his part of the mission.

"You'll remain in touch with us, in case we find out we need anything else, some kind of translation program or something," he said. "And I promise you, we'll leave if it looks like we're going to get into serious troubles with the locals."

The bridge was quiet for a moment.

"For the landing team," he said, "I want Yash, Perkins, Stone, Bridge, and two security officers. Rooney, make sure I have the folks who are the most up-to-date on weaponry."

"That would be me, sir," Xilvii said.

"You're not a security officer, Xilvii," Coop said.

"But I've been handling the weapons since we got to Lost Souls," Xilvii said.

"I want you on the *Ivoire*," Coop said. "We need people on the weapons systems here as well. I want security officers who are good with handheld weapons in case we come across something we don't like."

"I would suggest a second pilot," Rooney said.

"We have two," Coop said. "Me and Yash. That's enough."

Rooney opened her mouth as if she were going to argue with him, and then she didn't.

"One last thing, Rooney," he said. "The most valuable person going on this mission is Yash. Her skills are impossible to replace."

He knew that sounded brutal, particularly in front of Stone and Bridge, but he didn't care. He needed to be clear.

"Now that we're separate from the Fleet, I am not the most valuable person on the mission. Nor am I the most valuable person in the *Ivoire*. If something happens to me, she's your ship, Rooney. You have the skills and the talent for it. There are others who will captain just as well. They can take the other ships. I want you on the *Ivoire*."

She shook her head, disagreeing with him, as he knew she would.

"We're not you, sir," she said.

He smiled at her. "In this case, Rooney," he said, "that's a very good thing."

27

COOP DECIDED TO LAND THE SKIP on what should have been—according to the old maps—the City of Sandoveil. He had to fly between two mountain ranges to get there.

The maneuver was trickier than he expected. There were harsh wind currents in between the mountains, unpredictable wind currents, and they buffeted the skip. Not that it bothered any of the others on board.

The skip was one of the largest that Lost Souls built. Yash had overseen the design and had used Fleet tech, including nanobits, to create the hull. Unlike the skips Boss usually used, this one could easily handle a crew of ten or more—although half would have to sleep in their reclining chairs if the trip extended to an overnight.

Seven fit comfortably here. They were all in the large main area—not really a cockpit, more a ferry for tourists, with controls up front and passenger seats farther back.

The skip had no weapons, but Coop doubted he would need them. According to the readings they had gotten on the *Ivoire*, no one was in the general vicinity of what they all believed to be the old sector base.

He sat in the pilot's chair, Yash beside him. She was directing him nonverbally, pointing at the small holographic three-dimensional map that floated just above the console. Neither Coop nor Yash wanted to discuss their expectations of this part of the large planet; they didn't want to influence the other members of the landing team any more than they already had.

Those other members were engrossed in their own work. The two security team members, Monique Chen and Igashu Lankstadt, were completing a mostly silent double check of the gear that they wore. Perkins was monitoring local chatter from nearby areas, trying to get a sense of the language—any language—that might be spoken nearby.

Stone was using one of her many annoying tablets, holding it up to another tablet, comparing something that Coop couldn't and wasn't sure he wanted to see.

So far, the geography fit the descriptions he and Yash had found in the files. Sandoveil had been built in a long, narrow valley between two extremely tall mountain ranges, filled with dozens of natural wonders, including the largest waterfall on the entire planet.

A large waterfall was on the edge of this narrow valley. As he piloted downward, he saw so much spray rise off the waterfall that it looked like the entire area was covered in mist.

The edges of what had been a city were the best place to land. The valley wasn't quite a box valley because it opened onto a wide flat area that lead to one of Nindowne's oceans. It had become clear, as the skip got closer, that the wide flat area wasn't a good place to land.

He had partly ruled it out already because he had thought it was a sand-covered beach. But it wasn't. It was a mudflat that seemed to have some underground activity connected to it. The mud burbled and burped, making large bubbles.

There was another mudflat on the other side of the valley, which had led Stone to speculate that there would be no base here. She had only seen specs for sector bases that were built underneath cities.

Coop hadn't answered her speculation, nor had anyone else connected to the Fleet. He wasn't looking at the flat area where the city had been as a possible location for the sector base.

He was looking at the large mountain ranges.

Yash had been too. She had directed him to land near what appeared to be a large cave underneath a gigantic overhang on one of the mountains. She hadn't said anything about it, and neither had he.

She had simply pointed to the reading on one of the current scans, and he had nodded.

If the old maps were correct and there was a base here, then the skip was landing on what had been a road heading toward the base's entrance. This base had been built with a large parking area out front because the main entry wasn't in the very center of the city.

He suspected that the overhang was manufactured to hide the number of vehicles from the non-Fleet citizens of Sandoveil.

But he was guessing. He had no idea if the Fleet still followed its old procedures by the time it had built a base here. For all he knew, everyone in the city had known about the base, and the reason the city was gone now was because the Fleet had closed the base.

Because he wasn't certain of Fleet procedures and what had happened since the base closed, he had deliberately chosen to land far from that overhang. His team would have to walk to it.

He had a hunch they would be able to see more on the ground. If something currently existed in that overhang, they wouldn't be able to see the ship as well as closely from this distance.

He hoped.

"Humph," Stone said, "there are a lot more buildings standing than I would have expected, given the climate. If you want to see them, Captain, I suggest you move the landing site to one of the ones I recommended before we left the *Ivoire*."

Coop ignored that comment. But Bridge didn't. Out of the corner of his eye, Coop saw Bridge lean toward Stone, peering at the work she was doing.

"When do you think this place was abandoned?" he asked.

"I'm assuming it was abandoned when the base got moved," Stone said. "I'm using the calculations we came up with on the *Ivoire*, which would make the move about two thousand years ago."

"We don't know that, though, do we?" Bridge said in one of those tones that would have annoyed Coop if it was directed at him. The aggressive use of the word "we" when in reality Bridge meant "you." It was a criticism couched as a group mistake.

Yash had her back to them. She rolled her eyes. Coop smiled just a little, which was something only Yash could see.

"You're right, of course," Stone said. She wasn't upset by Bridge's tone at all. "We're almost to the site. We'll let it tell us what we need to know."

Coop had to manually correct the navigation to compensate for the winds. They were still swirling halfway down the mountainside. He had expected them to drop off before he got close.

But he had no real idea what the norm was here. Yash had looked at the history of the planet, as recorded by the Fleet, and was startled to learn there were twelve seasons in this region. The skip was arriving in one of the crossover seasons—Late Fall to Early Winter. Yash said in some places she had lived, weather could become extreme in times of seasonal crossovers.

Although he wasn't sure that was what was causing the strong winds. He thought perhaps the problem was the fact that this was not a box canyon, like he usually landed in near a sector base. This canyon opened on one end to a large ocean.

His controls told him that the wind, whatever the reason for its strength, was coming off the water, hitting the valley with a lot of force, and then creating eddies at the very back of the valley, where the mountains closed in and formed a single range.

It had been years since he landed somewhere this tricky. He enjoyed the challenge of it.

"You want me to stabilize?" Yash asked quietly, her finger over some of the controls on her side of the console.

He shook his head, but didn't explain. He didn't have to, at least to Yash. This mission wasn't regulation from the start, and he saw no reason to make it regulation now.

Finally, in the last third of the descent, the winds abated—not because they were less strong at ground level, but because of those buildings that Stone had noticed. They were blocking the worst of it.

Coop used a controlled descent. The runners touched so gently that only the rocking motion of the skip made it clear that they had landed. He secured the skip, and then shut down.

He unhooked himself from the pilot's chair, stood, and faced his tiny crew.

"Welcome," he said, "to wherever the hell we are. Let's grab our gear and go."

"Captain," Bridge said, sounding a bit surprised. "No environmental suits? No briefing on conditions?"

Bridge was used to being on missions with Boss, who was inordinately cautious about new environments. She always made sure her people were ready for anything that was coming their way.

"You can suit up if you want," Coop said. "I think that's a waste of time. The conditions are not quite optimal, but they're the best we've encountered on a planet in a long time. The temperature differential between this skip and the outdoors is about fifteen degrees. The wind will be annoying. It'll gust strong enough to make you stagger, but for the most part, you should be all right. Expect some dust and debris in the air, but the oxygen mix is better here than anywhere else on Nindowne. That's mighty fresh air blowing in off the ocean, which is only a few miles from where we are. All right?"

It was all he could do to keep from adding a somewhat snide, *There. You've been briefed.*

He didn't believe in coddling teams. They should have looked up the conditions on their own. Clearly, Perkins and the security team had both done so. Perkins had slipped on a light blue regulation jacket, not for the temperature, but to carry whatever gear she was going to bring.

Coop wasn't going to bring gear, not on this first outing from the skip. He wanted to walk around, look at everything, and make some decisions first. All he had done—and he had done it before leaving the *Ivoire*—was make certain he wore heavy boots and had a pair of gloves tucked into the back pocket of his pants.

Yash stood beside him, grabbed her favorite utility belt—which he hadn't seen in years—and fastened it around her hips. Lots of tools there as well, but no tablets. She had a pair of gloves in one hand. She wore sturdy boots as well.

The security team headed to the exit. Even though Coop would have liked to go first, he knew that some regulations were worth following. The security team was in full uniform, with utility belts and light jackets filled with everything from small tools to weapons. The jackets also hid some of the weaponry that they carried mostly under their arms for easy access.

Bridge stood next, looking a little stunned at the speed with which everyone was leaving the skip. He glanced around as if he was trying to figure out what he needed to bring with him.

Stone grabbed her own jacket, tucked one of the tablets inside one side and another tablet in the other. Then she grabbed the bag she had used on every single planet Coop had worked with her on. She had a lot of gear, much of it for finding underground materials and measuring them. She also had some tools that could read chemical composition.

Yash had something simpler—a small wand she had designed to recognize nanobits in all stages of their existence. Coop had mentioned making wands for the entire group before they left, but Yash had shaken her head.

I don't share prototypes, she had said.

But Coop knew it was more than that: Yash suspected this group wouldn't understand all of the readings—and she was probably right. She wanted to see all of the nuances herself, and she wanted to see them in real time.

He didn't wait for Bridge or Stone to gather all of their possessions. He joined Perkins behind the security team. She gave him a tight smile. There were fine lines near her eyes now that hadn't been there when he promoted her long before they had come to this time period. Back then, she had been one of the young members of the bridge crew.

He was a bit startled to realize she wasn't that young anymore.

He smiled, feeling more relaxed than he probably should have. She nodded at him. She shoved her hands in the lower pockets of her jacket, and waited as the security team entered the airlock.

The most annoying part of this skip was that it had a narrow airlock that fit at most two people.

The airlock slid open on the interior. The security team was already outside of the skip. He glanced at Perkins. She smiled at him again, and this time, it was a true smile.

He let the excitement he felt at this mission show in his eyes. He had a hunch they twinkled as he stepped into the airlock.

The door closed behind him. He leaned against the far wall, uncomfortably close to Perkins. She stared straight ahead. He did as well.

They had a minute to wait, even though the atmosphere on this planet was just fine. The skip hadn't been modified to allow the crew to exit quickly, something he probably should have thought of.

He'd been thinking about too many other things—too many hypotheticals. And he'd also been avoiding one.

Had he only brought mostly *Ivoire* crew (and a requisite few others) because there was an ever so slight chance he could send his entire ship back to its own time period?

Would he do that?

He was surprised to feel himself wavering. Six years ago, he would have immediately acknowledged his willingness to return to his time. Now, he was less certain, and it wasn't, as Yash would say, because of Boss.

He was beginning to like the new future spreading before him. He was trained to move ever forward and he had probably moved as far forward as any captain of the Fleet ever had.

He just couldn't report back to the Fleet he knew—and that was the only part of his mission right now that felt really wrong.

The exterior door swished open. Chen and Lankstadt were already several paces away from the skip. They had not drawn any weapons, but one hand rested near their sides so that they could grab something easily. They were facing opposite directions, their backs only about a yard from each other.

The air smelled of brine and fish. Saltwater oceans had similar scents no matter what planet Coop visited. And the smell was stronger at first; it would recede as he got used to it.

A wind played with his hair like a distracted lover. The air was damp with a bit of mist. That same mist gave everything a slightly soft edge and made him feel as if he was viewing the world through sleep-filled eyes.

The breeze was cold. Gooseflesh ran up his arms, leaving him slightly chilled. He stepped away from the doors, walking—as per regulation—to the security team.

"Nothing, sir," Chen said, her voice soft. "We seem to be alone here at the moment."

He nodded his answer, but scanned the area himself. It wasn't as wild as he had expected. He'd seen several former sector base areas, and in each case, nature had reclaimed the area.

This part of Nindowne or Sandoveil or wherever they were hadn't really been reclaimed.

The old maps were correct so far, because the team was standing on an old road.

The ground was brown, the road dirt-covered, but not overgrown. Long grass or weeds or some kind of green plants grew on the far side of the road, but he couldn't tell if that was by design or if they truly had grown wild.

If he looked toward the mountain where Yash's readings had found the cave, he saw cracked pavement, but it wasn't broken by lack of use. If anything, the cracks looked fairly recent, as if they had happened during the normal ebb and flow of the weather.

Sunlight filtered through the mist, reflecting off it and making his eyes ache. He shielded his eyes with his hand, and turned slowly, taking everything in.

Mature trees grew to his right—the direction that led away from the ocean and toward the second area of mudflats. The mountains on all three sides were extremely imposing. It wouldn't take long for the light to disappear behind them, leaving this part of the valley in shadow.

He hadn't paid any attention to the time of day when he had brought the skip down here. He hadn't realized that they had arrived toward the end of daylight for this part of the planet.

289

That wasn't like him at all. He used to be meticulous about when a landing party would arrive on a planet. But he hadn't done any planet-bound work in years, and when he had gone to planets, he hadn't been in charge of the mission.

Boss had been.

He heard the door to the skip swish open again—or was it closed? He didn't look, choosing instead to continue his scan of the area.

The flat pavement continued all the way toward that overhang that Yash had found on her readouts. It looked like a Fleet-designed protective roof, the kind that kept locals from seeing an aboveground entrance to a sector base, just like he had expected.

But usually, the Fleet destroyed features like that when it closed the bases, leaving behind rubble or creating something else in its place—a façade of some kind that would discourage locals from exploring here.

He wanted to explore that pavement and the overhang, but he didn't let himself do that, not yet. He wanted to see what was around him.

So he turned toward his left, and started as he got a faceful of mist. The wind plastered his hair back. The mist felt like soft tiny cold pellets caressing his skin. Water dripped off his nose onto his lip, off his cheeks onto his chin, off his chin onto his clothing.

And that was when he realized his clothing was already drenched. He wasn't wearing the right gear. None of them were.

Yash stepped up beside him. He hadn't heard the skip's door swish open and closed, announcing her presence. He doubted that was because it hadn't been loud enough.

He had been very focused on what he was doing.

"I didn't expect rain," he said to Yash by way of apology.

She wiped a hand over her face. "If this place is anything like one of the seasides I grew up near, this will pass soon."

"The wind guarantees that," Stone said. She had joined them as well. She pointed up. "See the clouds? They're moving fast."

Flat gray clouds, separated by slashes of light, floated past so quickly that Coop couldn't really keep track of them all.

"You going back to get the right gear?" Yash asked.

Coop shook his head. "I'm already wet. Besides, I'm interested in that."

He pointed toward the overhang.

"The settlement is to our left," Stone said. "Some of the buildings there appear to have been repaired."

"We got readings that suggested people lived on this continent," Perkins said.

"Yes, but nothing that showed people in this area," Stone said. "I'm a little disconcerted by it. None of the buildings showed up on the *Ivoire's* sensors."

Coop looked at her. Water dripped off his eyelashes. He wiped his face again, only to have the mist coat him one more time.

He didn't like what Stone said. It set off a warning bell in his head.

"Perkins," he said, "see if you can get readings on those buildings right now."

She pulled one of the tablets from the inside of her jacket, pressed the screen, and scanned the area. Then she shook her head.

"Nothing," she said. "Just flat ground, ruins, and emptiness."

"How are you seeing this?" Coop asked Stone.

"I'm using Lost Souls equipment," she said. "Modified, of course, to our needs."

Of course, he thought but didn't say.

"Yash," he said, "see what you get."

She gave him an irritated glance. Apparently she hadn't wanted the others to know that she had the wand.

"My equipment won't work at great distances," she said, not pulling out the wand at all.

"Those buildings are intriguing, Captain," Bridge said. "I propose we split up, each group taking one person from the security team, and seeing what we can find."

And that was why Bridge didn't command anything.

"We're not separating," Coop said. "We'll investigate the buildings later. Worst case, they're cloaked somehow, and we'd be alerting someone to our presence."

"You don't think they already know?" Stone asked.

Coop had become used to the civilians asking questions like that over the years.

"No," he said. "We didn't encounter anything that suggested the air space around here was being monitored. We set off no alarms and didn't trigger any kind of energy spikes."

"That we know of," Bridge said, nodding toward Perkins' tablet as if it contained proof of his point of view.

"That's one thing we do look for in depth," Coop said. "We don't want to initiate an attack, especially when a ship is on its own the way we are."

He glanced at the overhang.

"We're sticking together, and we're going to look at that formation over there," he said.

He trudged forward without waiting for a single response. The wind continued but the mist suddenly stopped. He wiped the water off his face for the third time.

It took longer than he expected to traverse the pavement. The road was much farther from the overhang than it had initially appeared.

He walked alone for several minutes, moving faster than the rest of the team. They were probably measuring things and doing everything that Boss asked of them during a dive.

This wasn't a dive. This was an investigatory mission.

Ah, hell. Who was he kidding? This was a mission of discovery; he felt closer to the Fleet than he had for some time.

The air wasn't as clear as it had been on the road, even with the mist. The sun was setting over the mountains, and he had stepped into the growing shadow. But he could still see underneath that overhang. As he suspected, it covered more pavement, and this pavement wasn't broken up at all. He couldn't see any cracks.

Lankstadt caught up to him, then passed him, with Chen only a yard or so behind.

"Slow down," Coop said. "I'd prefer it if you don't get there first."

"But sir," Chen said, "procedure—"

"Screw procedure," he said, then realized how harsh that sounded. But he was suddenly feeling very harsh. If anyone else said the word *procedure* to him again on this part of the mission, he would send them back to the skip.

"Yes, sir, all right, sir." Her agitated tone told him it wasn't all right at all. But he didn't care. He was going to see what was here, and see it with his own eyes.

Because he had heard the caution in both Stone's and Bridge's voices when it came to those buildings. They weren't normal.

He wouldn't put it past the Fleet that had built the Boneyard to set up some kind of external monitoring system, something that allowed them to know when strangers came to the site of the former sector base.

Why they would do that, he had no idea, because the Fleet never used to care about its past. But he had to keep that option as a consideration.

Yash caught up to him and snapped on her gloves, silently rebuking him for not wearing his. He pulled his out of his back pocket and slid them over his hands.

The material caught on his damp skin, pulling it. He had to yank to get them on firmly. Then he turned on the knuckle lights so that he could see what was ahead.

By the time he and Yash reached the edge of the open pavement, the sun had completely disappeared. A ribbon of sunlight still illuminated the skip because it was in the center of this narrow valley, but Coop knew that last bit of light would disappear soon.

It was darker under the overhang than it was nearby. He actually couldn't see in the inky blackness, even with his glove lights trying to penetrate the gloom.

Yash had stopped walking. She caught his arm, holding him back. Then, with her other hand, she signaled the rest of the team to stop behind them.

They did.

Yash slipped the wand out of her jacket and shoved the edge forward. Coop doubted anyone behind them could see what, exactly, she was doing.

293

She ran her thumb up and down the wand's edge. Pale gray lights appeared, blinking like running lights. Then they vanished, and a small green light glowed at them.

"Nanobits," she said softly so that no one else could hear. "The overhang, and whatever's in front of us."

"Can you figure out age with that thing?" he asked, just as softly.

"Not exactly," she said. "Not without touching some of them, which I'm loathe to do at the moment."

He was too. He didn't want to touch anything until he knew whether or not it would alert someone.

"But I can tell you," she said, "that these nanobits are still bonded. And they're replicating and repairing, just like they're supposed to. The ones on the top are either older or subject to a lot more stress than whatever is underneath."

"When we were on the *Ivoire*," Coop said, "you said there was a cave here."

She nodded. "I don't have the equipment out that will do the same kind of reading. But I doubt we have a natural cave in front of us. And if you look at what's beneath that overhang, what does it make you think of?"

He peered, trying to imagine this as if he were a hiker just stumbling upon it.

"The opening to a really large cave," he said.

She nodded.

"Wouldn't that attract explorers?" he asked.

"It might," she said. "I'm not a land-based explorer kind of person."

"It would certainly attract Boss," he said with a wry smile. The woman might have been cautious when it came to arriving somewhere, but she loved venturing into the unknown.

"Speaking of," Yash said to him, "she would tell us to don environmental suits."

"Yes, she would," he said. "I don't plan to enter this just yet, especially in the dark with the occasional rain. But I would like to know what we're seeing."

He glanced over his shoulder. The security team was flanking him, but they were back just far enough so that they couldn't hear the conversation. They had also kept Perkins, Bridge, and Stone back, following protocol. Following procedure.

Coop smiled. *All right*, he conceded to himself. *Sometimes procedure still has its place.*

Especially when the two senior officers were making a decision they didn't want the others to know much about.

"Perkins, Stone," he said. "Use your different equipment and scan what's ahead of us. See what kind of readings you get."

They both acknowledged him and glanced at their tablets.

"I'm getting a cave opening," Perkins said, "and something in Standard, our version of Standard, that claims this is one of the most dangerous places on Nindowne and we shouldn't approach without a registered guide. That warning is now scrolling through two other languages I recognize. I'm seeing other languages as well, and I'm assuming they say the same thing."

"Fascinating," Yash muttered.

For a half second, Coop thought she was being sarcastic. He glanced at her. She was still staring at that opening. He doubted she even knew she had spoken aloud.

"I'm not getting that at all," Stone said. "My readings show a thin curtain, and then a wall of doors. There seem to be doors beyond that—or a room—or something. I can't tell."

Coop frowned, thinking about that for a moment. "We're using Fleet technology older than this sector base," he said. "Could that be the problem?"

"I don't think so," Yash said. "The languages say otherwise."

"What does that mean?" Bridge asked.

"This barrier is designed to keep Fleet personnel away, and all the locals," Yash said. "This might have been put here when the base closed down."

"It's in good shape for something that lasted centuries," Coop said.

"Yes, but good tech is designed for that." Yash took one step forward, a frown on her face as well.

"Lost Soul's tech isn't more sophisticated…" Perkins said, then stopped, probably not wanting to offend Stone or Bridge.

"Depends on how you define sophisticated," Yash said.

Coop knew how they all defined it. They meant sophisticated in comparison to Fleet technology. But that lack of sophistication might be a benefit here.

"The differences in the tech might be enough to let the Lost Souls tech 'see' what's here clearer," Bridge said. He did not sound defensive at all. Just matter of fact.

"Or we all might be getting false readings," Yash said. "We'll have to go forward to find out."

"Not like this," Coop said. "We need to get back to the skip and get the proper equipment this time."

"You want to explore tonight?" Yash asked.

He was torn about that. He normally would have had them wait until daybreak. But they hadn't planned on staying longer than a few hours, and the skip itself didn't have proper sleeping quarters for seven people. The skip did have enough food, though.

"We could come back tomorrow," Stone said.

Coop smiled, glad one of the civilians suggested that. "There is a possibility that this place is being guarded," he said. "I think we might have slipped past, but I doubt we can do it twice."

"So we're exploring tonight," Yash said, as if he had answered her question directly.

"Just far enough to see which of our readings is correct," Coop said.

"If either of them are," Yash said.

"That's right," Coop said. "If either of them are."

28

As YASH STEPPED INTO HER environmental suit inside the skip, she found herself wishing that Boss was leading this mission. That wish surprised Yash; clearly, she had come a long way in her relationship with Boss. At first, Yash hadn't liked her at all, but over time, if she had to describe the relationship, she would have called it a grudging respect.

Only since their adventure on the runabout in the Boneyard, Yash didn't think that respect was so grudging anymore. Particularly as she was wishing for Boss to be here for this mission.

This mission was akin to a dive, and much as Yash loved Coop, she didn't think he was as good a dive master as Boss was. He hadn't even had them bring the diving suits that Yash had designed for Lost Souls.

To be fair, Yash hadn't thought to bring any either. She had been focused on figuring out if the sector base was here. Given what they had found so far, she was convinced they were in the right place.

They had found where Sector Base E-2 had been; the question now was what condition was it in—and whether or not it had information to share with them.

The others were gearing up as well. Stone was staring at her environmental suit as if she had never worn one before—which, given this type of suit, was probably true. Bridge was flailing his arms slightly, turning around in slow half circles, trying to capture the arms and torso of the suit, unable to quite sort it out.

The security team already had their suits on, but not the hoods. Coop was tugging his gloves over his hands, suit already adhering to his tall, broad-shouldered form. Perkins had her suit on as well, without the hood. She was adding some equipment to her belt, including a laser pistol.

Yash's stomach twisted. She was a lot more nervous than she usually was. She had tried hard to keep her emotions out of this entire mission, but she now knew that was impossible.

She was excited to be here, excited that there was another base, excited that they had found *something*. She loved that there were nano-bits and signs that the Fleet had been here, no matter how long ago.

She was so thrilled that she was shaking.

And Boss would have blocked her from diving with this kind of physical reaction. If they were in the Boneyard. If they were in space.

They were not.

Still, Yash had to calm down. Because, oddly enough, she was the person here with the most exploration experience. Not *Fleet* exploration experience. Boss-trained experience.

Yash wasn't going to point that out to Coop, though. He believed his emotions were in check, but she knew from having been on a similar mission with him that they were not. He was going to charge his way through the next few hours, no matter what happened. If he saw something that intrigued him, he would go for it without a lot of thought to procedure.

She half smiled to herself. He would behave like she had done in the lab. Then her smile faded. Here, his behavior could cost him his life.

She tugged the suit up, made sure it sealed around her arms and legs. She slipped on the gloves she had worn earlier and placed the wand on the suit's belt. Normally, she would have left the hood down on a planet, but she was going to be the one in charge of this mission, and she needed to follow the rules.

Boss's rules.

"Coop," Yash said, "we need to stop for a minute."

He finished adjusting the gloves, then frowned at her. He was clearly not ready to stop anything.

"We don't know what's behind that blackness," she said.

"Yes," he said. "That's why we're going there."

"And because we don't know," she said, ignoring him, "we might get into some kind of trouble, and get into it rather quickly."

He paused, eyes hooded. He clearly knew she was right. He might argue with her after she finished, but she had his attention for the moment.

"We need to keep someone on this skip," she said, "monitoring our vitals just as if we were exploring in space."

Coop raised his chin slightly but didn't say anything.

"We also need to keep the skip on standby just in case we need to leave quickly. We can't ignore the fact that we're finding evidence of others nearby." Yash didn't want to say anything more than that because she didn't want to alarm the civilians. But she didn't like the fact that some of the cloaking they had found was deliberately aimed at Fleet personnel.

It also bothered her that some of that cloaking had actually worked with their Fleet equipment—which should have been considered ancient by Sector Base E-2 standards, not counting the standards of this current time.

Coop sighed ever so slightly. Yash doubted the others even saw it. Then he nodded just once.

"Lankstadt," Coop said, voice sharp. "Can you pilot?"

"Yes, sir," Lankstadt said. "Both of us can."

Yash almost smiled. She recognized Lankstadt's attempt at manipulation. He didn't want to stay on board any more than she did.

"Good," Coop said. "You will take the first shift in the skip."

The first shift? Yash almost said something, then decided against it. She would argue with Coop later if need be. But this was a good start.

"The rest of us will see what we can find in that dark area," he said. "We'll run on a timer. Yash—forty-five minutes, you think?"

That was longer than any space dive she had gone on, but they weren't in space.

"Sounds good," she said.

"Then we'll return here and compare notes. We'll decide if we need to go farther, or if we need to go back for more equipment and personnel." Coop's gaze met Yash's. His eyes were twinkling.

She hadn't expected that.

"Think Boss will approve?" he asked, letting Yash know he knew exactly what she had been up to.

"No," Yash said. "She would want tethers, even though we're on land."

"I'm not tethering to the skip," Coop said.

"Which is why I didn't even suggest it," Yash said. Besides, she thought tethers on land would be cumbersome.

"Sometimes tethering going into the unknown is a good idea," Bridge said. He had finally grabbed the back of his suit and pulled it up where it belonged.

"If we don't like what we find at the edge of that dark area," Coop said, "we might tether on the next trip."

He was making it clear that they wouldn't follow anything other than Fleet procedure this time. Keeping one person back at the skip was a slight variation, but not a great one. Generally, a small team stayed behind when there was a possible threat.

He grabbed the last of his gear, then walked into the airlock alone. Yash had changed the settings so that they didn't have to go through the entire airlock procedure to get out of the skip. Coop didn't have to wait for the interior doors to close. He stepped outside without waiting for anyone else.

Yash wanted to hurry, to follow him, but she made herself remain methodical, checking every last bit of her suit and her equipment. She too added a laser pistol to her belt.

She was on edge here, and she wasn't quite sure why. Too many unexplained aspects to this place. Besides, Chen and Perkins would need backup if something went horribly wrong.

She went through the airlock and exit, gripping the side of the door with her right glove as she stepped down to the ground.

Coop was standing near the skip, his hands clasped behind his back. He was staring across that vast stretch of pavement.

Twilight had fallen everywhere in this part of the valley. The darkness wasn't absolute—it had a grayish brightness to it because the sun was still up on the other side of the mountains, and some of that light was still filtering into this area.

But the growing dark made it impossible to see the overhang and the possible cave opening from the skip. Yash's heart rate increased. Sometimes, her upbringing on land did not serve her well. There was nothing wrong with darkness.

Every dive she had done in space had been done in darkness.

But this wasn't space. The wind fingered her cheeks, messing her short hair. At least the mist had stopped. But the air had gotten decidedly colder.

Coop hadn't turned on any of his suit's lights. She didn't turn on hers either as she approached him.

Behind her, she heard faint conversation as the others left the skip.

"I'm thinking of having Stone and Bridge continue their work out here," he said.

"No," she said. "We need their eyes on that interior."

"Interior?" he said. "You're thinking it is the base, then?"

"Yes," she said. "And so are you. That's why you don't want tethers."

He tilted his head to one side. "No unusual *anacapa* drive readings here. I checked."

She had too, several times. Once from the *Ivoire*, figuring if they found unusual *anacapa* drive readings, they would know without landing that the sector base was below. They would also know that it was dangerous.

Then she had checked again as they were orbiting in the skip. And one final time as they had landed.

Nothing here, in the exterior of the potential base. But that didn't mean that the base's *anacapa* drives weren't malfunctioning below. The nanobit coatings she had found here were intact and continuing to repair themselves. They would keep any problematic energy spikes from reaching outside.

In theory.

"You and I are going in first," Coop said.

"I know." Yash wasn't going to argue with him. She had no reason to argue with him. She wanted to be the first one past that curtain. She wanted to see what was ahead.

The other team members joined them.

"Perkins," Coop said, "you and Chen are behind me and Yash. Stone and Bridge, the four of us are going to go in first. The two of you will monitor the readings with your equipment, since yours seems to be more accurate than ours."

If, of course, this was a real sector base. Otherwise the readings that the *Ivoire*'s equipment had would be the accurate one.

But Yash didn't say anything and neither did anyone else.

"I want hoods up," Coop said. "I want everyone to record everything. And as the group is moving, I don't want any member of this group monitoring equipment. We need our eyes. Let the suits tell us if something is awry. Is that clear?"

Everyone answered in the affirmative.

"All right," Coop said. "Lankstadt, do you have all of us?"

"Yes, sir. Visual, telemetry, and vitals. I will monitor the area as well." He sounded cool and professional. Yash hadn't trained him, though, so she had no idea how competent he was.

She hated having to trust someone she didn't know well.

"Ready?" Coop asked her softly.

"Ready," she said and started forward.

29

COOP HAD CHOSEN AN environmental suit with a clear hood all the way around. The very top of the hood had a light that he could control, so that it would illuminate anything he wanted it to all the way around. Right now, in deference to the rest of his team, he only had lights on facing forward.

He had also turned on the knuckle lights on his gloves and the lights all around his boots.

They illuminated the pavement. It was finely cracked, just like it looked, and incredibly smooth. He'd seen pavement like this before at Sector Base T shortly after it closed. The ship he had served on at the time was doing a post-closure inspection decades after the last worker had left the base.

The design of that base had been similar to what he suspected was the design for E-2. If, he had to remind himself, this actually was Sector Base E-2.

The hood blocked the wind and the distinctive odor of this region. His nose hadn't yet become used to that smell of brine and fish, but he found that he missed it. The smell had made it very clear where he was.

He was remarkably calm. He had thought he would be excited about seeing what they would discover. But he was focused now on the task at hand, focused in a way that felt familiar. He hadn't felt like this in a long time.

He glanced at Yash. Her hood was clear only on three sides. The back was covered. Her hood light was a focused beam that shut off whenever she faced someone, for which he was very grateful. Her hands and arms were lit up, as were her lower legs and boots.

Apparently, she wanted to see all of this.

The lights grew brighter as Chen and Perkins turned on their hood lights, then Stone and Bridge. Or at least, that was the order he figured they had turned on their equipment in. He wasn't going to double-check.

Even though Bridge had dived with Boss, he was inexperienced, at least as far as Coop was concerned. Stone was her own woman, never really hitting the level of professionalism that the Fleet aspired to—at least not on matters like entering an unknown area.

Coop wasn't going to babysit either of them. If something happened, he would let Perkins and Chen deal with it. Coop was going to focus on what he saw ahead of him, and nothing else.

The pavement was vast and went on farther than he had expected. The twilight had provided some kind of optical illusion, making the entire area seem truncated.

It wasn't. And as they got closer to the overhang and possible cave opening, the cracks in the pavement grew. Wind blew across it all, carrying leaves, dirt, scraps of cloth and what appeared to be paper. He didn't touch any of it.

Instead he focused on the spindly green plants growing out of the cracks. So the pavement near the old road was still in use, but the pavement here wasn't.

He held up his hand, stopping everyone, and then stopped himself. He had to take Yash by the arm. She hadn't seen him stop.

"Note the plants?" he asked, pointing at the spindly green things. "They weren't near the road. Let's find an area of this pavement where the cracks aren't as bad, shall we?"

Yash nodded. She understood. Coop half braced himself for a question from the civilians, but none came. Instead, all six members of the team pivoted, their backs to each other, and raked areas of the pavement with the strongest beams off their gloves.

Coop had moved somewhat kitty-corner to where he had been before. The cracks looked just as vast in the segment he was examining as they were where he was standing.

"Over here," Chen said. She was perpendicular to him, the light from her gloves pointing at the narrowing valley and the mudflats beyond.

Coop turned his gloves in that direction, adding to the light she had trained on the area. In the brightness, the pavement looked almost brown, like the road, not like the gray behind them.

That was odd in and of itself.

Yash had turned and so had Perkins. Coop couldn't see Stone or Bridge and he didn't really care what they were doing.

"See?" Chen said. "No weeds or whatever those are poking out of the pavement. And I'm not even sure that's pavement."

Coop trained his light along the brown area. It was clearly manufactured, but it lacked the smoothness of something made from nanobits. The brown material had bubbles and imperfections, as if someone had sprayed it over the ground and left the brown stuff to dry. It was uneven and looked a little unstable.

It hugged some kind of barrier wall that appeared to have been built out of nanobits. That barrier wall was black and absorbed the light, just like nanobits did.

He didn't ask Yash to take out her wand. If the barrier wall became relevant, he would have her examine it then.

He followed the brown area with his light. Keeping track of the brown material was easy because it covered part of the ground, creating a small lip. The brown led all the way to the edge of that overhang, precisely the place where it seemed attached to the side of the mountain.

"We'll walk over there." He marched toward the brown area, not waiting for the others to gather themselves or come with him.

For a moment, his shadow, long and skinny, extended almost to the brown area as the others kept their lights pointed in that direction. Then they toned down the beams and followed him, and his shadow became human-sized again.

The wind whistled around him. He had his hood set up for internal communications, but he had left the external microphones on as well so he could hear everything around them. The wind, gusting, was providing its own distraction.

He had no idea how anyone lived in actual weather. It was difficult at best, annoying at times like these. And his suit was registering small handfuls of sand pelting into him, as well as a drop in temperature.

The suit warned him that a storm was coming. He wasn't sure what to do with that information: he was in an environmental suit and it could handle severe weather, as could his gloves and his boots. They were made to create their own artificial gravity, so not even the wind should bother him too much.

He reached the edge of that brown area. His hunch had been right: it was made of the same material as the road. Although he had initially thought the road was old, he was reconsidering that assumption. Because the wind wasn't disturbing the surface of the brown area at all.

It was made to look old and carved out of the ground by usage, but it wasn't carved out of the ground. The road had been layered over the surface, just like the pavement had been long ago.

"Want me to see what that's made out of?" Yash asked him quietly. He realized suddenly that she had opened up a channel just for the two of them.

"Sure," he said. Better to be safe, after all.

She pulled out the wand, crouched, and extended it over the brown area without touching it.

Night had fallen completely, and that bit of gray that had come with twilight was completely gone. When she crouched like that, moving all the beams of light she controlled downward, the area around Coop had become completely dark.

That too suggested nanobits to him—not on the brown patch, but the barrier wall, the side of the mountain, and even the overhang— although it was still some distance from him.

Yash stood. "I don't recognize the materials. They're not naturally occurring, though. They're manufactured, somehow. I can take a sample, if you want."

"Are they safe to walk on?" he asked.

She shrugged. "I can't tell you without examining it all closely, but I can say on first glance that I'm not seeing anything dangerous."

He was about to walk on the brown area, then he paused. It might signal whoever had put it there.

Of course, if that was the case, then the skip itself had done the same thing when it landed. Not to mention the lights on their gloves.

He turned, and shined one of the beams toward the overhang and darkness beyond. As the light got closer to the overhang itself, the brown area spread out, covering three times the distance it had up here. He scanned as far as he could toward the edge of the overhang on the ocean side, and thought he saw brown going all the way.

Someone had deliberately placed this here, for what reason he could only guess.

"You think the Fleet manufactured it?" he asked Yash.

"Possible, I suppose," she said. "But why? Nanobits would coat the surface quickly and would replicate themselves easily. There's no reason to make them turn that shade of brown that I can see on first glance."

She was still using the personal channel, as was he. The others were just standing near them, waiting to see what Coop would decide.

He took a deep breath and braced himself. He was here to explore, so that was what he was going to do. He was going to have to walk on that brown stuff no matter what.

So he stepped on it now, half expecting some kind of reaction around his boots.

Nothing happened. He didn't even make footprints in the surface, given how wet everything was.

Yash stepped beside him. He assumed the others would do so too, but he didn't tell them to.

Instead, he followed the barrier wall, the farthest edge of the brown patch.

"That wall's made of nanobits, right?" he asked Yash through their channel.

She used the wand again. "Yeah. Really old too. Some of the bonding is starting to decay. I can see why. This environment is harsh. Salt, strong winds, and bad weather. You saw that a storm is coming."

"Yeah," he said. "I'm not sure what that means for us."

"We'll find out." She trudged beside him. He turned slightly, double-checking to see if his feet really weren't leaving an impression on the surface. They weren't, and neither were anyone else's.

The entire crew was walking with him. Stone was staggering a bit whenever a gust of wind hit her. She apparently didn't know how to use the microgravity in her boots to steady herself.

"You want to explain to Stone how to keep upright?" he asked Yash.

"Not particularly," she said, but then there was a slight hiss as she flicked over to the group channel and explained the procedure to Stone, who thanked her.

The barrier wall rose higher the closer the team got to the mountain itself. He recognized the design: it really did look like a similar design to Sector Base T. In that design, the rising wall would merge with the mountain. The architects would have built a false mountain's edge so that the locals wouldn't know that the Fleet had commandeered some space aboveground. No one would have cause to come this close.

Coop held up his hand and stopped everyone again, then peered at that overhang. Its edges were too rounded to be natural. It probably wasn't part of the mountain that the Fleet coated in nanobits. Unless he missed his guess, the overhang was made entirely of nanobits.

Underneath the overhang, the darkness looked impenetrable. As he got closer, that darkness should have receded some, or some natural formations should have shown up. But they hadn't.

So this was all manufactured, just as he and Yash surmised.

The barrier wall on his right was almost as tall as he was. A broad expanse of pavement extended to his left, but at the very edge of that, he thought he saw another barrier wall.

In most Sector bases, walls like these shut down outside communication equipment.

"Lankstadt," he said on the group channel. "You still able to monitor us?"

"Yes," he said. "Everything is clear."

Which meant there were three possibilities: the walls no longer had that function, the walls never had that function, or the walls recognized the Fleet-based equipment and let it continue to function.

Coop glanced at Yash, who shrugged one shoulder. She wasn't going to comment on anything until she saw more.

Neither was he.

They walked the remaining distance. The wall narrowed in on them and got even taller. The smooth edges didn't replicate the natural edges of a mountainside. Instead they sort of vanished into a general darkness.

The area underneath the overhang remained dark as well, absorbing the light.

Yash double-checked her readings and nodded at him. Without saying so, she let him know that they faced more nanobits.

"Captain," Perkins said softly on a third channel. "I've moved the screen from my tablet to my hood. I'm getting a lot of warnings here, in a variety of languages, just like we got on that road. They're getting more and more dire the closer we're getting."

Coop called up an outside communications channel on his hood—designed to see exterior warnings.

The clear panel was suddenly covered with red marks, flashing red words, and a large circle with a line through it, signifying *stop*.

"Wow," Yash said beside him. Apparently Perkins had included her on that channel as well.

"I know," Perkins said. "We're really being warned away."

Coop powered that channel down, so he didn't see it anymore. "And yet we're not," he said. "Because those warnings should be broadcast to everyone, no matter what their technology."

"This is Fleet-directed again," Perkins said. "What the hell?"

She usually didn't curse. Coop agreed with the comment, though. Why would a former Fleet base warn away any members of the Fleet and no one else?

"Is anyone else getting readings that make this area dangerous?" Coop asked on the group channel. "Are we missing something?"

"I'm not reading anything out of the ordinary," Lankstadt said, "but I am using Fleet technology."

"We're not," Stone said from behind Coop. "Bridge and I see nothing out of the ordinary."

Coop didn't like the fact that someone was trying to keep the Fleet away—or had tried to keep the Fleet away—but he didn't feel alarmed by it either. If someone had taken over this base, then of course they would want to keep the Fleet away from it.

"The only thing that bothers me," Yash said, "is the area we're heading to. All of the nanobits around here are too smooth. That overhang is too obvious. That opening is clearly the opening into something else. If they had followed protocol—*our* protocol, granted—they should have demolished this opening. It should have rockfalls or something."

Coop made a small sound of agreement in the back of his throat. She was right. The fact that no one had done that was as unusual as the fact that a city that used to surround a sector base had become a ghost town. Usually cities around sector bases grew. Only in areas that had not really had much of a community around them in the first place did the community vanish centuries after the Fleet left.

"We can't make assumptions about procedure anymore," Coop said, "much as we want to. The Fleet might have changed the way they closed sector bases."

"Yeah." Yash didn't sound convinced. "Okay."

Coop started forward again. The darkness ahead seemed profound. He didn't call up the readings or any telemetry, since his suit was Fleet technology—modified, of course, but still Fleet-based.

The wind had grown even stronger. It eddied near the wall. Then rain started, big fat drops at first, followed by a complete downpour. Water started to puddle, getting inches deep in a matter of seconds. It didn't drain into the brown path like it would have in the pavement cracks.

Coop was going to comment on that when ice chunks started falling out of the sky.

Yash cursed.

"What is that?" Perkins sounded panicked for the first time in Coop's memory.

"Hail," Yash said.

The ice chunks were the size of small peas. They hurt when they hit.

Either the team had to go forward—quicker than they were—and hope there was shelter under that overhang, or they had to head back.

Bridge swore, and someone cried out in pain.

"Stay in this too long," Yash said, "and our suits'll be compromised. They're not made to stand up to this kind of barrage."

Coop made his decision. He loped toward the overhang, hoping that it would protect them.

The team followed. They arrived in seconds and managed to get underneath that overhang just as the hail pellets got smaller and more numerous. Coop's microphone caught the sound of the pellets hitting the ground. The repeated rat-a-tat-tats were violent, almost as violent as the blows from the pellets themselves.

He shook some of the water off his suit, then looked out into the area the team had just come from. The hail was white in his lights. A long patch of bumpy whiteness that appeared both slick and treacherous.

"This is normal?" Perkins asked. Coop couldn't tell if she was asking it of everyone, or just as a rhetorical question. He certainly didn't know the answer.

"I don't know about here," Yash said, "but it's normal in a lot of places. I lived in areas that got hail at least once a year."

"No wonder we had warning about the storm," Bridge said quietly. As if to punctuate his sentence, light split the sky, followed a few seconds later by a loud bang.

311

"Thunder," Yash said, as if they didn't know what that was. And maybe a few of them didn't. Coop had experienced thunderstorms before, although he'd only seen lightning once before this.

Hail, though, that was something else entirely.

It continued, so he turned his back on it. Since they couldn't leave right away, they might as well explore where they were.

"Let's examine this overhang," he said to the team, "and whatever this is in front of me."

Because he truly didn't know. The light from his headlamp kept vanishing into what appeared to be a curtain, at least to the visor on his hood. But information in that visor was processed through Fleet technology, so he didn't entirely trust it.

"There is a curtain," Perkins said, "and faint readings of doors beyond. I'm having trouble getting a fix on anything, though. These warnings are extreme."

"I'm not getting any warnings." Stone moved to Coop's side, holding her tablet so that he could see what she saw. "And while I see a curtain, I don't see doors. I see a sturdy barrier beyond, and I don't like some of the readings coming off it."

Yash leaned closer, then took the tablet from Stone's hand. Yash scrolled through, moved the tablet to different areas, then handed it back.

"Make it a holomap, would you?" Yash asked. "One we can all see. And superimpose it over this opening."

Stone gave her a sideways glance. Coop couldn't see Stone's expression from where he stood, but he had a hunch he knew what she was feeling.

Stone didn't like taking orders. She never had.

Still, she had learned to overcome that on the handful of trips she had taken with Fleet personnel.

She tapped the tablet, and a holomap appeared in front of the curtain. The map was part science, part guess since they didn't have any information except what their sensors were providing.

The map showed a solid block of something, like a heavy wall or door, beyond the curtain. There weren't even ghostly doors or outlines of doors, just a solid surface, which the holomap projected as brown, just like the ground.

"Perkins," Yash said, "add a holomap of what you're seeing—without the warnings, if possible. Don't let the map show color. Just white."

Perkins stepped next to Coop, holding up her tablet. He could see the image to his side, lots of blaring red like he had seen earlier.

She tapped the tablet, and the red vanished. Then her holomap merged with Stone's.

The white layer showed the same curtain as Stone's. Nothing had changed because of that. But the doors Perkins showed were several yards behind the barrier that had shown up on Stone's holomap.

"Are the Fleet maps using the sector base's actual layout?" Coop asked.

"Possible," Yash said. "But I don't think this is a real map of what the sensors are picking up. I think it's a spoofed map."

"It's what Fleet personnel would expect if they showed up," Perkins added.

"I don't like this," Stone said. "The warnings strike me as real, kind of like, keep away or get hurt."

"But the hurt being promised is a decay and dangerous hurt, not something from this wall," Perkins said.

Coop looked at it all—the curtain, the image of the wall behind it, the doors beyond.

"Can you show me what's past those doors?" he asked Perkins.

"It's a projection," Yash said.

"Based on the schematics, you said." He continued to wait for Perkins, who wasn't moving yet.

"I said that was possible," Yash said. "I didn't say it was accurate."

"Let's see the possibilities, then," he said. "Kjersti?"

He spoke gently, and didn't use Perkins designation, trying to get her to work with him. Not that she usually had troubles. He was just being cautious.

Or maybe he was shedding Captain Cooper as bits of a plan formed in the back of his mind.

Perkins tapped her screen, then more white appeared, showing a large cavern, even more doors, and the faint outlines of corridors that led deep into the mountain.

There were also small rectangles and signs and tiny squares. It took Coop a moment to process that. Those were symbols for desks and chairs and the locations of various departments.

He had been right: these were schematics.

"Son of a bitch," Chen said. "They're projecting the map of this place, using the plans. Why would they do that?"

Coop jumped at the sound of her voice. He hadn't expected a member of the security team to speak up. Normally, they wouldn't speak at all. But he was the one who was changing the rules; no reason why they couldn't, too.

The hail continued to pelt, creating a rustling noise that constantly had him check the pavement behind them. The sound made him uneasy; he wasn't used to constant noise caused by something unpredictable. Usually noises like that had a mechanical source—at least in his world—not one that came from the elements.

"I don't think they expected anyone from the Fleet to examine this stuff closely," Yash said. "I think they were showing what we'd expect to see, and then the warnings, hoping we'd stay away."

"Make sure you get as much of those readings as possible," Coop said to Perkins. "That's probably as close to the specs as we'll find, at least right now."

She nodded and continued to tap her tablet. No more extra places showed up on the white version of the holomap. It faded as it went deeper and deeper into the mountainside.

But Yash's speculation didn't answer Chen's question. Why would anyone do that? A basic misunderstanding of the Fleet? Or something else?

Because anyone from the Fleet who needed to be here would try to see what was causing the warnings, and maybe try to repair that.

"You said there were things you didn't like in the readings about that barrier." Coop turned toward Stone. She was leaning slightly, peering at Perkins' tablet.

Stone glanced back at her own, then shoved it toward him. He took it, even though he didn't want it. He didn't look down at it either. He wanted her to tell him.

"That wall is alive," she said. "Not in an organic way. But tiny energy spikes rise off it. I think it might be the source of the transmission going to the Fleet technology."

"That's logical," Yash said.

"But I don't like the spikes," Stone said. "I don't know how to read them."

Yash took the tablet from Coop, and dug into it just a little. "Stupid outdated tech," Yash muttered, which he found amusing because that tech she disliked was younger than she was by centuries.

But he knew what she meant. She meant that the tech wasn't as sophisticated as the Fleet tech, which was actually what this team needed right now.

"Yeah," Yash said. "That barrier is active."

"Is it gathering information and transmitting it?" Coop asked.

"No," Yash said. "Not that I can tell. That doesn't mean it isn't. But it seems to be more concerned with preventing entry than it does with communicating that someone is nearby."

Coop frowned. "That barrier is made of the same material as the ground we're standing on."

"In theory," Yash said. "I'd need an actual sample to compare."

"And we didn't register any energy spikes off this ground cover," Coop said.

"But it's wet, not shielded," Bridge said.

With Fleet tech that would make no difference. But whatever they were standing on wasn't Fleet tech. And it had been subjected to weather like that hail behind them, over and over again.

The sound was easing. Coop glanced behind him. Right now, every part of the pavement exposed to the weather was covered in inches of white pellets. His suit registered the air around him as significantly colder than it had been when the hail started.

Thunder cracked again. This time Perkins jumped.

"I am not fond of that," she said.

Coop smiled. He didn't like it much either, but they wouldn't be near it long.

They were standing on the same brown material, in theory anyway. But they stood just barely underneath that overhang. The material they were standing on was subject to the same weather conditions as the material they had walked across.

But if they took a few steps closer to that curtain, the weather would probably cease to be a factor.

He took Stone's tablet from Yash, then pointed it downward. Out of the corner of his eye, he saw the holomap shift, then adjust itself.

The energy readings were similar to the readings on that wall behind the curtain. So if his team had taken a few more steps forward…something would have happened, but he didn't know what.

He handed the tablet back to Yash, not to Stone, even though Stone reached for it. Then he pushed back his hood and peeled off his gloves. He handed them to Yash as well.

"What are you doing?" she asked.

He opened his environmental suit and struggled out of it. A blast of ice-cold air hit him. The wind was whipping around in this protected area, like it had done near that wall. The air was damp, but that briny smell was gone.

Instead, the air smelled frigid and wet.

He stepped out of the suit, leaving it in a pile on the ground.

"What are you doing?" Yash asked again. Only this time, he couldn't hear her. He could only see her lips move through her hood.

He held up one finger—one cold finger—and stepped over his suit. He hadn't quite reached the curtain yet, but he was nearly there.

His heart was pounding, feeling how contrary all of this was to his training, and fighting that as well as the displeasure he could feel coming from the entire team.

He extended that hand, and touched the curtain, half expecting to get zapped with some kind of energy.

The holomaps wobbled, sending rings outward, as if he had stuck his hand in a bowl of water. But he hadn't. And he couldn't feel anything. Which meant that the curtain barrier was made of energy or was an illusion, not something real.

He stepped through the curtain, half expecting to feel some kind of surge.

He didn't. He felt nothing.

His boots touched the ground behind the curtain, and again, nothing happened.

Yash started to follow him, but he held out a hand, keeping her back. He shook his head.

"All of you, stay away," he said, hoping someone had their outside microphones on like he had.

Then he turned.

There was a wall here. It was brown. But glitter ran through it. Silver lines that looked like some kind of power source.

He couldn't be certain of that, but he knew he wasn't going to touch those.

Instead, he scanned the wall in front of him, then looked to his right, where this wall met the barrier wall.

There he saw, at his eye level, a slight depression that seemed a bit long.

He walked over to that. It was flat and had no silver lines on its surface. But the silver lines seemed to originate from it.

Unless he missed his guess, this was the control panel.

The wind blew even colder. His fingers were blocks of ice. The dampness in the air had become mist again, and because the air was so much colder, the mist had become colder too, adding to his chill.

He ran his almost-numb fingertips over the smooth surface of that depression. It was warmer than the air, and he almost wanted to lean into that entire wall just to warm up.

Nothing happened when he touched it. He didn't get hurt or feel a shock of energy. And nothing opened or closed or sent out warning signals.

He had moved away from the holomaps, so he wasn't seeing those anymore. And his team had followed orders. They hadn't come with him.

He didn't look at them, not wanting to see their distress.

Instead, he clenched his hand into a fist, rather surprised at how difficult it was. His hand was moving slower because of the cold. He pressed the side of his fist against that depression, and it popped open, revealing more silver lines and bright silver controls.

They were labeled in Standard. *His* version of Standard. And they were laid out like the Fleet would have laid out controls in his time.

That stopped him for a moment, wondering if it was another Fleet-based trap. Then he made himself read.

One of the controls—in theory—shut off the energy to the barrier. Another raised it up. But one was marked *reveal doors*. That was the one he touched.

Every six feet or so, doors appeared in the barrier wall. Doors with actual handles, also silver, so that they could be opened from the outside. One appeared in the very small space to his right.

He stepped over to it, his heart still pounding. Then he put his hand on the silver—again, expecting some kind of zap, and again, not receiving one. The door creaked open, and musty warm air, dry as dust, cascaded over him.

He had a choice now. He could go inside alone, without lights or equipment, or he could see if he could get Fleet equipment past this wall.

He walked back to Yash. She still clutched his gloves, but she also held the tablet tightly, peering over it as he walked.

She opened her mouth as if she was about to say something, but he couldn't hear her, and he really didn't care to hear any admonitions anyway. He pulled the gloves out of her hand as she shook her head.

Maybe she understood what he had done—he had taken off all of the equipment that had any taint of the Fleet. His clothing had come from Lost Souls, and his boots weren't Fleet-issue or Fleet design either.

But the gloves, they were Fleet design and Fleet issue. The *Ivoire* had had so many duplicates they still weren't used up.

"Thanks," he said, even though he suspected she couldn't hear him. He tugged the gloves on. The gloves warmed his hands immediately, which warmed him just a little. Then he walked back to that opening, his nerves jumping.

He half expected someone on his team—Chen, maybe—to grab him, trying to stop him. But no one did.

One benefit of being captain, he supposed, even if everyone thought what he was doing was crazy.

He paused near that opening in the wall. Yash was staring straight at him, her eyes barely visible inside her hood. But they were visible enough, and they were wide.

He glanced over his shoulder at the team. They were all watching him intently.

Then he stepped in front of the opening and shoved his hands through it.

30

COOP HALF EXPECTED TO FEEL extreme pain as he shoved his hands into that darkness. He thought maybe some kind of laser weapon or something would bite into his skin, repelling the invader (him) with some kind of force.

Instead, the light illuminated doors at exactly the places where Perkins' holomap had showed they would be. The walls near the door had a black surface that absorbed the light.

Nanobits, and they looked to be in fine shape.

The doors were clearly part of an entrance. Two doors, then a black wall, then two more doors, then a black wall, heading to his left. He turned his left arm's lights in that direction, but couldn't see the end of that parade of doors.

Nor could he see behind them.

So he trained the light up. The black overhang (nanobits) absorbed the light, reflecting nothing except where there were panels for exterior light. There he saw some kind of clear reflector that ran the length of the ceiling.

It all looked Fleet made.

He brought the lights down, examining the ground. The brown stuff formed a path about three feet wide behind the wall. It also provided a path before him that led to the door as far to the left as the doors went.

He let out one of those vapor-filled breaths, feeling a bit creeped out by the way that the vapor looked ghostly in the thin light.

Either he could step in and see what was going on, or he could step out and gather the team.

He had no weapons, no way to communicate, no tether (*thank you, Boss*, he thought with a smile). Going in would be foolish, even for him, even at this moment. No matter how much he wanted to see what was before him.

Disappointment filled him. He had the odd sense that he might not be able to see anything if he stepped back now.

But he might not survive if he didn't.

Nothing had attacked him or his gloves, so he could put the environmental suit back on, with all of its safety equipment.

He owed the team that much.

He squared his shoulders, then stepped back, shutting off his glove lights as he did.

He mimed pulling off the hood to Yash. She did with her free hand. So did Perkins. Chen, to her credit, did not. Stone and Bridge watched, waiting, most likely, for instructions.

"Did your readings change as I touched that wall?" he asked.

"Not then," she said. "When you put on the gloves, though. Everything sparked. Just a tiny release of energy, but I caught it."

"Meaning what?" he asked.

"I don't know," she said. "This technology looks familiar, but it isn't. I could guess."

"Guess," he said.

"Something was alerted, something local. There was no great big transmission that I saw, more like a silent alarm."

He nodded once. "Yeah," he said. "I've been worried about that. I think we only get one shot at this, and that shot is right now."

Her lips thinned. He couldn't tell what she was trying not to say. So he added a piece of information she might not know.

"The control panel is written in Standard," he said. "Our version of Standard."

Her frown grew deeper. "You think that the Fleet set this up before they shut down the sector base?"

"I think it would be odd if they did," he said. "Especially with all of the warnings against the Fleet itself. And this brown coating isn't uniform. It looks like it was made of some material that wanted to be nanobits but couldn't quite achieve it."

She bit her lower lip and looked down. He recognized her expression. It meant that she was intrigued. She wanted to investigate more.

"If Boss were running this as a dive," Yash said, "she would have us go back to the skip now, even though we're not done."

She sounded hesitant. He tried not to smile. He knew Yash well enough to know that she was suggesting the sensible thing while hoping he wouldn't be sensible.

"Boss isn't here," he said, "and this isn't a dive."

Yash didn't move, which he found a bit odd. Normally, she would have agreed with him, and they would have jumped right into the rest of the mission.

"I think we only have one shot at this," he said.

Yash's lips thinned. Then she looked pointedly at Stone and Bridge.

He got the message. Yash thought what they were about to do was too dangerous for the civilians.

He agreed.

"Stone, Bridge," he said. "Do you two think you can make it back to the skip without us?"

"I'd like to go in there," Bridge said. Coop noted that Stone didn't speak up at all, and that was unusual. She always spoke up when she felt she needed to do something.

"We'll take good readings," Coop said, "and with luck, we'll be able to go back in. But in case we can't—"

"We're not experienced enough to join you." The way Stone spoke, it wasn't a question.

"Boss trained us. Well, me," Bridge said. "I've gone on dives."

"Yes, I know." Coop tried not to sound curt, but he was feeling the time pressure. "I need a team who understands all of my commands. Even the unspoken ones."

Bridge sighed. His breath made that same white vapor. Coop found it so strange. The white vapor floated around everyone, just a bit, but enough to be disconcerting.

"All right," Bridge said. "I'd like to take some samples of this brown stuff, though."

"From here," Coop said. "Not from behind the curtain." Which was where it was active—or so he thought.

Bridge started to protest, but then seemed to think the better of it. He nodded once, and put a hand on Stone's arm. "Be careful on the way back to the skip," he said to her. "I suspect it'll be slippery crossing that pavement."

"Yes, it will be," she said curtly. Then she turned to Coop. "You'll keep my tablet."

Again, that wasn't a question.

"Thank you," he said, as if he hadn't had that idea all along.

Bridge and Stone started across the pavement.

"Yash," Coop said, "let Lankstadt know they're coming. And make sure he's watching the entire area. I suspect we'll have company soon enough."

Yash put up her hood and sealed it. Then she spoke, but Coop couldn't hear.

He grabbed his own suit and slipped it back on, making certain that all the seals were tight. The suit warmed him. He hadn't realized just how cold he had become.

Then he checked his belt and equipment. He double-checked his laser pistol.

It was charged and ready.

Perkins and Chen were doing the same with theirs. As he sealed the hood, he heard Yash finish up with Lankstadt.

"I don't know how long we're going to be," she said. "Can you monitor us behind that curtain?"

"No," he said. "I lost Coop when he went in there."

So that curtain created a sensor blackout for the Fleet.

"See if Stone and Bridge have more tablets," Coop said. "Attach one to your sensors and monitor us that way."

He hoped that would work. Yash was shaking her head as if she thought it wouldn't.

"I really would like a timeline, since you'll be out of contact," Lankstadt said.

"We'll be at least an hour, maybe more," Coop said. "Use your judgment. If something feels wrong, assume it is. Don't come in yourself."

"Sir—"

"A lot could happen," Coop said. "Someone else could be arriving here. We could run into someone inside that area. And you are the only remaining pilot. Your job is to get the team and what information we already have off this planet. Is that clear?"

"Sir—"

"Also," Coop said, not willing to hear any objections. "Notify the fighters and the *Ivoire* that we might have inadvertently alerted someone hostile to our presence. Have them monitor."

"Sir—"

"If it looks dangerous to land here," Coop said, "you all must leave us here."

"Sir," Lankstadt said. "What do you mean by dangerous?"

Coop suppressed a sigh. He really wanted to get into that area before anyone arrived.

"The *Ivoire* is one ship. Yes, it's DV-Class, but it can't handle a squadron of similar ships by itself. Get out, and wait until everything dies down. If we're alive, we'll figure out how to make it through. If not, then I don't want you risking the *Ivoire* on some misguided rescue attempt." He glanced at the other three.

They were watching him closely.

"And," Coop added, "you will play that order for Captain Rooney when you return to the *Ivoire*."

"If, sir," Lankstadt said.

"If." Coop decided to give that to him. "Now, let us get inside before something else goes awry."

He glanced at Stone and Bridge. They were leaning on each other, carefully picking their way across the pavement. Bridge seemed to have forgotten that he wanted a sample, or maybe he took it when Coop wasn't looking.

Then Coop turned his attention to his team.

"Let's go," he said.

31

THE WAY THIS MISSION WAS GOING was sixteen different kinds of wrong. Yash knew it in her gut, knew they were probably courting some kind of disaster, and yet she agreed with Coop: this was probably their only chance to get inside Sector Base E-2.

She did a gut check. Would she be willing to die for information on the Fleet?

Yes. Of course. She wanted to know and she was willing to take risks to do so.

She was relieved that Coop sent Stone and Bridge on their way. Yash didn't want to translate Coop's near-crazy to the two civilians. She also didn't want to justify failing to follow the training they had all received from Boss.

Perkins and Chen knew that Coop wasn't following Fleet procedure, and they hadn't spoken up. Lankstadt didn't like the position Coop had put him in, but Coop didn't care.

He wanted inside this base, and he was going to get there. No matter what.

He had finished checking his gear. He had turned on all of the same lights on the exterior of his suit. He now glowed like the rest of them, but his lights were aimed downward so that he didn't blind any of his teammates.

"Ready?" he asked, and just from his tone, Yash could tell that he didn't want anyone to say they were not. "Let's go."

Without waiting for a response, he walked as fast as he could back to that open door in the wall. Yash had to hurry to keep up, which irritated her. She wanted to stop and examine everything.

She would have felt safer if she could have stopped and examined everything.

But he was right: they had to move fast. Besides, he had already viewed that control panel (which she would have liked to at least examine before entering that door).

Perkins kept pace with Yash, and Chen brought up the rear, constantly moving her head to see if someone else had arrived or something was sneaking up on them.

The weather had settled. It had turned extremely cold, but the wind was dying down. There hadn't been thunder since the last of the hail, and no more rain to speak of.

Yash had no idea whether or not that weather would help or hinder someone else from finding them. Or if they were walking into an ambush inside.

Coop stopped just outside that open door. Inside looked very dark. Yash shot a glance at the control panel and was startled to see that, in addition to being in Standard, it was also set up the way that she had been trained to set up a control panel.

She had seen some of the later control panels built in the years after she left her timeline, and those panels had a different layout. A few of them didn't even label the controls on the panel, assuming that whoever was using it had already been trained in whatever they needed to make the panel work.

This panel did not look old enough to have been assembled when she was still with the Fleet. This panel looked relatively new—as in the-last-few-years kind of new.

Then Chen caught up to Coop and Yash. Chen kept her back to the group as she examined the area around them. Then she peered into the darkness, clearly doing her job whether Coop wanted her to or not.

"That brown path continues inside," Coop said to them all. Yash noted that he was using a channel that only went to *Ivoire* crew. He wasn't including Stone or Bridge. "It lines the side of the wall, but there's only one area where it goes directly into the back. I'm of two minds about that. Either that leads to whoever is running this place, or it leads to the only working part of the base."

"Or both," Yash said.

"Or both," Coop said. "I was thinking we split up and investigate one section that doesn't have the brown path, and the one that does."

Yash didn't like splitting up. She was beginning to dislike this entire enterprise, primarily because she didn't understand it. Something was going on here, something that wasn't immediately evident.

"I don't think we should split up," Chen said. "I think we should investigate one first and then the other."

For the first time, Coop seemed to hesitate. He had clearly only thought of splitting up. He seemed uncertain as to which path to choose.

"I think we need to find out what we're up against," Yash said.

"I agree," Perkins said. "For all we know, this elaborate setup was established centuries ago and no longer communicates with anyone."

Yash shot her a glance but couldn't see Perkins' face in the dimness. The light from her hood and around her neck pointed downward, keeping her face in shadow.

Yash wanted to send her a message without saying anything, but couldn't—not when she couldn't see Perkins's eyes.

"From small hints that I'm getting," Yash said, "I suspect this addition is newer than we thought."

She didn't want to elaborate any more than that.

"Maybe." Nothing in Coop's tone gave away what, exactly, he thought of all this. "But let's find out, shall we? Because if no one has been here in a very long time, then we can explore this sector base to our heart's content."

Yash hoped "exploring to our heart's content" meant bringing in proper teams, filled with historians and archeologists and techs who specialized in older technology. She also hoped that "exploring to our heart's content" meant bringing in more than one DV-Class vessel.

Coop met her gaze. She could see his face, and he looked defiant. He was determined to find out what had happened here. Normally she would prevent him from going forward, but not this time.

Maybe they all had a bit of the crazy that had taken Dix down a dark hole. Maybe, no matter how much the crew of the *Ivoire* pretended, the loss of their original time period and all they knew had a greater impact on them than they could ever imagine.

Or maybe that loss gave them a recklessness they wouldn't have otherwise had. After all, they really did have nothing to lose.

Coop stepped inside the door. Yash followed, as did Perkins and Chen.

The space they entered was wider and bigger than Yash expected. After looking (quickly) at those specs, she realized that once upon a time, this was the main aboveground entrance to the sector base.

That the base even had an easily accessible aboveground entrance surprised her. The bases she had grown up around had kept their aboveground accesses hidden. The workers at those bases had had to slip through designated doors carved into the local landscape before ever entering the base proper.

A lot had changed between Sector Base V and Sector Base E-2. But then, centuries had passed, and change was inevitable.

Yash let her light sweep over the area between the wall and the doors. This was some kind of grand entrance, the kind most often found in a big complex or some kind of venue open to the public.

She had never seen anything like it in a Fleet building, particularly a sector base. But if this were a major sector base, and the city around it only catered to the base, then maybe this design would work.

In the past, this entrance must have seemed imposing. A large frame ran the entire length, and inside that frame were sets of double doors. The pattern was deliberate: two doors surrounded by a fairly thick frame. The frame would butt against the next frame for the next set of doors, so between the sets, there was something that looked like a wall with a line through it.

She could almost imagine this entrance in its heyday, with lights behind those doors inviting people inside—or signs warning people away. Right now, though, the entire entrance looked sad, tired, and lost, as if it had once had glory and now only knew defeat.

"See how strange this all is?" Coop asked, echoing Yash's thoughts. He pointed toward his left with his knuckle lights, revealing even more doorways, curving away from them.

The lights lingered on the walls between the doorway.

"Nanobits," he said.

Then he aimed his knuckle lights upward, revealing the darkness of the ceiling above them.

"See?" he said. "More nanobits."

He swept the knuckle lights downward, nearer to the doors' entrances. The ground in front of the far doors also absorbed the light.

"And even more nanobits," he said.

His tone told her that he was feeling as odd about this design as she was. They had found the sector base, and it was designed in a way that the Fleet they had known wouldn't have designed it.

Yash shivered, beginning to feel the chasm of years in a completely different way than she had ever felt it before.

Coop swung his hand to the right, revealing door, door, black wall, door, door, black wall, door…and that strange brown material around the door, and maybe—they were too far away to see—but maybe, a bit of brown just beyond the door.

Nothing had come out of that door since Coop had activated whatever he had activated. From Yash's vantage—which she had to admit wasn't the best—she didn't see anything moving beyond that door either.

There were no lights flashing, no sirens blaring.

Nothing except the reflection of the direct pale light from Coop's knuckle lights, and a more watery reflection of the four of them, standing near the wall.

Yash pulled out Stone's tablet and tapped it, trying to see if she could get information as to what was beyond that door. But nothing registered.

The doors showed up.

But nothing beyond that door to their right.

Perkins had pulled out her usual tablet, repeating the same actions that Yash had done. Trying to see what kind of readings she could get on the Fleet equipment.

"I'm not getting anything beyond those doors," Yash said. "Nothing real, anyway."

"I'm not getting any readings in here at all," Perkins said, clutching her tablet.

"They're blocking Fleet signals," Coop said to Perkins. "Just put your tablet away."

"But not our comm links," Perkins said.

"I suspect they're monitoring those," Coop said.

Then Yash heard a faint rustle and clunk as the comm channel between her and Coop opened. At least, that was what she assumed she heard.

"We're doing this," Coop said. "I still think we should split up."

She glanced at the doors. "If you think we're only going to get one shot at this, then I agree."

She wasn't sure she should have said that at all. He might take that as an invitation to do something rash.

"I don't think we're only going to get one shot," she added. "I think—"

"We have to proceed as if this is our only chance," Coop said.

Then he walked to that far door. Yash followed, slowly, not sure what she should do here.

Although if he was going to make them separate, then she needed a team and he needed a team.

Or maybe the two of them took the risk, and Perkins and Chen waited here.

Yash held up her tablet and inspected the wall between the far door and the double doors near them. That wall was made of both nanobits and the brown stuff. The brown stuff coated the door side, and not the side near the other door.

Coop peeled off his glove, which startled Yash. Then she realized what he was doing. He had managed to open the door they had come through with his bare hand. He was going to try the same thing here.

"Wait," she said through their private channel.

He paused, then turned toward her, revealing to the rest of the team that the two of them were talking without communicating with anyone else.

She continued, "If you're going to insist on splitting up, here's how I want to do it. Perkins and Chen wait out here, ready to go in if one of us gets into trouble. Neither of us goes very far, just far enough to see what's beyond the doors. If that works, and we get out of here unscathed, then we plan a more coordinated exploration of what we're seeing, based on what we find."

Yash said all of that in a great rush, as if Coop would stop listening if she spoke slower.

"Yeah," he said, almost dismissively. (Or was he actually being dismissive? She couldn't quite tell.) "All right. That's what we'll do."

He stopped in front of that brown part of the wall, then added, "Logically, there should be similar controls for all of these doors."

He was right. Yash walked to the nearest full nanobit wall and stopped in front of it. She left her gloves on.

"What are we doing?" Perkins' voice was soft in Yash's ear. Yet another private communication. They were so far off-book now that everything felt clandestine.

"Let me check something," Yash said, turning on the lights on her fingertips.

Sure enough, there was a small, rectangular cutout in the nanobit wall in front of her. She activated her most general Fleet identification onto the palm of the glove and then pressed that palm against the cutout.

Coop was watching her, as was Perkins. Chen had her back to them, looking at the pavement behind them.

Yash's heart started pounding. This too could be some kind of notification to whoever—whatever—had put that brown stuff along these walls.

If that had happened somewhat recently.

Assumptions. Everything was an assumption.

Just like the fact that she had assumed an old identification would activate a Fleet doorway—

The door slid open, and a thin light rose inside another wide and long room. Yash let out a small breath of surprise.

"What are we doing?" Perkins asked again.

"You're staying here," Yash said. "I'm going to find out what the hell is going on."

32

THE AIR WAS FRIGID. Coop's hand got cold immediately. He clutched his glove in the other hand, then glanced at Yash. She had opened a panel and was working on the door.

Perkins was standing just a bit too close to her, and, he realized, they were talking as well. Perkins was probably wondering what he was thinking, and asking Yash to explain it.

So he would instead.

He flexed his fingers, feeling the muscles tighten from the cold.

"Perkins, Chen," he said on the channel to everyone, "I need you to stay out here. Chen, I'd like you to keep an eye open to see if anything changes on that wall or the brown whatever or behind these doors."

Chen nodded. She appeared unfazed, although he really couldn't tell since she was suited up.

"Perkins," he said, "see what you can monitor with that tablet. I'd like you to go back and forth between the doors that we'll open here in a minute, and keep an eye on us as best you can."

"On you?" Perkins asked.

He couldn't tell if she was being disingenuous, if Yash had already told her the plan.

"I'm going in this door; Yash is going in the other." He flexed his fingers again. The cold was getting to them.

Yash had opened her control panel. It would only be a moment before she opened the door—if she could open the door.

"Three things, Yash," Coop said. "First, if there's equipment that might have files or information on it, download as much as you can. Second, record everything."

He could almost imagine the look she was giving him now. He deliberately avoided her eyes. Of course, she would record everything. But he needed the command on record, just in case something bad happened to one or the other of them.

He wanted to make sure the team knew to pull all the data from their suits and any devices they might be carrying.

"And finally," he said, "we're going to time this, just like Boss would want."

Yash let out a small laugh, which surprised him. Apparently he had pleased her.

"Thirty minutes," he said.

"That's not enough time," she said.

"I know," he said. He had given it a lot of thought, and figured thirty minutes would get them in and out quickly enough, and not allow either of them to wander down corridors or access lower levels.

Even though he had a hunch this was their one shot at exploring E-2, he wanted to make sure they got out with any information they found.

"Thirty minutes," he said. "I'm activating timers. I doubt we'll be able to work comms inside. So fifteen minutes in and fifteen minutes out."

"You're no fun," Yash said, but there was a smile in her voice. "Don't activate those timers until your door is open."

Hers already was. A pale light had activated inside the area just behind the door. If he had been standing there as long as she had, he would have been antsy.

But she seemed calmer than he would have expected.

He flexed his cold fingers one last time. Then he pushed on the rectangle carved into the brown whatever it was. The panel door opened, just like the one outside had, and it revealed the same kind of controls that he had seen in the previous panel.

Only this time, the controls were lit from behind.

His breath caught. He hadn't expected that.

The labels were exactly the same. The position of the controls was exactly the same.

The words were exactly the same. Standard. His version of Standard, not the version that Boss used, and not some kind of hybrid.

The lights made him nervous. The version of Standard that he had grown up with made him curious. The language should have been subtlety different, considering how much the language had changed to become the language Boss spoke.

Or, perhaps, the language had only changed in her sector of space. Maybe here, it remained the same.

He pressed the right spot to open the door.

This time it slid back easily, as if it had opened just a few hours before. For all he knew, it had.

"Activate your timer," he said to Yash. "We're a go."

He activated his timer, setting it to count at the bottom of his hood, as well as in his ear. He hoped that the timer would continue working as he went inside.

He would do his best to monitor the time without the timer, just in case it shut down or time got elongated the way it sometimes did around a malfunctioning *anacapa* field.

His heart was pounding. He slipped his glove back on, grateful for the warmth, turned on the knuckle lights, and then aimed them inside.

No light had come on immediately behind his door, although as he got closer, he saw some dim lighting way in the back.

He had no idea if that lighting had been on before the door opened or not.

He examined the interior before stepping inside. A brown wall to his left divided this space from the larger space. The right wall curved along the mountainside and was made of nanobits. The blackness gleamed.

Piles of equipment were pushed against each wall. Whoever had piled that equipment had left a narrow space between the piles, a trail that went as far as he could see, heading toward the dim lights in the back.

He stepped inside, then looked down.

The floor was white, but it was clean. It also gleamed. It was clearly made of nanobits, not the brown stuff.

He frowned. Someone had deliberately cut this part of the base off from the part that Yash was in. Even if he pulled off his hood and shouted, she wouldn't be able to hear him. That brown wall looked thick. Whether or not it was, he couldn't quite tell.

He kept the door open and all of his lights on, even though he wanted to be a bit more stealthy. He felt like he was being watched—and not by his team.

He couldn't tell if that feeling was his own paranoia or not.

He paused right between the first two piles of equipment. They weren't attached to anything. They looked like junk piles. Consoles and chairs and recyclers tossed one on top of the other. Each piece of equipment looked old, and most of them were not intact.

If he had time, he would toss some of the consoles out of this room before he left. But right now, he needed to move forward to see what was here.

The jumble of piles was almost as tall as he was, and they went back nearly ten paces. The room itself was long, and it curved to his right.

He suspected that along the wall, behind the piles, were doors that accessed the rest of the base.

Either those doors had been deliberately blocked off, or whoever had piled this junk here hadn't known that the doors existed.

Considering all the work someone had put into this space, he was going to assume that they knew the doors were there and were either blocking them off to prevent outsiders like him from accessing them, or to prevent some employee or minion or guest from accidentally stumbling into them.

Or maybe the path between the piles led to the only door whoever had set this area up felt important.

He was breathing a little too shallowly, and despite his best intentions, he had lost track of time.

He glanced at the small numbers scrolling at the bottom of his hood. Eight minutes, twenty-seven seconds.

If he wanted to see what was near those lights, he would have to pick up his pace.

He didn't dare go too fast, though, because he didn't want to knock something over, or kick something, or step into a trap.

He moved slowly, still taking in the equipment. Some of it was deeply recognizable, bits of DV-Class vessels, parts of beds or chairs or control panels like the ones he had used in the past.

Other equipment wasn't as recognizable, but still seemed to be in the same family. Consoles with rounded edges instead of sharp ones. Hard flat surfaces that seemed to be made up of nanobits. Open (and empty) *anacapa* containers, all in different sizes and shapes.

Then he reached a pile of those containers that made him stop. They too were empty, but they were brown, made of the same material as that wall.

He frowned at them. They were very much out of place with anything he had seen before. *Anacapa* containers were—by very stringent regulation—made of nanobits, and nanobits only.

He almost picked one of those containers up, then decided against it—again.

Eleven minutes had gone by. He wasn't going to make it to the back, even though he wanted to.

This room was longer than he expected. And all he was finding was more questions than answers.

He gave the back a longing look, thought of running there, and immediately decided against it. Then he frowned at it.

Were the lights brighter? Were there more of them? And did he see an open door back there or was that simply an optical illusion caused by a nanobit wall?

He couldn't tell.

He crouched and used his knuckle lights to peer between some of the pieces of equipment, hoping against hope he would see a console that was attached to the floor or something that made sense of this mess.

But he found nothing.

He stood, looking toward the back again.

Those lights definitely were brighter. And there was an open door.

Now, the question was, should he violate his own rules for this mission and take the extra time to go back there?

This might be the only shot.

But he was alone. And if something happened, he would be trapped here, maybe for good.

He let out a small exasperated breath.

He hated being responsible. He hated following the rules in a situation like this—particularly when he made them.

So he tried one last-ditch thing.

"Yash," he said on that private channel. "Yash, can you hear me?"

He could tell, even before the words were out of his mouth, that she couldn't hear him. The signal was either dampened by the room or couldn't get out of the room.

He tried one last time on the overall channel, hoping that maybe Perkins or Chen could hear him because that door was open.

But they didn't answer him either.

He had to turn back, with more questions than answers, hoping that he would get at least one more chance to explore this space and doubting that would ever happen.

33

THE PALE LIGHT IN THE LARGE ROOM had once been stronger. Yash could tell time and use had diminished the light the moment she stepped through the double doors. The light came from the ceiling above. Nanobits had created a series of lights that ran along certain panels in the ceiling. She had worked on buildings with that design early in her career.

The lights were supposed to be very bright. If the nanobits stopped replicating, the lights would fade. At that point, the building's engineers would know that they either needed to add a new layer of nanobits or replace that part of the ceiling altogether.

The fading light meant that the nanobit bonding was slowly starting to fail.

And bonding like that didn't fail in the first five to eight hundred years unless something had gone wrong.

There were no signs of anything going wrong.

Except for the large brown wall to her right. It blocked her off from Coop. They both had known, without saying, that the different doors led in different directions.

She had, however, expected a nanobit wall between them, not a wall made of that same brown material that they had seen outside.

The presence of foreign material bothered her more than the weirdly retired sector base. She didn't like that someone was using this area for their own purposes—had *redesigned* this area for their own purposes.

Although the design wasn't familiar to her. The interior looked like the reception area for a big business. Rows of desks, with chairs behind them and signs that glowed ever so faintly above them.

She could barely make out the words on the signs closest to her— *Security, Employment Matters, Information*—all written in the same Standard as the control panels.

She took a step forward, feeling a bit stunned. The light from her boots flared, and it took a half second for her to realize that the floor was white, not black.

She glanced at that brown wall. The floor beneath it was white as well. That looked like it had once been the floor of the sector base.

She walked up to the desks, half expecting someone to stand up and ask what she wanted.

But that didn't happen. The signs didn't get brighter, either. The room seemed to end just behind them, but she knew that was some kind of optical illusion. There had to be more to this base, both aboveground and underground. She just didn't know how to access it.

She looked to her right, saw more desks and a few furniture groupings. Nothing looked untoward until she realized all the furniture should have been gone.

Sector Base E-2 was supposed to have been closed, and closed bases were emptied. No desks, no equipment, no chairs, no furniture groupings.

In fact, there should have been piles of rock-like rubble or dirt or something to make whoever entered here think this was part of a weird natural cave.

No one had done that here.

She let out a small, nervous breath.

"Anyone hear me?" she asked into her comm, just to make sure.

No one responded. Four minutes in, and she finally realized just how alone she was.

She had eleven minutes before she had to think about leaving. Eleven minutes to get what information she could from this part of the base. Either she could see what was in the back or she could try to pull information from here.

She opted to pull information.

Which meant the desks. If they were standard-issue from her time, there would be a lot of information stored in them.

Fortunately, she had brought more than one data strip. She peeled one off her belt, walked to the nearest desk, and set the device on it.

The desk flared to life, sending little bits of blue light across its surface as if it were answering a summons.

The desk next to it also flared to life.

She stepped back and watched all of the desks heading down the row turn themselves on.

Her breath caught. She hoped she wasn't activating something she shouldn't have.

She was a lot more nervous than she wanted to be.

Then she thought of diving that runabout with Boss—how Boss had gone in, even though the damn thing had nearly killed her, and how she had braved the runabout again, just for bits of information.

Yash could handle pulling information off these desks—as many as possible—before she had to leave.

Then she smiled at herself. Boss would find it deeply ironic that more than once today, Yash had taken inspiration from her.

Yash let out another shaky breath, then took another data strip off her belt. She set that device on the next desk.

She had one more data strip, and she placed it on the third desk.

No lights flashed at her, nothing in her suit showed a change in energy readings. No *anacapa* energy surged around her.

Nothing was any different except that the lights on the desks had activated.

Eleven minutes had gone by, faster than she had expected, and she had barely gotten inside the door. There was so much to see and absolutely no real time at all.

If she could communicate with Coop, she would have done so, asking for more time. Much more time.

But she couldn't.

More lights flicked on. Above her, what appeared to be skylights opened, sending sunlight down on her.

Only it had been storming outside. Even if it hadn't been, there shouldn't have been sunlight. It was night.

She looked at the ceiling. Those lights were designed for employees, people who were trapped in this entrance, day in and day out, without any natural light.

The system was malfunctioning ever so slightly. It did not seem to know that outside this area, night had fallen.

The environmental systems were off, and so, apparently, were the systems that monitored date and time.

Movement caught her eye. She looked backward at the door into which she had entered.

Perkins or Chen stood there, waving her arms. She was completely encased in her environmental suit, making identification from this distance impossible.

Since the comm system was Fleet-based, it was blocked inside here. Yash couldn't hear that person if she talked to Yash through the system.

When that person realized Yash saw her, she beckoned—hastily, it seemed—telling Yash that she had to leave.

She shook her head: she had more than half her time left.

But that person was insistent. They had to go *now*.

Yash bit back a surge of irritation, followed by a flash of worry. Had something happened to Coop? Had those alarms that she feared brought someone here? What, exactly, had gone wrong?

She glanced at the person near the door, wondering if that was even Chen or Perkins. They were wearing the right suit, the suit lights were on just like they had been outside this room, so that part, at least, was just fine.

Yash had to trust whoever it was, because otherwise, she might end up creating more problems than they needed.

Still, she wasn't going to lose the data. She hurried back to the first desk, grabbed the data strip off it, then backtracked to the second, grabbing the strip, and the third, grabbing that strip.

The person at the door got even more agitated, signaling harder now. Yash nodded, shoved the data strips into their places on her belt, and hurried out of the room.

When she stepped out of the door and into that area behind the wall, sounds rushed at her.

"...hurry, Yash, because they're on their way. And Lankstadt says he's heard from the *Ivoire*. We have to get off this planet now."

The voice belonged to Perkins, and she sounded almost panicked, which was weird because Perkins never sounded panicked.

Yash would parse all of that information in a moment. But first she had a few questions of her own.

"What about Coop?"

"Chen's getting him," Perkins said. "We have to go, *now*."

"Wait," Yash said. She handed one of the devices to Perkins. "In case something happens to me, one of these gets out of here."

"Got it," Perkins said.

Yash glanced at the other door. That was when she realized there was another person here, peering inside.

"Who the hell's that?" she asked.

"Bridge," Perkins said, with a bit of irritation, as if she'd already told Yash that. Of course, Perkins had no idea what Yash had heard and what she hadn't. "He volunteered to come get us. We're losing precious time, Yash. We have to go."

"Take him and go," Yash said. "I'll get Coop."

"No." Perkins grabbed her arm. "I'm under instruction to get at least one of you out of here."

"Lankstadt doesn't have the right to give that order," Yash said.

"That's correct," Perkins said. "Rooney does. And I agree. Now move."

She yanked Yash toward the still-open door at the far end.

Yash shot one last look at Bridge, hovering near the door Coop had gone through. Rooney, Lankstadt, and Perkins were right: they had to get either Yash or Coop out of here. Or both of them.

Both of them.

Yash pulled her arm away from Perkins.

"Neither of us," Yash said. "Hell, *none* of us can get caught. We don't want anyone to know about the Boneyard or Lost Souls or Boss. We have no idea what we're facing, Perkins. Let's get Coop, and let's go."

Perkins cursed, but through her hood, Yash could see a smile on Perkins' face.

"I was afraid you'd say that," Perkins said. She pulled her laser pistol off her belt. "So much for being sensible. So much for orders."

So much for any pretext that they were operating like members of the Fleet, Yash thought but didn't say.

Yash pulled out her laser pistol, too, and followed Perkins to the door that Coop had disappeared into a little over fourteen minutes before.

34

COOP HAD JUST FORCED HIMSELF to turn around, feeling disappointed that he hadn't discovered anything he understood, when he saw some-one slide in the door.

He grabbed his laser pistol, kept it low, and shut off his knuckle lights. He toyed with shutting off every light on his suit, but decided against it. For all he knew, the person near the door was one of his, not one of theirs—whoever they might be.

The person was wearing an environmental suit, and from this distance, it looked like one of the suits his team wore. Communications would be impossible from that suit to this one, though, because of the blockages.

He was about to mime that the person should remove their hood so the two of them could shout at each other when the person used some gestures he hadn't seen since he'd been in officer training. Hand signals for when the communications equipment failed.

We need to evacuate. Now. We're in danger.

He cursed and sped up, not quite allowing himself to run. He passed the brown *anacapa* containers and every single piece of equipment he had thought of snagging. He wanted to take something now, but that would only slow him down.

Whoever had come to get him—and considering the signals, it was probably Chen; Security personnel trained in hand signals for nearly a year—was extremely clear. Only a fool would ignore the word *danger.*

He scurried forward and then, as he rounded yet another batch of equipment, he decided he wasn't moving fast enough.

Two more people appeared behind Chen, making his heart stop. Were they going to attack her? Help her? Kidnap her?

He gave up on being cautious. He wasn't going to risk the whole team.

He ran to the door and realized at that moment that four people waited for him, not the three he expected. Still, they had followed his orders. No one had gone inside the base—if that's what it was—except him and Yash.

He stepped out, and as he did, Chen said in his ear, "We have to hurry. Reports from the *Ivoire* say a lot of ships are heading toward this planet, and some are already in orbit around it."

He had no idea how anything could orbit Nindowne, not with all the space junk around the planet, but he wasn't going to question that.

"We're okay here, then?" he asked. He wondered if they could just go deeper into the sector base and wait until the problem passed.

"No," Chen said. "Small ships are landing nearby, and Lankstadt says he got chatter that a group of locals are gathering weapons to drive us out of here."

Great. A full-blown army of some kind was advancing on them. Well, that answered the question of whether or not he had activated something in touching the brown stuff or opening the doors.

He was still having issues—why were there four people?—and then he recognized the suit. One of them was Bridge. His suit was scuffed and one arm was covered with white.

Bridge saw Coop looking at him.

"We really have to hurry," Bridge said. "It took me longer than I wanted it to getting here. It's icy out there."

"We need to activate the gravity in our boots," Yash said.

"It doesn't work," Bridge said. "Or, at least, mine didn't. The boots need something to attach to, and the ice..."

He shook his head.

Coop toyed with closing that door behind him, then decided he wasn't going to worry about it. If the group made it back to the skip—which was sounding like a big if—then maybe the open door would mislead whoever was coming for them. Maybe that person—that army—would think that Coop's crew was still inside.

He peered out the door in the brown wall, noted that indeed, the pavement was covered in white. And it didn't appear to be hail now. Now it looked like snow. Or maybe it was a combination.

Pellets were still falling from the sky, but they were clear. And, since his external microphones were still on, he could hear the pellets hit the nanobit wall. They sounded loud, louder than he would have expected.

But, he noted, when they hit the brown part of the ground, they didn't seem to stick.

"Follow me," he said and, with his head down, hurried out the last door.

The white was slick. His right foot slid away from him, but he took the weight off it and somehow managed to remain balanced on his left, which was on the brown stuff. He brought the right foot back, hands out, maintaining his balance, now walking on the brown stuff, heading back toward the skip.

He was tempted to order Lankstadt to move the skip closer to the entrance, but didn't. This sector base was too odd. There were active controls and possible silent alarms.

He had no idea what would happen if an actual ship of any size drew close to the doors.

He didn't want to risk it.

The white—snow? Ice? Hail?—was thicker than he expected, but down the middle of it, he saw boot impressions and then some skid marks and long holes that might have been made by a body, probably Bridge's. The man had fallen more than once trying to get here.

Coop's sense of urgency grew as he saw that. Bridge might have been on his way even before Coop and Yash went into the sector base.

Coop glanced over his shoulder. The four were following him, single-file. They weren't sliding either.

He now wished he was wearing regulation boots. They would tell him what the temperature of the brown stuff was, how it was defeating this white layer that was covering everything.

The farther he got away from the overhang, the stronger the wind became. One gust nearly blew him into the nanobit wall. He put out a hand to prevent himself from hitting that wall, and the hand slipped.

His suit sent a warning along the hood. *This suit is not made to handle severe ice storm conditions. Seek shelter immediately.*

Well, that answered his question. The storm had evolved into an ice storm, and the pellets were ice. He had no idea if there had been a bit of snow earlier or if the pellets were now coating the hail, making it a lower level of ice.

But that explained why Bridge had trouble getting here.

Coop could only hope whoever was coming to defend Sector Base E-2 would have trouble getting here as well.

The wall curved back toward the road, away from the skip. Coop was going to have to step off the brown stuff, onto the ice. He wished his boots had spikes or something other than the minimal features built into the average Fleet boots.

He hadn't expected to need other features since he was going to be planetside. The boots had helped him earlier, but they hurt him now.

He glanced back at the four. Bridge actually pointed in the direction of the skip as if Coop didn't know where he was going.

It didn't irritate him, though. He understood the gesture. It was almost impossible to see as the pellets of ice rained around them. He certainly couldn't see the skip from this distance.

He had his suit plot the most direct course to the skip. On his hood, a small map appeared. A three-dimensional path appeared over the white surface, showing his route in red, and telling him he was only about twenty yards away.

Twenty yards seemed like twenty miles.

But he squared his shoulders, braced himself, and started across the surface. He had walked on ice maybe a dozen times before, at least in real gravity. But usually he'd been walking on an ice-covered lake, and he had been wearing boots made for that trip.

He'd also walked on ice coating some of the ships in space, but the gravity in his boots had kept him in place, often interacting with the ship itself. Plus in that situation, he often used other tools—grapplers in his gloves or a tether—so he felt like he could fall and not hurt himself.

Falling here would be painful.

Even though he wanted to run, he didn't dare. His boots slipped with every step. His suit warned him again about the ice storm, and as it did, the wind nearly blew him backward.

The visibility had diminished just in the last few minutes. Only the path that the map carved out for him showed him where to go. He could barely see a few yards in front of him, and he certainly couldn't see the skip—not even the shape of it.

"Go slow," he said to his crew, without looking backward. He didn't dare look backward, afraid it would unbalance him. Every movement felt precarious, including every step forward.

"Something's coming," Chen said. "Above us."

She had barely gotten the words out when an aircar wobbled past. It was having trouble in the wind and ice as well, unable to maintain some kind of balance. It buzzed low, but didn't land. It seemed unable to do so.

If it was flying on automatic and it was like aircars Coop had ridden in, the controls wouldn't allow the car to land on a surface like this, not without the proper gear.

He wondered if there was proper gear.

"Where there's one, there's bound to be more." Yash sounded out of breath.

"Ignore them," Coop said. "Let's just get to the skip."

It was all he could do to stay on his feet. He had trouble maintaining a straight path. He veered all over the imaginary line created by his map overlay. Sometimes he would veer to his left, and sometimes to his right, depending on the wind.

Then he heard a whumpf, accompanied by a grunt of pain. He looked behind him, nearly lost his own balance, and had to shuffle his feet, and pinwheel his arms to stay upright.

One of the four was down. Bridge, Coop was guessing, but he couldn't quite tell.

He backtracked, even though someone—Chen?—waved her arms at him, telling him to go on. The other two were crouched, trying to help Bridge up, but they were losing their balance as they did so.

Pretty soon, everyone would be in a pile on the ground.

"I've got this," Chen said, her voice authoritative. "Move aside. Get to the skip. I've got him."

Of course she did. Security officers trained in all kinds of adverse conditions. If they were good—and clearly Chen was—they kept up that training on their own, usually simulating strange situations.

She was probably the only one of them who had actually trained for this.

"Yash, Perkins," Coop said, "step back."

Bridge was leaning to one side, but he was sitting up. The two who were trying to help him stood, then staggered in the wind.

Chen approached him from the back. "I'm going to lever you upright," she said. "Can you walk?"

"Hurt my arm, not my legs," Bridge said. He sounded annoyed.

Above them, the aircar wobbled past. It was flying too low. Another was flying higher than that, also wobbling. They seemed to overshoot the pavement again, or maybe they were just trying to record what was going on here.

Either way, Coop didn't like it.

He waited for Yash and Perkins to reach him, waited for Chen to get Bridge on his feet.

"Need my help keeping him upright?" he asked Chen.

"I can stay upright on my own," Bridge snarled. Coop hadn't used a private channel, and probably should have.

Coop didn't tell them that they had to hurry. They already knew that. So he pivoted—carefully—and headed back toward the skip.

His steps from earlier remained, but even in that short period of time, they had filled with fresh ice. He didn't think he could see as far ahead as he had a moment ago.

But the map told him that he only had about eight more yards.

Seemed like forever, particularly since he couldn't see the skip.

"You managing, Chen?" he asked. He didn't want to turn around again.

"We're fine." That was Bridge, still sounding annoyed.

As long as he sounded irritated, he was all right.

Coop bent his head, walking into the wind, feeling it push back at him as if it were an actual living being. He didn't remember ever being in weather conditions like this, not even simulated conditions.

But he kept his head down and followed the red line his map created on the surface in front of him, hoping it would take him to the skip.

He walked for what felt like forever and nearly walked into the skip itself.

It was coated with ice. Its sides gleamed, and icicles hung from every surface.

"Another one," Yash said from behind him.

Coop looked up, saw yet another aircar wobbling in the wind. He could only see it because its lights reflected on the ice pellets and rained down onto the ground below.

This aircar looked even more unstable than the others. It flipped sideways and started down.

"Watch out," he said to the others, hoping they could get out of the way.

It landed with a bang that he felt more than he heard.

If whoever was inside was suited up and belted in, they would be fine. And they would get out near him.

At that moment, the skip door opened. Lankstadt stood there in his environmental suit.

He grabbed Coop under his shoulders and yanked him upward, something Coop wouldn't have thought possible in full gravity.

"I thought I said that we would—"

"Orders later," Lankstadt said. "We have to get out of here. They need help, I can do it, and you're a better pilot."

He had a point. Coop staggered into the main part of the skip, feeling slightly unnerved. No longer pushing against the wind and ice unbalanced his entire body.

His muscles felt heavy with exhaustion, but somehow he made it to the pilot's chair.

Stone stood nearby, her hood down, monitoring everything on her tablet.

"I need something to drink," Coop said, pulling down his hood. "The others will too. And some kind of food."

He didn't know what kind. He didn't want to think about it. He just knew they had expended a strange kind of energy out there, and they needed refueling just like a ship would.

Lankstadt had several holographic screens open. They showed the distance between the skip and the sector base, the actual view of it, and the entire valley.

He hadn't been kidding: more aircars were on the way, as were vehicles that Coop couldn't identify. Some were actually driving on the roads.

The holomap off to his left showed the entire planet. Ships were coming in—what size, Coop couldn't tell at a glance—and were entering orbit.

A third holomap near the first showed the pavement itself. The aircar, on its side, was already covered in white, and it appeared that someone was trying to get out of it. A door was open, or so it seemed. Coop couldn't be certain.

Too many maps, and not all of them useful. He peeled off his gloves and dropped them on the floor.

Another holomap showed one of the mountain ranges. Coop squinted at it because something looked off. He couldn't quite tell what.

"You're dripping." Stone handed him a bottle of blue water—the kind that Lost Souls kept around for emergencies after a dive. He didn't argue, took it, and took a swig from it.

The water tasted metallic.

"Maybe you should take off your suit…?" she said.

"No time," he said. He leaned forward, shut off some of the holomaps because he couldn't process this way. He called up screens filled with telemetry—showing the area around them, showing the area beyond. He even brought up one that explained the weather.

It was going to continue storming for hours.

A bang behind him made him swivel. Yash was on her side, leaning against the skip's far wall.

"What the—?" he asked.

"It looked like she got tossed in here," Stone said.

Yash held up a gloved hand. "I'm fine. I'm fine."

Yash wouldn't have entered before the others, not voluntarily. Perkins or Chen had forced her.

Or something else was happening.

He glanced at the holomap of the area outside of the skip. Impossible to see much, with the weather clouding everything. But he thought he saw more figures around the crashed aircar.

"Got her," Yash said from behind him.

He glanced one more time, saw Yash near the door now, saw someone else roll in.

He couldn't concentrate on that. He had to focus on getting this skip ready to leave.

Lankstadt had the skip in standby mode. Coop activated the skip, then ran a quick systems check. The skip told him that the ice outside would create a problem if he tried to take off with the ship still covered, but he wasn't going to have the nanobits clear the ice until his entire team was on board.

Besides, he had a lot more to worry about. The telemetry told him that, in addition to ships arriving in orbit, one had entered Nindowne's atmosphere.

And the holomap of the mountain, the one that made no sense, made sense now.

The mountain's top was open.

Someone was operating the landing protocols inside the sector base. It had been occupied after all.

He opened a channel to the *Ivoire,* only to have it shut down immediately. He'd never experienced that before.

Then another channel opened, one that he hadn't expected.

He toggled it. "Boss?"

"No, Captain, it's Lynda Rooney." The *Ivoire* after all. "We're using this channel because we don't think they can access it easily. They're all over the Fleet channels. We're going to have to keep communication to a minimum whatever we do."

"They?" he asked.

"Whoever is arriving," she said. "There are a dozen more ships heading to Nindowne. They're all large vessels, the kind that can easily take on a DV-Class ship. You stirred up something big, Captain. I'm just not sure yet what it is."

He looked at the imagery she sent him. Dozens of ships, with a long trail of more.

There had been no indication of this when he arrived, nothing that showed some large group was using this base.

"The Fleet?" he asked.

"I don't know," she said. "But it doesn't matter if they blow you away before talking with you. Move fast, Captain. You don't have a lot of time."

He glanced back at that open door. The others weren't inside yet. Stone hovered, her hood up now. He couldn't see Yash anymore.

"Inside," he said on the group channel. "*Now.*"

But no one answered him.

No one answered him at all.

35

YASH'S CHEST HURT. When Lankstadt had tossed her inside the skip, it had knocked the breath out of her. Still, somehow, she managed to stand up, legs shaking.

She beckoned Stone to her side, then handed her the data strips. Stone had her hood down, so she wouldn't be able to hear any comm chatter.

Yash pulled her own hood down just enough to talk to Stone.

"Put those somewhere safe. Make sure that even if we get tossed around like a child's toy, they won't get destroyed."

Then she pulled her hood back up. Stone nodded and wandered toward one of the cabinets as if she had never given any thought to hiding or protecting anything.

Yash couldn't worry about that, though. Lankstadt had his hands full. The wind was making it almost impossible to get anyone on board the skip. Bridge was injured, and Chen was holding him up, barely staying upright herself. And Perkins—

Perkins had stepped away from the skip after shoving Yash toward Lankstadt. The last thing Yash saw was Perkins pulling her laser pistol.

Yash grabbed hers and reached the interior of the airlock. Lankstadt was bent over, trying to get his hands around Bridge's shoulders.

Yash shoved Lankstadt closer to the wall so that she could grip Bridge as well.

Chen was behind him, supporting Bridge's weight.

The wind was whipping, even inside the airlock, and the edges of the skip were covered in ice.

"We're lifting on three," Yash said, glad they were communicating inside the environmental suits. Their voices would be lost outside in that wind. "One. Two. Three."

She grunted as she pulled Bridge up. Lankstadt did too. Yash's chest hurt with the maneuver, and she wondered if she had done more to herself than have the wind knocked out of her as she had gotten tossed inside.

Bridge was dead weight and heavier than she thought a person should be. As they got him inside, she realized why.

He was unconscious.

Surely he hadn't hit that hard when he had fallen, had he? He hadn't because he had gotten up, acted like it was no big deal.

Lankstadt propped Bridge against the airlock walls, then put one gloved finger to his hood, urging Yash to remain silent.

Outside, in the ice storm—or was it an official blizzard now? Looked like one to her barely experienced eye—flashes of red glimmered through the moving darkness.

Lankstadt used hand signals, which Yash didn't understand. Except one. *Wait here.* Everyone learned that one.

Then Lankstadt jumped out of the skip and into the weather.

She leaned out, saw shadows moving in the darkness, saw more red lights, and realized that some of them were coming from the side of the skip.

The weather continued to swirl into the airlock. Yash looked down, saw Chen standing over Perkins and Lankstadt beside them, firing his laser pistol away from the skip.

Yash took out her laser pistol, then toggled the display on her hood so that it used infrared.

Five people—giant green blobs on her screen—wove their way toward the skip. More green blobs appeared in the distance, probably getting out of another aircar.

The first had crash-landed, but apparently someone had survived.

Yash crawled back into the skip, toggled her hood view back to normal, opened one of the lockers, and removed a laser rifle. Stone watched her, gape-mouthed.

Yash pulled down her hood. "Get Bridge out of the airlock," she said to Stone.

And then Yash pulled her hood up again, walking back into the airlock, feeling the wind buffet her. She changed the screen again, saw that the green blobs closest to the ship hadn't moved, but the ones farther away—ten of them—were advancing.

She sure as hell hoped Coop had the skip ready to fly.

Then she crouched in the doorway, leveled the rifle at the blob closest to the ship, and fired. The blob blew backward. She targeted the next blob, but didn't shoot before that blob spun away, as if it had been hit by someone else.

The skip rocked, and for a moment, she thought it was the wind. Then she realized that the advancing group had higher-powered weapons than the group up front. They were shooting on the skip.

Lovely. This was just getting better and better.

Yash leaned out, waved a hand downward, and hoped she got someone's attention. Because if she didn't, she was going to speak on the comms.

She assumed that Lankstadt wanted silence because he believed that the group coming toward them could hear the chatter. She had to trust that.

Chen looked up, and pointed toward the blobs. Yash nodded once, then caught the next one in her sites.

She fired, and didn't look for the result, turned and fired at the next blob, and the next.

The skip rocked. Chen grabbed the edge of the door and lifted herself inside. Then she crawled beside Yash, and reached down. Lankstadt hoisted Perkins up to the skip.

Perkins did not assist. It was at that moment that Yash realized Perkins had been hit too.

Something hit the edge of the exterior door, taking off a chunk of it. And then another hit at the door, and another.

Yash helped Chen pull Perkins inside. She turned, saw Stone struggling to drag Bridge out of the airlock, and knew she would get no help from that quarter.

So Yash pointed at Chen, then used her thumb to indicate the back of the skip. Chen shook her head, but Yash made the gestures again, wishing she knew the sign language that Lankstadt had used earlier.

Then Yash crouched in the doorway again, sighting the blobs with her rifle. They weren't quite close enough for her to use it, not in these conditions.

Chen grabbed Perkins and pulled her deeper into the skip. A red laser beam, clearly from Lankstadt's pistol, flew from beneath the ship toward the nearer blobs—apparently one of them was moving.

Yash decided to risk one quick communication.

"Inside, *now*," she said in Old Standard to Lankstadt.

He didn't need to be told twice. He placed his hands on the edge of the door and levered himself inside. Dozens of shots hit the area around the door, and at least one flew past, inside, hitting the edge of the airlock door.

Yash waited until Lankstadt was all the way in, then hit the door commands.

She scooted toward the middle of the door, shooting as it closed. Then she shoved Lankstadt out of the airlock. She followed, rolling back into the skip.

She yanked off her hood.

"Coop!" she shouted. "Get us the hell out of here."

Then she hit the controls for the inner airlock door. It wouldn't close, which didn't surprise her, given the hit that it had suffered. But they needed the door to close.

She reached into the control panel, working the controls from the inside, until the door shakily slid shut.

Then she turned around, her heart pumping, her breath coming in small gasps. Stone had a medical kit in one hand and was leaning over Perkins, whose environmental suit had been torn open by some kind of fire.

Lankstadt was struggling to open Bridge's environmental suit. His right arm was bent at a normally impossible angle, his head tilted to the left.

Yash could barely see Coop, sitting in the pilot's chair, maps around him. The floor of the skip was sopping wet as ice dripped off all of the environmental suits.

Yash replaced the laser rifle in the locker, hands trembling. Something awful had happened out there.

The skip was still shaking—so the something awful was still happening.

She knew nothing about medicine except the basics she had learned as a cadet. She'd had to use those skills in the past but only for a few minutes until the medical team arrived.

Right now, there was no medical team. And there were other aircars and more people with weapons, a terrible storm, and Coop by himself up front.

"Get them to a secure place," she said to Stone, Chen, and Lankstadt, referring to Perkins and Bridge. "Then strap yourselves in."

Because Yash knew, just based on what she had seen, that getting out of here was going to be difficult at best.

36

THE MOMENT THE AIRLOCK DOOR CLOSED, Coop activated the exterior cleaners—deploying an entire series of nanobits that would scrub the ice off the outside of the skip and maybe start repairing some of the damage from the shots.

Those shots shouldn't have penetrated the hull like they had, but they did. It was as if those shots had started unbonding some of the nanobits, as if those weapons were designed to attack Fleet equipment.

He didn't want to think about that—not now.

Yash dragged herself from the airlock to the copilot's seat. Her environmental suit was coated in ice, which had started to melt. Her hood was down, and her hair was plastered against her head. Her eyes seemed bigger than they usually did.

"What do you need?" she asked as she peeled off her gloves.

"Communications. We're using Boss's favorite channel, since the *Ivoire* says all of the Fleet channels are being monitored."

"Whoever these people are," Yash said, "they're smart and there's a lot of them. They'll find any channel we're using consistently. I'm going to tell the *Ivoire* that we'll roll communications backward, using the current favorite on this communication and then go backward toward the oldest ones with each successive communication. Someone on the ship will remember what we did."

Coop hoped. He couldn't remember. But at least on the *Ivoire*, they would be able to look up that information. And they had used rolling channels for communication before, usually in some kind of battle.

He couldn't remember the last time they had done so, though, and hoped the team on the *Ivoire* had been part of whatever battle had participated in the rolling channels.

Yash strapped herself in. Coop nodded at the reminder and did the same.

"What happened back there?" he asked.

"We have injured. I don't know how bad." Yash twisted slightly. "They're strapped in as well as they can be."

Injured. He didn't ask who, because he needed to focus instead of worry. Besides, the best thing he could do for them was to get them to the *Ivoire* as quickly as possible.

"All right," Coop said. "We're getting out of here, then. Let the *Ivoire* know, and tell them to deploy the fighters. Not to shoot at anything, though."

Yash did both of those things, then leaned back. She studied the screens in front of them, as well as the remaining holomaps. Then, without asking him, she shut off the one that showed the close-up view of the front of Sector Base E-2, calling up yet another holomap.

Only it wasn't a map of geography. It was of the ships coming in, including the one that was now disappearing inside the top of the mountain.

"Notice anything weird?" she asked.

"Besides the attack at a long-closed sector base in the middle of some kind of ice storm?" he asked.

She let out a laugh. It sounded involuntary and unexpected. "Besides that."

"No," he said. "Standard day, nothing to see here."

"The ships," she said. "They're all Fleet vessels."

"Saw that." He didn't want to contemplate the idea that he and Yash had found the Fleet and it was shooting at them.

"But they're not Fleet vessels," she said.

He wasn't sure he had heard her right. He tilted the skip as it lifted off. The wind did not buffet the skip because he had compensated for it.

The ice wasn't a factor yet, but at some point, the cleaners wouldn't be able to keep up.

He hoped the skip would be out of here before that happened.

"Yash, I don't have time for guessing games," he said, spiraling toward the ocean, hoping that maneuver would help the skip shed at least some of the vehicles following them. Aircars shouldn't be able to function over the ocean, at least the kind of aircars he was familiar with.

Which meant exactly nothing. He had no idea what the technology was like elsewhere on the planet.

"The ships," she said. "They're—"

Then the *Ivoire* pinged in. "The fighters are tracking you," Rooney said. "They'll meet up with you as soon as you get out of the atmosphere. We don't have enough fighters to take on these ships, nor do we have enough firepower ourselves. If more than one of these ships is outfitted like we are, we're in trouble. They don't know where we are yet, but it's only a matter of time."

And whoever *they* were, they'd follow the skip to the *Ivoire*.

"Maybe you should leave without us," Coop said. "We'll land somewhere on this planet and wait it out."

"No," Rooney said. "I want us all out of here. Together."

Contradicting him. That was new.

The skip rose above the storm, finally. The skip itself seemed to be breathing a sigh of relief. Nothing had followed them through the clouds, but that didn't mean anything.

There were enough ships in orbit that some of them were probably monitoring the skip. They'd be waiting for it.

Coop was waiting until the last minute to shield the vessel, using the shields that Lost Souls had designed. Those shields were based on what they called stealth tech, which was some weird version of *anacapa* energy. He didn't pretend to understand how it was created, but he did know how it functioned.

It masked the skip's signature from most screening methods, so it seemed like the skip wasn't there at all. And, the best part, it didn't leave a gap in the readings like so many other screening signatures.

But anyone looking out a portal would still be able to see a skip, particularly if they already knew it was there.

He set up the shield, ready to activate it with the touch of his finger. Once it engaged, he would sprint in a different direction—which one, he didn't yet know—before punching out of the atmosphere.

The space junk would help him. If he maneuvered through it properly, he might confuse the ships coming for them.

"The ships," Yash repeated. "This is important, Coop."

"Fine," he said, monitoring everything, trying not to think about the fact that he had two injured people in the back, and part of the skip was shuddering, a part that shouldn't have been shuddering. "Just tell me."

"Some of those ships," Yash said. "They're wrong."

God. She was still playing guessing games.

"I don't know what that means," Coop said.

Yash was monitoring the ships as well. And she was watching behind them to see who followed them across that ocean.

He couldn't see the water anymore, just the cloud cover below them, thick and heavy.

"The ships look like Fleet design with weird, unnecessary parts grafted onto them. Like an extra wing or a fin or I don't know. It looks strange."

He glanced at her. She was pointing to a few of the vessels coming into Sector Base E-2.

"You mean, like the stuff on the doors going into Sector Base E-2," he said. "Like that wall."

"Yeah," she said. "And the ships that are Fleet vessels? From what I can see, they're old. They're suffering nanobit decay. They're not moving as fast as they should if they were actual Fleet ships."

"The weapons," he said, "where they connect, they unbond nanobits."

The skip had told him that. But he had been monitoring the damage, and as far as he could tell, the nanobits had rallied and were repairing the holes caused by the weapons.

But the repairs were being conducted as if the material had been destroyed, not unbonded.

Again, something he couldn't think about. Because if he thought about it, he would worry that the unbonding was causing the shudder. The shudder originated on the same side of the skip.

On the upside, the damage had not expanded, which it should have done if the unbonding was contagious somehow. At the moment, the repairs were holding.

"Unbonding," Yash said, sounding surprised. "Well, that explains how their shots went through the environmental suits."

He shot her another glance, surprised. Somehow he had thought the injuries were more mundane than that—a broken bone, a concussion. He hadn't expected actual blood.

Yash ignored his look, or maybe she was so involved in the telemetry coming at them that she didn't notice.

She was half shaking her head.

"But with weapons like that," she said, "you'd think that the old Fleet vessels they had would have repaired themselves."

"Unless they're not the Fleet," Coop said. "Maybe they came up with a way to defeat some of the Fleet's tech, but not how to build it."

Yash ran a hand over her face, nodding just a little. "That makes sense. That explains the brown stuff. It's an attempt at nanobits. A failed attempted."

"Don't assume," Coop said.

"I'm not," she said, in a tone that told him she was. "Do you think those ships are spoils of some war?"

Like he had thought the ships in the Boneyard were damaged in some war? He had no idea. And he wasn't going to bring that up.

"We don't need to know who they are," Coop said. "We just need to get away from them."

"I wish we knew who they were," Yash said, more to herself than to him.

Knowing who they were was a luxury. Coop needed to concentrate on flying the skip.

"How many ships are behind us?" Coop asked.

"Too damn many," Yash said. "And I can't get a fix on the type. It seems like every single type of ship the Fleet ever invented is either in orbit, heading into the sector base, or chasing us."

"Every single type...?" Her words made him think about the Boneyard, about the fact that it had fired on them, about the way the ships were gathered there. He had assumed that was a Fleet-designed place, like the Scrapheaps he had heard about in school, but he could have been wrong.

The jumble inside Sector Base E-2, the haphazard equipment. Was some group trying to emulate the Fleet? Or were they just using old, found ships to create their own armada?

Which gave him an idea.

"Tell the *Ivoire* to call off the fighters," he said.

"What?" Yash sounded stunned. "We'll never get out if we do that."

"Sure we will," he said with more confidence than he felt. But he was convinced they wouldn't escape even with the fighters.

As Rooney had said, there weren't enough of them, and the *Ivoire* didn't dare try to rescue the skip. That was why he had offered to stay.

Staying on Nindowne would have at least given his people a chance to survive. Although the *Ivoire* might not have escaped, not with all these ships.

Yash shifted slightly in her chair as if she was going to argue with him.

"Can you do something weird?" he asked, hoping to forestall any complaints about his new plan. He hadn't even shared it yet, and she opposed it.

Although he probably would have in her shoes as well.

"Weird?" she asked.

He nodded.

"From what I'm seeing," he said, "they're using some old DV-Class ships, right?"

"Yeah," she said.

"Using the Lost Souls tech, we can mask our ships from their sensors, right?"

"Yes," she said, starting to sound irritated.

"Which means that we can change our signature," he said.

"Yee-ah." She was speaking slower, as if she was trying to figure out what he was trying to do.

"Can we change the signature of one of the DV-Class vessels, one of the ones that's not close to Nindowne yet?"

"I suppose," she said. "I've never done it, but it should be possible. Although not for very long. Why?"

"Because," he said, "I want them to think that ship is an outsider vessel."

"You want them to think that ship is the *Ivoire*?" she asked.

"Close but not quite," he said. "Use the *Shadow*'s signature, or the signature of one of the other DV-Class vessels we have at Lost Souls. If this doesn't work, we don't want to help them find the *Ivoire*."

"Meanwhile, we head to the *Ivoire*," Yash said. Then she leaned back. "Chen, what kind of shape is Perkins in?"

Coop felt a pang. He hadn't wanted to know that Perkins was one of the two injured people.

"Still unconscious," Chen said.

"Dammit," Yash said. "Lankstadt, I need you here. You need to do everything I tell you."

"Yes, ma'am," he said.

"One last question, Coop," Yash said, as her fingers started dancing on the control panel. "How are we going to prevent them from following us to the *Ivoire* anyway?"

"You're going to ghost us," he said.

She let out another involuntary laugh. "I haven't done that since school."

"I'm glad you did it then," he said. "I was too tight-assed to try anything like that."

"Which is why you were on the captain track and I became a lowly engineer," she said. "You're asking me to do a lot of work in a short period of time."

"Yes," he said. "I am."

Because he knew, if anyone could do this, Yash could.

He was gambling all of their lives on her skills.

But, he reminded himself, it wouldn't be the first time—and he doubted it would be the last.

37

GHOSTING.

Every kid learned how to do it. Or rather, every kid with a technical bent.

Or every kid had heard of it. Like Coop—so upright he hadn't tried it, but he had known it was possible.

To create a ghost, all someone had to do was replicate the ship inside the sensors, making a false image of it, and sending the fake signal to any ships nearby as if it were a real signal.

Some kids only used the signal, but the truly advanced ones, like Yash herself, created a complete three-dimensional ghost of the ship, sending it along that same trajectory, creating a dual spoof of the sensors. The unsophisticated spoof could be discovered with a simple glance out the portals of any ship; the advanced spoof crossed the human visual range as well, making it seem like there was an actual ship outside the portal, when all that was there was an elaborate hologram that managed to travel on a trajectory of its own.

Ghosting of both kinds was unbelievably simple to do, and not that easy to crack unless you knew what to look for. It would also have been easy to design around it, prevent it, to make it nearly impossible to do.

Yet the Fleet never had—and Yash always believed that someone, somewhere, had decided it needed to stay so that kids had a relatively safe way to rebel without endangering any ship they were on—especially the school ships, where hundreds of smart kids crowded together, alone too long with nothing to do.

Lankstadt joined her at the controls. Coop was maneuvering, zigging the skip for a moment or two, then zagging in the opposite direction. He went up, and down, back into the clouds for a few moments, then rising back up.

He couldn't continue doing that for long.

"You ever ghosted?" Yash asked.

"Who hasn't?" Lankstadt said as he crouched beside her. There were only two chairs near the control panel of this skip.

She glanced at Coop. "He hasn't."

"So that's how you become captain," Lankstadt said. "Why do I always get information like this too late?"

"Yash, please," Coop said, apparently not appreciating the levity—which surprised Yash. He usually didn't mind it at all, even in tight situations.

"I need you to ghost this skip," Yash said to Lankstadt. "And when I give you some coordinates, you send that ghost in that direction."

"Yes, ma'am," Lankstadt said, and immediately got to work.

"Can you do a dual ghost?"

"That's all I ever learned," Lankstadt said, which relieved her. Because if he didn't know how to make a dual ghost, then she would have had to do some of the work herself.

She was busy enough trying to figure out how to convince the ships out there that one of their own was the *Shadow*, which was the ship Lynda Rooney usually commanded, one of the ships they had left at Lost Souls. Yash had those specs at her fingertips, and right now she needed everything to happen quickly.

"This is not going to last very long," she said to Coop.

"I just need whoever is commanding those ships to look in the wrong direction while we leave the atmosphere and head to the first moon," he said.

She suspected her work wouldn't even last that long.

"We could time it," she said. "Ghost first, then layer in the trickery."

"Whatever you think will work," Coop said. "I'm not going to have time to help."

As if he thought that she wanted help. She was only informing him so that he could coordinate his own actions.

And then she understood what he had been saying all along: there would be no coordination. She was going to do what she needed to do, and he was going to fly the skip, and they were going to hope that this trickery would work.

"Tell me when you're ready to go," Coop said.

"Lankstadt?" Yash asked.

"Ready now, ma'am," he said.

She half smiled at him. "You did this a lot as a kid, didn't you?"

"More than I should have," he said primly.

Yash would have laughed again—usually laughing relieved the tension—but Coop didn't seem all that appreciative at the moment.

She picked her vessel—a DV-Class ship that looked like it had been built around the same time as the *Ivoire*, only the other ship was in terrible condition. It limped its way toward Nindowne, which was just perfect for Yash's purposes.

The farther back that ship stayed from the pack of ships heading toward the planet, the better for her ruse. The other ships wouldn't be watching that one—not until they believed they saw the skip heading toward it.

"Here are the coordinates," she said to Lankstadt. "You'll go first."

"We fly out of the atmosphere together," Coop said. "I'm going into the thickest pile of space junk I can find."

She understood why. He was hoping for a little extra distraction.

"As soon as we're out of the atmosphere," Coop said, "I'll shield."

Shields didn't work well coming out of atmosphere, so Coop was going to have to activate the shield the second the skip emerged.

"We don't want them to see two ships," he said. "So you're going to activate your ghost—"

"Ghosts," Yash said.

"—right after I activate the shield."

"There'll be a nanosecond or more of emptiness," Yash said. "Someone observant might see it."

"That's why I'm using the space junk," Coop said. "And I'm gambling on two other things. I'm gambling that their equipment isn't as sophisticated as it should be. I'm also going to gamble that they've never seen this little maneuver, so they don't know what to look for."

"You think the Fleet doesn't allow ghosting anymore?" Lankstadt asked. He sounded almost sad.

"We don't think they're the Fleet," Yash said.

"Ready?" Coop asked. "Because here we go."

38

AT THE VERY LAST MINUTE, Coop realized that Lankstadt wasn't strapped in.

"Lankstadt," Coop said, "turn on the gravity in your boots and hang on tight. I don't trust the attitude controls on this baby."

"Got it," Lankstadt said just as Yash asked, "Is there something wrong with the skip?"

Was there something wrong? There were a lot of things wrong. She apparently couldn't feel the shaking, but Coop could. It felt like a tremor that a nervous person had in his hands, something that he couldn't quite control.

Only the skip had the tremor, not Coop.

"Just a precaution," he said, not wanting to distract her. "Now, everyone. Hang on."

He programmed the *Ivoire*'s coordinates into the skip.

He changed the skip's position ninety degrees from where it had been just a moment before and accelerated as he headed out of the atmosphere.

He was taking another risk he hadn't mentioned to Yash. By waiting to shield after he got out of the atmosphere, he risked hitting some of that space junk.

He figured he was a good enough pilot to head into the thick of the junk and avoid hitting any of it.

He also hoped there was nothing too small coming at them.

He didn't have time to process that junk, to see where the safest pieces were.

He was going to fly this skip as fast as it could go, maybe faster than it should go given the condition it was in, and he hoped he could outrun the illusions that Yash and Lankstadt were creating.

It took maybe five seconds to launch this skip into orbit. The moment the skip broke through the atmosphere, Coop said, "Now, Lankstadt!"

Coop threaded past pieces of metal and other things he couldn't identify. Collision alerts were activating all over the board, some beeping at him.

He ignored them as he activated the shield around the skip.

The shield flickered for a second and then held.

Nothing had hit the skip after all.

On his own equipment, he saw an image of the skip appear right next to his position. The fake skip moved at the same speed he was, mirroring their path for a good ten seconds before veering off.

The path it needed to take to go to the fake *Shadow* curved toward a cluster of planets much farther away. Coop had to negotiate around a small moon, and then an asteroid belt, and then into the wide-open expanse of space where the *Ivoire* waited.

Rooney had moved the *Ivoire* there so that the jump to foldspace would be easy. Something about the jump to foldspace niggled at Coop too, but he couldn't think about that right now.

He needed to get the skip to the *Ivoire* first.

A rumble started toward the back of the skip.

"Hey, Captain," said an unfamiliar voice from the back. Had to have been Chen. "Things are vibrating back here."

"Yeah," he said. "Just hang on."

The weapon the Not-Fleet had hit them with had been damaging after all. It hadn't affected the exterior of the skip. Instead, it had burrowed into the skip and started unbonding the nanobits inside. Maybe the repair on the outside would hold long enough for them to reach the *Ivoire*.

And if that weapon was unbonding nanobits while it burrowed into the skip, what was happening to Perkins and the other injured person? Did the weapon they got hit with operate in the same way?

Probably, since whatever had hit the skip had been used in that ice storm.

Coop cast those thoughts from his mind. He couldn't do anything about that right now. He just had to pilot as fast as he could and pray this skip would hold together.

"We have two fighters on our six," Yash said, "and they're not ours."

Great. This skip didn't have its own weapons system. Normally, he would try to outrun them, but they were fighters. He wouldn't be able to.

"You think they're tracking us?" Coop asked.

"They're close enough to," Yash said.

"Are you done with the *Shadow*?" he asked.

"No," she said.

"Then finish that and let me worry about the fighters," he said. He wasn't going to monitor what was happening with the fake skip and the fake *Shadow* and all the other ships. He was only going to monitor this skip and hope to hell he could get it away from this planet without losing any more lives.

The fighters continued to trail, but they didn't shoot. That seemed odd to him. Either they didn't have weaponry (not possible, right? That couldn't be possible), or they weren't entirely sure he was here. Maybe they had seen the ghosting start, or maybe they were tracing the echo on their systems, the kind of echo that the stealth tech occasionally created.

He made a sharp veer to his left, then piloted down, backward, and up behind the fighters.

A small cry echoed from the back, followed by a sliding sound and a sharp bang. He tried not to pay attention to that. Clearly, though, he had been right: the attitude controls were failing. Other parts of the skip were failing too.

He hoped the inertial dampeners were still intact because he would need them when he reached the *Ivoire*.

But that was a long way away.

Right now, he had to shed those fighters—and it looked like he had.

They continued on the same path.

They had no idea where he was. They had seen him leave, plotted their trajectory based on his path, and matched his speed.

Their tech was better than he wanted it to be.

However, they were the only ships following him. No one else was. Which meant that everyone else was fooled—at least for the moment.

He hoped no one had seen the *Ivoire's* fighters or had thought much of them. He also hoped those ships were already back at the *Ivoire*—and had not been followed there.

That wasn't his problem though. If they were followed, Lynda was going to have to deal with whatever ships crossed her path.

Coop had to get to the *Ivoire*, and he had to do so before this little skip fell apart.

He flew beneath the Not-Fleet fighters—directly beneath them, staying close enough that if they saw an echo, they would think it was being caused by their own equipment. They were going fast enough, maybe a little too fast for this skip, and since he needed to go fast, he kept pace.

"You done yet, Yash?" he asked.

"As done as I'm going to be," she said. "Let's hope this holds."

He glanced at the holomaps, saw the *Shadow*—or what looked like the *Shadow*—at the end of a long string of vessels.

And then his breath caught. In that string of vessels were two fold-space search vessels. They were three models up from the *Arama*, which he had served on as a young man. He had made recommendations on how to improve foldspace search vessels, including ways to track where a ship went into foldspace and also have a better chance of figuring out what its trajectory in foldspace was.

The newer ships (newer from his timeline, anyway) could track a foldspace opening up to twenty-four hours after a ship left a region. The newer ships could read energy signatures that wouldn't entirely dissipate—sometimes for days.

"Dammit," Coop said.

"What?" Yash asked, not looking at him. She was still doing whatever she was doing to make some other ship look like the *Shadow*.

He couldn't consult with her—not that he had time.

"Nothing," he said, although it wasn't nothing. Because getting to the *Ivoire* was now only part of the goal. The *Ivoire* had to get out of this system without some ship following it all the way to Lost Souls.

He didn't know if the foldspace search vessels could do that now, but he also didn't know how much tech had changed in the past 5,000 years. Also, if these Not-Fleet people were advancing their own tech, tech that destroyed Fleet tech, then they might have figured out on their own how to do something Coop's Fleet had never learned how to do.

The Not-Fleet people might be able to track through foldspace.

He had to consider tracking through foldspace an option, just to protect Lost Souls and everyone in it.

He frowned.

Lost Souls…

The fighters peeled away, apparently no longer able to track anything. Or maybe they had been called to deal with the *Shadow*. They were heading in the direction of the fake skip.

Coop changed his trajectory slightly, not wanting them to come back and be able to trail him by energy signature or something else.

The skip was still rumbling, and the rumbling was getting worse.

But he didn't have too much farther to go to get to the *Ivoire*.

"Yash, you too busy to contact the *Ivoire*?" he asked.

"I'm not busy at all," she said. "I'm just monitoring our fake *Shadow* and hoping it sticks long enough for us to get out of sensor range."

Coop glanced at the skip's internal monitors. The very center of the walls was crumbling, or being eaten away by whatever that weapon was. The skip would end up looking just fine, but someone would be able to put their hand through it.

"You gotta strap in, Lankstadt," Coop said, envisioning Lankstadt sliding into the walls and going right through. "Everyone, hoods up. Full environmental suits."

Just in case.

No one asked why. They trusted him. He wasn't sure he trusted his abilities to get them out of here, but they did.

"I got the *Ivoire*," Yash said, "but I don't recommend you chat long. I'd like to cycle through quickly."

Coop didn't have time to chat long, nor did he have time to tell Yash that.

"Lynda," he said, "we're coming in hot. You're going to need to separate us from most of the ship, and you'll need to set up a shield for the interior of the ship. We're going to be going faster than I want, and you're going to have to siphon off some of that energy."

He took a breath, glad he had an experienced crew. They didn't look at him sideways at all. They knew if this failed, everyone would be flattened against the interior of the *Ivoire*.

Plus there was one other problem.

"And, Lynda," he said, "we're going to need to be quarantined. We might be bringing in something that could unbond nanobits."

"Got it," Rooney said. She was such a professional. She didn't ask why or what, knowing they didn't have time.

"Finally," he said. "I'm going to be cagey here, just in case. But you need to set coordinates to get us out of here. I don't want you to go to base. I want you to set coordinates to that starbase where Dix went off the deep end."

"Will do, Captain," Rooney said.

"We'll be there in about five," Coop said, and signed out.

"What the hell?" Yash asked. "Starbase Kappa?"

Coop nodded. He'd explain to her later. "How's our ruse?"

"It's about to expire," she said. "And then they're going to search for us."

Lankstadt had made it to one of the chairs and was strapped in. Coop looked over his shoulder, saw that everyone in the back was protected—conscious or not.

"How fast do you think I can make this thing go?" he asked Yash.

"And keep it intact?" she asked. "You're already there."

"That's what I was afraid of," he said, and hoped the skip hung together long enough to get them to the *Ivoire*.

39

YASH PULLED UP HER HOOD. Coop hadn't yelled at her for leaving hers off. She wasn't even sure he had noticed. He hadn't pulled his up either. He was looking wild-eyed, something she had only seen a few times in all the years they had worked together.

He didn't think they would make it to the *Ivoire*.

She called up one small holoscreen and looked at the skip's specs. Something was eating it from the inside. That something was heading toward the engines, and if that something hit the engines, then the skip would stop functioning.

They'd continue forward, but slower, and eventually, the other ships would find them.

This far out, the *Ivoire* wouldn't be able to rescue them. Even up close, the *Ivoire* might not be able to rescue them, depending on what was happening there.

However, the shields were holding, which was good, considering. Because the skip was now far enough away from that group of ships that the work she had done to spoof one of them couldn't be sustained.

At least Lankstadt's ghost version of the skip still functioned. That was a self-sustaining image that would only dissipate if something hit it.

She saw the moment the *Shadow*'s signature vanished from the other ship. She saw it in two ways: first on her own equipment, which told her that it couldn't sustain the spoof, and then in the ships heading toward the fake version of the *Shadow*.

Those ships slowed, like people did when they thought they saw someone they knew, and then realized that the person they were looking at wasn't their friend after all. The ships stopped then, as their commanders started searching for the actual destination of the fake skip.

It would only be a matter of time before someone on those fighters mentioned the trajectory they had been following, and the ships would retrace those steps.

"Okay," Yash said, "they just figured out that they were chasing one of their own ships."

"Got it." Coop was actually leaning in, toward the console, as if he could physically push the skip forward. He kept moving his hands along the console, monitoring everything, but not changing anything.

Yash had to look away. She wanted to tinker, to force this little skip to move faster, and she didn't dare, especially since something was eating at it.

She hoped to God that whatever was eating at the skip wasn't eating at Perkins and Bridge too.

The ghosted skip vanished.

"Damn," she said.

"What?" Coop asked.

"They're going to start searching for us now," she said.

"Yeah, they already have an idea where we are." He didn't sound panicked, just matter of fact.

Yash nodded, even though he wasn't looking at her. Why had these skips been built without weapons? She was so going to add weapons to every single ship that came out of Lost Souls.

If she ever made it back there.

40

THERE IT WAS—the *Ivoire*—a big blob on one of his screens, an actual ship on the holomap right in front of him, and a vast array of telemetry on the screen he used the most.

He felt relieved, but worried at the same time. This close to the finish line was where most commanders screwed up. They slowed down, they thought they were safe, they thought it was over.

He still had a lot of things to do.

"Fighters," Yash said.

He glanced at the wider two-dimensional screen next to Yash. A dozen fighters, from a variety of makes and models, had locked onto them and were heading this way.

They had clearly found the skip, so Coop dropped the stealth tech and diverted as much energy as he could to the small little shield that some stupid designer had put into the skip, clearly thinking no one would use it.

He hoped it would hold up to one or two shots, if it worked at all.

"Just got a coded message from the *Ivoire*," Yash said. "Cargo Bay Three is ready and about to open on our signal."

Cargo bay. He hadn't expected them to go into a cargo bay, but it made sense. The cargo bays were mostly empty on the *Ivoire* since it rarely traveled long distances any longer.

"Those fighters are a lot faster than anything we have," Yash said. "Or they have *anacapa* drives too, and used them to get here."

Short range *anacapa* usage? In a small ship? That would be suicidal. Coop didn't have time to think about it.

"They're almost in firing range," Yash said.

"Tell Rooney to fire on them the moment they get close enough. The last thing we want is some modified version of that weapon to hit the *Ivoire*," Coop said.

Plus, he and Yash both knew that the *Ivoire* couldn't use its shields for that moment when the skip entered the cargo bay. If a fighter was close enough, it could hit the *Ivoire* at that moment and do a lot of damage.

"Done," Yash said.

Coop was not monitoring the fighters. He wasn't doing anything except planning the quickest course to that open cargo bay door.

That weapon's destruction was nearly to the engines, so it no longer mattered if he overloaded them. They would be gone in a matter of minutes.

He pushed the engines, taking them to their very limit.

The skip shuddered so hard it felt like it was about to come apart— which it actually was.

The *Ivoire* loomed large on the exterior screen. All he could see were the sides of the ship, gleaming darkly in the light of distant stars.

He had never seen anything so welcoming.

The cargo bay was just to his left.

He had to maneuver slightly, barely turning the skip. He could no longer program the changes into the helm. He had to do it by hand, and he was, sweat coming down the side of his face as if he had been yanking the skip forward by hand.

Maybe he had been.

The side of the *Ivoire* disappeared. All he could see now was the mouth of the cargo bay, open and ready to receive the skip.

The interior of the cargo bay looked unfamiliar—filled with white webbing—and he realized he had never landed a ship into a quarantined bay before.

First time for everything.

He hoped Rooney had set up internal shields. He hoped she was prepared for them coming in too fast.

He hoped they had some way to siphon off the extra energy, because he couldn't double-check for it.

The skip entered the bay much too fast. Coop immediately let up the speed, hoping something would stop them. The shuddering was so extreme that bits of the ceiling panels started falling.

He hoped someone was monitoring this, because the engines had overloaded and they could explode.

Yash was trying to stop that from her console. He could have told her it wouldn't work, but he let her try. She knew a lot more about all of these ships than he did.

He leaned back as the skip slowly stopped shuddering.

They hadn't shot through any walls in the cargo bay. The crew hadn't been flung forward as the skip came to a hard stop.

Everything had worked.

He really hadn't thought it possible.

"We're here," he said, and didn't sound as triumphant as he wanted to. "Somehow, we're here."

41

THEY HAD TO GO THROUGH decontamination, which was the last thing Yash wanted to do. She had already called for medical assistance, but—per Coop's order—warned the medical team that whatever had happened to Perkins and Bridge might hurt the entire ship. Everyone needed to be warned.

The back of the skip looked like it had been hit with a dozen weapons, even though it hadn't. Bits of the wall were gone, leaving gaping holes. Some of the furniture, normally attached to the skip itself, had been flung into an interior wall, narrowly missing Bridge.

The moment the skip stopped, Stone had gotten up to tend to the patients. She seemed calmer than Yash expected.

"My data strips?" Yash asked as she stopped near the remaining members of the team. She knew she sounded insensitive, but the strips had the only information anyone had been able to pull from Sector Base E-2.

"I've got them," Chen said. "I had Perkin's strip, and I grabbed the others when the skip started shuddering."

The relief Yash felt was more profound than she realized. She had been worried this had all been for nothing.

"Oh, thank you," Yash said.

"I'll get them out of here, if you like," Chen said. "Can they make it through decontamination?"

"I don't know," Yash said. She had no idea what level of decontamination Rooney had ordered up or what type. "But I'm going to stay here. I'll take the data strips and upload them."

"Won't that harm the systems on the *Ivoire*?" Chen asked.

Yash almost smiled at how deep a security officer's training actually went.

"I don't think so," Yash said. "But I'm going to layer the files with as much protection as I can. I'll also isolate them inside the *Ivoire*'s systems."

If she could even access the systems.

At least the skip's shuddering had ceased. Coop had shut down the engines. He had already scrambled off of the skip.

The danger wasn't over yet, and he needed to be on the bridge. Yash didn't. There were people who could handle everything from this point forward.

She needed to secure the data, and maybe help the med techs with the injured.

"You get out of here," Yash said. "You've done everything you can."

"I'm going to stay until they're out." Chen nodded at Bridge and Perkins. Stone was still working with them. Lankstadt had walked in their direction, looking no worse for the wear.

They were in good hands.

Yash took the data strips from Chen, then headed back to the console.

Despite the confidence she had expressed to Chen, Yash wasn't sure she could keep the data isolated. She had to hope the system would flag anything that was amiss.

She usually didn't rely on hope. But she had no real choice here.

She had to rely on it in a dozen different ways. Including hope that this skip would hold together long enough for her to get the data transferred.

She didn't even want to think about that.

So she sat down and got to work.

42

DECONTAMINATION HADN'T BEEN PAINFUL, but it had been messy and unpleasant. Coop submitted to it to save his ship, leaving his environmental suit behind along with his clothes and his boots.

He showed up on the bridge wearing the white, loose weave clothing that was standard in any decontamination chamber. He hadn't wanted to risk more time heading to his cabin for a proper change of clothes.

No one on the bridge seemed to notice. Anita Tren was the only one who acknowledged his arrival. She nodded at him and gave him a small smile before returning to work.

Rooney stood near the captain's chair, one hand resting on the chair's arm. Xilvii was still at the farthest console from the chair, his dark hair in spikes around his head, not as a style, but because he'd been running his hands through it.

He looked years older than he had before the *Ivoire* left Lost Souls.

The other three people on the bridge seemed calm—the kind of calm that came in the middle of a prolonged battle. Coop didn't say a word to any of them as he headed to the chair.

Rooney stepped aside. "Captain," she said.

"Stay," he said. "You're running this mission."

Which wasn't entirely true. He needed to have input, but he didn't even know where they were at the moment.

Then the *Ivoire* stuttered its way out of foldspace. On the single open screen that covered the far wall, the remains of Starbase Kappa appeared. Coop's stomach twisted.

The last time he had been here, he had started an incident that had nearly sent the Nine Planets Alliance into a war with the Empire. He didn't see any Empire ships nearby, however, and that disappointed him. Where were they when he needed them?

Starbase Kappa was called the Room of Lost Souls by everyone in this time period. It had had a malfunctioning *anacapa* drive that Coop's people had managed to shut down. The starbase still drifted now, empty and abandoned. Apparently, ships in the Empire still avoided it.

"We're here," Rooney said. "What's next?"

"Send a distress signal," he said.

She blinked at him. She had fought alongside him against the Empire less than a year ago. He had wrestled them to a stalemate at the border between the Empire and the Nine Planets, a stalemate that still held.

"You want to announce our presence?" she asked.

"No," he said. "Sorry. A standard distress signal. Then move away from the starbase."

"You heard him," Rooney said. "Distress signal. Move."

His team didn't need to hear more than that. Nor did they question what he was doing. But Rooney did. He could see it in her eyes.

It only took a few moments to move away from the starbase.

"We've gotten a response," Anita Tren said. "Two ships, less than three minutes out."

"Good," Coop said. "We've got less than two minutes then. Program the *anacapa* with the coordinates for home."

Home. He hadn't expected to use that word. He wasn't sure he ever had in this context.

"To be clear," Rooney said. "You want to head back to Lost Souls Corporation."

"Yes," he said. "Right now."

She waved a finger at Anita, who set to work. Coop didn't even look at the *anacapa* drive.

He was about to tell Rooney why he was doing this when one of the foldspace search vessels appeared near Starbase Kappa.

Coop's heart jumped. He had hoped that the Not-Fleet didn't have that technology, but they did.

He also hoped the *Ivoire* was far enough away that they wouldn't notice it, not before the *Ivoire* jumped to foldspace.

At that moment, the *Ivoire* entered foldspace a second time in ten minutes, leaving Starbase Kappa behind. The ship bumped ever so slightly, the transition into foldspace so much smoother than it used to be.

Coop let out a small breath.

"Son of a bitch," Rooney said. "How did you know they could track us?"

"I didn't," Coop said. "I was kinda hoping they couldn't."

He was both thrilled and worried about the fact that they had the technology to track a ship through foldspace. Thrilled, because that meant no one would get lost in foldspace again. Worried that they might follow the *Ivoire* to the Nine Planets Alliance.

"You solved the problem though," Anita said. "One of those ships answering the distress signal was nearly at the starbase. That Empire ship will deal with whatever ships emerge from foldspace—and do so quickly. Great distraction."

Coop nodded. He hoped the distraction would work. But he wasn't going to know if it did, not really. The Not-Fleet ships might not follow the *Ivoire* to foldspace, but they might make note of where he was going.

More likely, though, was that the Empire would keep those ships from getting anywhere near the *Ivoire's* most recent foldspace entry point.

"The Empire's going to think those are our ships," Xilvii said. "Aren't you worried they'll think we violated the truce?"

"It's not a formal truce," Coop said. "Besides, either those strange ships will go back into foldspace or they'll be captured by the Empire. If they're captured, the Empire will know right away that the ships aren't ours."

"And whoever is using those ships will find out about us," Xilvii said.

"Maybe," Coop said. He didn't believe it, though. They hadn't obviously stolen anything from Sector Base E-2. The arrival of all those ships might have been the way that whoever ran Sector Base E-2 now ran their defenses.

Or they had seen the entry into Sector Base E-2 as an act of war.

Whatever it was, the *Ivoire* couldn't go back there. No one from Lost Souls could go back there.

If they stayed away, then whoever ran Sector Base E-2 now might see the entire thing as someone exploring the wrong place at the wrong time.

Then he shook his head at himself. He was being hopelessly optimistic.

Coop and his crew had arrived in a working Fleet vessel; they had used Fleet technology, albeit old tech. They understood old versions of Standard. They had used a skip augmented with Fleet tech. And they had activated an *anacapa* drive, not once, but twice.

The Not-Fleet was now on notice: there were others using Fleet tech in areas that the Fleet should have abandoned millennia ago.

If the Not-Fleet even cared about the Fleet, even understood Fleet history, then they would know this was a problem.

The Not-Fleet had to know about the Fleet, right? Because the Not-Fleet had to have a reason for developing weapons that unbonded nanobits.

Coop now wished he had gotten information out of his section of the sector base. He had no idea who had been chasing them or why.

"I think we did the best we could, given the circumstances," Rooney said. "We've seen several abandoned sector bases now. We simply assumed this one had been too, and we were wrong. Next time we won't be that unprepared."

"We're not heading back to Sector Base E-2," Coop said.

"Never say never," Anita muttered.

He smiled at her, but she didn't smile back.

"I mean," she said, "what if they find out who we are from the Empire? They might come after us."

"They might," Coop said. "We'll have to make sure Lost Souls is ready. But I don't think they'll find out about us."

"Care to share why?" Anita asked.

"The Empire," Coop said. He had been studying the Empire ever since he had to fight against it. "They're extremely difficult to deal with. They won't know what these vessels are or how they got so deep into Empire space. The Empire will deal with them as invaders first, which means the Empire won't share information with them. About anything."

"If only one ship followed us to Starbase Kappa," Rooney said, "then they're screwed."

She'd been studying the Empire too. Coop figured it was only a matter of time before the Empire tried to subdue the Nine Planets again, and Rooney agreed. They both wanted to be prepared before they went into battle against it.

"The Empire is going to try to do everything to find out how that ship got into Empire space," Rooney said, "which means they'll deal harshly with the crew."

"If the crew doesn't fight back," Xilvii said.

"Empire ships are not made of nanobits," Coop said. "Their ships will be a lot harder for one foldspace search vehicle to defeat. I think we're safe enough for now."

"They'll know we went into foldspace," Xilvii said.

"They might not even have registered our presence," Rooney said. "Besides, I scanned Starbase Kappa. It's still abandoned, and it doesn't have any monitoring equipment. There should be no record of our presence in this part of space, provided the ship chasing us didn't see us."

Coop nodded. He didn't tell the crew about his other gamble. He was hoping that the Empire's vessels still had a stealth tech energy signature, one that would interfere with any tracking that a foldspace search vessel might deploy.

"Heading out of foldspace," Anita said.

Coop looked at the screens in front of him. They had gone white for that half second between foldspace and regular space.

He felt no trepidation at all about being in foldspace anymore. Apparently this mission—or the series of trips he had taken recently—had gotten him past the trauma of getting lost in foldspace.

"When are we?" Xilvii asked, sounding tense.

But, apparently, not everyone was past that trepidation.

The screen cleared, and Lost Souls appeared. The starbase that the corporation had commandeered floated in the distance, looking smaller than Coop expected.

When were they indeed?

"Pinging," Xilvii said. Most ships coming out of foldspace pinged now, getting a reading from Lost Souls as to the date and time, rather than having some poor hapless person inform them that something had gone wrong with their trip.

Rooney was looking at the floating screen to her right, her body tense. Maybe Coop was the only person who wasn't worried about being in foldspace any longer.

"We're fine," Rooney said after a moment. "We didn't lose or gain time."

The bridge crew let out a collective sigh of relief—everyone except Coop.

He tapped the controls on the arm of his chair, without sitting in it since, technically, he had given the comm to Rooney.

The skip was still intact, the engines powered down. As far as he could tell, the quarantine was working. Only one life sign remained on board the skip.

Yash. She was working at something.

She was always working at something.

The medical team had managed to take the injured to a quarantined medical unit in another part of the bay. The unit was updating in real time: no one had died yet, although Bridge was critical. Apparently, he had been hit full-on with one of those weapons.

Two injuries, some information, a Not-Fleet, and a narrow escape.

Coop suddenly felt giddy. He had missed command. He had missed those moments when every decision had to be made quickly or something awful would happen.

He hated the day-to-day routine of Lost Souls.

He clearly needed to be back, doing some form of this, some kind of work, leading missions, running point.

"Captain?" Rooney asked, glancing down at what he was doing. "Are you all right?"

"Yeah," he said. "I am."

In fact, he was better than he had been in a long, long time. But he didn't tell her that. He needed to process what had happened, figure out what that meant for who he was and where he was going.

Although he did know where he was going.

He was heading forward again.

Into the future.

Just like he had been trained to do.

43

THREE NIGHTS LATER, Yash met Coop in their favorite bar on the *Ivoire*. Entering the bar made her feel like she had gone back in time. The floor-to-ceiling windows overlooked the space station that Lost Souls had just purchased.

Lost Souls had grown so large it was going to move its command to an even larger station, one that continually added wings and layers. Ilona Blake was supervising building, and sometimes, in quiet moments, Yash wondered if Blake was building her own empire.

Other than the view, the bar looked the same. The same twenty-five tables were still organized in the same small groups. Different plants ran along the counter, plants that were actually real, plants that hydroponics believed would thrive in this environment, so close to the main commissary.

Someone had polished the brass. The teak-colored wood shone as well. And alcohol bottles still lined the two interior walls, although most of the bottles were from this time period now, and from the Nine Planets.

The crew had worked their way through the bottles from their past, although Coop once told Yash he had taken some of his favorites and stashed them in his captain's cabin for important occasions.

She wondered if this was one of those occasions.

She didn't see him as she walked deeper into the bar. He had asked her if she wanted to join him, and she had almost said no. She wanted to dig through the information she had pulled out of Sector Base E-2. She had finally gotten the information out of quarantine and realized that she had a treasure trove of data.

The Fleet had not properly cleared the files when it shut down Sector Base E-2 if, indeed, it had shut down Sector Base E-2 rather than simply abandoning it. She had a hunch she would find the answer to that mystery as she looked through the data. She hoped she would find out about a lot of things as she combed it.

She felt that obsession she had felt weeks ago—the one that had led to the trip to Sector Base E-2 in the first place—return. Coop probably sensed it too, which was why he brought her here.

Or maybe he was just lonely. Boss hadn't come back yet, and he had no one to talk with. Not about things that really mattered.

Yash was about to wander to the alcohol wall when she saw Coop, sitting at a table deep in the bar. The chair he was sitting on rested on two legs only, and his feet were crossed on the tabletop. A glass of peach-colored liquid rested on his chest, a glistening square bottle with the same liquid open on the table beside another glass.

Anything that peach color should be sweet, but Yash knew from experience the drink had a bite to it. She couldn't remember the name of the liquid—some kind of weird hybrid that most resembled a vodka mixed with peach-flavored hot sauce. Coop had always liked it, though, and Yash could tolerate it.

He must have seen her reflection in the windows because he leaned forward, poured two fingers of liquid into her glass, and handed it to her as she reached his side.

She sat down on the bench seat. The view from here wasn't so much of the space station as an array of stars beyond.

She sipped the liquid. It was sharper than she remembered, with a tang at the back of the tongue that was almost sour.

"I called this place home," Coop said. "In the middle of everything. I was standing on the bridge of the *Ivoire*, and I called Lost Souls home."

He didn't have to explain any more than that. Yash understood what bothered him: A captain of the Fleet should consider his ship home.

But Coop no longer did.

He had changed—and he had just realized it.

She let out a small sigh. She had changed too. That trip hadn't changed her as much as cemented what she had been slowly realizing—that no matter how hard she tried, no matter what she sought, the past was long in the past. She would never be able to revisit the Fleet, not the one she knew. She would never regain her friends or her family.

She would never again have that comforting naiveté that she had grown up with. She had been raised to believe the Fleet was constant, that while other things changed, the Fleet never did.

And that had been wrong.

"I felt it too," she said. "Going into my lab. It's so big. You can't have a lab that big on a ship."

Coop gave her a sideways glance, maybe checking to see if she truly understood. She smiled at him—not a happy smile. Just a sympathetic one.

Then he put his glass on his chest again.

"Perkins is going to be just fine," he said. "She'll have some rehab, but nothing major."

Perkins had been shot in the back. The shot had destroyed her environmental suit. As the nanobits unbonded, some of them invaded her skin, but hadn't caused any permanent damage.

Bridge, on the other hand, had been shot in the stomach, and by the time they had returned to Lost Souls, the mingling of the unbonded bits with his colon had caused a terrible infection.

"Bridge is still critical," Coop said, "but they're willing to say he'll survive now."

"Good," Yash said. There was nothing else she could add. Because that was one of the other lessons that kept getting reinforced.

People died. One day they were here and the next they weren't, and no matter how much she wanted to believe she could control that, she knew she couldn't.

She didn't take another drink. She didn't want it. She just leaned her head back, still tired from the entire trip.

No ship had followed them to Lost Souls. There was no chatter from the Empire either about an armada of ships invading or anything else. Although that meant nothing. Starbase Kappa was on the other side of the Empire from the Nine Planets Alliance. Even if something major had happened there, the chance of the news arriving at Lost Souls was pretty slim.

"I got the data to my lab," Yash said. "They didn't shut the base down properly. We should have some kind of history of the Fleet once I organize everything."

Coop nodded, slowly twirling the glass as if it were a dial that would open his chest.

"We'll get some answers then," he said.

"Just not the ones we need."

He looked at her sideways, a frown creasing his face.

Yash shrugged one shoulder. "The Fleet's right, you know. We were raised right."

He stopped twirling the glass, still looking at her, waiting for her to continue.

"We wanted to know what happened to everyone so we could go into our future," she said. "But that was the wrong question. What happened that far in the past, it doesn't matter now. It's just a curiosity."

Coop nodded, then looked away from her. He took a sip from his glass, setting it down between them, his hand resting there as if resting the glass on his chest was too much work.

"The questions are what's around us now," she said. "And what do we do with it? Where do we go from here?"

"Or do we go from here," Coop said.

He swung his feet off the table and sat up, then put his glass beside the bottle.

"I need to command a ship, Yash," he said.

"I know," she said.

"But I don't need to live on one."

Her breath caught. That was a hell of an admission from a captain of the Fleet. Only Coop wasn't a captain of the Fleet anymore. He was someone else, and this was an acknowledgement of that.

"Those ships," he said. "That's what the ragtag force we're building here will look like."

"Prettier ships, I hope," Yash said. "They had no sense of design."

He grinned at her. "Yeah. But you know what I mean."

She did. Not a Fleet, per se. They'd been wrong when they talked about building a new Fleet.

They were building something else here. Blake was building a gigantic business. Boss was building knowledge in the form of old ships. And Yash could stop tweaking old technologies and make some newer ones, ones that would actually benefit the Nine Planets, Lost Souls, and whatever it was that Coop wanted to do.

"Boss explores the present to find out about the past," Coop said. "I've been trying that in my own way."

He had. Yash hadn't realized it, but he had.

"It doesn't work for me. I'm not an explorer. I thrive best in combat. Isn't that odd?" He sounded surprised by it.

But Yash wasn't.

"We don't have anyone to fight," Yash said. "We're safe here."

"Maybe," he said. "We don't know. We don't know what's out there, and what's around us. We don't even know what will happen with the Empire."

She set her glass beside his. "You had fun out there."

It sounded like an accusation. She hadn't meant it that way.

But Coop didn't seem to notice. "Fun's the wrong word," he said. "I felt alive. I was using all of my skills for the first time in a long time. I'm good at tactical. I'm good at being the underdog. I'm good at thinking on the fly. And I enjoy it."

"You're not going to go out and provoke fights, are you?" Yash asked.

He shook his head. "I'm not that person."

He was right; he wasn't.

"But I've been thinking," he said. "We need to take over all of Lost Souls' defenses. We need to do more than patrol the border with the Empire. We need to train a lot of crew. We need recruits, and we need good solid DV-Class vessels that we can trust."

"Those Not-Fleet people know how to unbond nanobits," Yash said.

"Yeah," Coop said, "and maybe we can figure that out. That's the first step toward defending against it, right?"

"I suppose," she said. She hated reverse engineering. It always led to mistakes.

"What I want," he said, "is their tech. They know how to track in fold-space. I want that."

Yash didn't have to ask who "they" were. The Not-Fleet people. The ones who attacked.

"You want to go on a raid?" she asked.

"Maybe," he said. "I don't know yet. What I want right now is a mission debrief. I want that from the entire crew. I want to know what worked and what didn't. I want to know how we can improve. And I want to know what they all think we should do in the future."

"That seems very democratic of you," Yash said. "What happened to the hierarchy?"

He shrugged. "It has its uses. But it seems like one of my life lessons—one of the ones I have to learn over and over again—is that rigidity is the enemy of the good. The more rigid I am, the poorer my decisions. And that goes to everything from procedure to hierarchy to assuming I know what the hell I want with my life."

Yash nodded. Then she said, "You remember being in here with Dix that last night?"

"I'll never forget it," Coop said.

"He said we'd lost the future, remember that?"

"Yeah," Coop said. "But at the same time, he'd raised a glass to that window and said, *There's the future. It's been there all along.* I always thought that was ironic, considering he then tried to take our futures away."

"He took his own away," Yash said.

"It frightened him," Coop said. "He was mourning what he called the expected imagined future. The rigid future. The one in which we kept traveling forward under someone else's command."

Yash picked up her glass. That weird bitter liquid seemed appropriate now.

"That's what I've been thinking about," Coop said. "Not the loss of a future. The loss of the hierarchy. Not in the *Ivoire*, but above the *Ivoire*. We're the ones in charge now, Yash. If we want to be. And while we were trained to run departments and ships, we were never trained to lead—not with a vision, *creating* the future."

She sipped, wincing at the taste. She had been bemoaning the loss of structure, saying she wanted to return to the Fleet to join the regimented life she had known. But the regiment was about knowing where you fit, how it all went together, and who expected what from you.

The Fleet had done the thinking. She functioned inside their vision and limited her work to whatever they needed.

Coop was right; there was no one above them now, no structure that showed them where the next step should be.

They could invent it from scratch.

She should have found that terrifying. Instead, it felt freeing.

"I take it we're going to stop searching for the Fleet," she said.

"Yeah," Coop said. "I think we found it."

She looked at him in surprise. "We did?"

He opened his hands, indicating the two of them.

"It was a community, Yash, filled with people, a shared vision, and a collection of ships. We have a community. We have people we care about. We're gaining a collection of ships. We just need a vision."

"It sounds like you're gaining one," Yash said.

"I think I am," Coop said quietly. "I finally think I am."

She nodded. She was too. She wasn't the same woman she had been six years ago. She wasn't the same woman she would have been if she hadn't gotten lost in foldspace.

She was someone new. Someone other. Someone with opportunities she had never had before.

It was time to embrace them, rather than lament what she had lost. It was time to step into the life she had, not the life she thought she deserved.

It was time to be herself—once and for all.

She held up her glass. "A toast to the future," she said.

"*Our* future," Coop said as he clinked his glass to hers. "Our unknown future."

"And everything it sends our way," Yash said, and finished her drink.

I value honest feedback, and would love to hear your opinion in a review, if you're so inclined, on your favorite book retailer's site.

Be the first to know!

Just sign up for the Kristine Kathryn Rusch newsletter, and keep up with the latest news, releases and so much more—even the occasional giveaway.

To sign up, go to kristinekathrynrusch.com.

But wait! There's more. Sign up for the WMG Publishing newsletter, too, and get the latest news and releases from all of the WMG authors and lines, including Kristine Grayson, Kris Nelscott, Dean Wesley Smith, *Fiction River: An Original Anthology Magazine,* *Smith's Monthly,* and so much more.

Just go to wmgpublishing.com and click on Newsletter.

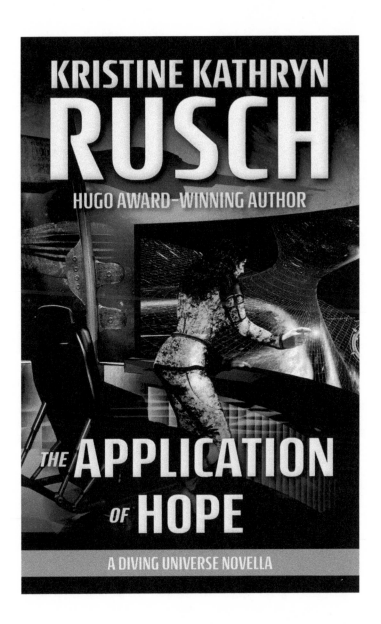

Learn more about foldspace and the history of the Fleet
in *The Application of Hope: A Diving Universe Novella*.

On Sale Now.

Turn the page for a preview.

1

"REQUESTING SUPPORT. The *Ivoire*, just outside of Ukhanda's orbit. Need warships."

The calmness in the request caught Captain Tory Sabin's ear before the name of the ship registered. She had stopped on the bridge just briefly, on her way to a dinner she had sponsored for her support staff. She wasn't dressed like a captain. She had decided to stay out of her uniform and wear an actual dress for a change.

At least she had on practical shoes.

But she felt odd as she hurried across the nearly empty bridge, covered in perfume, her black hair curled on the top of her head, her grandmother's antique rivets-and-washers bracelet jingling on her left wrist. She grabbed the arm of the captain's chair, but didn't sit down.

Only three people stood on the bridge—the skeleton crew, all good folks, all gazing upwards as if the voice of Jonathon "Coop" Cooper, captain of the *Ivoire*, were speaking from the ceiling.

Then Lieutenant Perry Graham, a man whose reddish blond hair and complexion made him look continually embarrassed, leaned forward. He tapped the console in front of him, so that he could bring up the *Ivoire's* location.

It came up in a 2-D image, partly because of the distance, and partly because Graham—the consummate professional—knew that Sabin preferred her long-distance views flat rather than in three dimensions. The best members of any bridge crew learned how to accommodate their captain's quirks as well as her strengths.

She moved closer to the wall screen displaying the image. The ship, marked in shining gold (the default setting for the entire Fleet), showed up in small relief, traveling quickly. Like Coop had said, the *Ivoire* wasn't too far from the planet Ukhanda. Whatever was causing the crisis wasn't readily apparent from this distant view, but Sabin could tell just from Coop's voice that he had been under attack.

Coop was one of those men, one of those *captains*, who didn't ask for help if he could avoid it. Much as she teased him about this, she knew she fell in that category as well.

Sabin didn't have to tell Graham to zoom in. He did, more than once, until the *Ivoire* looked huge. Around it were at least a dozen other ships, so small and feathery that they almost seemed like errors in the image.

"What the hell?" said Second Lieutenant Megan Phan. She was tiny and thin, her angular face creased with a frown. She probably hadn't even realized that she had spoken out loud.

Sabin doubted the other two had realized it either. Phan's words probably echoed their thoughts. In all her years in the Fleet, Sabin had never seen ships like that.

On screen, they looked too small to do any damage. If they were firing on the *Ivoire*, it wasn't obvious. But their position suggested an attack, and a rather vicious one.

"Let Captain Cooper know we're on the way," Sabin said to Graham.

"Yes, sir," Graham said, and sent the word.

The *Geneva*'s current rotation put it in the front line of defense for the Fleet, but the Fleet was in a respite period, which was why Sabin only had a skeleton crew on board. The Fleet had rendezvoused near an unoccupied moon. Six hundred of the Fleet's ships were engaged in maintenance, meetings, and vacations, all on a rotating schedule.

She'd been in dozens of respite periods like this one, and she'd never needed more than a few officers on the bridge.

Until now.

"Captain Cooper sends his thanks," Graham said, even though everyone on the bridge knew that Coop had done no such thing. Someone on his staff had. If Coop had done so, he would have spoken on all channels, just like he had a moment ago.

"We need other front line check-in," Sabin said. Technically, she wasn't the senior captain for all the front line ships on this shift, but no one took front line seriously during a respite period. Everyone had dinners and relaxation scheduled. Most bridges, even in the front line ships, were minimally staffed.

The only difference between a minimal staff in a front line ship and the other ships during a respite period was that the front line ships had top-notch crews manning the bridge, in case something did go wrong.

"Already done, sir," Graham said. "The captains are reporting to their bridges."

"What about our crew?" she asked. She felt almost embarrassed to ask. Graham was one of her most efficient crew members and she knew he had most likely pinged the bridge crew.

But she had to make sure—even in this respite period—that the crew was following protocol.

"Notified, and on the way," Graham said.

"Good, thank you." She sat in the captain's chair, and winced as the bow on the dress's back dug into her spine. A bow. What had she been thinking?

She knew what. The dress's tasteful blue fabric and demur front had caught her eye. But she had loved that bow for its suggestion of girlishness, something she wasn't now and would never be.

"Let's hear the check-in," she said.

Graham put the captains' responses overhead. In addition to the arrivals—all twenty of them—the captains seemed to believe it important to engage in a discussion of Coop's motives. A request for support was the lowest level request a captain could issue. Normally, a captain in distress asked for a battalion of a particular type, not a general support request of warships.

So it was curious, but it spoke more to Coop's conservatism than to the situation at hand. Besides, no one seemed to acknowledge that the *Ivoire* had gone to Ukhanda at the request of one of its nineteen cultures. The Fleet had agreed to broker a peace deal between the Xenth and the Quurzod, but didn't know enough about either to do a creditable job.

The *Ivoire,* which had the best linguists in the Fleet, had gone into Quurzod territory to learn more about that culture in advance of the actual peace conference three months away. The *Alta,* the Fleet's flagship, apparently believed that the Fleet knew enough about the Xenth to do more limited preparation.

It had only been a month since the *Ivoire* had sent a team to the Quurzod. Apparently things had not gone well.

She shifted, the dress's shiny fabric squeaking against the chair's seat. She wasn't sure she had ever sat in her chair without wearing regulation clothing—at least, since she had become captain. As a little girl, she used to sit in her father's captain's chair on the *Sikkerhet.* This dress made her feel that young and that out of place.

Stupid chatter from the other captains surrounded her. They were still speculating on what Coop wanted and whether or not this was a legitimate request. They hadn't made the transition from respite to action. And there was another issue. Coop's message was low-key.

Only people who knew him well understood that he was worried.

"Open a channel," she said, unable to take the chatter any longer.

Graham nodded. Then he signaled her.

"Coop's asked for support," Sabin said in her most commanding voice. "Stop arguing about why, and haul your asses out there."

The chatter stopped immediately. She had a hunch she knew how the other captains had reacted: a straightening of the shoulders, a nod, a deep breath as they all gathered themselves, a momentary flush of embarrassment as they realized they had conducted themselves like people on vacation instead of captains on a mission.

She didn't like respite periods, so she didn't understand the vacation mindset. But a lot of these captains believed in relaxation, and believed the crap that the civilians on the various ships peddled, that a rested crew was a healthy crew.

She believed a practiced crew was an efficient crew.

She followed regulations, gave her staff the proper amount of time off, and no more.

Because this respite period was so long—months, really, as the Fleet prepared for the work around Ukhanda—she had her first officer, Charlie Wilmot, continually run drills. Each department had to run drills as well.

Her crew was going to remain the most disciplined crew in the Fleet. If a member of the crew complained, that crew member got transferred. Often, she'd trade that crew member for someone else on a different ship. She'd stolen more good officers from other ships than any other captain. The good officers, she believed, were the ones who wanted to work, not party at every opportunity.

Wilmot had just arrived on the bridge. His uniform looked crisp and sharp. He glanced at her dress and his lips turned upward just enough to register as a smile to anyone who knew him. Fortunately, no one else on the bridge watched him.

"The *Ivoire*'s in trouble," she said to him. "Graham will catch you up."

Wilmot nodded, then walked to his station not too far from hers. As he did, he looked up at the screen, frowned, and glanced at her again. But he didn't ask anything, because she had already told him to figure out what was happening from Graham.

As if Graham knew. No one on the bridge did, and it was clear that no one on the other front line ships did either.

She tapped the right arm of her chair, bringing up the captain's holographic console. She'd designed this so she didn't have to move to another part of the bridge to get information.

Before she'd followed the captain's training route, she'd started in engineering. While she loved design, she hated the lack of control the engineering department had. Plus, she was a captain's daughter, and she had ideas from the start on the way a well-run ship worked.

Most of the ships she had served on were not well run. So she had gone back to school, and had risen through the ranks until she got the *Geneva.* That was fifteen years ago. Even though she occasionally designed upgrades for her baby—upgrades that other engineers eventually brought to their ships—she hadn't really looked back.

She preferred being in charge.

Which was why, as the five other members of her team took their places on the bridge, she looked up those small, feather-shaped ships herself.

The ships weren't in the database, no matter how she searched for them. She searched by the ships' image, the design, and the area's history. She also searched through the images of Ukhandan ships, not that there were uniform ships on a planet that housed so many different cultures. Not all nineteen cultures were space-faring, but five of them were, according to the database, and those five had no ships like this.

Small, efficient, and capable of swarming.

She wanted to contact Coop, but she would wait. He would let her—and the other front line ships—know if something had changed.

She almost closed the console, when something caught her eye. She had images of the ships for five cultures, but the information before her contradicted itself. Five cultures had ships, but six cultures had gone into the space around Ukhanda.

The sixth culture, the Quurzod, were the ones that the *Ivoire* had gone to Ukhanda to study before the peace talks.

Her stomach clenched.

Clearly, something had gone very, very wrong.

"How far out are we?" Sabin asked Lieutenant Ernestine Alvarez, who was running navigation.

"Even at top speed, we're half a day away," Alvarez said.

Too close to use the *anacapa* drive with any accuracy. The *anacapa* was the thing that enabled the Fleet to negotiate long distances. It put a ship in foldspace, and then the ship would reappear at set coordinates. The problem was that the ship would reappear blind, and in a battle situation, that wasn't optimum.

Plus, time worked differently in foldspace, and while the best crews could predict the time differences down to the second, sometimes even the work of the best crews went haywire. Engineers claimed the problem was with sections of foldspace itself; scientists believed the problem was with certain *anacapa* drives.

Even with centuries of study and upgrades, neither group could come to a complete agreement. In Sabin's opinion, the Fleet had forever messed with something it did not understand when it started using the *anacapa* drive.

She wasn't going to use it on something like this. Nor was she going to order the rest of the front line to do so—not unless Coop sent out a major distress signal, which he had not yet done.

She wasn't going to explain herself to her crew, but if she had to, she would tell them what she always told them—that portion of the truth that they needed to know. It was the same truth every time they considered using the *anacapa* drive. The *anacapa* put a strain on the ship and on the crew that Sabin couldn't quite quantify. She hated using it for that very reason, just like most of the captains did.

Which was probably why Coop hadn't used his drive yet. The *anacapa* also worked as a shield. The ship would jump to foldspace for a moment, and then return to its original coordinates. Depending on how the *anacapa* was programmed, the return could happen seconds later or days later, without much time passing on the ship at all.

"Another twenty-five ships have just left Ukhanda's orbit," Alvarez said.

"That settles where the ships are from, at least," Graham said.

"It was pretty obvious that the ships were from Ukhanda," Phan said. "The question is which culture controls them."

That *was* the question. It would have an impact on everything: how the front line ships would proceed, how they would fight back, *if* they would do more than simply rescue the *Ivoire*. If they needed to rescue the *Ivoire*. Coop might get away on his own.

Sabin hoped Coop would get away on his own.

She asked Graham, "Have you sent a message to the *Alta*, asking if they know which culture owns these ships? Because we need to get some diplomats on the mission here, to ensure we don't make things worse."

The *Alta* was twice as large as all of the other ships in the Fleet, including the warships, and it housed the Fleet's government when that government was in session.

"I notified them as soon as we got Captain Cooper's message," Graham said. "I trust that they're monitoring the *Ivoire* as well."

Sabin was about to remind Graham that one should never "trust" someone else to do anything important, when Wilmot snapped, "Don't make assumptions, Lieutenant."

He sounded a bit harsh, even for him. Sabin glanced at him. That small smile had disappeared, and she saw, for the first time, how tired he looked. She wondered what he'd been doing during respite, besides running drills.

His uniform was so crisp she knew he had put it on right after the call to the bridge. So he'd been either asleep or doing something else when the call came in.

"Sorry, sir," Graham said, sounding just a bit contrite.

"I want identification on those ships," Sabin said. "We have time— half a day, you said. So let's see if we can cut that time short, and see if we can figure out who or what we're dealing with. The other cultures on Ukhanda are a mystery to me. Maybe they developed some technology of their own that we're not familiar with."

"Do you want me to send for Sector Research?" Meri Ebedat spoke up for the first time. She usually handled navigation, but she'd been doing some maintenance on the secure areas of the bridge during the respite period. She had a streak of something dark running along her left cheek, and her eyes were red-rimmed. Her brown hair had fallen from its usually neat bun.

She had to be near the end of her shift, although now, she wouldn't be leaving. She was a good all-around bridge crew member, and Sabin would need her as the mission continued.

"Yeah, do it," Sabin said, "although I doubt Sector Research knows much more than we do. We haven't had enough time to study Ukhanda. That was one reason the *Ivoire* was there."

"You think they did something wrong?" Wilmot asked her softly, but the entire bridge crew heard.

She knew what he meant: he meant had the *Ivoire* offended one of the cultures in a severe way.

But she gave the standard answer. "By our laws, probably not," she said.

He gave her a sideways look. He wanted a real answer, even though he knew the real answer. They all knew the real answer.

Had the *Ivoire*—or, rather, its on-planet team—offended one of the cultures? Clearly. And if Coop didn't act quickly, the entire ship might pay the price.

ABOUT THE AUTHOR

New York Times bestselling author Kristine Kathryn Rusch writes in almost every genre. Generally, she uses her real name (Rusch) for most of her writing. Under that name, she publishes bestselling science fiction and fantasy, award-winning mysteries, acclaimed mainstream fiction, controversial nonfiction, and the occasional romance. Her novels have made bestseller lists around the world and her short fiction has appeared in eighteen best of the year collections. She has won more than twenty-five awards for her fiction, including the Hugo, *Le Prix Imaginales*, the *Asimov's* Readers Choice award, and the *Ellery Queen Mystery Magazine* Readers Choice Award.

To keep up with everything she does, go to kriswrites.com and sign up for her newsletter. To track her many pen names and series, see their individual websites (krisnelscott.com, kristinegrayson.com, krisdelake. com, retrievalartist.com, divingintothewreck.com). She lives and occasionally sleeps in Oregon.

CPSIA information can be obtained
at www.ICGtesting.com
Printed in the USA
LVHW031528120419
613988LV00001B/274